The **FIVE**

BOOKS *of*

MOSES

LAPINSKY

KAREN X. TULCHINSKY

POLESTAR
An Imprint of Raincoast Books

The author gratefully acknowledges the British Columbia Arts Council for a creative
writing grant to write the first draft of this manuscript.

Polestar and Raincoast Books acknowledge the ongoing financial support of the
Government of Canada through The Canada Council for the Arts and the Book Publishing
Industry Development Program (BPIDP); and the Government of British Columbia
through the BC Arts Council.

Editor: Lynn Henry
Cover and interior design: Ingrid Paulson
Typesetting: Teresa Bubela

NATIONAL LIBRARY OF CANADA CATALOGUING IN PUBLICATION ÐATA

Tulchinsky, Karen X
    The five books of Moses Lapinsky / Karen X. Tulchinsky.

ISBN 1-55192-556-7

I. Title.
    PS8589.U603S74 2003   C813 .54   C2002-911351-2
    PR9199.3.T76S74 2003

LIBRARY OF CONGRESS CONTROL NUMBER: 2002096018

Polestar/Raincoast Books	*In the United States:*
9050 Shaughnessy Street	Publishers Group West
Vancouver, British Columbia	1700 Fourth Street
Canada V6P 6E5	Berkeley, California
www.raincoast.com	94710

At Raincoast Books we are committed to protecting the environment and to the responsible
use of natural resources. We are acting on this commitment by working with suppliers and
printers to phase out our use of paper produced from ancient forests. This book is one step
towards that goal. It is printed on 100% ancient-forest-free paper (100% post-consumer
recycled), processed chlorine- and acid-free. It is printed with vegetable-based inks.
For further information, visit our website at www.raincoast.com. We are working with
Markets Initiative (www.oldgrowthfree.com) on this project.

Printed in Canada by Friesens

10 9 8 7 6 5 4 3 2 1

Contents

For my parents,
Jack and Marion Tully

And in memory of my grandparents,
Ben and Mary Tully
and Albert and Esther Jacobson

PROLOGUE

Notes on a biography of Sonny Lapinsky
by Moses Nino Lapinsky, Ph.D.
APRIL 1, 2003, VANCOUVER, B.C.

MY FATHER WAS a prizefighter. Perhaps you've heard of him? Sonny "The Charger" Lapinsky. He won the World Middleweight Title in 1948, lost it to the British fighter Tommy Foster in 1953, won it back in '54, then retired from boxing forever, when his body began to give out. He was thirty-one years old. Throughout his career, Sonny fought the top middleweight boxers of his day: Jake La Motta, Rocky Graziano, Sugar Ray Robinson, Tippy Larkin, Jimmy Doyle and Marty Servo, just to name a few.

In many ways, I am not my father's son. Where he was tough and athletic, I am sensitive and intellectual. He was an extrovert, vivacious with life, whereas I am rather quiet and calm. He dropped out of high school the moment he turned sixteen, partway through the tenth grade. I lived the first third of my life in the proverbial ivory tower, earning a B.A. in Liberal Arts from the newly built York University in 1965. I completed my Masters in History in '67 and earned my Ph.D. in 1974 — after a three-year absence from academia to, as we called it at the time, "find myself."

Since completing my thesis on the History of Eastern European Immigrants to Canada in the First Half of the Twentieth Century, I have not felt compelled to write. Until now. I suppose the urge has been brewing inside of me for the past couple of years, circumstances edging my writing ambitions to the forefront. In the fall of 2001 a journalist by the name of Roderick Matthews, a sports writer for the *Toronto Star*, published an unauthorized biography of my father. At first I was amused. Then I read the book, and I became enraged, not an emotion I regularly feel. I am a mild-mannered man, not given to erratic emotions. But the book, you see, is complete, unadulterated trash, three hundred and

twenty-three pages of half-truths and speculation, based on sketchy
interviews with people who barely knew my father, and inadequate,
sloppy research — if you can even call it that. The book, which is titled
Below the Belt, characterizes my father as a womanizing wife beater who
neglected his children, brought disgrace to his community and won the
middleweight championship on questionable terms.

I'd be the first to acknowledge that my father's parenting skills were
inconsistent at best. And yes, it's true, my mother left him when she could
no longer live within the confines of their tumultuous marriage. But there
are two things I know for sure. That he won the World Middleweight Title
fair and square, and that despite his personal failings, Sonny Lapinsky
brought nothing but honour to the fledgling Jewish community that was
just beginning to establish itself in Toronto when he was a boy. Therefore,
I find myself strangely compelled to set the record straight, as it were, and
to write my own biography of my father, Sonny Lapinsky, the Jewish
Canadian prizefighter.

These, then, are my first notes toward this large and rather ambitious
project. I plan to conduct my research through one-on-one interviews
with people still alive who personally knew my father, of which there are
a surprising number, an in-depth study of newspaper and other media
coverage spanning my father's career, plus my own personal memories and
analysis. The tentative working title of my book shall be "The Biography
of Sonny Lapinsky." These notes are simply the genesis of the project, and
are not necessarily recorded in chronological order. Here's what I know
off the top of my head about his boxing career.

My father was at the beginning of his professional career, having
proved himself in the amateur circuit, when in 1943 he was conscripted
into the Canadian Armed Forces. Later he volunteered to fight amongst
the infantry in France and Holland. When the war ended, he remained in
the Netherlands for several months, helping the Dutch people begin the
arduous task of rebuilding their broken country.

After the war, Sonny's hometown of Toronto was crawling with boxers.
While fighters around him were staying put, content to be "merely"
Canadian champs, my father got on a train to New York to compete with

the Americans. He was determined to go all the way to the top. It was hard work, but it paid off. Eventually, he was getting on fight cards in the holy shrine of pro-boxing — the one, the only, Madison Square Garden. And because he won almost every fight, he quickly became a top middleweight contender. For the world title.

On June 15, 1948, at the age of twenty-four, he got his chance, a shot at the prize. He won by a Technical Knock Out, fondly known in boxing circles as a TKO, when his American opponent, the world title holder "Tiny" Dave Johnson, was so battered by Sonny he couldn't come out of his corner for the tenth round. That was a great day for my father, a poor Jewish kid from an immigrant family, from the ghetto at College and Spadina, a neighbourhood in which you were more likely to grow up and become a thief, a bookie, a gambler or dead, than a world-renowned Boxing Champion. When the officials fastened the middleweight belt around his waist, my father cried. You can see the tears on his face in the newspaper clippings. Tears of victory, I suppose.

I didn't see my dad much in those days. My mother, Loretta Maria Mangiomi Lapinsky, was in the process of divorcing him and we were officially mad at Dad. I never really understood why. Around me, he was fun and exciting. My friends were jealous of his fame. His picture was constantly in the newspaper. Everybody knew Sonny. When he was between fights and he had a free afternoon, my dad and I would walk down the street and strangers would shake his hand, pat his back, get his autograph, have their pictures taken with the champ. We had lots of money; we never had to worry about that. We had a nice apartment in the Kensington Market area, on Palmerston, a spacious avenue with a tree-lined boulevard running up its middle. There were times when he and my mother even seemed happy and in love. But like a scary monster under your bed in the middle of the night, seething menacingly, poking its heavy, hairy arm up every now and then, there was something dark and frightening about my dad that I was only vaguely conscious of.

As the first son but second child, I suppose I was protected from the turmoil of my parents' volatile marriage. My sister Mary, three years older than I, got the brunt of it. My mother depended on her beyond the capabilities of her young age. Mary was helping take care of me before she was in the first grade. My sister remembers the violence. The tension. She's the one who was awakened in the middle of the night to witness my parents fighting. She never saw my father actually hit my mother (and I don't think he ever did), but she saw him pulverize our apartment walls more than once, enough to frighten all of us into submissive obedience. And there were the dents to prove it. All over our apartment there were holes in every wall, the exact size of my father's fist. There was plaster flaking onto the carpet, the inner workings of the wall exposed. This was the price of living intimately with an explosive, sensitive, sad and passionate, world-class champion fighter.

My father died in 1969, the summer of love, *olev hashalom* — the same year my life truly began — of a stroke. He was forty-five years old. It was probably all the years of getting repeatedly bashed in the head. He'd started fighting when he was a small boy. Only nine years old, in the 1930s, at the height of the Great Depression.

HELL IN A HANDBASKET

The Grudge Match
APRIL 1, 1954, MADISON SQUARE GARDEN
NEW YORK, NEW YORK

IT'S QUIETER THAN DEATH in the long narrow hallway. Sonny Lapinsky's breath moves in and out through his nose in a steady rhythm. With each step, the silk of his boxer trunks brushes softly against his thighs. The hem of his long blue robe flaps against the back of his knees. Rudy Gold, his trainer, stops at the door to the stadium, glances back to see if Sonny is ready. Sonny nods. No words pass between them. There's no need. They know each other more intimately than lovers. Rudy's been with Sonny since he was a boy. Over twenty years now. They know each other's silent signals. Rudy throws open the heavy metal doors.

The din is deafening. Sonny glances up, scans the seats of the stadium. In the stands above it's like an explosion when they spot him. People jump to their feet and cheer, hands above their heads, pushing and jostling for a view of the Champ. A jumble of sound. It vibrates through Sonny's chest to his heart. Cigar and cigarette smoke hangs thick in the stale, hot air. Beads of sweat collect on Sonny's forehead and under his arms. He raises one fist, the victory salute, and follows Rudy down the aisle, past rows of people sitting up front in the ringside floor-seats.

"There he is!" a young fellow shouts.

"Hey Lapinsky!"

"Knock 'em dead, Sonny."

In Sonny's corner, mugging for the newspaper reporters, Sonny's manager, Checkie Seigelman paces back and forth, smoke from his cigar surrounding his bulk like a shield, his white Panama hat tilted low over his forehead. He wears a crumpled white gabardine suit over a black cotton shirt with a colourful hand-painted tie. Checkie throws an arm over Sonny's shoulder, smiles broadly for the newspapermen as dozens of flashbulbs pop and flare.

Reporters leap up, pencils poised over notebooks.

"Sonny, Sonny. Will you win your title back?"

"How's that sprained wrist?"

"Foster says he'll beat you."

"Will you knock him out?"

"I'll win. You can bet on that." Sonny smiles, flashing his dimples for the cameras.

"Later, boys. Later," Checkie promises, and swivels Sonny around, nudging him toward the ring.

Sonny hops up onto the canvas and slips through the ropes. Hot, blinding light shines down from above. He holds both gloved hands high above his head and grins for all he's worth. It's a crooked, boyish grin he perfected years ago, a grin that drives women crazy. The crowd goes wild.

Sonny turns in all directions, nodding to his fans. Middleweight Champ of the World. He'd held onto the title for five years. Six months ago, Foster came out of nowhere and stole it from Sonny. This is a grudge match. He's going to win his title back. Sonny feels waves of love and admiration flow over him. Yeah. This is what it's all about. They love him. He's the underdog, the poor boy from a poor family who fought his way to the top. Sonny "The Charger" Lapinsky, of Clinton Street, Kensington Market, Toronto, Ontario, son of an immigrant, a two-bit door-to-door peddler, is an international hero.

A radio reporter in a rumpled brown suit leaps up onto the edge of the ring, sticks a round chrome microphone in Sonny's face.

"Sonny," he yells, "can you tell the folks at home how you feel just before the fight?"

"Yeah. Sure," Sonny grins. "I feel swell. I'm in great condition. I been training hard, and I'm going to win this fight."

"Sonny, Tommy Foster says he's going to keep the Middleweight Title …"

"Foster doesn't stand a chance. I'm the Champ. After tonight, you'll see." Sonny taps his gloves together in front of his chest, glances to the left, sees something and immediately stops breathing. His grin vanishes and his jaw sets. Ringside. Front and centre. *No. It can't be … Geez, he looks old. When did he get so old?* Sonny's breath returns in a cold gasp of air as he turns back to the reporter.

"Sonny? I said, who are you fighting for tonight?"

"Fighting for?"

"You gotta fight for someone — a girl maybe? Your wife?"

"Oh, yeah." Cautiously, Sonny glances again to the second row. His father is still there. Sitting beside his older brother, Sid. The old man's looking this way. Staring, chin stuck out arrogantly as usual, looking like he hates the whole world. "This one's for …"

"Sonny?"

"… my fans." He pulls away, dances to his corner.

"Sonny? You okay?" Rudy removes Sonny's robe.

"Yeah, sure." Sonny perches on his stool in his corner. Looking straight ahead. Breathing hard. The referee enters the ring.

Couple of Steaks

IT'S THE FIFTEENTH ROUND. Sonny is exhausted. His head hurts. His left wrist aches. He's losing steam. Can't last much longer. He goes into a clinch with Foster, leaning his weight on his opponent's shoulders. He must be leading in points. But what if he's not? He has to win the title back. After all he's been through, he can't go out a loser. Drawing strength from the centre of his being, he shoves Foster away, finds his rhythm, dances on the balls of his feet. Foster throws a hard right. Sonny sees it coming but dodges a half-second too late. The glove connects with his chin, tossing his neck back. He's been hit in both eyes over the course of the fight. He can feel the swelling. His vision is slightly skewed. He dances in his spot to find his balance. Fists in front of face, he stares out from under his eyebrows at Foster, who is grinning maniacally. A red hot fire burns in Sonny's belly. This is the rage he conjures up to give him the strength and the heart for fighting. Dancing and dodging, stalling for time, he digs deep inside, doesn't look, but imagines his father sitting in the stands, feels hate and love and grief rise up from the pit of his belly, through his chest, down his arms to his fists, which are now lethal weapons, powered by every wrong ever done him.

Foster strikes again. This time Sonny swings his head under the glove and charges forward in his signature style, throwing a hard left jab to Foster's ribs. Can tell Foster's hurting there. Feeling fury vibrate in his hands, Sonny pounds relentlessly in one spot, until Foster lowers his guard. With his powerful right arm, Sonny plows his opponent in the chin, sends him onto his back on the canvas. His injured left wrist aches from repeated blows, but it doesn't matter. It's all over anyway. Foster stays down. The referee begins the count. 1-2-3. Sonny steps back to a neutral corner, but stays on his feet, mustering his strength. 6-7-8. Foster struggles, tries to lift his head. 9 … "Ten!" the referee shouts, his arm hitting the floor. A knockout in the fifteenth round.

The crowd leaps to its feet, roaring. Flashbulbs explode as photographers scuffle for the best shots. Heavy, square television cameras follow Sonny's every move as the referee grabs Sonny's wrist, holds it high in the air, proclaiming him the World Middleweight Champion once again. Rudy jumps into the ring, drapes Sonny's robe over his shoulders, removes the mouthguard, kisses his cheek in triumph, proud of his boy. Checkie separates the ropes, steps inside, puts an arm over Sonny's shoulder, smiles for the cameras. Sonny breathes hard. Sweat rolls down his face. Reporters jump into the ring, toss questions at him.

"How's it feel to be the Champ again?"

"How's the hand, Sonny?"

The questions fly out, one on top of the other. He can barely make sense of them. There's a thumping in his ears. His heart beats fast. He strains to look into the stands.

Pop was here. Front and centre. With Sid. What the hell were they doing here? He pushes his way to the edge of the ring. Scans the second row. He can't see them. They're not in their seats. Damn.

"Later, boys. Later." Checkie pushes the reporters back. "Come by the dressing room in thirty minutes. Let the Champ have some room. Come on ya bums. Outa the way." Checkie takes Sonny firmly around the waist and leads him out of the ring. With his adrenalin seeping away, Sonny is beginning to feel the pain. In the kidneys, ribs, face, ears. His eyes are really beginning to swell. He can hardly see. He needs Checkie's help to get to the dressing room.

IN DARK GLASSES, showered and dressed in a freshly pressed linen suit with an open collar, Sonny takes questions from the reporters. It never ceases to amaze him, their stupidity.

"Did you plan to punch him that way?"

"Did you know you would knock him out in the fifteenth round?"

As if he could really plan each and every punch ahead of time. He had a pre-fight strategy worked out, based on Foster's style, but once you're in the ring, anything can happen. He answers their questions, as always, flashing his grin, making them laugh, a real charmer, then he's swept away by Rudy and Checkie to the victory party back at the hotel. There are hundreds of people at the party, by invitation only, carefully monitored by Checkie Seigelman. Boxers, pro-ballplayers, sports reporters, boxing officials, politicians, cops, lawyers, movie stars, models, film directors, singers, and out of respect, the requisite members of the mob. The champagne flows, along with Scotch and water, gin and tonic, whiskey sours and gallons of beer. A chef in white uniform stands behind the food table, cutting slices of rare beef, served with horseradish. The table overflows with salads, dinner rolls, potatoes and desserts.

Many beautiful women at the party are throwing themselves at Sonny. How to choose between them? A bosomy brunette attaches herself to his side, and somehow, hours later, he is back in his suite with her. Can't remember her name. Louise? Lois? What strikes him is her dark-brown eyes. They remind Sonny of his wife's eyes.

"Loretta …" he says when she climbs on top of him.

"Lucille …" she corrects him, bending over, her lips on his neck.

"Oh, yeah, sure." Sonny grunts as he reaches for her. A pink neon sign from across the street flashes on and off through the hotel curtains. Through the paper-thin hotel walls, they can hear a radio playing in the next room. Ethel Merman is belting out "There's No Business Like Show Business," from the recently released movie. Sonny is vaguely aware of the song. He has to agree with Ethel.

IN THE MORNING, Rudy barges in to wake Sonny. Lucille is already up and dressing.

"Excuse me, Miss," Rudy apologizes.

"That's quite all right," Lucille says, in a thick Brooklyn accent, "I have to be going."

"Nice to meet you, Miss." Rudy tips his hat as she leaves the room. "Come on, Sonny. Get up." He grabs Sonny roughly by the shoulder and shakes him. From the Manhattan street outside, there is the continuous melody of horns honking. A man yells for a taxi. A car screeches its brakes.

"What's a matter?" Sonny opens his swollen eyes. His vision is slightly blurred.

Rudy sits on the edge of the bed. Sighs deeply, lowers his head, depressed as if another war has just been declared.

"What the hell's going on?" Sonny rubs his jaw, sits up in bed. Every single part of his body aches, especially his head. Especially his kidneys. Especially his wrist, which throbs to beat the band.

Rudy hands over the telegram that arrived for Sonny earlier that morning.

"What is it?"

"Just read it."

Sonny reads out loud.

"DEAR SONNY STOP CAN'T TAKE IT ANYMORE STOP I'M LEAVING YOU STOP MOVING IN WITH MY SISTER GINA STOP THE KIDS ARE WITH ME STOP YOU CAN VISIT THEM WHEN YOU WANT STOP LORETTA STOP."

Sonny crumples the telegram into a tight little ball, then smoothes it out, reads it again.

"You okay, Sonny?"

Sonny stares at the telegram. "You think she means it?"

"I don't know, Kid. What do you think?"

"She always says she's gonna leave me. It's not the first time, you know, Rudy."

"I know."

"She'll come back. She always does." Sonny crumples the telegram a second time and tosses it toward the trash can in the corner. He misses. It bounces off the wall, rolls onto the hardwood floor. Despite his words, he's worried. Loretta's never sent a telegram before in her life.

"Sure she will, Sonny."

Sonny fumbles on the nightstand for his pack of Viceroys and slides one out. He opens the small drawer, searching for matches. Inside is the requisite hardcover Gideon's Bible, but no matches. He slams the drawer shut. From his trouser pocket, Rudy fishes out his Ronson lighter, offers the flame to Sonny, who takes a deep drag from his cigarette, blows out grey-black smoke forcefully, watches it rise to the ceiling.

"Listen, Rudy. Can you get me a couple of steaks? I can't hardly see." Sonny's eyes are swollen practically shut. His face is a big purple mess of bruising and cuts. His ribs ache, and he's been pissing blood. At thirty-one, it's starting to hurt more. His body takes longer to heal. And something else. Sonny's noticed his reflexes aren't as sharp. It used to seem like slow motion when his opponent threw a punch. He had plenty of time to roll under, or dodge the hit. Everything used to work in a split second. He saw what was coming and was already throwing his counterpunch without even thinking. Now he's off. It's just by a fraction of a second, but it's long enough to count. He's been taking more hits than he ever used to. For the first time, Sonny is scared. Worried he's losing his heart for fighting. Lately, he's even been thinking about hanging up his gloves, getting out while he still has some brains left. A few times lately, he's been walking down the street, and suddenly he can't remember where he's going or why. It only lasts a few seconds, but it's scaring the hell out of him. Sonny doesn't want to be one of those poor bastards, ex-fighters with their screws all loose. Sitting around the bar, drinking Jack Daniel's, not even able to remember their own mothers' names. Telling the same ring stories over and over, reliving their glory, with no future, just a past. Wives who won't speak to them. Kids who never call. Sonny doesn't want to end up like that. He shakes the thought away. "And some coffee, Rudy. Can you get me some coffee?"

"Sure, Sonny. How about breakfast?" The thought of food makes Sonny's stomach heave. A bitter taste rises in his throat. Sonny remembers that his father and brother Sid were in the stands last night and his guts churn in fury.

Rudy swipes one of Sonny's smokes, lights it, flicking his lighter shut with one thumb.

"Nah. Not hungry." Sonny says. "Listen, when does our train leave for home?"

"We ain't going till tomorrow, Sonny. Remember? I told you last night."

"Oh. Yeah." Sonny doesn't remember. "Sure. I meant what time tomorrow?"

"Ten o' clock. Be home the next morning. You gonna call Loretta?"

"Nah. I'll see her there. Give her some time to cool down. Know what I mean?"

"Sure, Sonny. Good idea."

Rudy closes the door to Sonny's room and heads for the restaurant in the lobby to get the raw steaks.

Down But Not Out
TORONTO, TWO DAYS LATER

"LORETTA, CAN YOU help me in the kitchen, Honey?" Ruthie calls.

Loretta weaves between the piles of boxes stacked on the hardwood floor of the living room in her sister-in-law's downtown apartment. The green sofa and matching big old easy-chair are set by the door, ready to be carried downstairs. The coffee table and tiffany floor lamp remain in the centre of the room, on top of the fake Persian rug, which has yet to be rolled. The living room windows are cracked open for the first time in months, letting a cool breeze inside the apartment. There is the faint smell of spring in the air.

Inside the kitchen, on the pink Formica table, there is a cardboard box that Ruthie is filling with dishes, wrapped in newspaper.

"What do you want me to do, Ruthie?" Loretta pushes a stray curl of dark hair off her forehead.

"Can you start on the other cupboard? You I can trust not to break anything. With Sid ... his hands are so big, he's always dropping my china."

Loretta reaches into the cupboard for a stack of teacups.

"How's everything going in here?" Sid kisses Ruthie on the cheek. His dark trousers are rumpled. He's wearing a white cotton shirt with the sleeves rolled up, top button undone. He is a tall, broad-shouldered man, with dark brown wavy hair and mahogany eyes behind thick round glasses. He's followed by his youngest brother, Izzy, who rocks back on his heels, a habit he has when he's nervous or excited.

"Cup." Izzy points to the counter, where Loretta packs her box.

Sid reaches up to ruffle Izzy's hair. At twenty-six, Izzy is taller than Sid by a few inches, though not as brawny. Izzy is lean, like their father. His hair is lighter than Sid's, a medium brown and without the wave; it combs back neatly with a little dab of Brylcreem. His eyes are hazel, and innocent like a small boy's. "That's right, Izzy. That's a cup."

Izzy steps forward and stands beside Loretta, tips his head to one side, watching as she wraps a cup.

"Don't touch the cups, Izzy." Sid warns. "They break easy. You can help me. There's lots of stuff to go downstairs into the truck. Come on."

"Where we going, Sid?"

Sid smiles at his brother patiently. Izzy asks the same questions over and over. He has no short-term memory. His comprehension is that of a six-year-old. Sid's used to it. Izzy wasn't born retarded, but he's been this way since he was little. Since the accident that damaged his brain. "To load the truck, Iz," Sid reminds him.

Izzy is still staring at the counter. "Why is she putting the cup away?"

"Cause we're moving. Remember?" Sid leads Izzy out.

"Oh yeah."

Loretta reaches for another sheet of newspaper and notices that it's the *Toronto Daily Star,* the sports section. There's a front-page article about Sonny. "The Charger Wins Title Back." And a photo, taken in the ring. Checkie stands beside Sonny, holding his right arm high in the air. Loretta sees the grief in Sonny's eyes, his swollen face, then his crooked grin. She wants to die of heartbreak, right here in Ruthie's kitchen. Instead, she crumples the paper up quickly and fiercely, crunching the photograph of his face into a tight little ball which she stuffs inside a teacup. She'd love to crush his real face. It was bad enough when she merely suspected he was having affairs. The letter from the woman in Brooklyn was the final straw. She almost wrote back to tell the girl not to waste her time—Sonny's forgotten all about her by now. Loretta's sure there's no shortage of girls in other towns. Loretta has put up with Sonny's affairs for a long time, but she has hit her limit. Mary's almost thirteen years old now. Loretta doesn't want her daughter to grow up watching her parents fight all the time. Moses is ten and Frankie has just turned eight. Loretta might not have a faithful husband, but she has children to raise. And she has her pride. "So tell me again exactly where you're moving to, Ruthie?" she asks her sister-in-law.

"It's north of Lawrence," Ruthie answers, pushing her thick greying hair from her face with the back of one hand. In her mid-thirties, Ruthie has hair that's beginning to grey, but she's not the type to use hair dye. She's a sensible, practical woman. She's a bookkeeper, not a movie star or a model. Anyway, Sid's starting to grey around the temples too and if he's not going to colour it why should she?

"All the way up there. Isn't it farm country? The middle of nowhere?"

"Not really, it's the new suburbs. They're building all kinds of houses. Lots of people are moving north. We bought a nice bungalow with a yard for five hundred down and two hundred dollars a month. The mortgage is for $18,000."

"But what's there besides new houses?"

"Well … nothing much yet, but there's going be a plaza at Lawrence and Bathurst, and it's only a thirty minute drive back down here. There's the Nortown Movie Theatre at Eglington, and lots of shopping. Even a kosher butcher."

"Seems so far from the neighbourhood is all."

"It's not so bad. It's nice. You'll see."

"It sounds nice."

Ruthie smiles at Loretta. Poor girl. Ruthie would like to punch her brother-in-law, Mr. Big Shot the Boxing Champion, right in the kisser. The way he treats his own wife. Running around with a different girl everywhere he goes. He doesn't even try to hide it. Everyone knows. It's embarrassing. The worst part is, Ruthie knows that Loretta is still in love with Sonny. Even though she's divorcing him. Finally.

Izzy dashes into the apartment, followed by Sid.

"That's a big truck," says Izzy.

"That's right, Iz," Sid says. "How are we doing here? Almost time for a lunch break?"

"Soon, Sid. Take a few more boxes down first."

"We're getting hungry, Sweetheart."

"Okay, okay. I made up some sandwiches. Nothing fancy." Ruthie opens the fridge and pulls out a plate of tuna fish on rye. Sid grabs two bottles of Coca-Cola and pops off the caps with a bottle opener. He hands one to Izzy, who takes a long drink, spilling some of it down the front of his shirt.

"Easy there, buddy." Sid opens a drawer. "Ruthie, he needs a towel."

At that moment, a familiar voice calls out, "Where is everybody?"

Izzy runs toward the door. "Sonny, Sonny, Sonny," he calls, hugging his favourite brother roughly, towering over him. Sonny has a boxer's muscular physique, but he's on the short side, just over five foot six. "I'm helping Sid," Izzy proudly announces.

"Good boy, Izzy."

"Sonny?" Sid calls from the kitchen. "I thought you were in New York." He swings through the kitchen door into the living room.

"I bet you did," Sonny says abruptly. At the sound of Sid's voice, his face clouds with anger.

"Holy cripes." Sid studies his brother. "You want an ice pack? Ruthie!"

"Don't strain yourself, Sid," Sonny spits out.

"What? What's a matter?"

Sonny closes in on Sid, pushes hard against his older brother's chest. "What was that all about, Sid?"

"What?" Sid takes a step back.

Ruthie rushes in, followed by Loretta.

"Oh God." Loretta is shocked, as always, at Sonny's bruises.

Sonny sees her. His face softens. "Loretta? What are you doing here? Come on, Sweetheart. Let's go home."

"No, Sonny." Loretta stands beside Ruthie. "I'm not coming home."

"Yeah, I got the telegram, but Sweetheart … come on Baby, don't be like this. We can work it out …"

Loretta squeezes Ruthie's arm. "I'm sorry Ruthie. I'm gonna go. I gotta pick the kids up anyway." She glares at Sonny as she pushes past him. Sonny knows the look in her eye. Has seen this look before. Stubborn as a mule. He knows to just let her pass. He turns his rage on his brother. "Come on Sid, I want the truth, damn it! I'm sick of being the last to know everything."

"Okay, Sonny. Take it easy." Sid's worried. Sonny hasn't been so bruised after a fight since the early days when he was just learning how to dodge and duck. "Let's just take it easy here," he repeats.

Sonny suddenly notices the boxes, the furniture stacked by the door.

He lowers his sunglasses. "What's going on around here? You moving or something?"

"Yeah. Uptown," Sid answers.

Sonny pushes his sunglasses back in place. "Oh yeah? With Pop? Is he moving in with you?"

"What? No. What are you talking about?"

"You know what I'm talking about, Sid."

"No. I don't."

"You don't know?"

"Come on, Sonny. What's going on? Why are you so mad?"

"Pop. That's why," Sonny says.

"What about Pop?"

"You know damn well what I'm talking about," Sonny snaps.

Sid studies his brother's face. "You mean New York?" he ventures.

"You mean New York?" Sonny mimics.

"No big deal, Sonny. We came to see your fight."

"No big deal?" Sonny laughs harshly, one short loud bark. "Bringing Pop to my fight is no big deal?"

"Sonny … come on. Sit down." Sid's heavy glasses slip down the bridge of his nose. With one finger he pushes them back in place.

"No, Sid. I don't wanna take it easy. I almost had a heart attack right in the ring. Seconds before a championship bout, I turn my head, and there's you and Pop. Why didn't you warn me? I coulda lost the fight."

"I didn't know you could see us from there."

"You were front and centre. I'm not blind like you Sid. I can see just fine."

"Sonny …" Sid draws back, hurt. "I didn't think it would bother you."

"Oh. You didn't think it would bother me. That's great, Sid. Just great." Sonny kicks at a box on the floor. The cutlery inside clatters. He bends down, pulls up a bread knife, points it at Sid, who instinctively steps back. "Why don't you just stab me in the heart?"

"Sonny! Put that down!" Ruthie yells. She grabs Izzy's wrist, yanks him behind her.

"Uh-oh, Sonny's mad." Izzy peers over Ruthie's head, rocks on the balls of his feet.

"Sonny, put the knife down." Sid holds both hands out, ready to deflect the weapon with the back of his hand. "You're scaring Izzy. Look at him."

Sonny glances at Izzy, smiles at him, then glares at Sid and tosses the knife back into the box. It clanks against the cutlery. "Don't worry. Geez. You think I would stab you?"

Sid drops his hands. Takes a deep breath. Relaxes slightly. "No. Course not."

Ruthie keeps her eyes on Sonny, her back tense.

"Sonny's mad, Sonny's mad, Sonny's mad," Izzy chants.

"The way you stabbed me?" Sonny continues.

"I didn't mean to hurt you."

"In the heart."

"I didn't mean anything."

"Oh no? Then why'ja do it?" Sonny stares hard at Sid. "Why, Sid?"

"Pop wanted to come."

"Pop wanted to come?"

"Yeah."

"He hasn't seen me in fourteen years!" Sonny yells, startling everyone.

"He wanted to come. I didn't think …"

"Oh … you didn't think."

"Listen, how about a drink? Calm your nerves. Huh? Ruthie, go and get the schnapps from the kitchen. Will ya? And take Izzy in there."

Ruthie takes Izzy's hand and leads him into the kitchen. "Come on Izzy, how about some Coca-Cola?"

"Coca-Cola-cola-cola!"

"I don't need a drink, Sid. I need some respect here. That's what."

"Come on, Sonny. I respect you."

"No you don't!" Sonny raises his voice again. "Otherwise you wouldn'ta brought Pop!"

Sid holds out his hands, in a conciliatory gesture.

"That's my turf, Sid. Mine." Sonny thumps his own chest. "Did I say

Pop could come there? No. If I'da known earlier, I'da had security toss him out. That's what."

"He's your father," Sid says quietly.

"What?"

"You should have some respect for him," Sid says.

"He don't respect *me*," Sonny shoots back. "He don't even talk to me."

"You have to meet him halfway Sonny."

"What do you know about it?"

Ruthie returns with Izzy on her heels and hands Sonny a water glass half-filled with Canadian Club whiskey. Not a drinker, Ruthie has no idea how much to pour. Sonny accepts the drink, swallows a large gulp, wipes his mouth with the back of his hand, sits the glass on top of a box.

"Huh? What do you know about it, Sid?" he persists.

"All I'm saying, Sonny, is maybe you're just as stubborn as he is."

"Me stubborn? He hates me!" Sonny yells.

"He doesn't hate you."

"Shut up, Sid."

"He doesn't," Ruthie adds.

"What do you know, Sid?" says Sonny, ignoring Ruthie. "You had it easy. Ma and Pa danced at your wedding. Pop made a speech at your wedding. I didn't ask for that, did I? I didn't ask for nothing. Not one damn thing. And he hates me. Just 'cause I married Loretta — the girl I love."

"You don't love Loretta. You're never home," Sid says.

Sonny charges at Sid, grabs the collar of his shirt, and pulls back his fist to strike.

"Stop it!" Ruthie yells.

Sonny freezes, his fist in mid-air. He pushes Sid back against the wall.

"I'm sorry, Sonny. But it's true." Sid adjusts his glasses.

"I oughta kill you. I swear to God I love her." His fist tightens on Sid's shirt.

"Then how come she spends more time in my house than in yours?"

"Why, you lousy creep." Sonny pushes harder against Sid's chest, banging his head against the wall.

"Crying her eyes out half the time."

"You're lying."

"No. I'm not."

"Damn you, Sid."

"It's true," Ruthie adds.

"True, rue, rue true," sings Izzy.

"Wondering where her husband is. And with who," Sid continues.

"She gets lonely," Ruthie adds.

"She cries?"

"Course she does, Sonny."

"Over me?" Sonny loosens his grip on Sid's shirt.

"You should call her more, Sonny. When you're away."

Sonny drops his hands, fishes in his pocket for his cigarettes. "It ain't easy … being on the road all the time … you know."

"If it was me, I'da called." Sid straightens out his rumpled shirt. "That's all I'm saying."

Sonny lights a cigarette. Sid's right, of course. He should have called Loretta more often. Maybe he wouldn't be in this mess if he had. His belly swirls with the familiar tension and guilt he's lived with for years. Damn it.

"If it was you?" Sonny inhales deeply, then blows the smoke out violently. A wave of nausea rolls over him. A sharp pain slices through his head then melts into a slow dull ache. Black spots dance in front of his eyes. A ringing sounds inside his ears. He staggers away from Sid, grabs for the sofa to keep from falling.

"Sonny." Sid steps forward, catches his brother by one arm and gently lowers him to the sofa. Sonny leans over, head between his knees. *Breathe,* he tells himself. *Just breathe.* "Sonny …?" Sid repeats.

BOOK ONE

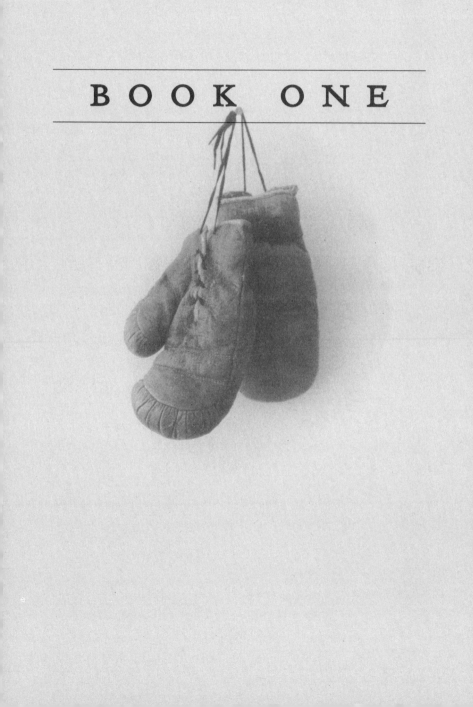

Notes on *The Biography of Sonny Lapinsky*
by Moses Nino Lapinsky, Ph.D.
APRIL 15, 2003, VANCOUVER, B.C.

I'M SITTING ON A HARD vinyl chair in the windowless, fluorescent-lit, concrete grey basement of the Vancouver Public Reference Library, in the west end of the city, where I am scanning through old archives of the four major newspapers that were in print in Toronto in 1933, the year my father was nine years old. the *Toronto Daily Star,* the daily *Mail and Empire,* the *Globe* and the evening *Telegram.* I've taken from the shelves microfiche from all four papers for the week of August 14, 1933. The front pages are filled with stories about the riot in Christie Pits.

The headlines scream out:

"Swastika Gang Drives Citizens from City Park."

"Scores Hurt as Swastika Mobs Riot."

And in the right wing, *Telegram,* "Swastikas Rid Beaches of Undesirable Persons."

I'd heard about the so-called Christie Pits riot when I was a small boy. It was unavoidable in my family. My father and all three of his brothers were in the park that day and had fought in the riot. It would have been hard to be a boy in that neighborhood and not be involved in some way. It's my theory that in my family it was a terrible, devastating, defining moment, a moment in which everything changed. I believe it holds the clue to the strained relationship between my father and grandfather. And, I suspect that day influenced my father's decision to become a boxer. But of course, I'm getting ahead of myself. Here are the bare facts.

On August 16, 1933, a group of British Canadian boys from the Beaches area in the east side of Toronto, part of a group called the "Swastika Club" who modeled themselves on Hitler's Nazis, instigated a riot in Willowvale

Park. The park, which still exists today, is known in the neighbourhood as Christie Pits because it looks exactly like a big pit, dug into the ground on Christie Street, near Bloor. At one time, around the turn of the twentieth century, it had been an open hollow from which sand and gravel was mined. All summer long in 1933, the Swastika Club, whose mission was to drive Jews and other "foreigners" from the east side beaches, patrolled up and down the lakefront boardwalk, wearing Swastika badges and armbands. On that fateful day in mid-August they upped the ante. They traveled across town to the Jewish quarter, and, as we say today, all hell broke lose.

I try to imagine what it must have been like, for my father and *his* father. My grandfather, Yacov Lapinsky, came to Canada in 1913, when he was barely fifteen. He came on his own, leaving his entire family behind in Russia. Canada was good to Yacov in the early years. Or so it seemed to him, compared to how Russian Jews were treated. It's true there were few options open to a young, Russian, Yiddish-speaking Jew in 1920s Toronto, but at least Yacov was left alone to his business, as long as he didn't break any laws or attract attention to himself. With his cousin, known to me as Great-Uncle Max, he eked out a living, peddling door-to-door. How could he possibly understand his Canadian-born sons, whose sense of entitlement was beyond anything Yacov had ever dreamed of?

In 1933 it was the height of the Depression. Jews and other immigrants were mostly worried about paying their rent, putting food on the table, staying warm in the winter — plain old simple survival. The older generation, like my grandparents, had fled the pogroms of Russia and Poland and were used to a certain degree of oppression. As long as there were no pogroms, they were better off in Toronto than in the old country. They kept to themselves, their families and their own tight communities. The more invisible they were, the safer they felt. Their children, who were born on Canadian soil had a different take on things. Unlike their parents, Jewish youth were prepared to fight. They were street-smart ghetto boys, used to fighting their way through school, the streets, the parks, their own neighbourhood. When the Swastika boys came into the ghetto, they didn't count on the Jewish boys fighting back. My grandfather was terrified of his sons' resistance. He'd built a life upon staying in line, not questioning authority, turning the other cheek. I try to imagine what he must have gone through, watching his sons put themselves in the line of fire. I try to imagine Sonny's opinion of my grandfather, whom he surely saw as a coward.

My theory is that it was in the aftermath of the riots that my father's family began to unravel, steeped in guilt and tragedy over what happened to the youngest son, Izzy. This was also the moment that strengthened my father's resolve to become a champion boxer. These feelings were buried deep inside the family. People didn't talk about their feelings in those days, and there certainly was no money for therapy. I surmise that after the riots my father realized two things. One, that with his fists he could hit his mark nine times out of ten, while easily dodging blows from the other guy. And two, that as long as he remained focused on the fire in his belly which came from his rage and sorrow, he would possess a natural ability, what boxers call "the heart for fighting." With this secret weapon, as a boxer he was virtually indestructible.

GUILTY *as* CHARGED

The Aftermath
AUGUST 17, 1933, TORONTO

SONNY LAPINSKY STRIKES OUT at his homemade punching bag, which hangs from the backyard apple tree. It's not a large tree, but nine-year-old Sonny is short for his age, and the bag, made from an old potato sack and stuffed with rags, is at just the right height. There is no technique in Sonny's workout, only raw talent and a heart full of grief. His hands, wrapped in rags, ache, he's been punching for so long, but it's the only thing keeping him from crying. And there's no way he's going to cry in front of his brothers. Leave that to Lenny, he thinks. Sonny can't yet look in the mirror, can't look directly at the guilt in his own eyes. But if he could, he'd think he looked rather like a raccoon, both eyes ringed in black.

It is tremendously hot, even though it's after seven in the evening. The city has been in the grip of an oppressive heat wave for the past two weeks. The air is still and the humidity makes it difficult to move fast or even breathe. The grass is dry and yellow. The earth bakes. Trees and flowers wilt. Neighbourhood dogs sit lethargic, panting. Tempers flare easily.

Lenny sits on the grass, leaning against the rickety, peeling picket fence that separates the Lapinsky yard from that of their neighbours, the Pincinnis. At eleven, Lenny is just under five feet tall, and thin. Not rough-and-tumble like his brothers, Lenny has his head in books. He is going to be a great writer when he grows up, like the Yiddish author Sholem Asch. His mother, Sophie, is pleased that one of her boys has a passion for books, but his father is worried. He knows Lenny's dream is impossible. He will have to learn a trade, or join his father in the peddling business. A writer cannot support a family. Although the family has great respect for books, writing them is not something anyone they know has ever done.

Usually Lenny would be devouring a book, but today he's reading all four of Toronto's daily newspapers. The headline in the morning *Globe* reads, "Swastika Feud Battles in Toronto Injure 4. Fists, Boots, Piping used in Bloor Street War." The subtitle reads, "Hail Hitler Is Youth's Cry: City in Turmoil. Trucks loaded with Jews and Italians rush to the scene." Four injured? Lenny scoffs at this. More like four hundred. Maybe even four thousand.

He tosses the paper down abruptly, aggravating his aching left wrist. Lenny has a shiner on his right eye and a split lip, which is puffed up to twice its normal size. His wrist is fractured and he has bruises all over his legs and chest. Unaccustomed to fighting, Lenny is suffering from the unfamiliar throb of a wounded body. But that pain is nothing compared to the ache in his heart, or the fear that churns in his belly every time he thinks about Izzy lying in a hospital bed with a bandage covering his little head.

The morning *Mail and Empire* screams out its bold front-page story: "Scores Hurt as Swastika Mobs riot at Willowvale." Scores hurt is slightly more accurate, although vague, thinks Lenny. The paper goes on to report, "Thousands caught up in park melee. Gangs wielding lead pipes and bats sweep streets, bludgeoning victims." The *Mail and Empire* claims that five were taken to hospital. What a joke. The emergency ward at Toronto Western Hospital was teeming with riot victims.

The article that makes Lenny laugh, almost — he would, but it hurts too much — is in the right-leaning evening *Telegram*, which claims "Communists Incited Riot," and "Jewish Toughs Began Trouble." The article is so ridiculous, Lenny would laugh his head off. If only his world wasn't falling apart at the seams.

Lenny turns his attention to the local Yiddish paper, *Der Yiddisher Zhurnal*, the Daily Hebrew Journal, and slowly reads the Hebrew characters. The report in the *Zhurnal* is not as sensational, but it puts the blame for the riot on the Gentiles. It reads, "It all began during the first inning when a few young Gentiles among the crowd began chanting, 'Hail Hitler' and other epithets aimed at the Jews." Lenny reads on.

Lenny's older brother Sid paces the backyard like a caged lion. His injuries are restricted mostly to his chest and back, which are covered in purple bruises, although he took several shots to the chin and a fist to the head during the riot in the park. As the eldest son, Sid bears the responsibility for what happened to their youngest brother Izzy. Sid has already had his bar mitzvah. Six months ago at the Shaarea Tzedec Synagogue he read from the Torah, and technically became a man. It's his duty now to look after his younger brothers, but yesterday he failed miserably in an unalterable way. Sid is big for his age, with broad shoulders and a strong chest, dark eyes and curly brown hair. He's a good boy, does what he's told. Never causes trouble. He resembles his Uncle Max more than his father. Sid is not exactly a genius, but he's good-natured, loyal and responsible.

As the eldest, Sid bears the brunt of his father's discipline. A traditionalist, Yacov believes it is the oldest son's duty to watch out for the younger brothers. If one of the younger boys gets in trouble, it is ultimately the responsibility of Sid, and he must take the punishment for not properly guiding or watching out for his brothers. The punishment Yacov delivers is a strapping with his leather belt, directly onto Sid's buttocks. At thirteen, Sid is really too old for strapping, but that doesn't stop Yacov. Years ago a pattern developed. It is an unjust system, but in the Lapinsky family, that's the way it is. Lenny is strapped occasionally, but he is such a quiet boy, Yacov can never believe he is at fault. Sonny is exempt simply because he is named for Yacov's little brother, Shmuel-who-died-in-the-pogrom of 1913, the year Yacov emigrated to Canada. To strap Sonny would be like hitting beyond the grave. It would be like hurting Shmuel, may he rest in peace. So it is Sid who bears the brunt of Yacov's anger.

Yacov and Sophie are at the hospital with Izzy right now, waiting to bring him home. Sid is sick with worry and guilt. The doctor says that Izzy was struck on the head by a heavy blunt instrument. Perhaps a rock. Maybe a brick or a bat. His wounds don't look particularly bad. The other boys look much worse. But something has happened to Izzy's brain and he will never be the same again.

Sonny too thinks it was all his own fault. He was supposed to keep an eye on Izzy. Earlier, at the hospital, he couldn't look at his baby brother Izzy. He tried, but when he did, a nausea rose from his belly to his throat and he had to run down the hall, barely making it to the men's room in time to vomit into a toilet. It isn't because he doesn't love dear sweet Izzy. It's because now, whenever he looks at Izzy lying comatose in the hospital bed, Sonny hates himself.

A lightning bolt flashes, followed by a loud crack of thunder. The clouds burst and a heavy rain suddenly drops on the baking city. The cool rain is refreshing after the heat wave. The boys don't budge as their hair and clothes are soaked by the cold rain.

They hear the sputter of their father's old Model T ford chugging down Clinton Street. They glance at each other nervously. Their father has been acting unpredictably since the accident and for the first time in their lives, the boys are afraid of him.

Yacov Lapinsky drives the old Ford, his hands gripping the steering wheel tightly. The windshield wipers slap rhythmically back and forth, away from each other and back. The window fogs up. Yacov wipes at it with his bare hand, his eyes straight ahead, not so much on the road as in the past. The last time his heart was torn apart so thoroughly was the day he left Russia for good in 1913, two days after the pogrom in which his younger brother Shmuel was killed. The familiar grip of doom tightens across his middle, making it hard to breathe. In his shirt pocket, the hospital bill burns, adding worry to his growing pile of misfortune. Sweat drips down the back of Yacov's neck and under his arms. He tries not to listen too closely to the sounds of his wife softly weeping on the car seat beside him, their boy Izzy curled up in Sophie's lap, looking more like five months than five years old. Like a baby, he leans against her bosom, quietly sucking his thumb, staring blindly ahead.

Sophie is in shock over the state of her youngest son, who only two days ago was reading, printing his own name, ready to enter the first grade at the end of the summer, the smartest of her boys, the one destined for college one day. Now he doesn't even know the sound of his own name. He can't form words, seems not to understand anything at all. The doctor said as the swelling in his brain recedes, his condition may improve, "but don't get your hopes up too high, Mrs. Lapinsky. His brain has been seriously compromised." How high of a hope is it to wish your son would be himself again? Gently she strokes his face, her eyes darting, searching for further danger. She is already developing the fierce protective shield she will need to envelop him in for the rest of his life. Izzy jumps in fear when the car backfires, something it always does. Sophie strokes his back to calm him.

Later in the kitchen, Sid pours his father a glass of schnapps. Yacov never drinks, but today he needs the numbing gauze of the liquor. He sips his drink at the table, by the wide-open window. The rain has subsided. There is no breeze, only thick hot air. Sonny and Lenny hover in the doorway, as Sophie puts Izzy to bed, in the cramped second-storey bedroom where all four boys sleep. Sid and Izzy in one bed, Lenny and Sonny in the other. For tonight, Izzy will have his own bed. Sid has volunteered to sleep on the floor.

Sophie removes the thermometer from Izzy's mouth, holds it up, but she can't read it. Maybe it's broken. She doesn't look at Sonny and Lenny as she passes them on her way to the kitchen.

"I'm running downstairs for a minute," she says quietly to Yacov. "I can't read this thermometer. Maybe Tessie can figure it out." Holding the handrail she walks down the stairs to the first-floor flat where Yacov's cousin Max lives with his wife, Tessie, their two small daughters, four-year-old Lillian and baby Esty, and old Mr. Tepperman, the boarder. Max took in Mr. Tepperman two years earlier to help with the rent. He sleeps on the living-room sofa. Max has considered taking in another boarder who could sleep in the hall. These days, people are happy to have a roof over their heads, even if it means sleeping on the floor or doubling up with strangers. Both families share the one bathroom on the second floor. They are happy to have indoor plumbing; some of the neighbours aren't so fortunate and are still using privies set out by the back lane.

Downstairs, Tessie wipes away the tears on Sophie's face as she attempts to read the thermometer. Sophie's heart lurches to her throat when she hears something crash upstairs. She takes the stairs two at a time, with Max and Tessie on her heels. The scene they encounter makes no sense. Sophie stands at the top of the steps trying to understand why Lenny is lying on the floor, Yacov standing above him, his belt raised in the air to strike. Sid is groaning in a corner, clutching his belly. Sonny is on his side, under a knocked-over chair. Yacov's arm freezes when Sophie screams his name. Sonny bolts up, almost knocks her over, stepping on Max's foot in his rush to get out of the house. Izzy wanders in and all eyes are on him as Sophie scoops him up, takes him back to bed.

A few minutes later she orders Yacov out of the house. He will spend three nights on the floor in the hall downstairs at Max and Tessie's flat before Sophie allows him back into the apartment where her children sleep.

Monkey Boy

ALL THE LAPINSKY BOYS have jobs for the summer, while school is out. They hand over most of their pay to their mother each week. It's the only way to make sure there will be enough money to get the family through the long, hard winter. Sid works alongside his father and Uncle Max in their small peddling operation. Lenny sells newspapers. He gets up early, buys an armful of copies of the morning *Mail and Empire* and heads down to the financial district on Bay Street, selling his papers to the businessmen on their way to work. Paperboys buy copies of the three-cent paper for two cents each, pocketing the extra penny per paper. Most customers toss Lenny a nickel, telling Lenny to keep the change — a profit of three cents. Izzy used to help Lenny fold the papers, and count the pennies, but now those days are over.

Sonny has a summer job at the College Lanes Bowling Alley, in the esteemed position of Monkey Boy. You have to be small to be a Monkey Boy; it's one of the few times in Sonny's life when being short is a good thing. The College Lanes hires boys to sit on small wooden perches, swings suspended by ropes on a pulley system just above the pins. The Monkey Boy waits in position until the player has thrown three balls, then he lowers himself down to the floor with a hand crank, leans over and rights the fallen pins, and raises himself up again for the next player's round. It isn't a difficult job, but there are risks. If you don't move out of the way fast enough, you'll get hit by a flailing bowling ball. Sometimes the pins are hit so hard, one or two bounce up and strike the boy. The boys call these pins "jumpers." Once in a while the ropes on the pulley system give way and a boy tumbles down to the alley from a height of three feet, which tends to cause embarrassment more than injury.

In the days after the riot, Sonny begins waking early every morning, long before anyone else stirs. He sneaks quietly into the backyard and performs his daily exercises — fifty push-ups, one hundred sit-ups, then twenty minutes on the punching bag. When he's done, he creeps back inside for his shirt and cap, grabs a piece of bread and runs out the door.

Since Izzy's accident, Sonny has been lying to his parents, telling them the bowling alley has extended its hours and he is now on early shift. He does this to get out of the house before anyone wakes. Whenever he's around his father, the look in Yacov's eyes burns a hole in Sonny's chest. When he looks at Izzy, staring into space and rocking like a retarded boy, not like his smart little brother — who could read when he was four and could name all the provinces in Canada, recite all ten commandments and knew the difference between a left jab and a right uppercut, but who now sits and stares, a puzzled expression on his face — the nausea rises in Sonny's belly. His guilt pulls him under where he'll drown if he sits in it too long.

Sophie knows Sonny is lying about the bowling alley. She walked by to check early one morning. It was locked up tight. The sign had not changed. They were open from eleven in the morning to eleven at night. Six days a week, closed Sundays.

Sophie tried talking to Sonny the day after the incident she thinks of as "Yacov's episode," the night he lost his temper and beat the boys. Sophie has never seen her husband behave like that before, and she prays she'll never see him like that again. She watches him closely and almost imperceptibly begins backing away from him as a partner in the raising of their children. She has always consulted him before on every little decision about the kids. She tries to tell herself it was an isolated circumstance. He's a good man. He works hard. In general, he is kind to the boys. And patient. But the man she saw in the kitchen, one fist raised, the other clutching his belt over his head while her sons lay cowering on the floor, that man is not her husband. He is not the man she's lived with for fourteen years. That man is a stranger. It gives Sophie chills to recall the look on Yacov's face. He had been vacant, in another time, another place. Sophie senses that a tiny crack, almost invisible, is weakening her family's foundation. That kind of crack has a way of widening slowly over time, until one day it bursts wide open, and topples everyone.

Steady as always, Sid seems to have recovered in the days following the riot, cheerfully leaving every morning for his summer job, helping Yacov and Max in their door-to-door peddling business. Yacov and Max started the business when they first came to Toronto in 1913. Nobody in their neighbourhood can get credit with the department stores, so peddlers like Yacov and Max sell a rug here, a lamp there, for fifty cents down and fifty cents a week, plus interest, until the item is paid off. Since the crash of 1929 they've been lucky to get a dime or a nickel from their customers. It's a terrible situation, but with no other options they walk up one street and down the next, trying to scrape out a living. At thirteen, Sid is tall and broad. He does the heavy lifting for his father and uncle. And he helps them collect on debts. Sometimes they have to repossess a rug or a table. It's Sid's job to carry the item outside and tie it to the roof of the Model T Ford. Other times, when business is so bad they haven't taken in a dime, Max and Sid will take a trip to the farmers' market and purchase a fifty-pound bag of potatoes wholesale, then sell a few potatoes to Mrs. Rosen, a few more to Mrs. Pincinni, a dozen maybe to Mrs. Cohen — the Cohens own a fish shop and are doing a little better than most of their neighbours. It's Sid's job to carry the sack of potatoes over his shoulder, while Max makes the sales.

Lenny, of course, is shaken for a long time after Yacov's episode. But that's to be expected. Lenny is, well, fragile. At least he goes to his mother for comfort. Sonny is too proud to do this. Sophie tried to soothe him that next morning, but he just sat stoney-faced and eventually said, "It's okay, Ma. You don't have to worry about me."

He sounded so old, so tough, it broke Sophie's heart. *He's only nine years old, too young to carry such a heavy weight on his shoulders.* Sophie knows he feels guilty for what happened to Izzy, and although technically it *was* his fault, she doesn't want him to be burdened with such guilt. It's bad enough that Izzy is permanently damaged. Does Sonny have to be also? She says nothing about the hours of the bowling alley. After the first week, she takes to packing him a bagged lunch.

"Sonny," she says, "take the brown paper bag from the bottom shelf of the ice box. If you're going to work such long hours, at least I want you should have something to eat."

"Okay."

Anger festers inside Sonny. He hates the Swastika Club for what it did to Izzy. He hates himself for not protecting his brother. He hates his father. He hates God. He hates everybody. He gets into fights with other kids. He looks for fights, provokes altercations, just so he can pound his fists into some other guy's flesh. It's the only thing that stills the tornado swirling in his heart.

In the mornings, to get out of the house, he walks around the city. He walks for miles south, and then miles east. He's never really gone outside his own neighbourhood much before. He hadn't realized there was a huge city out there. Some mornings he walks east through the Ward, still showing its Jewish immigrant roots, now changing into Toronto's Chinatown. He walks all the way to the Danforth and back. He walks through Cabbagetown and south to the waterfront. He walks west to Parkdale, even as far sometimes as High Park. And he has gone as far north as the ritzy neighbourhood at St. Clair, but feeling conspicuous, he never stays there long. Someone might think he's planning a robbery. He hangs around Christie Pits, looking for guys in the hateful Swastika Club, hoping they will pick on him, call him a dirty Jew or filthy kike so he can pulverize the creeps. They must be keeping a low profile since the night of the riots, because so far he hasn't uncovered a single *Swazi*.

THE SECOND FRIDAY NIGHT after the riot, Sophie invites her parents, Channa and Reuben Perodsky, for dinner. She tells Tessie and Max to come upstairs with their girls. Even Mr. Tepperman-the-boarder is invited. They sit around the big wooden table in the kitchen while Sophie and Tessie remove pots of food from the cast-iron coal stove. The Sabbath candles burn, dripping white wax onto the table. Through the open window come the sounds of a horse clopping down the street, followed by the rattle of a buggy. The neighbour's laundry flaps on a line strung across the front lawn, hanging over the street. Shouts of children playing stickball on the road drift upstairs.

Izzy sits in a chair next to Sophie. He can sit up, but he doesn't speak and doesn't understand what anyone is saying. He can't feed himself. Sophie indulges him with milk in a baby bottle, one she's borrowed from Tessie, whose youngest daughter, Esty, is still in diapers. Yacov sits at the head of the table, sullen. Sonny sits as far away from his father as possible, beside his grandfather. Channa and Reuben fuss over the boys' bruises and cuts, alarmed that their grandsons were part of the big riot they read about in the paper.

"So dat's it?" Reuben asks Sophie. "The doctors don't know?"

"No, Papa." Sophie's eyes fill with tears. She spoons food into Izzy's mouth, like she did when he was a baby. He has forgotten how to use a fork.

"Maybe in a little time, he'll get better," Reuben suggests, cutting the small roast chicken they're sharing into thin slices with a carving knife.

"He's not going to get better," Yacov cuts in, glancing sternly at Sonny, who lowers his head, studies his plate.

"You should sue, Yacov. That's what I been trying to tell you." Max stabs the air with his fork.

"Who's he gonna sue, Max?" Tessie asks, serving potatoes around to everyone.

"I don't know," Max says, "the police maybe. The city. It happened in a public park. I bet you could sue the city."

"Can you do dat?" The idea sounds fishy to Reuben. If it was so easy to sue the city, everyone would do it. People fall down and hurt themselves in public parks all the time.

"Sure you can. You just need a good lawyer."

"Who can afford a lawyer?" Tessie points out.

"Sophie," Channa says, "don't cry *mamaleh*. Please. You're gonna make me cry."

"I can't help it, Mama. Look at him. Like a baby."

"That's all she does now. She cries every day," Yacov says, scratching the back of his neck — a nervous habit.

"It's understandable," Tessie says. "You go ahead and cry, Sophie. Men just don't understand."

"I understand," Lenny says.

"Course you do, sweetheart," Tessie smiles at Lenny. "You're sensitive. Unlike some fellas I know." She glares at Max.

"What did I do? Yacov, pass the seltzer will you?"

Yacov grumbles under his breath. He reaches for the glass bottle of seltzer water and passes it to Max, who holds his glass under the pressurized spout and squeezes. Seltzer shoots into his glass. "If you boys had stayed at home, like I told you to …" Yacov tells Sonny.

"I'm sorry, Pop. I'm sorry. Sorry. Sorry," Sonny repeats.

"I should have stayed home. I could have gone to the library another day." Lenny wants to take some of the heat off of Sonny.

"It was my fault, too," Sid offers.

"That's what I mean. You all should have stayed home," Yacov snaps.

"You can't change the past, Yacov," Reuben points out. "What happened, happened." He takes a small slice of chicken, passes the plate to Max.

"That's right, Reuben," Max agrees, serving meat to the kids before taking any himself.

Tessie elbows him in the ribs.

"Ouch. What, Tess?"

"Stay out of it, Max."

"What did I say?"

"What are you saying about the past?" Channa asks, cupping her deaf left ear with one hand. Dr. Grossman says she has a sixty percent hearing loss, from an untreated infection. There's nothing that can be done.

"You can't change it," Rueben answers loudly.

"You can't what?" She leans her ear in closer to his mouth.

"Change it. Change it," Rueben hollers. "You can't change the past."

Sonny is about to go crazy. He wishes they would stop talking about it. He wishes his father would just hit him again. Beat him to a pulp. That, he could take.

Day of Atonement

AUGUST 26, 1933

SID GENTLY TUCKS IZZY into bed and sings him a song, tries to calm the rage that swirls in his chest whenever he thinks about what the Swazis did to his baby brother. He's not sure if Izzy even understands the song he's singing, but it doesn't matter. The tune seems to be working. Izzy's eyes are closed. His breathing slows down, ready for sleep. Sid has noticed that Izzy is constantly nervous now, rocking when he sits or stands. He settles down when you sing to him or stroke his face.

Sid had never intended to fight at Christie Pits. He went to the baseball game to prevent trouble. His friends are a bunch of hotheads. Sid is always keeping his best friend, Louie Horowitz, and Ralph Shapiro from fighting. Eddie Finkelstein, too. And the others guys who hang around with Sid's gang — Guido Toscano, Salvatore Ricci, Yossie Singer, Meyer Glass and his little brother Jerry. Because of his size, Sid can get other guys to settle down with just one look in his eye, a slight raise of one arm. A guy takes one look at Sid and backs off. Fighting with him would be like smashing your head against a brick wall.

The guys begged Sid to show up to the softball game that night. Ralph had already been in a fight on Balmy Beach with the Swastika Club the week before. Louie had never experienced the Swazi gang firsthand, but has relatives in Germany who are at this very moment being interned in labour camps and beaten in the streets of Berlin. He was itching to fight the Swastika Club boys. Sid tried to talk them out of it, but when the word spread that the Swazis were coming to Christie Pits, the Jewish area, he knew there'd be trouble. He couldn't leave the rest of the neighbourhood to take care of it without him. That would be shirking responsibility. And Sid is, if anything, responsible. He was helping his mother take care of his brothers before he could talk in full sentences. Lately, he has noticed that his parents will take whatever is dished out at them. They just want to stay out of trouble. Survival is enough for them, but for Sid it's not enough. He wants to thrive. He wants success. He has so many ideas. There are so many opportunities if you just apply yourself. As a Canadian-born Jew, he doesn't have to bend his head, look down and say *Yes sir, no sir, three bags full sir,* the way he's seen his father do.

Sid has a memory that burns in his belly. He couldn't have been more than five years old, barely as high as his father's waist. It was a Sunday. He was helping his father, going door to door as he always did on Sundays. It was the best day to find most of their customers in, Saturday being the day they'd be in synagogue. They stuck to the Jewish area, knowing what could happen if they knocked on Gentile doors on their holy day. It's against the law to work on the "Lord's Day," according to the Sunday Blue Laws. Might as well be back in Russia, bowing to the Cossacks, Sid figures.

They had just collected a payment from Mrs. Greenblatt, and were walking down the steps from her porch, when a group of churchgoers in their Sunday best blocked their path. Four men and two women. The women hung back. The largest man approached. Walked right up to Yacov.

"What cha ya think yer doing, Abraham?" he asked Yacov, his face an inch from Sid's dad, his voice full of hate. Other than the churchgoers, the streets were quiet and empty. An autumn chill was in the air.

His name's not Abraham, Sid wanted to yell. But his father's tight grip on his hand kept him silent.

Yacov looked down at the ground. "Nothing, sir. Visiting a friend, with my boy."

The man cleared his throat and spat on the ground by Yacov's feet. "Sure ya ain't peddling?"

"No, sir."

"It's the Lord's Day, ya know." One finger stabbed Yacov's chest.

"Yes, sir. I know."

Sid stared at his father. *Why doesn't he fight back?* A terrifying anger filled Sid's belly, and something else, too. Shame. He had no word for it then. He only knew he felt hot and uncomfortable.

"Fred, let's go," one of the women said to the man, who moved even closer to Yacov and said, "I see you on this block again on the Lord's Day, I'll personally show you some respect. You understand, Abraham?"

"Yes, sir."

Yacov let go the vise grip on Sid's hand only when the churchgoers were two blocks away.

"Shoulda told them, Pop," Sid said, bewildered.

Yacov stared at his son. "What?"

"Our Sabbath was yesterday. Why didn't you tell them?"

Yacov crouched down to look in his young son's eyes. "We don't want any trouble, Shimon." His Hebrew name. Sid hated it.

"Call me Sid, Pa."

"Oy." Yacov straightened up, took the boy's hand and headed for home. "I should call my son by an English name? For this I came to America?"

"Canada, Pop."

"Canada Shmanada."

They walked the rest of the way home in silence. But Sid never forgot the shame. Forced to grovel, just for being who he was. On someone else's holy day.

WHEN IZZY HAS FALLEN ASLEEP, Sid kisses his forehead and leaves the bedroom. They've been leaving the light on all night, because otherwise Izzy wakes up screaming in the dark. Sid checks the small window.

It's open as high as it goes, held in place by a small stick of wood. He hopes Izzy will not swelter in the heat.

In the kitchen, Sophie washes the supper dishes in the deep, wide, white enamel sink, her eyes filled with tears. Yacov and Lenny share the evening newspaper.

Sid sits by Lenny and grabs a section of the *Toronto Daily Star*. The riot is still on the front page. "Die with Boots On, Cry of Incensed Jews." *Die with your boots on* is the motto of the loosely organized gangs of Spadina Avenue Jews, according to Ben Steiner, 120 Denison Avenue, who claims to know and to have talked to hundreds of members of these gangs since the riot. "Rather than submit to the outrages that have been perpetrated against our race, we would die on the streets. That is the feeling amongst the younger element of our people," Steiner told the *Star* in an interview this morning.

That's right, thinks Sid, although he wonders who the hundreds of Jewish gang members are. His gang has five regular guys, and a few hangers-on, and they don't really think of themselves as a gang so much as a group of guys defending what little turf they have to call their own.

For his part, Lenny devours the news. Normally he wouldn't have been involved in the riot if you'd paid him. He'd been on his way home from the library that Wednesday night, carrying a new book by John Steinbeck called *The Pastures of Heaven*, another by the Canadian novelist Hugh Garner, and *Great Expectations*, which he'd already read and was studying under the mentorship of Mr. Cornwall, the evening librarian. That's when he came across the fighting. He would have continued walking straight home, eager to check on Sonny and Izzy and to crack open one of the new books, when he spotted Sid flat on his back, under a huge guy with a Nazi armband. Lenny stood frozen in his spot, watching his older brother being beaten, trying to think of what to do. He'd never instigated a fight in his life, didn't have a clue how to save Sid. Then someone pushed him down, and they were calling him names and hitting him and his arms flew up to protect his face. He was worried they'd kill him, when he heard something crack in his arm, then Sid's voice. Somehow Sid had wrestled free of a hulking guy to save Lenny. Then there was more

fighting and Lenny practically passed out from the pain in his wrist and
the stress. He waited on the ground until the fighting stopped. He didn't
know what else to do.

Lenny is not a coward; he is brave, in his own way. He's just not a
fighter. Nor is he particularly athletic. Lenny knows that his ambition to
be a writer worries Yacov, but Sophie is proud of her second-born son.
He's the only one in the family she can talk to about the finer things in life
— or what little she knows of such things. If they were middle class,
Sophie would spend her afternoons at the museum or in art galleries,
soaking up culture. But this is an impossibility, given her situation in the
middle of the Depression. Sophie spends every waking moment finding
ways to feed her growing family on the small income her husband brings
home each day, and the rest of the time, she keeps the house clean, scrubs
the laundry, does the washing and the cooking. In the precious moments
she has to watch Lenny read, or discuss a book with him, she feels pure.
The drudgery of her life melts away. She tries to treat all her boys the
same but the truth is, she loves Lenny more than the others. His sweet,
gentle nature appeals to her. His literary ambitions make her proud.

Lenny knows there are finer things in life he can only dream of now,
but he intends to partake of them fully when he's older. He will spend
most of his time writing his own works, but of course, to make a living,
he imagines becoming a journalist for one of the local newspapers. Or he
could teach. But he'd need a degree for that, and the way things are going,
it's doubtful there will be any money to send him to college. Perhaps he will
find a rich benefactor who will recognize his budding literary talents and
send him to school. After he finished reading Dickens' *Great Expectations*
he became enchanted with the idea of finding a benefactor. It's a big city.
Surely to God there is a rich man out there who'd like nothing better
than to help a poor but intelligent boy get a start in life. Lenny just has to
figure out where such a man could be found. Perhaps he could wait
around outside his home or work, then accidentally bump into the man.
What he'd say after that, Lenny hasn't quite figured out, but there's plenty
of time for that. He's only eleven, about to begin the sixth grade. As long
as he figures it out by the end of high school he'll be fine, and that's six

years away. But now Izzy's hospital bill weighs heavy on the family's tight budget. It's possible that in six years they'll still be paying it off. Every morning since the accident, Lenny has woken up thinking about how he could have stopped the tragedy from happening.

Lenny's guilt looks like this: I should have stayed home with Izzy and let Sonny go to the ball game. I could have gone to the library any old day. Sonny wanted, needed to be there. He was crawling out of his skin to be at the park. It makes sense that he disobeyed Pa and took Izzy to the game, and look what happened. Izzy will never be the same again, never be normal and it's all my fault because I went to the library. It's all my fault, my fault, my most grievous fault. I wish it was *Yom Kippur,* the Day of Atonement, already so I could atone for my sins.

Sid's guilt looks different: I am the oldest. I am my brother's keeper. I should have known better. I should have stayed home with Izzy. There was trouble in the neighborhood and I let my family down. The family is the most important thing. Honour thy father and thy mother. Honour thy brothers. As the oldest, it is my responsibility. It's my fault that Izzy got hurt. All my fault. My fault, my most grievous fault. I should have stayed home. Should have stayed home. I'm responsible for my brothers and I failed. It's all my fault that Izzy will never be the same again.

It doesn't really matter how much Sid and Lenny chastise themselves for their part in the calamity. Sonny, sitting silently at the table, knows it was all his fault: He's the one who was entrusted with their baby brother. He's the one who brought Izzy to the riot. He's the one who left Izzy, a sweet little five-year-old boy, standing all alone at the top of the hill while all around him big boys and large men were fighting, tossing stones, throwing bricks, swinging bats, pounding fists, hurtling sticks, crashing bodies, flailing limbs, biting, kicking, punching, screaming, yelling, wailing, cursing, hating and rioting. It was he who couldn't keep still, who couldn't just stay at home like his father asked him to, couldn't just stay in the backyard where it was safe, and amuse his sweet baby brother until his parents came home. It was his stupid idea to follow Louie Horowitz to the park, with Izzy in tow, to jump into the fray while his brother stood terrified on the hill. It was he who couldn't stand the thought of being left out of the fighting when the cursed Swazis had the nerve to take the streetcar all the way to his neighbourhood just to kick them out of their own park. It is Sonny's fault. There is no doubt about it. It is all his fault. His fault, his most grievous fault.

It doesn't matter that Sid is willing to shoulder the burden as the oldest son, that Lenny has admitted he already had a couple of books at home he could have read. Sophie knows this: that she should have taken Izzy with her that night to the *shiva* visit. That Sonny is too young to babysit. That a boy of nine doesn't have the sense of an adult. That really, when you got down to it, as Izzy's mother, she is responsible for his welfare. She is responsible for all the boys and it is her fault for not taking Izzy with her that night. It's her fault, her fault, her most grievous fault. And now she aches for her baby boy Izzy who will never be the same again, just as she aches for her other boys who feel guilty and will never be the same again. She can see it in their eyes, even if they refuse to talk about it.

Yacov knows it's all his fault: He's the father. He came to this country to have a better life. To escape the pogroms. To raise a family in peace. To stay out of trouble. To make a decent life for his wife and children. At the very least, to protect them. They're in a Depression and it's really not Yacov's fault that he can barely provide for his family, but it doesn't matter. He still blames himself. He chokes on his tears every night because he knows his boys go to bed hungry, even if he eats half as much as he should, is growing thin, giving most of what food he can bring home to the kids. It's not his fault that a bunch of hothead British Canadian boys formed a club modeled on Hitler's storm troopers, emulating Nazi terror here in the New World, where the streets are supposed to be paved with gold, where all men are supposed to be equal, where a poor man can dream of becoming rich and where all men are supposed to be free.

Yacov slouches over the *Star*. It is still all over the front pages. Jews fighting Gentiles. His boys involved. Yacov thought he'd left all that behind in Russia, twenty years ago. This isn't supposed to happen in the new country. His family is supposed to be safe. But they are not safe at all. Izzy hasn't spoken a word since they brought him home from the hospital.

He sleeps most of the time. When he is awake, he rocks back and forth, staring stupidly ahead, as if he doesn't even know where he is. The sight of Izzy rips a crater of grief in Yacov's chest. He knows Sonny is suffering terribly, but there's nothing Yacov can do about it. How can he ever forgive his son?

To Sonny it doesn't matter that Yacov is consumed with guilt over Izzy's tragedy, that Yacov has been consumed with guilt since 1913 when he couldn't save his little brother Shmuel from the pogrom. It doesn't concern Sonny that Yacov has barely slept a wink since the riot, that to him it's 1913 all over again and the Cossacks are riding into town, death and destruction and hate are thundering down the streets of Toronto just as the horses carrying soldiers thundered down the dusty roads of Tiraspol when he was a boy and tore up his family, leaving a dead baby brother in their wake. It doesn't matter to Sonny how guilty his father feels, because Sonny knows one thing for sure. He is bad. He is a bad boy. Because of him, his brother almost died, and will never be the same again. Sonny is so full of fear, hate, guilt, and shame his body vibrates with sensation. All the feelings under the sun, every emotion known to humans and God ricochet relentlessly through Sonny's battered nine-year-old body.

Kiting Cheques
AUGUST 30, 1933

AT THE BOWLING ALLEY, Sonny has taken to hanging around after his shift is over at seven o' clock. He's supposed to be home by eight every night, but since the accident Sophie has not said a word when he lets himself in at nine and even sometimes at ten. Yacov doesn't seem to notice what Sonny does, as long as he stays out of his way. After his shift Sonny hangs around the back room, watching the tough guys play poker and billiards. Sometimes he makes himself useful, fetching them a hot

dog or a glass of whiskey. They usually let him keep the change. The
bowling alley doesn't have a licence to serve alcohol, but like many businesses in the Spadina-College neighbourhood, it has found that a little
cash in the hands of the beat cops buys an unofficial licence to run a small
bootlegging operation in the back room. No off-sales. Strictly belly up to
the bar, lay down fifty cents, and you get a shot of cheap, watered-
down rye. No credit, no tabs, no money, no drink.

It's a Wednesday night. Sonny has one more hour on shift. He crouches
on his wooden perch three feet over the pins. By this time in the night, his
legs are so stiff from sitting in one position, there is a dull ache in his hip.
The heat wave broke at last, but it's still stifling hot at the back of the
bowling lane. Sweat gathers in Sonny's thick wavy brown hair inside
his woollen cap and runs down the sides of his cheek and the back of his
neck. There's no time between throws of the bowling ball to reach into
his pocket for his handkerchief, so periodically he wipes the sweat with
the back of his shirt sleeve. His back is drenched, his shirt sticks to his
skin. It's getting almost hard to breathe in the tight airless space at the end
of the lane. He feels a bit faint. He glances at the clock. Fifty more minutes.
He is stationed on alley number ten, farthest in the back. The players are
the tough guys he sees hanging around the billiard tables. Small-time
hustlers, and crooks. Some are only a bit older than his brother Sid and
have already dropped out of school and been in trouble with the law. He
knows they have associations with the Jewish Mob, but he doesn't really
know what they do. One guy bowling on his lane is around his father's
age, only fat instead of thin, wearing an ultra-flashy suit made of white
cotton, with a thin black stripe. His shirt is black, his tie a swirl of colours.
He wears old-fashioned spats on his black-shined shoes, and when he
sits, his trousers ride up his calves and Sonny can see the garters holding
up his socks. He leaves his hat on, even indoors — a crisp brown fedora.
He reeks of money. Thick smoke billows from the fat cigar between his
lips. They are playing for cash. There's a little pile of five-and ten-dollar
bills on the score keeper's desk. Sonny works efficiently and smoothly.
The second each player's last ball is thrown, he lowers himself down, the
pulley wire squeaking as he goes, leans over, and rights the pins. He is

trying to impress the tough guys, but they barely notice the boy on the swing. They take the Monkey Boys for granted and treat them as if they are part of the machinery. Some people tip the boys. Most don't. Sonny keeps one eye on the fat rich man, the other on the pins, watching for "jumpers." Occasionally he glances at the clock. Ten minutes left in his shift. The game is almost over. Thank God. His left knee is cramping up. He can't wait to stretch his legs.

The last round. The fat man is in the lead. Each player takes his turn. The balls thunder down the lane, clattering against the pins. A jumper flies toward Sonny; he dodges it, and without missing a beat continues his work. The last ball is played. A strike. The fat man is the winner. He doesn't jump up and down like Sonny would do if he'd won. He merely slaps one hand hard on the score keeper's desk, and says, "Hah!" Then he puffs on his cigar and scoops the pile of bills from the table, folds them and stuffs them in his pocket.

The men stand and head for a table farther back, to drink shots of whiskey. Sonny glances at the clock. Five minutes to seven. The rule is that when a game finishes, if there are ten minutes or less left on a boy's shift, he quits early. It's too disruptive to a game to switch boys after just a few minutes. Sonny rights the pins for the last time of the evening, lowers the swing and unfolds his aching legs. He tugs his suspenders higher on his shoulders, adjusts his woolen knickers that creep up from squatting for so long. He emerges from the pit and stretches his legs, stifling the urge to cry out. His left knee is really bothering him. He leans over and rubs it. He tries to remember if he got injured in the leg during the riot, or maybe on the night his father hit him.

In the tiny staff room behind the shoe rentals, he punches his time card, then strolls toward the back. He orders a bottle of Coca-Cola and leans against the counter, trying to look older and tough, his cap low on his forehead.

"Hey kid." It's the fat man. "Come 'ere." He holds out one hand and beckons Sonny with his finger.

Sonny saunters over, trying to walk like a gangster, cocky and dangerous. "What's your name, kid?"

"Sonny Lapinsky."

"Lapinsky," the man repeats. "Sit down, Lapinsky. Take a load off."

Sonny's heart speeds up. He pulls back the chair opposite the man and sits. His feet don't quite reach the floor. He wraps his ankles around the chair legs, to keep from swinging his feet. Behind him a pool game is in progress. The cue ball clacks against the eight ball, landing it plunk in the corner pocket with a satisfying thud.

"Do you know who I am?" The man looks Sonny right in the eye.

Sonny thinks hard. Nothing comes to him, so he shakes his head.

The man laughs. Hard and loud, throwing his head back, and his stomach out. "Good. That's good. You like working here, Sonny?" The man wipes the back of his sweaty neck with a white handkerchief.

Sonny shrugs. "It's okay."

The man rolls his cigar around in his thumb and forefinger. A thin stream of smoke drifts into Sonny's face. "They pay you good?"

"Okay, I guess."

The man replaces his cigar in his mouth, takes a puff, blows the smoke out between his lips. "Lapinsky. Sonny Lapinsky," he says again. Then it dawns on him. "Say … are you any relation to Max Lapinsky?"

Sonny sits up straighter. This guy knows Uncle Max? Sonny had no idea that Uncle Max knew guys like this. "My uncle. Well, I mean, I think he's really my cousin, but I call him Uncle Max on acounta he's old, like my pa."

"Uncle Max. All right. That's funny." The fat man laughs loudly. "Uncle Max. So then, we're practically *mishpochah*."

"We are?"

"Sure. Practically related. Your Uncle Max and me we go way back. My girl Lila is girlfriends with your Aunt Tess."

Sonny doesn't remember hearing about a Lila before.

"My name's Shlomo Seigelman. Everyone calls me Checkie, but you can call me Mr. Seigelman on account of you're just a kid. You call me Shlomo and I'll have you killed, understand?" He stares Sonny hard in the eye.

Checkie Seigelman! Holy cripes! Everyone's heard of Checkie Seigelman. Made his fortune kiting cheques. Sonny doesn't really understand how it works, but it has something to do with writing rubber cheques on out-of-province bank accounts so Checkie can float the cash and loan it out at high interest rates to guys who can't get a loan at the bank. By the time his out-of-province cheque is processed ten or twelve days later, he's been partially paid back for the loan and slipped the money into his account just in time for it to clear. That's how Checkie got his nickname, on account of he's a genius with cheques. Everyone knows about Checkie Seigelman. He's a local legend. Grew up right in Sonny's neighbourhood. But now he's so rich everyone goes to him for loans instead of the bank. Sonny gawks at Mr. Seigelman and keeps his mouth shut.

"How'd ja like to do me a little favour, Sonny?"

Sonny shrugs. "Sure."

"That a boy. How old are you?"

"Nine. And a half."

"Nine and a half," Checkie repeats, then laughs. He laughs so hard he starts to cough. His assistant Gershon "Romeo" Schwartz, a tall young man with movie-star looks, leaps to his feet instantly and hits Checkie on the back hard. "You all right, Boss?"

"Yeah yeah," says Checkie. "Get yer hands off me." Romeo takes a step back.

Checkie puts out a hand. "Give me that item," he snaps at Romeo, who opens his jacket, fishes in his breast pocket and hands Checkie a small white sealed envelope. Sonny tries not to stare at the gun strapped around Romeo's chest in a leather harness. Checkie holds the envelope out, fingering it. "You see this, Sonny?"

Sonny tears his eyes from the gun, stares at the envelope and nods.

"I want you to deliver it for me. Can you do that?"

"Sure."

"You know where Ossington Street is?"

"Sure I do."

"Atta boy. All you gotta do is take this here envelope to a building at the corner of Ossington and Bloor. You know the building?"

"Red brick, with a green awning."

"That's right, kid. I want you to go inside and knock on apartment 302, see? A man wearing a straw boater, you know one of those hats from the '20s, you seen one before?"

"In pictures."

"In pictures, all right. Tell me what one looks like."

"White, kind of flat on top with a round brim, and a black band around the middle. Everyone knows that, Mr. Seigelman."

Checkie laughs. "Ain't he cute? All right, good. So a guy wearing a boater should answer the door. Only, not just any boater. This one has a red band. Red, not black. You got that?"

Sonny nods.

"Okay, so if it's him, the guy with the red and white boater, you hand him the envelope. You don't gotta say nothing. Just wait. He'll give you a different envelope. See? You take the new envelope and you bring it right straight back here to me, see?"

"Sure." Easy, thinks Sonny.

"On your way there, you keep the envelope nice and safe in your pocket, all right. You don't take it out until you get there. Okay?"

"Yes, sir."

"And when the guy gives you the new envelope, same thing. You put it in your pocket till you get back here, and then I'll take it out. You got that?"

Sonny nods.

"Now, let's say a guy answers the door, and he ain't wearing a straw boater, I want you to pretend you're calling on a little friend. Okay? You say something like, uh … hi, is Davey there? See? And then you leave. Only you don't come back here right away. How long you been living around here, Sonny?"

"My whole life."

"So you know your way around pretty good, huh?"

"Sure. I know all the streets around here. And the alleys. The shortcuts. The rooftops. Everything."

"Good boy. So if it's a guy and he's not wearing a red and white straw boater, you ask for your little friend, Davey, then you leave and I want you to take your time coming back here. In fact, take at least an hour. Climb over fences, stop and play in a park for a few minutes, go down back alleys. Join a stickball game. You get it? Make it look like you're just a little kid out for a good time. See?"

"Sure I do, Mr. Seigelman."

"Then you come back here and bring the envelope to me. Okay?"

"Yes, sir."

Checkie asks Sonny to repeat his instructions, including the address, three times.

"Okay," he hands Sonny the envelope. "Scram, kid."

It's only a twenty minute walk to Ossington and Bloor. It's a warm evening, not too hot. In postage-sized front yards are tiny gardens with tomato plants, pole beans, pepper and garlic. Along the side of one house, a small group of chickens squawk, running free in the yard. Sonny is dying to know what's in the envelope. It burns a hole in his trouser pocket. A couple of times he considers pulling it out and examining it, but then Sonny thinks about the gun on Romeo's chest. He has no doubts the guy would use it. What if they're following him to make sure he delivers the envelope like he's supposed to? If he opened it, Romeo would shoot him. He imagines the bullets ripping through his chest as he pitches forward onto the sidewalk, dead at age nine. He can't do that to his mother, so he resists the urge to peek. At the building on Ossington, he walks inside, finds apartment 302 and knocks. Just like Checkie said, a thin man wearing a red and white straw boater opens the door. He looks down, surprised to see such a little boy at the door.

"Yeah? Whadya want, kid?" the man barks in a deep voice.

Sonny gulps, reaches in his pocket and extracts the envelope. His arm shakes as he hands it up to the man.

"Oh." The man takes the envelope, scoots back inside, shuts the door. Sonny waits. A minute later, the man opens the door, hands Sonny an identical envelope, waits and watches while Sonny stashes it in his pocket.

"How old are you, kid?"

"Ten."

The man looks Sonny over, shakes his head and slams the door. Sonny walks straight back to the bowling alley, presents the prize to Checkie.

"What a guy!" Checkie says enthusiastically, then he takes Sonny on both sides of his face, pulls him forward and kisses the top of his head. "What a genius. Look at that Romeo, and in record time too."

Sonny beams. This is the first good thing he's done since Izzy got hurt. The hollow ache in his chest fills, just a little. He basks in the glow of Checkie's praise.

"Sit down, kid. Romeo, get the kid a Coca-Cola, will ya."

Romeo raises his eyebrows, insulted. What the hell is he? A babysitter? But Checkie's the boss, so he walks over and orders the soda for Sonny.

Checkie reaches inside his trouser pocket, pulls out a bulging billfold, peels off a two-dollar bill, hands it to Sonny. "Here ya go, kid. That's kind of like a tip, for such a good job done."

Sonny's eyes bulge. Two dollars is almost a week's pay at the bowling alley.

Romeo returns and plunks the soda in front of Sonny. A splash of pop sloshes to one side of the bottle and onto Sonny's hand. He wipes it on his pants.

"So, kid. Tell me, how's your Uncle Max? I haven't seen him for quite some time, you know."

"He's okay, I guess."

Checkie stares at Sonny for a long time, as if he's planning to say something, but he's not sure if he should. "All right, Sonny. Listen, how'd ja like to do me another little favour tomorrow?"

"Yes, sir."

"All right. What time you finish work here?"

"Seven."

"Every day?"

Sonny nods.

"Okay. Tomorrow I'll be right here. Come see me when your shift is over. All right?"

"Sure."

Checkie takes a cigar out of his front handkerchief pocket. Romeo steps forward and lights it. Checkie takes a long puff, then lets the smoke out slowly. "Ahh," he says. He glances over and sees Sonny still sitting there. "Go on. Scram."

Sonny bumbles to his feet, grabs his soda and backs away.

"See you tomorrow, sir."
"Yeah yeah."

A Right Uppercut
SEPTEMBER 1933

SONNY BEGINS WORKING for Checkie. It's something he's good at, and he craves the praise that Checkie doles out with the two dollar bills. Every day it's the same task. Take a small white envelope and deliver it somewhere. One day it's a hat box. Inside is a hat. Under the hat, a false bottom. Sonny knows this because Checkie shows him before he leaves. He wants the kid to see that there's actually a hat in there. In Checkie's experience it's always easier to lie if there's at least some truth in it.

Sonny makes two dollars a night delivering packages for Checkie. His salary at the bowling alley is three dollars and fifty cents a week, but he keeps the job because he's scared his mother will find out if he quits. He wishes he could give her more of the money he is earning from Checkie, but she'll want to know where he got it from, and he can't tell her, so he stashes it in an empty coffee tin that he keeps under the back porch, in a hole in the ground, under an old rotting two-by-four. He turns over two dollars and seventy-five cents to her every week from his bowling alley pay, keeping seventy-five cents for himself so she won't get suspicious.

IN SEPTEMBER, SONNY has to go back to school. Checkie asks Sonny if he wants to keep on doing him favours, only maybe a little earlier in the afternoon, after school is out. Sonny can't fit in both jobs, so he quits the bowling alley. He doesn't tell his parents. It's obvious they wouldn't approve. On the first day, Checkie asks Sonny to meet him outside the pool hall he owns on Queen Street in the Ward, where he has an office on the second floor. Checkie bought the pool hall in early '20s, long before the Depression. Over the years, it's become a local hangout. Besides playing a game of billiards, a man can buy a fifty-cent shot of rye, a fifteen-cent glass of beer, play a few rounds of poker, and bet on everything from the horse races to the heavyweight title, to the ball games at Maple Leaf Stadium and the hockey games at the new Maple Leaf Gardens. There are three bookies who rent space and pay a commission to Checkie for operating out of his place. One of the operators, Benny Chicago (who is not from Chicago but from Brooklyn) will take book on just about anything. Just last week, guys were laying bets six to one that Joey Applebaum, who had just been paroled, would be back in jail by the end of the week. And he was. Checkie is paid thirty-three and a third on all the bookmaker's profits, a good deal when you consider that everyone from both the Ward and Kensington neighbourhoods drops into Checkie's pool hall at some time or another, and anyone wanting to place a bet always knows where to find the bookies.

It takes Sonny a little longer to cross town than he thought it would, so he is late. He runs from the streetcar stop to the pool hall. Checkie is standing out front, talking to Romeo and another large man. A crisp autumn breeze knocks bright red leaves from a streetside Maple tree and swirls fallen leaves in the nearby gutter.

"There he is," Checkie says. "Okay kid, come on." He grabs Sonny by the collar and steers him along. "See ya later, Silverman," he says to the large man.

"Wait a minute, Boss. What do you want me to tell the bank manager?" Silverman asks.

"What?"

"The bank manager. He's all the time bothering me. Ask Mr. Seigelman about loaning money, he says. So what do you want me to tell him?"

"Aw right. Aw right." Checkie reaches in his pocket, extracts a thick wad of bills. "How much does he want?"

Silverman laughs. "You got it all wrong. He wants to loan you money."

"What?"

"Yeah. He wants to make you a loan."

"What the hell I want to borrow from a bank for?"

"I don't know."

"Get outa here, will ya?"

Silverman shrugs, turns and enters the pool hall.

Sonny has learned never to ask questions, so he doesn't ask where they are going. He walks along on one side of Checkie. Romeo is on the other side. His legs are much shorter than theirs, so he has to trot to keep up. They walk a block and stop in front of a shiny black Buick. It's a brand new, sleek 1933 model with a silver hood ornament of a diving dolphin, heavy grated grille in front, spare tire mounted on the running board, and a small trunk perched on the back fender. Checkie holds open the back seat door. The immaculate brown seats smell of fresh leather.

"Get in," he commands Sonny.

Checkie plops his bulky frame into the front passenger seat. Romeo slips into the driver's seat and starts up the car. Sonny steps onto the running board and onto the fine soft leather of the back seat. The only other car he has ever been in is the broken-down Model T his father shares with Uncle Max, with its ripped seats, hand-crank motor and unreliable engine that coughs and sputters its way up the street. This baby rides smooth, and shifts like a dream. Every surface is clean and polished. Sonny leans back against the seat and imagines what it would be like to be rich. They drive toward Sonny's neighbourhood and stop in front of the Cecil Street Athletic Club. Sonny's heart leaps.

"Come on, kid," Checkie says. "I got something for you to deliver, but first we gotta stop in here." Wide-eyed, Sonny follows Checkie inside and up the narrow staircase to the second floor.

It's his first time inside a gym. He cranes his neck around, looking everywhere all at once. His heart races with excitement. They walk into a large room with high ceilings and two regulation-sized boxing rings, one in each corner. There are several small round punching bags hanging from the dropped ceiling along a side wall. Heavy bags are scattered all over, fastened by thick chains to steel beams above. Over on one wall is a rack filled with barbells of different sizes, beside an exercise mat. On another wall is a series of pulleys. One of the rings is empty. In the other, a boxer spars with his coach. Sonny stops and watches, trying to figure out exactly what the boxer is doing with his feet.

"Come on, kid." Checkie grabs Sonny's shirt collar and pulls him along. They pass a large man working out on a heavy bag, thumping it with gloved fists, then a smaller man jumping rope, never missing a beat, the rope slapping the polished hardwood floor in rhythm. Slip slap. Slip slap. An older man is yelling at a young boy in the corner, instructing him on the proper rhythm required to hit the speed bags. The boy tries again, his fists a blur, punching in a quick circular motion. Rat tat tat tat tat. In the back corner are a few scattered card tables with men playing poker, jackets off, shirtsleeves rolled up, ties loosened, cigars and cigarettes dangling from pursed lips. There are stacks of money piled on the card tables. In one of the rings, there is a sparring session. The boxers, dressed in trunks, boots and gloves, dance and jab. The thud of leather gloves against skin echoes through Sonny's heart. He watches the boxers in awe. The room is smoke-filled, noisy and sweaty. Sonny is in heaven.

Checkie glances back at the kid, sees him ginning like an idiot. "What's a matter kid? Never been in a gym before?"

Sonny shakes his head. "Not really. Except for once. For a fight. Sammy Luftspring was boxing."

"No kidding?"

"I'm gonna be a fighter," Sonny says to the floor.

Checkie glances back at the kid again. He's so little. Checkie can't imagine him fighting. He tips his head back and laughs from deep in his belly.

Sonny blushes, more out of anger than embarrassment. He hates being laughed at. *I'm short*, he thinks, *but strong. I'll show you. Just you wait. I'll show you all.* Checkie is still laughing when they reach the occupied ring. The men in the ring have stopped for a break.

"Hi, Tony. How ya doing?" Checkie searches in his trouser pocket, pulls out a handkerchief and wipes his face.

Tony spits his mouthguard into his coach's hand. "What's so funny?"

"The kid here," he points to Sonny, "wants to be a fighter."

"I can fight," Sonny says quietly.

"What?"

Louder. "I can fight."

Tony laughs, puts up his dukes, and says, "Why don't ya step into the ring and take a crack at me then?"

Sonny looks up. Tony isn't that much older than he, maybe fifteen he figures, only two years older than Sid, and he's shorter and thinner than Sid. Sonny's had lots of play fights with his older brother, so he knows how to take on a bigger guy. Rapid-fire punches to the body, then a left jab followed by a hard right uppercut to the chin from below. Piece of cake. He figures the worst that could happen is the guy kills him. He's already humiliated, which is worse. "Okay," he says, through clenched teeth.

They all laugh some more. Tony stops laughing first and sees by the look in Sonny's piercing brown eyes that the shrimp is dead serious. "Okay, kid," he says, "come on up." Tony won't hurt the runt, just dance around the ring with him for a few minutes, land his punches softly, let the kid hit him once or twice. Make him feel like a hero.

Sonny looks at Checkie, who says, "Go on. Let's see your stuff." Checkie is always up for a bit of entertainment. "This oughta be good," he tells Romeo.

Sonny takes off his cap and shirt, lays them down on the floor. He is wearing a white undershirt, short pants and knee socks when he steps into the ring. The coach finds the smallest pair of sparring gloves in the gym and slips them on Sonny's hands. Laces them. They're just a little large. They feel wonderful to Sonny. Real leather boxing gloves. He puts his fists up in front of his face to protect his chin, like he's seen boxers do. Tony takes his position. The coach signals to start. Sonny wastes no time. He has no technique, but he has speed, power, determination, talent, and heart. For a little guy, he can sure pack a wallop. And keep 'em coming. Using his rapid-fire style, he charges at Tony, catching him on the chin on his second punch, hard enough to knock the older boy back a few inches.

Checkie removes the cigar from his mouth and stares. The coach watches with great interest. Tony rubs his jaw and shakes his head. *Jesus, the squirt can pack a punch. Maybe I shouldn't go so easy on him.* They get back in position and Sonny does it again. Bam bam bam bam bam. He strikes out so fast Tony doesn't have a chance to dodge and again Sonny connects hard, a direct hit on Tony's chin.

"Jesus," Tony mumbles through his mouthguard, then steps in and swings at Sonny, but the kid is so short, he misses his mark. Sonny successfully dodges every punch. Checkie's eyes light up. Even Romeo is impressed.

"Holy fuck, kid," Checkie shouts. "Do that again."

And Sonny obliges. He moves in and bam, bam, he makes two more direct hits. Everyone can see the kid has natural talent. Dollar signs ring in Checkie's head. *A goddamned gold mine. The kid is a gold mine and I discovered him.* "Hah!" Checkie says, when Sonny hits his opponent again. "Hah! Did you see that?" he asks Romeo, who nods with wide eyes.

"Amazing," Romeo concedes.

The coach calls time and the fighters stop. He removes Tony's gloves, and Tony sticks out a hand for Sonny to shake. Sonny's still in his gloves so all he can do is touch Tony's outstretched hand with his right glove. "Nice work. Who's your trainer?"

Sonny shuffles his feet. "Don't have one."

"Yet!" shouts Checkie. "That's one of the reasons we came down here today. Gotta find the kid a good trainer. Right, Romeo?" He digs an elbow hard into Romeo's ribs.

"Yeah, sure."

"Course, as his manager," continues Checkie, "I only want the best for the boy. Anyone can see he's gonna go far. Come 'ere Sonny." Checkie holds out his hand and helps Sonny out of the ring. He ruffles his hair affectionately. "What a guy," he says. "Knew it the first time I laid eyes on the kid." He steers Sonny away from the ring. "Why didn't ya tell me, kid?"

Sonny shrugs and smiles. Pure happiness.

"You don't know? All right. Fair enough. What a punch."

"Come on. Let's get outa here. We got some thinking to do. Romeo, get the kid outa his gloves."

Checkie takes Sonny to a delicatessen on College Street for a pastrami sandwich on rye, coleslaw and a soda. He sends Romeo on an errand. For the first time, Checkie looks Sonny in the eye and treats him with respect.

Sonny can't remember a time when he has felt happier. Or eaten meat. He takes huge bites of his sandwich, chewing fast, in case someone takes it away from him. He'd like to stuff half in his pocket and bring it home to share with his brothers, but he doesn't see how he could do that in front of Checkie. So he eats it all himself. And fast.

SONNY ARRIVES HOME LATE. The apartment reeks of boiled cabbage, a smell he despises. The family has already eaten dinner. Yacov is reading the *Toronto Daily Star* in the living room, Lenny is doing homework, Sid is playing with Izzy and Sophie is cleaning up. Yacov says nothing when Sonny walks in, just glances up, catches his son's eye, then looks back down at his paper. Yacov has become silent around Sonny. Whenever he looks at Sonny his head throbs with tension and his neck aches. He doesn't know how to make it stop. He has started attending services at the synagogue in the mornings before work and in the evening. He is hoping God has some answers for him.

"Sit down," Sophie says to Sonny. She has saved him a plate from supper — boiled cabbage with potatoes. Sonny is not hungry, but he doesn't want to hurt his mother's feelings, and he can always eat. He's dying to tell everyone about his good fortune, but everything has been so tense in the house since the riot. He's scared to say anything. What if his parents won't let him fight? Checkie is going to "do a little asking around," to find the best trainer for him.

"Now, as your manager," Checkie said, "I'll pay all the expenses for your training and equipment and whatnot, and then later on, when you go pro, which ain't gonna be tomorrow, let's face it kid, I take forty percent of your winnings. That's the going rate. You can ask around." Actually, the standard manager's commission is thirty-three and a third, but Checkie figures he deserves a little something extra on account of the kid is so young and it's going to be a long time before his investment even begins to pay off.

Sonny is thrilled that Checkie will pay for the trainer and everything. He doesn't have trunks or boxing shoes or even a jockstrap. He doesn't mind paying his manager a percentage. He's thrilled to have a manager. He can tell by everyone's reaction that he's got what it takes. He is going to be famous. And rich. A world champion, like Joe Louis or Maxie Baer.

"This is great, Ma," he says, shovelling her supper into his mouth in big heaps. She eyes him suspiciously. He is smiling for the first time in weeks, and besides, Sonny doesn't really like cabbage.

LATER IN THEIR BEDROOM, Sonny spills the news to his brothers.

"That's swell," says Sid. "The Cecil Street Gym. Terrific."

Even Lenny, who abhors sports, is impressed. "That's great, Sonny," he says.

Izzy stares at Sonny, trying to figure out what the guys are talking about. He giggles, caught up in the happy mood.

"Why don't cha tell Pop?" Sid asks.

Sonny sighs.

"He can't," Lenny answers for Sonny.

"Why not? This is great news. Geez, a fighter in the family. You're gonna be famous, Sonny."

Sonny rubs his head. It is starting to ache.

"Pop don't like Sonny any more." Lenny speaks the truth they've all been avoiding.

"Aw come on, that's not true," Sid ever-the-optimist says. "He's just sore. Give him some time. He'll come around."

"I don't think so," Sonny says, sadly.

"Well, tell Ma, then," Sid says loudly.

"Shhh," Sonny says. "What if she forbids it?"

"You think?" Sid has never considered this. "Lenny?"

"I don't know. I don't think she'd be as excited as you are, let's put it that way."

"I'm not telling," Sonny affirms. "Not yet anyway."

"Geez," grumbles Sid.

"Geez," Izzy imitates him. They all swivel around to look at him. It's the first thing he's said since he's been home from the hospital. First thing in six weeks.

"What did you say?" Sid asks Izzy gently.

"Say?" Izzy repeats.

"Hey, he's repeating the last thing he hears. Maybe he's getting better now. Hey Izzy, say Mama."

"Mama," says Izzy.

"Hah!" says Sonny. "See that?"

"See dat," Izzy says.

"Oh my God," says Sonny. "He's talking! Come on Izzy. Ma!" He grabs Izzy by the hand and leads him into the kitchen to show his parents.

THE BOYS, ESPECIALLY SONNY, pay close attention to Izzy, talking to him, patiently repeating everything over and over. He seems able to repeat the last word he hears. They believe for a while that the more information they feed him, the more he will learn. But Izzy's disability doesn't work that way. There seems to be just enough room in his memory to remember the last thing he hears, but he doesn't retain anything else for very long. And his comprehension is sketchy. He may seem to understand a simple concept one day, but then be at a total loss the next day, sometimes the next hour.

No one really knows how much he understands. His doctor says it's possible that Izzy's understanding may be greater than it seems. He peers at Izzy through the round metal eyepiece then listens to his heart with a stethoscope. In the corner of Dr. Milne's office is a human skeleton, mounted in a standing position, staring at patients from its empty eye sockets. An eye chart beginning with a huge E hangs on the wall. From the next examining room over, a little girl cries.

"Izzy's speech, or his ability for speech, has obviously been badly affected, but he seems to understand a great deal," the doctor surmises. "On the other hand, since he can't tell us ... well, we'll never know for sure." Dr. Milne pulls a cigarette from his pack on the desk, lights it and writes something on his clipboard.

Sophie hates the doctor's answer. "But what should we do?"

"Let's just take it one day at a time, Mrs. Lapinsky."

Sophie hugs Izzy and strokes his head softly. He looks up at her with his soft hazel eyes, a world of trust.

LATE ONE NIGHT IN September, Lenny, a bad sleeper, wakes. His throat is parched. In his cotton pyjamas he pads into the kitchen for a glass of water. The light is on. His mother sits at the table with a cold cup of weak tea, staring out the window at the empty street below.

"Ma?" Lenny says quietly.

Sophie offers a weak smile. Lenny can see she's been crying.

He fills a glass with water from the sink, and sits across from his mother. He knows she has been up most nights since Izzy's accident, worrying. He tries to think of something to say, something that would make her feel better, but there really is nothing. If only he could turn back the hands of time and change the circumstances. He sits with his mother in silence for a while. All is silent from the street below.

"I don't know what's going to be," Sophie finally says.

"Be?"

She sighs deeply. "When he grows up. After your father and I ... pass on."

"Oh." This is somewhat beyond Lenny's scope, but he knows he must say something. "You don't have to worry about that, Ma."

Sophie looks at him hopefully, as if he has the magic answer.

"I'll take care of him." It's almost imperceptible, but Lenny notices a fleeting expression of relief cross his mother's face.

"Sure," Lenny runs with his idea. "As long as I'm around, Izzy will be taken care of."

His mother shakes her head. "You'll get married. Have children of your own. Your wife won't want to put up with — with Izzy."

Married? Who said anything about married? It's certainly not anything Lenny has ever considered before. When he thinks of his future, of being an adult, he thinks about his writing career, about having his own apartment with a separate room for a study. He thinks about getting rich so he can fill his study with books. He thinks about things he has never experienced but has seen in the movies, glamorous things like cocktail parties, New York art galleries, the theatre, the opera. He sees himself as a bachelor. A playboy even, although he's not exactly sure what that means, only that it sounds like fun. But married? To a woman? Kids of his own. These are not part of his fantasy, so he says to his mother, "No. Not me."

She almost smiles. He's just too young to realize what will be. "Sure you will, sweetheart. Everyone gets married. Eventually."

"Not me," he repeats with such assurance it stops Sophie in her tracks. She studies her boy Lenny.

"Then what will you do? You'll be lonely," she suggests.

"Not if Izzy lives with me."

And this time Sophie does smile. Somehow dear sweet Lenny has found a silver lining in the midst of their tragedy. Somehow he can picture a future that contains Izzy, damaged though he is, and it's not completely bleak. She reaches over and pats Lenny's hand.

"You should go back to bed, Sweetheart. It's late."

"You should go to bed, too, Ma."

"In a little while."

He kisses her cheek on his way back to the boys' bedroom.

Road Work
NOVEMBER AND DECEMBER, 1933

"COME ON KID, hurry up," Checkie says as Sonny enters the pool hall. Come on, come on." He drapes one arm over Sonny's shoulder and hustles him outside and over to the Buick parked by the side of the road. It's a cool afternoon in early November. The clean scent of snow is in the air, although the streets are clear. Romeo is already behind the wheel. Checkie opens the door to the back seat and motions for Sonny to get in. Silverman is leaning into the window talking to Romeo. Checkie drops his bulk into the back beside Sonny.

"Wait a minute," Silverman runs around the front of the car. "Boss," he says into the window. "Carmello wants to be paid. He says you owe him five bills."

"So?" Checkie puffs on his cigar, blowing small clouds of smoke toward Silverman.

"Well. What should I tell him?"

Checkie shrugs. "I owe him money. He can worry about it. Why should we both worry?" He removes the cigar stub from his lips, tosses it out the window by Silverman's feet and bellows, "Romeo, let's get the hell outa here. Drive. Will ya?"

Romeo puts the car in gear, lifts the clutch and floors the accelerator, leaving Silverman on the sidewalk.

"Okay kid, guess what?" Checkie pulls a fresh cigar from his jacket pocket, bites off the end, spits it out the window and stuffs the cigar into the corner of his mouth. "Can you guess?"

"No, sir."

Checkie ruffles the hair on Sonny's head. "No, sir," he mimics. "Ain't that cute, Romeo?"

Romeo stares at Sonny in the rearview mirror. "Yeah, real cute."

"No guesses?"

Sonny shakes his head.

"None at all?" Checkie pulls out his silver lighter and lights his cigar, puffing and blowing smoke in Sonny's direction. "Aw right, aw right. I'll give you a hint. How's that?"

"Fine, sir."

"We're going to the gym."

"Swell."

"Right. So why do you think we might possibly be going to the gym, Sonny?"

Sonny shrugs. "Watch a fight?"

"Nope."

"You want me to deliver something?"

"Nope."

"You got a meeting?"

"No, but you're getting close."

Sonny is out of ideas. He stares intently at Checkie and tries not to choke on the cigar smoke that catches in his throat.

"Aw, forget it. You're lousy at guessing. *You* got a meeting."

"I do?"

"Yeah. I got you a trainer."

Sonny practically jumps out of the plush leather seat. He feels like kissing Mr. Seigelman but he knows he shouldn't do that, so he grabs Checkie's hand and pumps it wildly, squeezing tightly. "A trainer. Oh boy. That's swell, Mr. Seigelman. Thank you. That's swell. Boy, oh boy." He falls back against the seat.

Checkie laughs and gently pulls his hand back. "Careful, will ya? That's a good ring." Romeo slows the car and stops by the side of the road in front of the Cecil Street Gym. "Come on, kid. Let's go. Romeo, you go ahead and deal with that whatchacallit? Other situation. I'll meet you back at the office later."

Inside the gym, Checkie leads Sonny into the locker room. "Here ya go." He tosses Sonny a pair of boxing trunks, black with a white stripe down the side, a jockstrap and regulation boxing boots.

Sonny feels the shiny newness of the items in his hand. As the third son in his family, he's never worn a stitch of new clothing in his life. All of his clothes are hand-me-downs from Sid or Lenny, and even their clothes are usually secondhand in the first place, so they're third- or fourthhand by the time Sonny gets them.

"Come on kid, don't just stand there gawking. Let's get the lead out. Put that stuff on. Then come on out and meet your trainer." Checkie walks out of the locker room, smiling under his stern exterior. He is tickled by the kid's enthusiasm. Checkie is naturally generous. Of course, he doesn't miss the incredible investment opportunity before him in the form of this kid, who he is sure is going to be the next welterweight champ, maybe even middleweight, who knows? He's a little on the short side now, but he's seen scrawnier kids spring up once they get a bit older. As Sonny's manager, Checkie Seigelman is going to become not only rich but famous. Besides all that, he's getting a real charge out of the kid's excitement. Checkie hasn't had anything come along in a while that's made him feel this way: young again. Like he has the chance to do something big.

As Checkie leaves the locker room, Sonny strips naked. He's never worn a jockstrap before, but it's pretty obvious how to put it on. It's a little large, but he figures out how to tighten the adjustable straps on his thighs. He slides into the shiny new boxing trunks. The silk is soft against his skin. The thick Everlast waistband is snug but not too tight. His heart thuds in excitement. The boots fit perfectly. How did Mr. Seigelman know his shoe size? There is a mirror over the sink. Sonny stands before it. He can only see his reflection from the chest up, but when he looks down at himself, he looks like a real boxer. Grinning, he bounds into the gym.

"There he is," Checkie shouts and walks toward Sonny.

"That's him?"

"Yeah, that's him."

The man studies Sonny. "Kind of short."

"Yeah, yeah, Rudy. Wait till you see the kid swing."

Rudy Gold had been the Canadian amateur welterweight champ of 1925 when he was twenty-one years old. He'd gone pro in 1926 and out of twenty-two fights over the next two years, he'd won twenty. Eighteen knockouts and two by decision. In 1928 at a party in New York, he'd been drinking heavily and began sparring bare-fisted with another fighter, Patty Nicholson. Rudy took a hard right uppercut that sent him up and over the edge of the porch. The drop was only seven feet, but Rudy landed on his tailbone and cracked his lower vertebrae. After six months in traction he recovered. He could walk and even fight, but his back was never the same. He fought for a few more years but the pain got the better of him. He lost more fights than he won. He was knocked out seven times and badly beaten seven more times. Rather than go out a loser, he quit while people still remembered his good fights. He's been coaching ever since. At twenty-nine, he's starting to think about retiring from boxing altogether. A guy he knows, Jimmy O'Hagen, is opening up a nightclub on Yonge Street and looking for a manager. Rudy's thinking about it. How hard could running a club be? He agreed to take a look at the kid only as a favour to Seigelman. Plus he owes Checkie over a thousand bucks in gambling debts and Seigelman says he'll wipe the slate clean, plus pay him seventy bucks a week to train the kid.

Watching Sonny Lapinsky walk out of the locker room, Rudy has second thoughts. Kid's a shrimp. Seigelman says the kid is ten, but he looks about eight. That sticks in Rudy's jockstrap. At one time, he was the champ. Now here he is — a has-been, reduced to babysitting some damn runt. But Rudy hasn't had a steady gig in three years. He referees part-time when he can get the work, and does some sparring by the hour for some of the guys in training, but nothing steady. Not for a long time. Wiping his debt clean, plus seventy bucks a week would sure sit pretty with Rudy. So he grits his teeth, and smiles for all he's worth when Seigelman introduces him to the brat.

"It sure is good to meet you, Mr. Gold," the kid says in a quiet voice.

"Yeah yeah." Rudy wraps the kid's hands with tape, and helps Sonny into a pair of gloves, a small pair Seigelman bought especially for the kid. Rudy eyes the sparring chest protector on the floor by the wall, but decides not to wear it. With this shrimp, he doubts he'll need it. He steps into the ring. "Come on. Let's see what you can do."

Sonny has to reach way up to get his foot onto the edge of the ring. He pulls himself the rest of the way up by the ropes. When he pries apart the top rope to step into the ring and his foot touches the sacred inner circle, he almost dies of happiness. This is a magical moment. Everything moves in slow motion. He can feel the spring-loaded flooring under his new boots. He pulls at the ropes with his gloved hand. He looks down at Checkie, who nods and gives him the thumbs-up. He's aware of the sounds around him in the gym: the clicking of chips at a poker table below, the slow thudding crash as a boxer works on the heavy bag, the rumbling of barbells dropped on the hardwood floor, the rhythmic pop of a speed bag in motion. He looks down at his feet in the new boots. He is standing in a ring across from the man who is going to be his trainer. Sonny has a keen sense of well-being, of power. And of something unusual for Sonny these days — a sense of peace. Mr. Gold stands right in the middle of the canvas, beckoning Sonny with a wave of his hand.

"All right. Let's see what you got." Rudy faces Sonny, his hands at his sides.

Sonny hesitates.

"What's a matter? Come on. Hit me."

Sonny is concerned. "You're not wearing any gloves, Sir."

Rudy laughs. "That's all right. Hit me right here." He points to his chest area. "I want to see your stuff."

Sonny looks Mr. Gold in the eye, worried. He seems kind of old. Not as old as his father, but close, and he walks with a slight limp, as if he's in pain or something. Sonny doesn't want to hurt the guy.

"Come on. I ain't got all day."

Sonny glances at Checkie, who winks and nods approval. Sonny turns back to Mr. Gold, checks his foot position, puts up his dukes, then he charges forward and lets fly a series of punches, using his whole body. Each blow lands hard against Rudy's chest and belly. Not hard enough to hurt Rudy, but enough to impress him. Sonny's final punch, in which he packs all seventy pounds of his body weight, catches Rudy smack on his chin and sends him backward several inches toward the ropes.

"Whoa. Jesus Christ," Rudy curses. "Damn." He rubs his chin.

Checkie pulls the cigar out of his mouth and laughs loudly, almost choking.

"Jesus Christ," Rudy says again. He stares at Sonny, moves closer. "Let me see your hands."

Sonny thrusts out his hands. Rudy unlaces and pulls one glove off to examine Sonny's hand up close. The palm is square and strong. Large for a kid his age and size. The muscles in the boy's hand are rock hard. Rudy runs his fingers up the boy's arms. Same deal. Like a rock. He bends on one knee, checks out the kid's legs. Huge muscles for a kid his age and size. His abdomen. Same thing. Tight, lean and muscular. Jesus Christ. Seigelman is right. This kid is a natural. Rudy nods to himself and smiles. Drops Sonny's arms, leans his hands on top of the ropes. "Seigelman, you son of a bitch."

"I told you, Rudy."

"You son of a bitch."

"So we got a deal or what?"

"You're a crazy bastard."

"Deal?" Checkie rolls his cigar around in his mouth.

"Deal," Rudy says, then bends down and sticks out a hand for Checkie to shake. "You bastard."

Checkie laughs.

Rudy turns back to Sonny. "All right. Gimme your hand." Sonny holds out the bare hand as Rudy replaces the glove. "Let me see that again."

SONNY'S TRAINING PROGRAM begins the next day. He runs to the Cecil Street Gym the second school lets out. Rudy is waiting for him outside, leaning against a car, a blue and white, two-toned Ford convertible coupe.

"Hi, Mr. Gold," Sonny pants with excitement.

"Get in the car, kid." Rudy opens the driver's side door and sits on the bench seat.

Sonny hops in beside him, confused. He thought they'd be going inside the gym. He is anxious to change into his boxing trunks, to slip his fists inside the new gloves Checkie bought for him. Rudy puts the car into gear and drives off. "Where we going, sir?"

"Road work." Rudy reaches inside his shirt pocket for his package of Players Navy Cuts. Taps it against his other hand which holds the steering wheel, slips a cigarette into his mouth. "And cut it out with the Sir business. You can call me Rudy. That's my name. I ain't that old." Rudy raises his butt off the seat, searches in his trouser pockets for his lighter, a sliver Ronson.

"Yes, sir. I mean … Rudy. What's road work?"

Rudy lights his cigarette. The faint scent of lighter fluid wafts under Sonny's nose. Rudy inhales deeply, turns to the side. A steady stream of smoke pours from his mouth toward Sonny, who tries not to choke. "You'll see."

Unlike Checkie's immaculately neat Buick, Rudy's Ford is a mess. The floor in the back is littered with old Coca-Cola bottles that clink together whenever he accelerates or brakes. Empty cigarette packs are crunched up on the front seat. There is the faint smell of spilled whiskey on the upholstery. The ashtray overflows with butts. The side mirror has been broken off. There's an oil leak Rudy hasn't gotten around to repairing, and the trunk is crammed with sweaty gym clothes, empty whiskey bottles, a rotting long-forgotten pastrami sandwich in a paper bag, and a disorganized tool box. There is a periodic knock in the motor which Rudy ignores.

They drive to High Park and enter through the front gates. Rudy stops the car. "Okay, kid. Get out."

Sonny opens the door of the car. Gets out, waits. Rudy does not follow. He remains in the car. Sonny doesn't know what to do.

"Come 'ere." Rudy shouts impatiently. "Let me see your feet."

Sonny holds up one foot. He's wearing a pair of well-worn leather shoes, passed down from Lenny via Sid. They look as though they're about to fall apart. Colour rises in Sonny's cheeks.

"That's what I thought." Rudy reaches into the back seat for a pair of rubber-soled sneakers and tosses them to Sonny. "Come on. Put 'em on. I ain't got all day."

Sonny sits on a tree stump, changes shoes, and tosses his old pair through the open window into the back seat. He needs to save them for Izzy, even though they are old and tattered. The brand new shoes fit perfectly. Just his size. He tries not to smile.

"Okay, now. Get in front of the car, and start running."

"Running?"

"Yeah, you heard me. Running. Go on. Scram."

Running? What does running have to do with boxing? Sonny wants to ask, but Rudy is kind of crabby. Sonny wonders if his trainer is in a bad mood today, or if he's always like this.

"Now," Rudy shouts.

"Yes, sir. Rudy." Sonny begins to run. Rudy follows behind in the car. Sonny runs toward a foot path under a canopy of large old oak trees. Rudy leans on the horn, blaring loudly, startling Sonny. He looks back, adrenalin soaring.

"Not there, kid. How am I supposed to follow you? Huh? Stick to the road. Over there." He points. "Just run in the centre of the road. Jesus Christ. It's not that hard."

"Yes, sir." Sonny runs back to the road. He runs for ten minutes, fifteen, twenty. His legs begin to ache. His lungs pound. His breathing is heavy. The cold November air is freezing the inside of his nose. His ears are red and frozen, his bare hands are cold. Nose drips. He wants to stop and rest. He slows down.

"Keep going. No stopping," Rudy yells out the window.

Sonny looks over his shoulder. The car chugs on relentlessly behind him. He keeps running. His legs burn. He pounds his feet hard on the pavement. The rubber-soled runners absorb the shock. There is no way out of this. He has to keep going. He concentrates on the road ahead. Don't think about your legs, or the cold, he tells himself, wiping his dripping nose with the back of his hand. Don't think. Just run. Right left right left. He swings his arms widely at his sides. Back and forth. The wind through his hair. The fresh smell of pine cones and cedar trees. A black squirrel crosses his path, runs up the side of a tree. Sonny sucks air in greedily. His heart races. A sense of euphoria washes over him. Adrenalin and endorphins are released naturally by his body. He feels high. Riding on air. The burning in his legs cools, soothed by the air with every breath he takes. His body is warm, the cool air refreshing, the scenery peaceful and calming. He speeds up. He could run forever. He could leap as high as the tallest tree. He is invincible. He is Joe Louis, Jack Dempsey and Maxie Baer, all rolled into one. A Champ. He can do anything. Thirty minutes, forty, one hour. How many miles has he run?

A light snow begins to fall. Thin, dry flakes float down, collect on the road and grass, dust the roof of the car and the top of Sonny's cloth cap. Rudy switches on the windshield wipers, flips his collar up around his neck. He opens the glove compartment, finds his whiskey flask, takes a swig against the chill, lights a cigarette, inhales deeply. He watches the kid run and remembers being that young himself and in training, his whole life ahead of him, on his way to being a world champ. What the hell. Rudy stops himself abruptly. This train of thought will only lead to depression.

"All right, kid." Rudy's voice punctures the silence in Sonny's mind. He glances over his shoulder, keeps running. He's on automatic pilot now. Rudy honks the horn. Sonny doesn't notice. Rudy honks again, three times in a row. Sonny finally registers and stops. "Okay. That's enough now. It's starting to snow, for chrissakes." Rudy pulls the car to the side of the road. "Get in."

Sonny opens the car door, slides inside. Slumps onto the seat. His breathing is heavy, but steady.

"How's that feel?"

"Aw right." Sonny says between breaths.

"Here kid." Rudy hands him a cold bottle of Coca-Cola. Sonny tips it back. The sweet bubbly liquid washes over his dry mouth. His heart pounds in his chest. Sweat pours down his back and chest inside his shirt. But it's a good sweat. Cleansing. "Good. That was good. Not bad for your first day." Rudy backs the car onto the grass to turn around, drives back the way they came. "That's enough for today. Where can I drop you off?"

"Oh." Sonny is disappointed. Running? He wants to learn how to box, not run.

Rudy can see the confusion on Sonny's face. "It's called road work. Every day you run. It builds up your legs and your stamina. Also you gotta learn how to take punishment. A boxer has to know how to stand pain. You got that?"

"Yeah." Oh, that, thinks Sonny. He knows how to stand pain. He is practised at that. Since Izzy's accident, he feels pain every day. Rudy stops at College and Spadina. Sonny gets out of the car.

"One more thing." Rudy says through the open window. The snow is coming down thicker and wetter now. An inch has piled up on the ground, settling on the roof of parked cars, blanketing the city in a quiet soft stillness. Sonny is chilled from sweating inside his jacket. He's starting to shiver. He looks at Rudy, eyes wide.

"Here's the most important thing, see?" says Rudy. "I'm your trainer. You got that?"

Sonny nods.

"I know what's best. Whatever I say goes. Got that?"

"Sure Mr … Rudy."

"I say run — you run. I say sleep — you sleep. I say you wash my windows …" he raises an eyebrow, gestures with one hand for Sonny to finish.

"… I wash your windows."

"That's it. You got it. I'll see you tomorrow after school. Three-thirty sharp, outside the gym. And when you get home, take a hot bath."

"A bath?" Sonny usually has a bath once a week, on Friday afternoons when his mother boils pots of water on the coal stove, slowly filling the tub with hot water. She forces each of the boys, starting with Sid on down, to take a turn in the hot bath. It is usually only lukewarm by the time Sonny gets his turn. How the hell is Sonny going to explain an extra hot bath to his mother?

"You don't soak in a hot bath, your muscles will seize up," Rudy says.

"Uh, sir?"

"For Christ's sake. I told ya to call me Rudy."

"It's just that," Sonny looks at his feet, "my father doesn't approve of boxing."

"What?"

The anguished look on Sonny's face explains everything. Rudy's own father is a religious man. He didn't break the news that he was a boxer to his family until he had won the amateur contest and knew he had no choice, because his name was going to be in the newspapers.

Rudy reaches for his wallet, hands Sonny a dollar. "Go back to the gym. Take a shower there. Go on."

Sonny accepts the dollar. "Thank you, sir."

Rudy raises his eyebrows.

"Rudy," Sonny corrects.

Rudy watches Sonny cross College Street, then he guns the motor and turns south onto Spadina.

The hot water pounding over Sonny's chilled body in the athletic club's locker room is a godsend. He stays under as long as he can, then dresses quickly and runs home. Sonny doesn't tell either of his parents about his trainer. He is scared they will make him stop boxing if they know. He continues to lie, says he's still working at the bowling alley after school. He earns money delivering packages for Checkie, so he continues to hand over two dollars and seventy-five cents every Thursday to his mother, from his "bowling alley pay." The rest goes into the coffee tin under the back porch.

For two weeks Rudy drives out to High Park with Sonny for road work. It's road work and nothing but. Sonny is getting bored of running around the park. He's dying to get into the ring, but like he promised, he does whatever Rudy tells him to do.

On the second Friday of his training, he arrives at the gym and looks for Rudy's car. It's parked by the curb. Rudy is nowhere in sight. Sonny enters the gym. It is hazy with smoke. In one of the rings a sparring session is in progress. Sonny hears one man grunt as his gloved fist pounds against his opponent's chest. The room is filled with the aroma of sweat and fear and smoke. Along the back wall, at the portable card tables, older men play poker. Sonny passes one table. There is a large pile of money in the centre. Fives, tens, twenties. A man is skipping rope. Another rhythmically taps the light bag, fast and furious, with both fists. Tap, tap, tap, tap, tap.

"There you are. You're late," Rudy barks. He wears loose grey sweatpants and a white T-shirt. He tosses a small-size sweatsuit to Sonny. "Go get changed. Hurry up. Keep your undershirt on under the sweatshirt. I want you to stay warm."

Sonny dashes into the locker room with the new suit.

"OKAY, KID," RUDY SAYS, after he laces Sonny's gloves. "We're going to work on the heavy bag today. Stand before it. Knees bent, just a bit, feet spread. Like this." He kicks Sonny's legs apart, shoulder-width. "Now take your best swing."

Sonny pulls back his right arm and rams his fist into the bag. Heavier than Sonny's backyard potato-sack bag, it swings forward, then thumps back against Sonny's chest, knocking him to the floor heavily. The men at the card tables laugh. Sonny's face flushes.

"Stand up. You all right?"

Sonny nods.

"Aw right. Let's start at the beginning." Rudy shows Sonny how to throw his whole body into the punch, so it will have more power and balance, not just what is in his arm. How to keep his chin down and protected, peer out from under the eyebrows and how to weave and dodge out of the way. How to punch going in and coming away. Sonny learns how to use his body properly, so his shoulder becomes a solid launching pad that sends his fist straight and hard at the target. By the end of the day, Sonny is hitting the bag without getting knocked over. The poker players stop laughing and start watching. They recognize talent when they see it. They can see that, even at nine years old, Sonny's punch can do a lot of damage.

That night every muscle in Sonny's body aches. He feels terrific.

Rudy works out a training regimen. They alternate: one day road work, the next day gym work. Every day after school Sonny trains. On Saturdays he trains all day — road work in the morning; break for lunch; gym work in the afternoon. Sundays, he delivers packages for Mr. Seigelman — he still has to make money to bring into the house. He develops strength with the heavy bag, speed with the light bag. He jumps rope. He does push-ups, sit-ups, knee bends and stretches. Rudy teaches him basic footwork. He practises until he is ready to drop. He shadowboxes. There are exercises to strengthen his hands. Others to improve his endurance, his balance, rhythm, his ability to withstand punishment. He lies on the floor, contracts his abdominal muscles as Rudy drops the heavy medicine ball on his belly. He practises one-armed push-ups, running on the spot, wrist curls, bench presses, hamstring curls and knee bends. He trains and practises. Practises and trains. Improving steadily, he spars with Rudy. Some evenings he watches movie reels of championship bouts on a projector Rudy sets up in the living room of his downtown apartment. The same movie clips, over and over, to learn ring craft. Watching the pros to see how they do it. Rudy has films of Joe Louis losing to Max Schmeling at Yankee Stadium, Jack Sharkey up against Jimmy Maloney. He has footage of Jack Dempsey fighting Luis Firpo, and Jack Sharkey's battle against Dempsey. Sonny watches all the great fighters. Rudy plays the films until Sonny can get on his feet and imitate the fancy footwork, has memorized the moves, the ring craft of the greatest fighters in the world. Sonny grows restless with all the training. He wants to fight.

In December, school is out for two weeks for Christmas vacation. Checkie books Sonny into his first "Smoker" — fights held in athletic clubs where promising young fighters begin their careers. His first is at the old Leonard Athletic Club on the second floor, at Queen and Spadina, right across the street from the Pickford Theatre. There is a boxing ring in the middle of the dusty room and chairs for 150 people all around it.

The boys fight three-round bouts at the Smokers. Each round is three minutes, with a sixty-second break in between.

On a Thursday in late December, at five o' clock, Sonny emerges from the locker room in his trunks. His hands have been taped by Rudy, his gloves laced up.

"There's my boy," Checkie paces on the floor below Sonny's corner. "This guy ..." Checkie announces in a booming voice to everyone around him, "... is the next Max Baer. You heard it here first. Huh? Wait till you see this kid fight."

In the stands, front and centre, Sid Lapinsky sits, proud of his little brother for getting this far. Imagine: an amateur fighter. The room is filled with smoke and sweat and overflows with testosterone and the anticipation of the boys and men in the stands. The ceiling lights are dingy and dim. The chairs are hard.

Rudy separates the ropes and Sonny climbs into the ring, takes his place on the low stool. He opens his mouth as Rudy slips his mouthguard into place, hard against his teeth. "Remember everything I taught you. But don't think too much. In the ring, you gotta rely on your instincts. You got that?"

Remember but don't think, Sonny repeats to himself. Nods. His belly twists and turns like a storm. He looks out to the audience. There are forty or fifty men and boys in the seats, ready to watch the fight. Sonny takes a deep breath. His opponent Nordy Stein, a talented ten-year-old, is three inches taller than Sonny, but scrawnier. Since he began training, Sonny's chest and arms have filled out considerably and though he is still short, he is sturdy. The bell rings. Sonny charges at Nordy Stein aggressively in his trademark style, remembering to keep his right hand covering his chin, to peer out under his eyebrows, to follow his hunches. Sonny leads with a left to the body. Stein drops his hands and with his right fist, Sonny connects cleanly with the other boy's chin. His first hit in a real fight. He feels powerful as he sends his opponent backward toward the ropes. Stein moves back in and swings. It's like slow motion. Sonny has all the time in the world to dodge the blow. He hears the crowd yell in appreciation. Adrenalin rips through the air from one side of the room

to the other. The bell rings. Fastest three minutes of Sonny's life. He backs
into his corner, sits.

The crowd cheers.

"That's the stuff, Sonny." Rudy removes the mouthguard and brings a
cup of water with a straw to Sonny's mouth.

The second round, Sonny is out in front. He hasn't been hit once. His
opponent moves forward and strikes Sonny below the belt into his lower
belly, just above his groin. The referee calls foul, breaks them up.

"Boo!" Sid calls from his seat. "Get 'im Sonny."

Sonny is mad now. He charges forward and lets loose a rapid-fire
combination: a left to the chest, a hook, a right, a left, and a final right
uppercut to the chin, hard. The bell rings. Sonny keeps punching Stein in
the head.

"Break it up," the referee says as he pulls the boys apart. Sonny glares
at the man. "Easy son. Easy." Sonny retreats to his corner, madder than
hell. Some boys in the stands boo.

In the third round, Nordy Stein fakes a left jab to the body. Sonny,
expecting the blow to be close to his groin again, drops his hands and
takes a hard right in the face, which opens a cut above his eye. Blood
spurts and trickles down Sonny's face. Stunned, Sonny shakes his head.
Drops of blood splatter onto Stein, who tosses a quick combination and
hits Sonny on the lips, the cheek and chin.

"Charge him," Rudy shouts from below Sonny's corner. "Charge!"

Sonny slips under the next blow, charges and jabs Stein in the face,
with a left, a right and a left. He can taste the salt of his blood in one
corner of his mouth. He charges again.

"Atta boy, Sonny," Sid yells.

Other spectators get on their feet to see better. It's not a bad fight for
a couple of kids.

Stein fakes a jab to Sonny's body again. Sonny is enraged. Red-hot fire
in his belly fuels his power. He keeps his guard up, contracts his stomach
muscles, absorbs the body blow and charges forward with a right uppercut, connecting with his opponent's chin. He keeps close and swings with
his left hook, a straight right, and a left, pulverizing his opponent's face.

The bell rings. In mid-swing Sonny completes a hard right uppercut, sending Stein sprawling to the canvas.

"Great job, kid," Rudy says, as Sonny sits in his corner, breathing hard, waiting for the judge's decision. Rudy removes Sonny's mouthguard and tends to his cut with iodine on cotton batting. It stings. Sonny pulls back, but Rudy persists. Sonny hears his name called out over the cheap tin PA system, hollow in the cavernous room. Rudy pushes him to stand. The referee holds his arms up high in the air. His first fight. Won by decision. He glances over at Rudy, who gives him the thumbs-up.

Sid is up on his feet, exuberant. "Sonny!" he shouts. "You won! That's my brother," he tells the guys all around him. "That's my brother. The winner." Sid inserts two fingers in his mouth and whistles loudly. The sound echoes through the club.

Checkie dances in the front row, both arms high above his head. "That's my boy!" he shouts. "Sonny Lapinsky. Remember that name," he yells to the crowd. "Sonny Lapinsky. Gonna be a world champ someday." He grins madly. "Okay," he drops his hands, "pay up," he says to the man on his left.

An unfamiliar sense of well-being courses through Sonny.

UNLIKE SID, LENNY HAS no interest in boxing, although he's proud of his brother Sonny. Earlier, he declined Sid's offer to accompany him to the Smoker to watch Sonny fight. He had somewhere to go that was much more important. Mr. Cornwall, the evening librarian at the Shaw Street library a few blocks from their house, has invited Lenny to an art show opening, at a gallery north of Dupont Street, in a Gentile neighbourhood. Lenny has never been to an art show opening. He is not even sure what one is, but he knows it has to do with the life he aspires to. Mr. Cornwall has invited Lenny to such events in the past — a poetry reading once, and a lecture — but Lenny always assumed there would be an admission price beyond his means and he politely declined. Mr. Cornwall must have caught on, though, because this time he made a point of informing Lenny that the opening was free of charge. As long as you didn't bid on a painting, which Lenny has no intention of doing. Before leaving home, Lenny parts his curly brown hair in the middle, combing it to each side neatly and slicking it down with a few drops of olive oil that he nicks from his mother's kitchen. It works as well as hair tonic. He slips into a fresh shirt, which he tucks into a pair of dark trousers, and carefully knots his one and only tie. He wishes he owned a dress jacket, and vows right then to save a penny each week from his newspaper earnings until he has enough money to buy one. If he's old enough for long pants, he's old enough for a dinner jacket. He'll have to wear his threadbare woollen tweed jacket. It's all he's got. In the bathroom, he pinches a squirt of Uncle Max's aftershave and pats it on his face and neck. He doesn't need to shave yet — his face, still smooth as a peach, with perhaps just a hint of fuzz — but he likes the fresh masculine scent. Spicy and sharp.

To save the streetcar money, Lenny walks up Bathurst Street to Dupont. Clutching the address on a small slip of paper, he passes houses, shops, restaurants not much different from those in his neighbourhood, although perhaps a trifle more upscale. He finds the gallery without too much trouble, right on Dupont, just east of Bathurst. Nervous, Lenny stands outside for a few minutes. He sees a young man dressed in a sleek brown suit and tie enter the gallery, followed by two other men, dressed as elegantly. Lenny looks down at his secondhand, threadbare trousers, hand-me-down tie and brown tweed jacket, and feels underdressed. Ashamed, he turns away, heading back home.

"Lenny?" It's Mr. Cornwall. "Is that you?"

Lenny turns to face the librarian.

Mr. Cornwall is dressed in a nicer suit than the one he usually wears to work. This one is jet black, neatly tailored. His white shirt is crisp with starch. His tie is silk, with a tasteful polka-dot pattern. His tie clip is silver and gleaming. His hair is slicked back. He is freshly shaved. He looks like a movie star. Lenny is in awe. "So you made it," Mr. Cornwall smiles.

Lenny grins back, still intent on running for cover, but how can he do so now?

"Come along then. Shall we?"

Mr. Cornwall throws one arm casually across Lenny's shoulder and steers him inside the small storefront shop.

Lenny looks around, wide-eyed. The room is crowded with elegantly dressed people, more men than women. The walls of the gallery have been painted white. Hanging every couple of feet apart on the walls are oil paintings — landscapes mostly and some portraits. Mr. Cornwall leads Lenny to the far wall.

"I like the portraits myself. What do you think?" Mr. Cornwall asks Lenny, who feels more grown up than he ever has before. This is the life he envisions for himself. A cultured man, out for the evening with a good friend, discussing art.

He nods, not really sure what to say in response.

"Although I really wish we'd get more of the modern art brought in. There are artists in Paris who are working in astonishing new forms. Have you seen any?"

"No, sir." Lenny has no idea what modern art might be.

Mr. Cornwall smiles at Lenny. "Why don't you call me Ted?"

"Sure," says Lenny, although it feels weird to call a grown-up by his first name and he's not quite sure he can do it.

"Shall we sample the pastry table?" Ted steers Lenny to a table near the back that holds tea and plates of cookies and cakes. All around are civilized people, engaging in intelligent conversations and lively debate. Lenny looks around the room, grinning. Yes, this is the life.

BY THE TIME HE gets home from the Smoker, Sonny's left eye is swollen shut, his chin is bruised and there are tiny purple blotches from burst blood vessels all over his cheeks. He sneaks through the kitchen quietly, hoping to get past his mother. Sid follows. Sophie turns from the stove.

"Oh my God! Sonny! What happened? You were fighting again? Oy vey."

"Ma ... it's not what you think." Sonny stops, holds out his hands.

"Oh my God. Who's the other boy? What's his name? I'm calling his mother."

"Ma, you don't understand."

"Yeah, Ma. Let Sonny explain," Sid adds.

Lenny wanders into the house, and skips up the stairs, back from the art gallery. "Holy toledo, Sonny. Did you lose the fight?"

"Nah. I won by decision."

"You shoulda seen him, Lenny. Sonny was great. Looked like a real champ. He almost knocked the other guy out."

Lenny smiles politely, knowing he'd much rather have the evening at the art gallery.

Sonny puffs out his chest in pride.

"What are you boys talking about? Decision? Knocked out? I don't understand."

"Ma ... maybe you better sit down," Sid suggests.

"I fought in a Smoker, Ma. That's an amateur fight-like. At the athletic club. Just down the street."

"Fighting?"

"Boxing, Ma," Sid corrects.

"Boxing? In a boxing ring? With those heavy gloves?"

"That's right, Ma."

"I don't understand, Sonny. Why do you want to beat up another boy, and let him beat you? What for, Sonny?"

"Ma ..." Sonny struggles for the right words.

"It's a sport, Ma." Sid saves him. "Boxers make a lot of money."

"They do?"

"Sure. Sonny's gonna be famous. And rich," he adds.

"Rich?"

"Yeah. The purse for the latest Joe Louis fight was twenty thousand dollars."

"A purse?"

"Not a purse. That's what they call the prize money."

"Twenty thousand dollars?"

"He's a world champion."

"I think I need a cup of tea."

THE NEXT DAY, Yacov takes the news surprisingly well.

"So? You're a fighter now?"

Sonny chokes on his vegetable soup. Waits.

"Well..." Yacov continues, "... that's not so bad. If you're going to fight, at least you're in a ring. And not on the street. Did you win any money?"

There is no prize money at Smokers. The winner receives a dime-store watch or sometimes a silver cup. Sonny got a watch, which he has already hawked at the pawnshop for two bucks. "I won two bucks," he lies. "Gave it to Ma already."

"Two bucks." Yacov is only half-impressed. "That's it?"

Sonny hangs his head and quietly eats.

The Principal's Office
JANUARY 1934

IZZY IS OF AGE to begin First Grade. On the first day back at school after Christmas vacation, Sophie fills the bathtub with hot water boiled on the stove and bathes Izzy, scrubbing off the dirt from playing in the yard. Sonny stands in the kitchen doorway, watching. His brow is crinkled. The coal stove in the kitchen burns, warming the house.

"I want to come with," Sonny says.

Sophie washes behind Izzy's ears. "You run along to school," she tells Sonny.

"Please, Ma."

Sophie sighs. "Then help me dress him." She stands Izzy up, dries him off. He smiles; such a good-natured little boy, thinks Sophie. Sonny takes his brother's hand and leads him to their bedroom. "In his good clothes." Sophie yells from the other room.

"You should come to school," Sid tells Sonny. "You'll be late."

"I'm going with Ma. Lift your arms," Sonny orders, as he pulls a fresh white undershirt over Izzy's head. He helps him into underwear and his one pair of good wool pants, hand-me-downs, that used to be Sonny's and, before that, Lenny's or Sid's.

"What for?" Sid asks.

Sonny can't explain it. It's more of the same — the terrible guilt ripping him apart from the inside out. The hurricane might be calmed, at least momentarily, if he walks with his mother and Izzy. At least it's something he can do. "You go ahead. With Lenny." Sonny feels it's his duty to watch out for his brother Lenny, who is always getting picked on by bullies.

"Okay," Sid relents.

"You guys coming?" Lenny pokes his head in.

"Just me," Sid says. "Come on."

Lenny looks at Sonny. "What's going on?"

"I'm going with Ma. That's all," Sonny grumbles.

"I understand," Lenny nods. He knows it makes Sonny feel better to do something nice for Izzy.

Sonny finds Izzy's one unpatched shirt and wool jacket and helps him on with them. He plasters Izzy's hair down, declares him ready and goes to find their mother.

Sonny and Sophie each hold one of Izzy's hands as they walk up the street to find Yacov. Izzy skips between them, happy to be on an outing. Sophie spots the Ford parked by the side of the road on Manning Avenue. Yacov is standing on a front porch speaking to a woman, his collection book in his hand. His cousin Max is two doors down. Yacov finishes his call, sees his wife and walks down the stairs. He stares hard at Sonny, challenging him.

"I want to come." Sonny answers. "Ma said it's okay."

Izzy beams at his father. Yacov kisses his wife on the cheek, bends down and kisses Izzy's head.

"Ready?" he asks.

Sophie nods.

Yacov waves to Max and takes Izzy's other hand and they walk in the direction of the school. Sonny walks a few paces behind, hands jammed in his trouser pockets.

In front of the school they stop. Sonny leads the way inside. At the principal's office, Yacov gestures with a nod for Sonny to get going. Reluctantly he ruffles Izzy's hair and leaves in the direction of his classroom.

The secretary asks Yacov and Sophie to please wait. "Principal Stuart will see you just as soon as he can," she says. Yacov and Sophie sit on a hard child-size wooden bench, in front of the secretary's desk. Sophie pulls Izzy onto her lap. He rocks slightly, as he does when he is nervous. Sophie can see that the secretary is trying not to stare. Finally the principal's door opens. A middle-aged man steps out, wearing a dark grey suit, white shirt and blue-striped tie. He smiles, calls them into his office.

Yacov and Sophie sit on hard wooden chairs opposite the principal's desk. The office is all dark wood and heavy bookcases, less the office of an elementary school principal than a scholar's darkened study. This room belongs to a man of letters, of the book, thinks Sophie. The dusty venetian blinds are closed tight, blocking out any sunlight that might accidentally spill into the room. The ashtray on Principal Stuart's desk overflows with crushed cigarette butts. There is a copy of yesterday's evening *Telegram* on the corner. His university degree is framed and hanging on the wall.

Izzy stands in front of his mother, leaning against her legs. The principal pulls open a file and studies it. Then he removes his bifocals and looks sternly at Yacov. Principal Stuart's formerly blond hair is streaked with grey, and is balding on top. He wears a three-piece suit, his slight paunch straining at the seams of his tweed vest, threatening to pop a button. Yacov notices that the principal has a nervous tic above his left eye. His steel-grey eyes stare across the desk.

"Mr ... La ... pin ... sky," he struggles with Yacov's name. "I've reviewed your request, and well, frankly I'm afraid I can't allow your son to attend regular classes ..."

Yacov puts his hands on the principal's desk and leans forward. "What? Why not?"

Principal Stuart takes a deep breath and folds his hands carefully on the desk in front of him. He has expected an outburst. The Italians, the Poles and the Jews, he's discovered, are passionate, hot-tempered people. Not reserved and dignified like the British. They fly off the handle at the slightest provocation. This morning, he is prepared. He took a tranquilizer while the Lapinskys waited outside his office. And he made them wait until his pill took effect. He would not make the same mistake again. Last year, an Italian named Carducio came in complaining about his son's grades and he, William Stuart, had reacted to the man's anger. The father had threatened the principal physically and William had lost his temper and screamed right back. Nothing ever came of it, but if the superintendent had found out, well, at the least, he'd have received a reprimand, and Principal Stuart wants his record to remain absolutely spotless. He has ambitions of becoming the superintendent himself one day.

"Mr. Lapinsky, I'll ask you to please not shout," Principal Stuart says, with an eerie calm to his voice, an unnatural stillness in his eyes.

"Yacov …" Sophie pulls at her husband's arm.

Yacov slumps back in his chair, glaring at the principal. He pays the school fees. They don't have the right to keep his boy out of school.

Principal Stuart waits a full beat before beginning again. The effects of the tranquilizer are coursing pleasantly through his veins. He can wait forever.

"Mr. Lapinsky …" he repeats. "I'm sure you can understand my position. The classrooms are quite full. Our teachers have a lot on their hands as it is. Times are hard for everyone these days, you know. We just can't accept retarded children …"

"He's not retarded!" Yacov shouts, leaning forward, hands on his knees. Izzy recoils against Sophie at the outburst. She squeezes Yacov's arm to quiet him.

Principal Stuart breathes in and breathes out. Then he continues, "… in our regular classes, and while some of the schools in other districts have classes for slow children, we just don't have the resources here at Shaw Street Public School."

"But my money you'll take." Yacov can't keep silent. "My money is good enough for you, but not my son, is that right?" Yacov stands, takes Izzy's hand. "Come on. Let's get out of here." Izzy shrinks back against Sophie's legs, a look of terror on his confused face. Shouting makes Izzy nervous.

Sophie remains seated, determined to do the best for her son. She pulls Izzy close to her. "Then, Mr. Stuart, where can my son go to school?" she asks calmly.

Principal Stuart consults his file. Referrals he can do. Paperwork is his pleasure. He feels calmer as he scans the list. "There is a school for retarded children …"

"He's not retarded," Yacov insists again.

"Yacov …" Sophie glares at her husband.

"… in the area. It's called the St. Joseph's School for the Retarded."

"*Gai in drerd arein,*" Yacov curses, under his breath. *Go to hell.*

Principal Stuart raises his eyebrows. He understands no Yiddish, but he has some idea what Mr. Lapinsky has just said to him. He has half a mind to withhold the information.

Sophie frowns. "That sounds Catholic," she says to the principal.

Stuart looks down at his notes. "Ah, why yes, so it is. Is that a problem?" He peers over the top of his bifocals.

"We're Jewish," Sophie says quietly.

"Yes, but the school is subsidized, Mrs. Lapinsky. The only other school of its kind in the city is uptown and well … beg your pardon, but I'm quite sure it's beyond your means …"

Yacov interjects again. "Come on, Sophie. Let's go home. Some school. What's the use?"

"Can you write down the name and addresses of both schools, please, Mr. Stuart?" Sophie asks as calmly as possible. Inside she is shaking. She is furious at Yacov for behaving as he is, irrational and with emotion. She is furious at the school for failing her son, and she has nothing but contempt for this scared little man sitting across the desk from her who will offer her no help at all. She nestles Izzy's head against her bosom, as if she could protect him from the world's cruelty with her body.

"Certainly," Principal Stuart says through clenched teeth. He knows it is a waste of his time. They obviously can't afford the Forest Hills school and the Jews never accept his advice of a good Catholic school. Stubborn people. Rather keep their boy out of school than let him attend the Catholic school. He bites his tongue and copies down the information on a small piece of paper, which he hands to Sophie.

"Thank you," she says tersely. Then she stands, takes Izzy by the hand and pushes her husband toward the door. Yacov has to draw on every ounce of internal discipline to keep from slamming the door on the way out. He manages to restrain himself only because his other sons still have to go to this miserable excuse for a school. He walks his wife and son home in silence.

On the way, Sophie considers her options. Izzy will just have to stay home with her. She will teach him herself. They will all teach him. The other boys will help. She bends down and kisses the top of his head.

From this moment on, Sophie will not treat Izzy like an invalid. And she makes this clear to the rest of the family. Since they don't know the full extent of Izzy's brain damage, the family acts as though he understands everything. He gets out of bed, gets dressed and eats breakfast every morning with everyone else. When the boys go off to school and Yacov to work, Sophie spends two or three hours every morning with Izzy's studies. They begin with the alphabet. She goes through the motions of teaching him to read. He is great at repeating the last sound he hears, but beyond that it isn't clear that he understands. She keeps him busy with projects — colouring, cut and paste, anything she can think of. And he helps her around the house. He has an amazing capacity for detail, although he isn't great with large tasks. So she gives him a rag and shows him how to dust, or sits him on a chair to help her snap peas for dinner. The other boys teach him things as well, especially Sonny, whose patience is boundless. He sits for hours while Izzy painstakingly draws a picture. He reads Izzy's favourite book over and over, until the rest of the family is about to go out of their minds. The more repetitious something is, the more Izzy seems to enjoy it. Sonny offers to take Izzy with him whenever he goes out with his pals. Anyone who doesn't like it has Sonny to deal with. The only time he leaves Izzy at home is when he's training with Rudy or working for Checkie.

Small Miracles
JANUARY AND FEBRUARY, 1934

AFTER THE NIGHT of the art opening, Ted Cornwall begins to introduce Lenny to the pleasures of poetry. He has secured permission from the library to organize a reading series featuring local writers.

"I only wish my budget was larger," he tells Lenny. "Then I could bring in poets from New York or even Montreal. Still it's a start, don't you agree?"

Lenny, of course, agrees with everything Ted has to say. How could he argue when everything he currently knows about poetry he learned from the librarian. He confesses that he'd like to be a poet himself one day.

"My dear boy," Ted counters, "unless you'd come from greater means, you'd better forget that idea. Poets literally starve. Especially these days."

Lenny feels foolish for having admitted his idea.

"A passion for the art is splendid, Lenny. I'm merely suggesting you follow more, shall we say, realistic dreams. Even a novelist can eke out a tiny living, if he develops an audience."

"You think so, Ted?" Lenny feels a ray of hope.

"Absolutely. Now, you must help me arrange the chairs. Our poets will be here shortly."

To Lenny, Ted Cornwall seems old and wise, but the truth is he's only twenty-five. When Sophie listens to Lenny talking excitedly about Ted, she doesn't understand why a grown man would want to spend time with an eleven-year-old. She's not sure what could be going on, but something nags at her.

"Leave him be," Yacov suggests. "Maybe the man has no kids of his own. There's no harm in it."

But Sophie worries all the same.

After the poetry reading, Ted invites Lenny to his apartment for tea. It's only eight o' clock, so Lenny doesn't see any harm. Ted's apartment is everything Lenny imagined: a spacious one-bedroom on Grace Street, not far from Lenny's neighbourhood. A living room, bedroom, kitchen and bathroom all to himself. Lenny shares his bedroom with three brothers, the living room and kitchen with his whole family, and the bathroom is shared by all of them, plus Max, Tessie, their kids and Mr. Tepperman the boarder. How luxurious it must be to have all this space for just one person.

The hardwood floors are polished. The apartment is filled with books on shelves, and paintings adorn the walls.

"Mostly by my friend Jacques," Ted informs Lenny. "He's from Montreal. He's not famous yet, but he's going to be a major talent. You can see he has a vision. Don't you agree, Lenny?"

For his part, Lenny wouldn't know good art from bad, but he nods emphatically and says in his most sophisticated voice, "Oh yes. I do."

Ted doesn't have a wet bar as Lenny imagined, but he does have a bottle of brandy on the kitchen counter, and even though Lenny is only eleven, Ted pours a tiny shot into Lenny's tea and an altogether larger amount into his own, until his cup contains more brandy than tea. Lenny feels elegant and mature, sitting in the living room with his friend Ted, sipping his brandy-laced tea, discussing contemporary art. Lenny looks around Ted's apartment and he knows that one day he'll have his own place and it will be exactly like Ted's.

SID TURNS FOURTEEN in the middle of February. Technically, he's been a man according to Jewish law since his bar mitzvah last winter. He's tried his best, but now he figures it's time to quit school. He's a smart boy, just not a scholar. He decides to convince his parents of this and to beg his father to let him work full-time, like he did all summer, and forget about school.

"Pop, please," Sid tries the day of his fourteenth birthday. "I like working with you and Uncle Max. I'm doing good, right? Uncle Max says I'm good with sales."

"You are, Sid, but your mother wants you to finish school. An education is important."

"Pop, I'm no good in school." In fact, he is terrible. It's painful. Sid can't read what his teacher writes on the blackboard and he's so busy struggling to read that he can't pay attention to the lesson. It's humiliating. Whenever he is called on to answer a question, he makes a fool of himself. He can't bear the thought of staying in school.

"I said no. That's it. You can quit when you're sixteen."

Two more excruciating years. Sid wonders how he can make it. The only good thing about school is his young new teacher, Miss Jennifer Miller. She's fresh out of college; this is her first post. She took over Sid's class in January after the first-term teacher retired. She is twenty-three years old, bright, young and energetic. Miss Miller has clever new ideas about teaching. From an upper-class family, she doesn't need the job; she's interested in educating the masses and in progressive ideas. More significantly, Miss Miller despises Principal Stuart and she loves the children under her charge. She is determined to provide them with the best education she can and with the utmost respect.

As the tallest boy in his class, Sid has been assigned a seat in the back row, as always. There is barely enough room for his long legs under the wooden desk. His knees bang up uncomfortably against the bottom of the wood. He is constantly worrying he'll tip the jar of ink that sits in the shallow well on the right corner of his desk. At the front of the class, pinned to the wall, is a map of the world. Over the blackboard is a chart of the alphabet. On a bulletin board hang clippings of current events, mostly about unemployment and the Depression. The windows on one side of the classroom look out to the schoolyard. The blinds are up, letting in as much sunlight as possible. Miss Miller asks Sid to stand and read something she's written on the blackboard. Sid removes his cap, squeezes his long legs out from under the desk and stands in the aisle, squinting. As usual, he can't read a thing — the words look like white squiggles on black. Embarrassed, he tries to wisecrack his way out of it, and is sent to the principal's office.

Miss Miller has a hunch, though, and the next day she asks Sid to read again. He stands by his desk and leans his head slightly forward, which elicits giggles from his classmates. Sid tries to focus, but it is hopeless. Nothing but white shapes. Before he can open his mouth to make a joke, Miss Miller asks him to step toward the front of the class.

He moves a few inches forward.

"Closer, Sidney," she says.

He moves an inch closer.

"No. I want you to stand right here." She points to the floor beside her desk, way up at the front of the class.

There is nothing for Sid to do but oblige. He lumbers right up to her desk.

"Now, read what is written on the board."

And a miracle occurs. Sid knows what Moses must have felt as he stood over the Red Sea, held out his staff, and watched the mighty waters part. Or what Abraham must have thought when he witnessed the burning bush and the voice of God. Sid stares up at the board, shocked. The white squiggles are letters. The letters are words. The words a sentence. He can read it just fine.

"A noun can be a person, place or thing," Sid reads out in a steady voice, grinning, amazing himself and everybody else.

There is a hush in the room because Sid's classmates have known for the past four years that Sid can't read. Sid is so excited, he reads it again, his voice booming. "A noun can be a person, place or thing."

Miss Miller writes a note for Sophie and sends it home with Sid.

"GLASSES HE NEEDS? *Ich vais nicht.* I don't know." Yacov is skeptical. No one in his family ever wore glasses, and everyone can see perfectly fine.

"I'm taking him to the doctor tomorrow," Sophie declares. "Imagine all this time and he couldn't see. Sid, why didn't you tell us before?"

"I don't know, Ma."

The next week, Sid Lapinsky gets his first pair of glasses — round with heavy black frames. The world becomes a wondrous place. For days, Sid walks around looking closely at everything. He can't believe how beautiful the world is. He had no idea that grass was made up of individual thin blades, that clouds had definable shapes, that his own face was actually handsome, or that Ruthie Snyder, the girl who has sat in front of him in school four years in a row, was so incredibly pretty.

BOOK TWO

Notes on The Biography of Sonny Lapinsky
by Moses Nino Lapinsky, Ph.D
MAY 1, 2003, VANCOUVER, B.C.

MY MOTHER WAS a child bride. She and my dad had a shotgun wedding. She was only sixteen when she was pregnant with my older sister Mary, so my father hastily married her at City Hall with no family around, only Sonny's manager, the famous Toronto gangster Checkie Seigelman, and Checkie's longtime girlfriend, Lila Rubinoff. Given their mixed marriage — a Russian Jew and a Roman Catholic Italian — my parents had agreed to practise no religion. She would not recite the Hail Marys, nor attend Midnight Mass. He would not ask her to light the *Shabbes* candles on Friday night, nor go to *shul* and pray on Saturday mornings. They agreed they would not celebrate Easter Sunday or Passover, the high holy days of Rosh Hashanah and Yom Kippur, or even Christmas morning. They were modern Canadians and religion was old-fashioned superstition brought over from the old country by their immigrant parents. (Although, when we were kids, they gave in on celebrating a mixture of Christmas and Chanukah, not wanting to deprive us of the presents.) Mixed marriages were rare at the time, and my parents had no support, no role models. They had not a soul they could talk to about their differences. They didn't have a clue what they were doing.

When Mary was born, and my father was away competing in the National Amateur Boxing Championships, my mother had her baptized without his knowledge. All the years of Sunday school catechism were so embedded in her psyche, she worried her infant daughter might end up in purgatory forever if she was not properly blessed by a priest and dipped in holy water. When my father returned from Vancouver, depressed and defeated, having lost the championships, he blew his stack when he discovered his daughter had been named after the Virgin Mary and had been welcomed into the world by the Catholic Church.

In 1941, when my parents hastily married, Orson Welles released his classic, "Citizen Kane," Bogart was staring in "The Maltese Falcon," Judy Garland and Mickey Rooney were singing their hearts out in "Babes on Broadway," and the Germans invaded Russia. Purchasing Canadian Victory Bonds entitled buyers to Honour Cards to display in their windows and Torch badges for their lapels. The first cruising tank rolled off a Canadian assembly line in Montreal and the City of Toronto failed its first blackout test, when despite warnings by press and radio, there were dozens of lights in nearly every section of the city.

When I was born in 1945, three years after my sister's birth, my mother decided to make it up to my father for Mary. I was named Moses — the most Jewish-sounding name she could think of. With the help of her sister-in-law, my Auntie Ruthie, and my Uncle Sid, I had a proper *bris*, the ritual circumcision performed by a *moyel*, a religious Jew trained in the ancient art of penis snipping, seven days after the birth of a Jewish boy. I was named Moses, after the Biblical leader who led the Hebrew slaves out of bondage, centuries before, in Egypt. Such a heroic name I had to live up to. I can assure you there have been times in my life when it has been a burden. Can you imagine?

I was the first member of my family to go to college. In 1962, I was admitted to York University at the new Glendon Campus, which had opened the year before at Bayview and Lawrence. It was an hour's commute from downtown where I lived with my mother and younger brother, Frankie. Mary was already married and living with her husband, Phil Tanenbaum, a grocer. (They divorced in 1980, after their kids were all away at college. Phil eventually remarried, a much younger woman. My sister Mary declared herself through with men and has since put her emotional energies into her grandchildren, of whom she has plenty.)

My father and I were never close. Not the way a father and son should be, but I guess it runs in our family. Sonny was estranged from his own father for fifteen years. All because he married my mother, a Roman Catholic Italian. My mother, God bless her, is seventy-eight and still going strong. To her credit, she never gave up on my father, never remarried, never so much as dated another man and remained in love with Sonny until the day he died. She divorced him because it hurt too much to stay with a man intent on destroying himself. But she took care of him from afar, and raised me, Mary and my younger brother Frankie, mostly on her own, with a little help from my paternal grandparents, Sophie and Yacov Lapinsky. Mostly *Bubbe* Sophie. *Zayde* Yacov had officially disowned us, on account of we weren't exactly *according to hoyle*, being only half-Jewish. But he came around eventually. Unfortunately, his change of heart was a well-kept secret, one that would have given my father a great deal of pleasure if only he'd known sooner.

Was it painful to not be close to my father? I suppose, although in some ways, one doesn't miss what one never had. After my parents divorced, my father stayed away for a long time. I didn't see him at all for three years, until the morning of my bar mitzvah, when he mysteriously reappeared. He had retired from boxing the same year my mother left him. He had to. The headaches had grown worse, the dizzy spells more frequent. He hung on to his title until the end of 1954, when he was challenged by a young African American fighter named Bobo Washington. Sonny made it to the tenth round, when he was KO'ed so hard, he fell right through the ropes and landed in the lap of the newspapermen in the front row, which, as you can imagine, was the focus of the headlines. Shortly after that, he travelled with Rudy Gold, his longtime trainer, down south, where they spent a year in Florida, lying in the sun, shooting craps, getting drunk and dating showgirls. He came back to Toronto later that year and opened a nightclub with Rudy, but we didn't hear from him for a long time. He kept his distance.

I suppose it made me angry. I was an eleven-year-old boy and my father had disappeared from our lives. I guess I reacted like most kids with divorced parents. I assumed it was my fault. Something I had done had driven my father from us, I figured. It was because I wasn't like him, not an athlete. If only I was the son he'd dreamed of, perhaps he would have stayed. This, of course, was ridiculous. My brother Frankie was just that sort of boy, a natural athlete, a jock. His sport was baseball — he was a talented pitcher — and he could have boxed if he'd wanted to. But my father didn't stick around to witness Frankie's athletic achievements. The truth was, my mother took us kids and left *him*. He'd have done anything to have remained with us. I realize now that he must have stayed away out of shame. He probably felt like a failure. As a husband, a father, even as a world champ. His career had been illustrious and glorious, but he'd gone out with a fizzle.

I vividly remember the moment when I finally saw him again. I was up on the raised *Bema*, the stage in the synagogue, standing beside the cantor, reciting the Torah portion I had been practising all winter. The synagogue was quiet as I sang. I looked up at one point, to see my mother in the front row, smiling proudly, beside my paternal grandparents. *Zayde* Yacov was silently singing along with me in encouragement. Just before my eyes returned to the Torah, something at the back of the temple caught my attention. My father was walking in, his hat in hand, struggling to keep the black silk *Yarmulke* perched on top of his unruly curly hair. My heart leaped to my throat at the sight of him. I had no idea he was coming, or had even been invited. I stopped singing, watched him walk up the aisle, looking for a seat near the back. The cantor peered at me, gesturing with the ornate silver pointer to the spot where I'd left off. People in the pews looked at me expectantly. Some followed my eyes, which landed on my father, as he dropped heavily into a seat, nodding at me silently.

"Moshe?" the cantor quietly prodded, addressing me by my Hebrew name.

I returned to the Torah, and when I picked up singing where I had left off, I know that my voice was stronger, more vibrant, deeper and more soulful than it had been before my father had arrived. In that moment, I let go of my anger at him for having stayed away for three long years. My heart filled with love for him. He had come back to be at my bar mitzvah, to witness my entry into manhood, to stand at my side on this, the biggest day of my young life. And I was filled with pride and love. He looked older than I'd remembered, although he was only thirty-four. The years in the ring were catching up with him. He had put on weight around the middle, the way ex-athletes tend to do. His hair was beginning to thin and turn grey at the sides. And for the first time ever, he looked small and vulnerable. As I finished my Torah reading that would take me over the threshold into symbolic manhood, I realized for the first time that the day would come soon when I would be called upon to take care of my father. That as I grew up, he would become more frail. I was on the cusp of my prime, my greatest moment of youthful virility, while he was on his way down, heading quicker than most — a legacy of his profession — into old age.

As I sang out, loud and clear, a part of me ached for my father and I realized — astute as it may have been for my young age — that whatever relationship we'd had in the past, it was about to change, forever.

TRADITION

Another Great War

SEPTEMBER TO DECEMBER, 1939

ON SEPTEMBER 3, 1939, as the Nazis invade Poland, three generations of the Lapinsky family gather around the RCA radio in the cramped living room of Yacov and Sophie's second-storey flat to hear the news. Prime Minister Neville Chamberlain is making a speech, broadcast via the BBC to all of Britain and her colonies.

"This country is now at war with Germany," Chamberlain announces, solemnly. "In this grave hour, perhaps the most fearful in our history, I send to every household of my people at home and overseas this message: for the second time in our lives, we are at war."

"Oy. War again over there." Yacov shakes his head, reaching for his package of cigarettes in his shirt pocket.

"I can barely understand a word the prime minister's saying." Tessie picks up her cup of tea, plops a sugar cube between her teeth, sips the tea over the sugar. "With that English accent."

"Thank God we're here, is all I can say." Sophie purses her lips, grabs Yacov's cigarettes, lights one herself.

"I remember the Great War," Reuben says. "Everyone was excited. All the young men were running over themselves to sign up." He helps himself to another slice of Sophie's famous sponge cake. So light and sweet.

"What for?" Yacov asks, inhaling deeply.

"To fight for their countries," Sid says simply.

"I'll give you something to fight about." Yacov raises a hand as if he's going to hit Sid.

"It's true."

"War is for Neanderthals," Lenny says.

"What?" Sid doesn't know what Lenny is talking about.

"Are we going to get drafted?" Sonny is fifteen and a long way from conscription age, but there's no way he's going to war, not if it stands in the way of boxing.

"You're too young to worry," Sid says.

"Listen. No one knew the last war would last so long. Who knows? They called it the Great Adventure. Like a game. *Ich vais nicht.*"

This does not reassure Sonny.

Reuben savours the last bite of cake, contemplates taking another slice, but his blood sugar is high. He's not supposed to eat a lot of sweets. His wife makes sure of that. He knows she's watching him now.

"What's that?" Mr. Tepperman-the-boarder asks. Mr. Tepperman is near-deaf now and just this side of senile. "A pogrom?"

"No, Mr. Tepperman. Germany invaded Poland."

"Poland? I never liked the Polish," Mr. Tepperman says. "We had pogroms over there too, you know."

"Do you think they'll attack Russia?" Yacov is worried about his family in Tiraspol. He puffs hard on his cigarette.

"Who knows? Yacov, don't get excited." Sophie pats his arm.

"This might be good for business," Max speculates. Not one with a sweet tooth, Max is sipping a glass of seltzer.

Yacov can't believe his cousin sometimes. How can a war be good for business? He butts out his cigarette, reaches for another.

A LITTLE LATER, Sid walks down to Manny's Deli on College Street to find his friends. He's restless with all this talk of war. Maybe he should sign up, fight for his country. Save the world for democracy. He's nineteen years old and in perfect health.

On his way into the deli, he waves to Manny, who sits up front with his regular customers, their ears glued to the small Westinghouse tabletop radio Manny keeps by the cash register. What a night. All shows have been interrupted for a special broadcast. The liner *Athenia* bound for Montreal with fourteen hundred passengers, including one hundred and twenty Torontonians, was torpedoed by a German submarine two hundred miles west of the Hebrides. Canada is officially at war.

Sid heads directly to the back table. His best friend, Louie Horowitz, is holding court. Eddie Finkelstein, Guido Toscano, Ralph Shapiro, Salvatore Ricci, Yossie Singer, Meyer Glass and his brother Jerry are all there. Sid slides into the booth beside Louie. The deli is warm and heavy with the scent of smoked meat, fresh rye bread, dill pickles and coleslaw. The front windows are steamed up. The sombre voice from Manny's radio echoes throughout the restaurant.

"I signed up," Louie tells Sid. "Royal Regiment of Canada, armed forces. I'm gonna fight those lousy Nazis."

"You did? When?" Sid's heart flutters. He feels hurt, as if someone had just stabbed him in the heart. Louie's his best friend. Louie and Sid tell each other everything. Usually. Sid's thick black glasses slide down his nose. He pushes them back up with one finger.

"Today. This morning. Told my father I was feeling sick and couldn't come to work and as soon as he left the apartment, I went down to the recruiting office."

"Does your father know?"

Louie lowers his voice. Glances to the front in case Manny can hear them. "Not yet."

"Louie, he's gonna kill you."

Louie sticks out his jaw. "Naw. He's not. Anyway, I'm nineteen. I'll be twenty in five months. There's nothing he can do about it."

"What about the shop? How's he gonna manage without you?" Louie's father runs his own tailor shop. After Louie's mother died ten years ago, Louie started helping out after school, on weekends, and full-time in the summer. Since he finished school two years ago, he's worked full-time alongside his father, as an apprentice. One day he'll take over the shop, maybe train his own son in the trade. Louie knows how to measure an inseam, a waist and a chest, baste a hem, cut the bolts of cloth, do a quick stitch, work a foot-powered sewing machine, replace a bobbin, match thread colours, oversee the bookkeeping and the cash, order material and thread, and court the customers. He is temperamentally suited to follow in his father's footsteps as a neighbourhood tailor. Only problem is, he hates it. He doesn't know what his future holds, but he dreams of something more exciting than tailoring.

"I don't know," Louie says. "There's a war on. Anyway Pop'll be glad I'm gonna be fighting Hitler and the Nazis. My Pa's from Germany, you know."

"I know." Sid is offended. Of course he knows. It's like his friend Louie is slipping away already.

"They killed his father and brother. They were arrested in a huge roundup of teachers a long time ago, like in 1935 or something. We don't even know what happened to his sister and her kids. They were arrested two years ago. Sent to a labour camp somewhere in the east. Haven't heard a word since then."

"I'm gonna join the navy," Eddie announces, taking a huge bite of his corned beef on rye. "I'm going down tomorrow."

"The navy. That's where I'm gonna go," Jerry Glass decides. "You learn how to sail."

"Aw, you're only fifteen. The war'll be over by the time you're old enough, Jerry."

"You think?"

"I wanna sign up. But I don't know what my Ma would do without me," says Guido. His father died a long time ago, when he was little. At eighteen, Guido supports his mother, grandmother, his younger brother and two younger sisters. He has a good job with the city, hauling garbage.

"What about you, Sid?" asks Louie.

"You guys are nuts," says Ralph, stealing a bit of meat from Eddie's sandwich, when he's not looking.

"What?"

"Who wants to go to stinking Europe and get your heads blown off? I'm gonna stay here and make a fortune while you suckers are lying in filthy trenches, dodging bullets."

"Oh yeah?" says Louie. "What kind of fortune?"

"I got ideas," boasts Ralph, puffing his chest out.

"Like what?"

Ralph leans forward and whispers. "Scrap metal. Think about it. If there's a war on, metal's gonna be in short supply."

"So what are you gonna do about it, Ralph?"

"Go into business for myself, wise guy. That's what."

"Aw, they're gonna get you anyways, Shapiro," says Louie.

"Who?" asks Ralph.

"The army, dummy. There's gonna be conscription. That's what my Pa says."

"There won't be conscription. Not here. Not after the Great War. People voted against it. That's what the prime minister says," Ralph counters.

"Oh yeah?"

"Yeah, besides, they can't get me. I'm supporting my Ma now." Ralph's father died the year before of a heart attack. His married older brother runs the poultry shop so Ralph got a job procuring scrap for Weinstein's Wrecking, the biggest scrap-metal business in town. He gets paid by the weight of the scrap he brings into the yard. Meantime, he's observing and learning. Ralph can see what a lucrative business this could be. He wants to be his own boss one day. *Shapiro's Wrecking,* he'll call the business. Or maybe *Shapiro's Scrap Metal.*

"That's true," Sid says, "he's needed here. They can't take you if your family needs you."

"That's right," confirms Guido.

"Says who?" asks Louie.

"I don't know. The prime minister, I guess," Guido says, although he really has no idea.

"Anyway, the army wouldn't want me," Ralph reminds the others. "Not with my bum leg." He pats the thigh of his shrivelled leg in its steel brace.

Ralph barely survived childhood polio. His left leg is scrawny and five inches shorter than his right, with almost no muscle tone. He wears a special shoe with a built-up sole, and a metal brace for support. He manages to walk without crutches, in a lopsided way, but with a kind of habitual grace. The guys are so used to his limp, most of the time they don't notice it.

"What about you, Sid?" Louie asks again.

"I don't know." Sid hasn't given it serious thought. He is brave, but in a quiet way. He doesn't need to prove anything. These days Sid has his mind on Ruthie Snyder. They've been dating. He finally got the nerve up to ask her out. To his surprise, she seemed delighted. He took her for a soda. He didn't know what to say at first, but Ruthie is so easy to talk to. It's as if she really listens to what he has to say. And she laughs at all his jokes, even the corny ones. Ruthie is so sweet and kind, he feels confident around her, like a man. She looks at him with love and is constantly telling him how handsome he is. They haven't done anything more than kiss, and a little light petting. Sid respects Ruthie and would never push her, but he's about to die from arousal these days, whenever he's around her. He's thinking of asking her to marry him, but he's scared. What if she says no?

"Hey Sid, go for the armed forces. We could go together. Be in the same company."

"It don't work like that, Louie," says Ralph-the-expert. "You don't get to pick your company. You might get sent to different countries even."

"We could pick the same company," argues Louie.

"Could not."

"Hey you guys," Sid says. "Stop it. There's a war on. We can't fight each other. We gotta stick together."

Ralph and Louie glare at each other for a moment. Then Louie breaks his gaze. "Okay, you're right Sid. No hard feelings, Ralph?"

Ralph nods. "Sure, Louie. No hard feelings."

"I gotta go," Eddie stands. "I'm supposed to pick up my Pa at the track. See you guys."

"Me too," Ralph follows. "Gotta help my Ma shovel out the coal cellar."

LENNY ALSO STEPS OUT after dinner, to meet Ted at a coffee shop on Bloor Street. Ted is now thirty-one and still unmarried, a fact that has not escaped Sophie, but Lenny doesn't see anything wrong with it. He pulls open the glass door and spots Ted sitting at a table near the back. Beside him is another young man, dressed in a neat, pressed suit, with an ascot at his neck rather than a tie. Lenny approaches a little slowly.

He was expecting Ted to be alone, which Lenny prefers. Ted's friends tend to patronize Lenny for being so much younger, whereas when it's just the two of them, he feels like an adult, not like a gangly boy of seventeen at all.

On a radio in the restaurant, the sweet melodic sounds of a new song from the hit movie, "The Wizard of Oz," is playing. A young actress, all the rage, Judy Somebody — Lenny can't remember her last name — is singing. Her voice is so clear and strong and full of emotion, he can't help but notice as he walks toward Ted's table.

"If happy little bluebirds fly
Beyond the rainbow,
Why, oh, why can't I?"

"Lenny." Ted stands as Lenny approaches. "This is James. My friend."

James looks Lenny over in a way that makes the younger boy uncomfortable, and offers his hand to shake.

"Well, Lenny. What do you think of the news?" Ted asks, sipping his coffee.

"I don't believe in war. It's barbaric," Lenny answers.

"Good for you. I wholeheartedly agree. What do you think, James?"

"Quite so."

"So you're not going to sign up?" Lenny worried all the way over that Ted would be one of the young men running to sign up. After all, he's single. He has no wife or children to worry about.

James and Ted laugh uproariously at Lenny's question, until his face burns in shame. He's not sure what is so funny, but he feels as though he is the brunt of a secret joke.

"Don't worry, Lenny, they wouldn't take us anyway," Ted manages.

"Why not?"

Which sets the older men off again, until they're laughing so hard they choke, and James has to down the water in his glass.

"Flat feet," Ted finally answers. "We have flat feet."

"Oh."

And they laugh some more. Lenny laughs a bit with them, although he doesn't see what's so funny.

Later, when he says goodnight and heads for home, Lenny decides not to see Ted for a while. He's sure Ted and James were making fun of him. Anyway, he has a lot on his mind these days. His last year of high school is upon him. By the end of the school year, he needs to figure out how he's going to get to college. At one time he'd hoped that Ted would be the benefactor he'd dreamed of, but he quickly realized that, like himself, Ted was from humble beginnings, and though he made a weekly salary, a librarian was not particularly well-paid. Lenny had hoped he'd meet his benefactor at one of the poetry readings or art shows Ted took him to, but no matter how many people he introduced himself to, not one emerged as a rich benefactor. If he doesn't find one soon, Lenny will never get to college. The song from the radio floods Lenny's head, and he hums to himself as he heads down Clinton Street for home, the lyrics resonating deep in his hopeful heart.

"Somewhere over the rainbow,
Way up high,
There's a land that I heard of,
Once in a lullaby …"

THREE DAYS LATER, Sid waits in line at the recruiting office, which is really a big open makeshift room hastily thrown together from an abandoned warehouse. A hundred young men sit on hard wooden folding chairs, stripped down to their boxer shorts, clutching in their hands the forms they were asked to fill out. In the corner of the room, a Union Jack on a pole sits in a floor stand under a portrait of the King. Sid signs his form and hands it to the sergeant. He is told to sit in the waiting room, which is stuffed to the rafters with half-naked men. The air is stuffy and stale; smoke and sweat permeate what little air exists. Outside, the queue runs for three blocks. Young boys ready for adventure, unemployed men, guys who've been down on their luck so long, three square meals a day sounds like a good deal, even if they have to wear a scratchy woollen uniform, shoot a gun and salute every time an officer walks by.

Sid looks around the room at all the hopeful recruits. He's determined to pass. He's in great shape, over six feet tall, with broad shoulders and a chest hard as steel. If Louie's going to fight the Huns in Europe, then Sid's going to go too. He knows his mother will be upset, but he doesn't want to be a coward. Anyway, once he is in uniform, he can ask Ruthie to marry him. He is sure she'll say yes. He'll look handsome and be doing something brave. Something more important than peddling door-to-door. The heroes in the picture shows he takes Ruthie to are always doing things more exciting than Sid. How could a girl as beautiful and kind as Ruthie want to marry a common peddler? Especially when there were men in the world like William Powell, Errol Flynn, Henry Fonda and Robert Taylor? If Sid goes to war, his family will miss the income he helps bring in, but he'll send home most of his army pay to his mother. *Besides, Lenny is seventeen. It's time for him to quit school, get a full-time job and help out more,* Sid thinks. *It's Lenny's turn now.*

"Shee-mon La … pin … sky," a corporal sounds out Sid's Hebrew name. Sid stands. "Here, sir."

"Follow me." The corporal turns swiftly on his heels and marches down a long hall to a room with an open door. He gestures for Sid to go inside. Sitting behind a table is the recruiting sergeant. His nametag reads "Sergeant L. McClusky." His blond hair is cut in a severe crewcut. He is in his early forties, barrel-chested, with a slight gut hanging over his belt, yet to Sid he is strong and impressive in his Royal Regiment of Canada uniform, his sergeant's stripes proudly displayed on each shoulder under his regimental crest.

"Sit down, Lapinsky," says Sergeant McClusky.

"Yes, sir." With passion.

Sergeant McClusky reads over Sid's forms. Then he glances over the top of the papers at Sid. Shame, he thinks. Big strong healthy-looking boy. "Son," he says, "I'm afraid we can't take you."

"But, sir," Sid is on his feet before he realizes what he has done.

"I'm sorry, son. I'd love to enlist you, but your eyesight. It's below acceptable levels."

"But, sir, I can see perfectly with my glasses." Sid touches the earpiece to accentuate his point.

"That's the problem exactly, son. What if you're out in a battlefield and your glasses get knocked off? Why, you'd become a liability. Your buddies would have to take care of you."

"Sir, I can buy a strap that fits around my head. My glasses would never move an inch."

"I'm sorry, son. Regulations." The sergeant stamps Sid's form and places it in a file.

Sid sticks his chest out. "But Sir. I want to fight for my country."

Sergeant McClusky sighs deeply and rubs the back of his neck. It is going to be a long day.

"YOU WHAT?" Sophie says sharply at the supper table when Sid tells his family he tried to enlist, but not to worry, he was refused anyway.

"Oy," Yacov says. "You know how many boys left Russia in my day to stay out of the army? Your Uncle Max for one."

"Pa, Louie's going."

"So because Louie Horowitz is going, that means you should go too?" Sophie admonishes Sid.

"I had to stay in the bottom of a dry well, for seven days. Just to get out of Russia. And he wants to run back there." Yacov takes a bite of bread. Furiously.

"We know the story, Yacov. We've heard it a thousand times," Sophie reminds her husband. Izzy sits beside her, quietly eating. He has learned how to eat by himself, with a spoon, but he is uncoordinated and gets just as much food on himself as in his belly. He wears a towel around his neck as a bib. Drinks are even worse. When he tips a glass to his mouth, most of it pours over his clothes. But Sophie refuses to let him use a baby bottle. He's eleven years old, and he's creeping up on Sonny already. He's much brawnier than Lenny, who has remained slight, although of medium height.

"I could have been a hero," Sid says to his full bowl of soup. Now he will never do anything great. He is nothing but a crummy door-to-door peddler. He feels as if he's shirking his responsibility somehow, even though he tried to enlist.

"I'll give you a hero," Yacov says. "You want to be a hero? Stay by your family and help out."

"I always do, Pa," Sid says glumly.

"I'm going to be a hero," Sonny declares, puffing out his growing chest, although at fifteen he has a few years to wait before he can even think about signing up. Not to mention the fact that Checkie Seigelman would personally kill Sonny for doing so. He hasn't spent a fortune training and grooming Sonny for the pro-boxing world so he could sign up and get his keister blown away by lousy Nazis halfway across the stinking world. If he wanted to, Sonny probably could be a hero. Athletic and graceful, strong and brave, he'd be the kind of soldier who would run behind enemy lines, carry a dying comrade to safety, do something heroic that would win a battle and garner him the coveted Victorian Cross. Sonny has no fear. His fearlessness is a part of him now. He doesn't worry about his own hide, because in his wounded mind, he doesn't deserve to be whole while his brother Izzy is damaged.

"I'll give you a hero." Sophie waves her fork in the air and reaches for the pack of cigarettes Yacov tossed on the table earlier. "That's all we need." She drops her fork, inhales deeply, blows smoke out through her nose.

"I'd rather be a war correspondent than a soldier," Lenny announces quietly. "Think of the primitive conditions a soldier has to contend with."

Sonny gives Lenny a look; he feels like slugging him. Lenny reads the dictionary every day to improve his vocabulary, then he springs fancy words on his family. Sonny figures Lenny does it just to make him feel stupid. Sometimes he'd like to pound Lenny out, if he wasn't so busy protecting his skinny brother from the neighoubourhood bullies.

"There's nothing for us over there, in Europe. That's why we came here," Yacov asserts, a little too loudly. His heart is beating in his chest. Thank God Sid wears glasses. He can't imagine one of his boys crossing back over the ocean that saved him from the horrors of Russia, to fight in a war. For more than twenty years he's been safe. He doesn't want any of his boys going back over there.

"Pop. I don't want to live there," Sid says, "I want to fight the Nazis."

"Never mind. There's plenty of Nazis here you could fight."

"There's Nazis here?" Sophie asks, alarmed, her soup forgotten.

"No, Ma," Sid says.

"There could be," Sonny argues. "Remember the Swazis back in '33."

"Those guys are washed up," Sid says.

"Maybe with the war on, they'll be around again. You don't know," Sonny maintains.

"Where you going, Sid?" Izzy asks suddenly.

"Sid's not going anywhere, Sweetie." Sophie moves Izzy's soup bowl an inch; it looks too close to the edge. He carefully slurps up another spoonful, spilling only a little.

"There was one good Gentile family in Romania. They hid me in the bottom of their well for seven days. Saved my life."

"Yacov, we know about the well." Sophie puffs on her cigarette.

"Aw, what's the use?" Sid says to his plate. "You just don't get it, Pop."

"I get. I get. You wanna be a big shot. Everybody wants to be a big shot."

"Ma, I'm not so hungry tonight." Sid pushes his half-full bowl back and stands. "I'm going to meet the guys. Okay?"

Sophie sighs. "Go on." She'd rather have him home on a night like this, but boys are restless. She knows he needs to do something with all his energy. Especially now that he isn't going to the war. She thanks God silently that Sonny is too young and Lenny, well, she can't imagine Lenny wanting to sign up. The last thing she wants is to send any of her boys off to war.

IT TURNS OUT that Louie Horowitz is the first of Sid's gang to go overseas. On a crisp December morning in 1939, he stands on the deck of the ship that will deliver the first two companies of the Royal Regiment of Canada to England, where they will take a train to Aldershot for training, and become part of the 1st Canadian Corps. The ship is barely out of the Halifax harbour and Louie already feels seasick. Good thing he didn't sign up for the navy. He'd literally be sunk.

Louie's father, Sam Horowitz, has taken a new part-time job while Louie is away. Tip Top Tailors have converted its cafeteria into a uniform factory, and with Louie gone to war, Sam wants to help out in any way he can. The long, narrow cafeteria tables have been outfitted with foot-powered sewing machines, ten per table. Middle-aged Jewish tailors dominate the room, in white shirts, sleeves rolled up, ties tucked in, jackets hung on the back of their chairs. There is a dull roar, a din of sewing machines chugging mechanically, the huge cutting machine slicing through bolts of cotton and wool. Hanging in the air is a mixture of scents — motor oil used to lubricate the gears; cigarette smoke; sardines, pickled herring and smoked meat from the workers' lunch bags. A sense of great purpose abounds. The men are sewing Canadian Armed Forces uniforms, less for the money than to aid in the war effort. Most of the tailors have family back in Europe, some of whom have already been marched to their deaths inside Nazi concentration camps. Or like Sam, they have young sons newly overseas as Canadian soldiers and the chance to help in any way they can is the only thing soothing the pain in their hearts as the world marches back to war for the second time in their lives.

"Vat's dat?" asks Yossel Sipowitz, the tailor who works at the machine next to Sam, pointing to a pile of small pieces of paper.

"Have a look."

Yossel unfolds one of the papers. Handwritten on the note are the words "God Bless You."

"Who knows if it helps? My son is over there." Sam stuffs a *God Bless You* note into the front pocket of the uniform he is stitching.

"Couldn't hurt." Yossel stuffs a note into his uniform.

They bend over their machines and sew.

The Proposal
FEBRUARY TO MAY, 1940

SID HAS BEEN GOING STEADY with Ruthie Snyder for two years. He's not sure, but he might possibly be in love. He's confided in his father that he is going to pop the question to Ruthie. And soon. He has sworn

Yacov to secrecy. What if she says no? Sid has never been so nervous in his life.

"What's wrong, Sid?" Ruthie asks, sitting beside him in the front room of her house. He's been fidgeting and he's sweating even though it is terribly cold outside and not much warmer inside. With the war into its second year, there is a shortage of coal and people are conserving. They bundle up in sweaters, mufflers and long johns, even inside their houses, to keep warm. Ruthie's two younger brothers are listening to the *Chase and Sanborn Comedy Hour* on the radio, sitting on the floor at the other end of the room under a heavy quilt, laughing hysterically at the funny parts. Ruthie's mother, father and grandmother are sitting in the kitchen, drinking tea. Sid can see them through the doorway. It feels as if they're staring at him. The warm scent of their dinner of roasted chicken and potatoes hangs in the air. A large ornate fireplace takes up the better part of a living room wall, but with the wood shortages, there's no fire tonight. It's chilly inside the house.

"It's nothing, Ruthie," Sid lies. "Come on. We'll be late for the picture." They're going to see "Johnny Apollo," with Tyrone Power and Dorothy Lamour, playing at the Capitol on Bloor Street.

Ruthie glances at the clock. Actually, they will be early if they leave right away, even if they walk, even though there is ice on the sidewalks and the gutters are piled high with snow banks. But she knows Sid. He is shy. Whatever is bothering him will take some time on her part to draw out. And she knows he certainly won't tell her in front of her family.

Ruthie grabs her coat, scarf, gloves and hat, steps into the rubber boots that go over her shoes, says goodbye to her parents, and they leave.

Outside, Sid is still a bundle of nerves. He is silent as they walk, but he keeps glancing at Ruthie with a terrified smile plastered on his face. A light snow falls. It is bitter cold. Finally, Ruthie can't stand it any longer. On the sidewalk, in the middle of two huge dirty-brown snowbanks, she stops and turns to him.

"For heavens sake, Sid. What is it?"

"Will you marry me?" he blurts out. Oh no. No. That's not the way it was supposed to be at all. Sid has been planning this for a long time. He wanted it to be romantic, like in the picture shows. He wanted to take her to the movies, sit in the back row, his arm draped around her shoulder. Maybe they'd neck for a while. And then he was going to take her to the fountain shop. He has the ring in his pocket. He paid twenty dollars down and is paying it off at five dollars a week. He was going to order a soda with two straws, look her in the eye, tell her how much he loved her, and then he was going to pop the question, all confident and cavalier the way Robert Taylor would have been. Now he's blown it. Just blurted it out like a fool on the sidewalk. What must she think of him? He can feel the blood rise in his cheeks. His heart is beating so fast he's worried she can see it pumping, right through all his clothing. He glances at Ruthie. She is grinning from ear to ear.

"Oh Sid." She throws her arms around him. They are both wearing heavy overcoats and he can barely get his arms around her. "Of course I will. Of course, dear."

"You will?" He's feels faint from the excitement.

"Of course, Sid. I thought you'd never ask."

"OKAY MA, I DON'T KNOW. Maybe Ruthie knows a girl Lenny's age," Sid says doubtfully.

"It's not natural. He's shy. Can't you help him out?" Sophie is worried about Lenny. He's eighteen years old and he's never been on a date. She knows he'll find his way eventually, but would it hurt to give him a helping hand?

"I'll ask Ruthie. Ok? Don't worry," Sid assures her, just as Lenny arrives home.

"Ask her what?" Lenny removes his cap, tosses it onto a hook on the wall.

"Uh, nothing," Sid mumbles.

"I'm looking for a recipe," Sophie lies to Lenny, then silently asks God for forgiveness. She's never lied to her son before.

"Oh." Lenny passes into the living room with the afternoon newspaper. He's been following the war with great interest.

IT TAKES TWO WEEKS for Ruthie to dig up a girl of the appropriate age, the younger sister of one of her friends. The girl's name is Abigail. She's loud and talkative, not a good match for Lenny, but Ruthie tells Sid, "It's a start."

Lenny is unhappy, and at first refuses to go on the double date.

"What, Sid? You think I can't ask a girl out on my own?" Lenny objects.

"No, Lenny. I didn't say that. She's a friend of Ruthie's. We thought you'd hit it off is all."

"Well, no thank you." Lenny grabs his cap from the hook and heads for the door.

"Well, see, we already invited her," Sid confesses.

"What! Without checking with me? Well, just uninvite her."

"I can't, Lenny. She's already waiting for us at Ruthie's."

Lenny glares at his brother.

They go to a picture show, "Jezebel," starring Bette Davis. Lenny enjoys the movie, but he feels uncomfortable as Abigail inches her leg closer to his. He has to cross his legs and shift position several times to keep from touching her.

After the picture, they go out for a soda. On the radio, Benny Goodman and his orchestra serenade the customers with a cover version of *Blue Moon*.

Lenny relaxes. He finds that Abigail is quite a good conversationalist, if only she'd let someone else get a word in edgewise once in a while. He doesn't notice Ted and James enter the soda shop, doesn't see them until they are standing right by Lenny's table.

"Hiya, Lenny," Ted interrupts Abigail.

Lenny whips his head around. He turns beet red, although he doesn't know why. "Oh," he stammers, "Hi, Ted. Hello, James."

"Lenny." James tips his hat.

Lenny makes the appropriate introductions. Ruthie invites the men to join them, but thankfully they decline. Lenny watches them walk to the other side of the shop; his mood has now changed. He has no idea what he is doing here, talking to a girl he barely knows. He should be across the room, engaging in witty conversation with his older intellectual friends, who seem to be having a damn fine time without him. Lenny can't help but watch as Ted and James lean toward one another in deep and serious talk. Abigail continues her chatter, but Lenny is no longer responsive.

Sid is suspicious. "Those guys are kind of old for you to be pals with, Lenny. What do they want with a kid like you?"

Lenny is offended. "You wouldn't understand, Sid."

"They were laughing at you, Lenny. They're grown-ups and you're just a kid."

"Shuttup, Sid."

"Leave him be, Sid," Ruthie says.

"I think friendship can cross all age groups," Abigail declares.

It's on the tip of Lenny's tongue to tell her to shut up too, but instead he says, "I'm not feeling very good. Sid, can you please see Abigail home for me?" He stands and grabs his cap, jams it on his head.

"Lenny, where the heck are you going?"

Lenny doesn't answer. Instead, he tips his hat to Abigail, smiles sweetly. "Nice to meet you." It takes every ounce of discipline he possesses not to run out of the soda shop. He does not look at Ted on his way out.

SID AND RUTHIE'S WEDDING is held at the Orthodox synagogue on Baldwin Street at the beginning of May, with a small reception back at the house afterwards. Hope is in the warm spring air. Business is finally booming for Yacov and Max after the hard years of the Depression. Most of their customers are back at work in the factories and ammunitions plants that have sprung up all over the city, providing jobs to thousands of unemployed workers. Max and Yacov are being paid up on old accounts with years of interest. Rationing is the cause of shortages now, not unemployment, so anytime the cousins get their hands on something as scarce as flour or sugar, it is snapped up by their customers in no time.

Sid has saved up enough money to take Ruthie on a honeymoon. They are going to New York City, where they'll stay with Ruthie's cousin

Joe, who lives in Manhattan with his wife, Irma. They are going to see the Empire State Building, the Statue of Liberty and Broadway. Sid has never been on a vacation before. He has never been outside Toronto, has barely left his own neighbourhood. He is as excited as a little boy. After the honeymoon, Sid and Ruthie are moving into their own place on College Street, just two buildings over from Yacov and Sophie's first apartment together. It is a two-room flat in a four-storey walk-up, but they have their own kitchen and bathroom and Sid plans to save money for a down payment on a house some day, maybe even as far uptown as St. Clair Avenue. For now, Ruthie doesn't care where they live, so long as she is with Sid. Anyway, he is a good businessman. Ruthie has faith in him.

When Sid and Ruthie are finally alone together after the wedding, Sid lies back on the bed. He pushes his thick black glasses up higher on his nose, a habit he's developed. It's their first night as man and wife. They leave tomorrow for their honeymoon, but for tonight they're sleeping together in Sid's childhood bedroom. Sonny, Lenny and Izzy are camping out in the living room to give the new couple their privacy. With Ruthie in his arms, Sid can't believe he was worried. Making love to her was the most natural thing in the world. He kisses her beautiful face.

"Sid?"

"Uh huh?"

"I want to have lots of children."

"So do I, Ruthie."

"Five or six."

"We can have seven or eight if you want."

"Oh Sid." She reaches for him. He leans up on one elbow and kisses her.

"So, we better get started." She laughs into his shoulder as he gently rolls her onto her back.

The Scrapbook
NOVEMBER AND DECEMBER, 1940

THE DAY SONNY TURNS SIXTEEN he walks out of Harbord Collegiate for the last time. He tosses his schoolbooks into the trash can, but at the last second, remembers to scoop them back out and bring them home for Lenny, who will read anything he can get his hands on. Even school textbooks.

The next day Sonny takes the streetcar to the pool hall to find Checkie Seigelman and announce that now he's available to train and fight full-time.

"All right, *boychick*. Good," Checkie says. "School shmool. I quit when I was eight. And look at me today. Huh?"

Sonny has to admit Mr. Seigelman is rich, even if he's not exactly classy.

When Izzy turns twelve later that year, Sonny makes him his personal towel boy. It's a job Izzy can do well; it's simple, physical and repetitive. Sophie insists that Izzy's home education continue, but she is also relieved that Sonny watches out for his brother. What other kind of a job is he ever going to get? Checkie, on the other hand, puts up a fuss at first.

"Come on, Sonny. This ain't no playground. We can't have kids hanging around."

"He won't be hanging around. He's my towel boy. He'll help out." Sonny has become bold with Checkie. As his skill improves, he realizes just how good he really is and how much money he is going to make once he goes pro. He doesn't argue for things often. But on this he is immovable.

"Aw right, aw right." Checkie gives in. "Just see that he stays out of my way."

"Don't worry, Mr. Seigelman."

"A towel-boy he needs? Mr. Big Shot." Checkie affectionately makes a fist.

Sonny smiles triumphantly.

His training schedule increases. Road work every morning, three miles of running. Rudy picks Sonny up at five in the morning and they drive out to High Park. Rudy follows in his car as Sonny runs. In the afternoon they do gym work. Izzy meets him at the athletic club — it's only a three-block walk, and Izzy can manage that on his own. Sonny keeps him busy fetching water, holding his towel, unlacing his gloves, sweeping up and other odd jobs. Izzy is proud that he has a job.

Sonny has grown to five foot six and weighs in at 140 pounds of solid muscle. He is ready to fight as a welterweight in the amateur boxing circuit.

Checkie books Sonny onto amateur fight cards all over the city and out of town. Sonny travels by train, or sometimes by car with Rudy, to St. Catharines, Hamilton, Windsor, London, even Detroit and Buffalo. Checkie has Sonny fighting every two weeks, and when Sonny isn't fighting, he's training hard. He is in peak condition and winning more often than losing. His name begins appearing in the newspaper frequently.

"Seigelman's Boy wins on a TKO."

"Sonny Lapinsky, Hebe from Spadina, charges in and knocks out opponent in round two."

"Sonny 'The Charger' Lapinsky Wins Bout."

He is dubbed "The Charger" by Gordon Sinclair in his sports column, "Hook, Line and Sinclair," which runs for years in the evening *Star*. Every boxer needs a nickname, and this one sticks. It refers to Sonny's habit of charging forward like a bull the second the bell rings.

"Hey Ma," Sid roars up the stairs one evening in late December, holding out a copy of the *Star*. "Look. Sonny got in the paper again." Sid thrusts the sports section in front of Sophie.

"A Couple of Hebes Battle it Out," screams the headline. Sonny had knocked out another Jewish fighter, Benny "The Tiger" Katzman, in the first minute of the second round.

"Ach." Sophie complains, as she grabs the scissors to clip out the article for her scrapbook. Every article, every mention of Sonny in the papers, no matter how small, is carefully clipped out and glued into the scrapbook. Sonny's the first person to bring fame to the family. "Look, they spelled his name wrong again."

The sportswriters can't seem to wrap their pens around Lapinsky. The name has been recorded as Lewshinsky, Larinski, Larenzo, Lapinski. Sonny has toyed with shortening it to Lapin or Pinsky, but then he figures, what the hell, they'd get that wrong too, so why bother?

However often his name is misspelled, Sonny is the pride of the neighbourhood. When he's out in the streets, the neighbourhood men and boys clap him on the back, shake his hand, give him boxing advice and ask for his opinion.

"Hey Sonny," they shout as he walks by, "great fight Saturday night!"

"Hey Sonny, how's the hand?" they ask after he breaks his right hand against Tony "Bull" Conduccio's jaw.

Sonny loves the attention. He's the hero he always dreamed he would be. It is up to him to bring honour to his family and his neighbourhood. He feels almost good these days, not like a bad person at all, especially when he's in the ring.

There isn't much money in amateur fighting, but Checkie takes care of Sonny, makes sure he's in on a piece of the action. Sonny is paid thirty-five or forty bucks under the table by the promoters, forty percent of which goes to Checkie. Still, at twenty bucks a fight, Sonny is bringing home fifty or sixty a month — a fortune in his family. He keeps out a couple of bucks for spending money and hands the rest over to his mother for family expenses. Sonny isn't too worried about the money. He knows that in a couple more years he is going to go pro. That's where the big money is. He is only sixteen. He has lots of time. Meanwhile with every fight his skill increases, his reputation grows and his body develops.

And there is the coffee can. For years Sonny has been stashing the money he's made from working for Checkie under the back porch. Now he can finally bring it out and spread some cash around. He takes his brothers to Simpsons Department Store on Queen Street and tells them to pick out new suits.

"Are you crazy, Sonny?" Sid says. "You know how much that's gonna cost?"

Sonny smiles, reaches in his pocket and flashes the biggest billfold they've ever seen.

"Holy cripes, Sonny." Sid puts a hand over the money protectively so no one around them can see it. "Where'd you get it?"

Sonny shrugs. "Boxing."

Sid and Lenny look at one another. They have some idea how much Sonny makes per fight. This amount of cash seems excessive. He must be gambling or shooting craps. Maybe even betting on his own fights.

"Come on," Sonny says. "I ain't got all day. Pick out whatever you guys want. It's all on me."

Sid picks a simple brown suit, a white shirt, and a striped tie. He finds his size quickly and makes his decision. Lenny is ecstatic. He tries on every suit in his size, modelling them before his brothers, until finally they are exhausted and order him to pick one. So Lenny settles on a black, double-breasted suit with a thin white pinstripe, a white shirt and a classic silk tie, with a stick pin and matching cufflinks.

Sonny knows better than to produce a significant amount of money all at once in front of his mother without arousing her suspicions. So he continues handing over fifty dollars a month, telling her it's his pay from Checkie.

"Kinda like an advance. Sort of. On all the money I'm gonna make later on."

Sophie accepts the explanation, thinking of the food and clothing it will buy for her family. Fifty dollars a month: a fortune. After the lean years of the thirties when she worried every day how she was going to put soup on the table with nothing in the icebox, this is heaven. She can feed her family properly, even buy meat a few times a week. Sonny takes his mother to the department store and insists she pick out a new dress. She agrees only after finding a pair of trousers and new shirt for Izzy. Sonny offers to buy his father a new suit, but Yacov's pride gets in the way. He mutters something about his old suit being fine, and that's the end of that. Sonny is plotting a way to buy his father a new suit anyway. He's just not sure how to get his measurements without tipping him off.

"Sonny." Sophie ruffles his hair affectionately, leans over and kisses the top of his head. "This doesn't mean I approve of fighting …"

"Boxing, Ma." Sonny grins with pride.

The Newspaperman
MARCH TO JUNE, 1941

IF HE COULD, Lenny would go to college. He has the grades for it, and the passion. Lenny would love nothing better than studying and reading, debating philosophy and politics, spending hours in a university library, having access to all that knowledge, writing essays and term papers. Thinking, wondering, questioning. But this is a pipe dream for a boy from a poor immigrant family. As it is, last summer he graduated from Harbord Collegiate, finishing twelfth grade with honours. He is the first person in his family with a high school diploma, but college is out of the question. Even if the family had the money for tuition, even if Lenny had found his elusive benefactor (which he has not), the quota system is in full force in Toronto. Few Jews are admitted to any university. What would be the point in applying? Anyway, it's time Lenny brought money into the house. That's what Sid always says, although Sophie would love to find a way for her favourite son to stay in school.

Since graduating from high school, Lenny has been working with his father, Uncle Max and Sid. It is not an occupation he is suited for. He is not much help when it comes to lifting the heavy rugs and drapes — Sid takes care of that. He's not much of a salesman either. Lenny just can't muster up the enthusiasm to sell a customer on the wonders of silk stockings, or a particular brand of soap. Yacov puts him on collections. He carries the account book door to door, calling on people to pay their debts. With the war on, every man not in the army is working in a factory. Young people are working. Even women are working. Customers can pay again. The credit business is booming.

Collecting debts is a task Lenny — an intelligent boy — can certainly manage, but he hates every single second of it. He was not born to be a debt collector. He is a writer. His dresser drawer overflows with notebooks crammed with half-started stories, poems, plot lines, ideas. He reads all four newspapers voraciously, studying the articles, editorials and the review section. Lenny knows he could write articles like the ones he reads. He could write anything. When he was younger he planned to write his first novel by the time he was sixteen. He wanted to write a gritty modern urban novel, in the style of Hemingway or Steinbeck or even the Yiddish writer Sholem Asch. Lenny's novel would be set in Kensington Market. He'd write about people like his mother and Aunt Tess, poor immigrant women who held together families during the harshest time of all, the Great Depression when he was a little boy. He'd write about the other immigrants in his neighbourhood, the Italians, the Chinese and the Polish. Lenny has thousands of ideas for his first novel, but he's never had time to actually write it. After school every day since he was eight years old, he's been selling newspapers on street corners. Now here he is, trudging up the street behind Sid, and with every collection he makes, a little piece of Lenny's soul floats away, a piece he will never get back. Lenny is nineteen years old. If he doesn't pursue his dream soon, he will die.

EARLY ON A MARCH MORNING, Lenny wakes, shaves, washes and dresses in his one good suit, the suit that Sonny bought him last year. He knots his tie and stuffs a white handkerchief in his pocket just so. He shines his one pair of good shoes to a high polish. He adjusts his natty fedora with the red feather in its brim. Then he jumps onto the streetcar and rides it to the *Toronto Daily Star's* office on King Street West. He pauses outside, admires the formidable building, sucks in a deep breath, marches in and stands in front of the desk in the main reception area.

"Yes, sir," the secretary says. She's an older woman, dressed in a skirt and blouse. Her beige sequined sweater is draped over her shoulders, the top button fastened to hold it in place. A big black telephone, with a cone-shaped earpiece, perches on the corner of her desk and in the centre of the desk sits a solid Smith & Corona typewriter, white paper ready in its rollers. She puffs on her cigarette, sets it in her ashtray, smiles at Lenny. He cuts a handsome figure in his good suit and hat. "Yes, we are hiring staff reporters. Would you care to speak with Mr. Fitzgerald, vice-president in charge of hiring?"

"Yes ma'am, I would," Lenny answers optimistically. "Thank you."

She directs him to the twelfth floor, "and turn right," she says. She phones ahead to the secretary upstairs, who hands him an application form to fill out. He thanks her and sits on a hard wooden chair, pencil poised. The secretary goes back to her typing. The keys clack against the roller. Every twenty seconds she pushes the carriage back with the hand lever; *thwack.* Then on goes the clickety-clack of ninety words a minute. Her desk is positioned by a large window looking out to the street. Lenny can see a twenty-storey skyscraper through the window. A mail boy wheels a cart into the waiting room, tosses a stack of mail to the secretary, grabs her outgoing mail, smiles at Lenny and hurries out. The secretary lights a cigarette. Lenny follows suit, resting his in the black-marble floor ashtray by his chair.

The top of the form worries him. Name? Should he use his real name? Or something, well, less Jewish? There's probably no point in lying, so he writes his real name. Address is no problem. The next line asks religion. He wonders if he should lie, but what would he write? Catholic? Protestant? His name kind of gives it away. Anyway what if they ask what church he goes to? He wouldn't know what to say so he writes "Jewish" on the line. The rest of the form is easy, like writing an essay for school. He reaches for his cigarette. It has burned down to its filter. He stubs it out, finds his package of Chesterfields in his shirt pocket, lights another. Words float like magic in Lenny's mind, then down to the page like poetry. He knows his answers will dazzle Mr. Fitzgerald. When he's finished, he butts his cigarette and hands his application to the secretary, who asks him to please wait. "Would you like some coffee?" she adds.

"No, thank you." He lights another cigarette. Nervous.

The next fifteen minutes are excruciating. While Lenny waits, another young man enters the room and introduces himself to the receptionist as Thomas Willison Jr. He'd like to apply for the reporter's job. The receptionist hands him a form; he nods at Lenny and sits two seats away. Lenny watches as Thomas quickly fills out the paperwork and hands it back to the secretary. After another ten minutes, a well-dressed, handsome man in his mid-forties, with thick salt-and-pepper hair, emerges from the office behind the receptionist. Must be Mr. Fitzgerald. Lenny readies him-

self to stand, but the man calls out "Thomas Willison." Lenny settles back
in his chair as Thomas stands and follows Mr. Fitzgerald into the office.
The receptionist must have mixed up the order of their forms. That's got
to be the problem, Lenny convinces himself. There's nothing he can do
about it anyway. He waits another excruciating thirty-five minutes,
chain-smoking until he is out of cigarettes and has to mooch one from
the receptionist.

The office door opens again. Mr. Fitzgerald leads Thomas out. He
reaches forward and shakes the younger man's hand warmly. "Welcome
aboard, Mr. Willison. Report back to me first thing in the morning. Miss
Mills, may I see you in my office for a moment?" Mr. Fitzgerald glances
tightly in Lenny's direction.

Lenny's belly turns over. Something is wrong. He has his suspicions,
but forces himself to wait. The secretary returns and calls his name. He
stands.

"Mr. Lapin-sky," she drawls, as though his name is dreadfully long and
awfully inconvenient to pronounce. "Mr. Fitzgerald wishes me to inform
you that he is not currently hiring any more staff reporters, but we will
keep your application on file, and you may feel free to query him for free-
lance assignments."

"What?" Lenny moves forward and leans on her desk. "But downstairs
they said he was hiring!"

The secretary steps back as though there is a bad smell or unpleasant
noise. "Mr. Lap-*in*-sky. Please calm down."

Lenny takes a breath and closes his eyes for a moment to fight off the
fury, which is really just a mask for tears hovering just below the surface.
He turns away, puts a hand on the doorknob, then marches back to the
receptionist's desk, spots the application form with his name on it, rips it
from her desk, turns and leaves. He has only tried the *Star* because in
print it has been sympathetic to Jews. He should have known better. The
quota system. Everyone knows it exists. It's just not spoken of in polite
WASP company. The department stores and the banks aren't hiring Jews
either. Even the hospitals won't take qualified Jewish doctors. The *Star*

already has a few Jewish reporters. More than enough, as far as the publisher is concerned, Lenny figures. Lenny doesn't stand a chance, not unless one of them dies.

He is so angry he walks for hours, rage swirling in his belly with the injustice. He'd be such a great journalist, if only someone would give him a chance. He walks all over the city as a light rain falls. The bottom of his pant legs and his shoulders are damp. His hat brim is soaked. He ends up back on Spadina Avenue, not really sure until he is standing in the doorway that he is headed for the office of *Der Yiddisher Zhurnal,* the Daily Hebrew Journal.

"Mr. Lapinsky," the managing editor, Moe Berkov, strides out of his office, one arm extended heartily. "Please, come in. Sit down. Maybe I should get you a towel?" His mouth curls in a slight grin. Lenny is dripping all over the hardwood floor. Moe is an energetic man in his mid-thirties with brown hair, slicked back. His jacket is off, his shirtsleeves are rolled up and his tie is loosened at his neck. His vest buttons are open. There is a small coffee stain on his shirt, above the pocket. He smokes a pipe, which he waves in the air, and then sticks back into his mouth on the left side. Born and raised in New York, he moved to Toronto with his family when he was fourteen. He'd started at the *Zhurnal* as a paperboy and begun writing for the paper at sixteen. He's been Managing Editor for the past six years. On the second floor, overlooking College Street, the *Zhurnal* office is crowded with desks, paper, archives and printing equipment. It's a busy, noisy place with an infectious energy. There are newspapers piled on every surface and in every available corner. Desks back into each other, heavy with typewriters, phones, paperwork, files, and research. A bookcase that dominates the back wall is filled with Yiddish and English hardcover classics and modern bestsellers. There's a flurry of activity inside the *Zhurnal* office. It doubles as the unofficial headquarters of the Communist Party of Toronto, the Young Zionists, and the Paul Robeson appreciation club. The office is messy, cluttered and alive. Even the pigeons that gather on the outside ledge seem always to be debating. On one wall, Berkov has hung a world map, dotted with coloured pins that charts the progress of the war against Hitler.

"Please call me Moe," Berkov says, in his thick Bronx accent. "The Journal can't afford another staff writer right now. There is me, and two other writers who've been with the paper for years, but we welcome free-lance writers, young fellows like yourself. You see, we can't pay you a weekly salary, we pay by the word. You can make thirty dollars a week, on a good week. It's a nice way to make a living, Len. You work at home, only come down to the office to file your story."

Lenny imagines working at home. His mother is home most of the time cooking, cleaning, washing, mending. And Izzy is there most days, unless he's been sent to the store, or out with Sonny, who is not home much but when he is there, he is noisy. Tessie and her youngest kid, Morris, are home downstairs during the day — and the house isn't exactly soundproof. Sid and Ruthie are constantly dropping by, as are Sam Horowitz and Lenny's grandparents. His is a noisy, populated household. How could he ever concentrate? He doesn't have a typewriter and he's sure they'd want the stories typed, not handwritten. He swallows his pride and explains the situation to Moe.

"Let me think about it for a minute, Len. Maybe I can come up with something."

Berkov doesn't ask Lenny to leave his office. He merely stops talking and leans back in his chair across from Lenny with his hands folded behind the back of his neck, his face set in deep repose, puffing quietly on his pipe. This goes on for ten or fifteen minutes. Lenny begins to feel uncomfortable, wonders if maybe he should leave and come back later. He glances around the office. The desks are brown with wooden swivel chairs. Each desk has its own ashtray, Yiddish dictionary and a phone. From the street outside, there is the hum of the College streetcar, the chatter of pedestrian traffic, the racket of children playing and horns honking. Occasionally there is the clip clop of a horse slogging along the side of the road, hauling a bread- or milk-wagon. Lenny notices an impressive shortwave radio behind Moe's desk and figures it's probably for picking up the BBC and the Polish Free Radio stations in Europe.

Moe works hard and is passionate about journalism. A small "c" com-munist, Moe believes in equal rights for all and would lay down his life for the cause. He's looking forward to the later part of the century when he's sure the world will be a kinder place. In the meantime, he does what he can, marching for workers' rights, writing about the war in Europe, providing office space to progressive organizations and publishing the *Zhurnal.*

"I've got it!" Moe says suddenly, snapping his fingers in the air, leaning forward on his desk. "It's perfect, Len. Just perfect." He waves his pipe by its stem.

Lenny leaves the *Zhurnal* office half an hour later with instructions to return the next morning at eight a.m. sharp. He is so happy he hurries along College Street, tipping his hat at people whether he knows them or not. He stops in at the liquor board and buys a bottle of champagne — well, sparkling wine actually — to celebrate. No one in his family has ever tasted champagne, but Lenny read about it in a novel, *The Great Gatsby.* Cultured, artistic people drink champagne. Lenny is going to be a journalist. And this is only the beginning. He's still planning to write a novel, but in the meantime he will be paid to be a writer. There's only one small hitch, but Lenny figures he can deal with it. *Der Yiddisher Zhurnal* is a Yiddish paper. All the articles are in Yiddish, and although Lenny speaks Yiddish fluently, it being the language most often spoken at home and in his neighbourhood, he's never written much in Yiddish and will have to learn. Lenny doesn't care. He just has to keep this job. He cannot go back to peddling with his father and Sid.

"A WHAT?" YACOV SAYS as Lenny pours sparkling wine into water glasses and teacups. They don't own wineglasses.

"None for Izzy," Sophie says.

"That's okay, Ma. I got him soda pop," says Sonny, who is always buying treats for Izzy.

"Pop," repeats Izzy, excited. "Pop, pop, pop, pop."

"Take it easy, Iz." Sonny opens a bottle of Coca-Cola and hands it to Izzy.

"A proofreader," Lenny repeats. "My job will be to check the copy — uh, the articles for mistakes. Moe, that is Mr. Berkov, says I can use the office typewriter in the evening after my work is done and write my own articles, too. Kind of like being in training."

"That's swell, Lenny," Sid says wholeheartedly, lifting his glass and tasting the sweet bubbly liquor. He prefers beer, but to be polite he takes a second sip.

"*Mazel tov*, Lenny," Ruthie says, although she declines the champagne. This morning Dr. Grossman informed her she's pregnant and she wants to be careful, especially since her first pregnancy ended in miscarriage after six weeks. Ruthie and Sid have agreed not to share their news just yet. Not until they're sure everything is going to be okay.

"That's wonderful," Sophie says, coming around behind Lenny. With her hands on his shoulders, she leans forward and kisses his head. She always knew Lenny would go far. A newspaperman in the family. Imagine that. She is so proud of her boy.

"You can write in Yiddish?" Yacov is skeptical.

Lenny shrugs. "With your help, Pop, I'm going to learn."

"Atta boy," Yacov claps Lenny on the back.

"Of course," Sophie declares. "We'll both help."

"*Mazel tov*, son." Yacov picks up his glass and knocks back the champagne as if it were schnapps. "How much are they paying you?"

Lenny squirms. "Well ... they don't have a lot of advertisers, see? They depend on selling the paper ... and Moe says it's only a matter of time ..."

"But they're paying you something ..."

"Oh sure, Pop."

"So *nu?* How much."

Lenny studies his plate. "Eight dollars a week."

"Eight dollars?"

"A week."

"Not so bad," Sophie rescues him.

"Just to start."

"Sure, Lenny. You'll get a raise in no time."

"And I get extra for writing articles."

"Do they have a sports page?" Sonny asks.

"Sure they do," Lenny answers, not altogether certain that they do. With a flourish, he fills everyone's glass.

PROOFREADING IS BOTH harder and easier than Lenny had imagined. Easier, because he learns all of the rules within three days; harder, because it is tedious and tiring and hard on the body to be bent over a desk for hours at end, poring over the typeset pages, searching for the tiniest of errors. For the first two weeks, he is far too exhausted by the end of the day to think of article ideas, research and write them after his proofreading duties are over. He feels bad about it and goes in to talk to Moe.

"Don't you worry, Len. It takes a while to get used to the pace. Take your time," Moe says. Which only makes Lenny feel worse. Especially since he is now three years beyond the age by which he had vowed to write a novel. In his third month, on a Tuesday, he forces himself to stay late. Moe advises him to leaf through back issues from the previous week to look for article ideas. He sits at his desk with a hot cup of tea, poring over copies of the *Zhurnal.* The paper is filled with stories about the war, which is now into its third year. The *Zhurnal* can't afford a foreign correspondent, so its war coverage is expanded from short pieces it finds in other newspapers, the wire service and from listening to BBC Radio on the shortwave in Moe's office.

It's a humid, muggy June evening — hot as hell in the second-storey office. All the windows are open as wide as possible, but there is no breeze to speak of. Sweat pours from Lenny's scalp and down the sides of his face. His underarms are drenched. A small trickle runs down the front of his chest. He lights a cigarette and rubs his temples, which are pounding. Nothing in the back issues strike him, so he knocks on the door of Moe's office.

"Come on in." Lenny opens the door. Moe looks up, smiles. Moe's white shirt is soaked in sweat under the arms and at the collar. "Hello, Len. Have a seat." Moe is eating a cold corned-beef sandwich, drinking a Canada Dry ginger ale. Crumbs of rye bread decorate his loosened tie. The shortwave radio is switched on. Lenny sits in the chair opposite Moe.

A British radio announcer relays the news that the Nazis have marched into the Soviet Union and have occupied the cities and larger towns. The Russian peasants seem to welcome the storm troopers with open arms, angry as they are at the Bolsheviks and the Jews who "are the real source of all of our troubles." They cheer the invaders; they will take care of the problems in Russia. Moe grabs a small steno pad from his desk and tosses it to Lenny.

"Take notes," he says. Lenny scribbles furiously as the announcer continues with the details. When the report is over, Moe turns the radio off. "Why don't you write the story up, Len? Then bring in a draft to show me."

Lenny is scared. He is not sure he can do it. But he knows he has to try. He takes his notes back to his desk and he begins to write. After several hours have gone by, Moe is heading out for the night. "Don't forget to eat dinner, Len." He winks as he passes. Lenny gives a thumbs-up to Moe, and then bends back down over his typewriter. By nine o' clock he has a first draft, but he wants his first assignment to dazzle Moe, so he decides to rewrite the whole article before leaving it on his boss's desk.

"Oh no." He hasn't called home to say he'll be late. His mother will be worried. Sophie picks up on the third ring. She must have flown down the stairs to have answered that quickly. Lenny tells her that he's sorry, he got caught up in his work and will be late.

"Yeah," he lies in response to her question, "a smoked-meat sandwich. Right here at my desk." He hangs up and gets back to work. It doesn't occur to him to pass the terrible news on to his father: Nazi storm troopers have marched into Russia. His father's hometown, Tiraspol, near the city of Odessa, is one of the towns mentioned.

THE NEXT DAY, Lenny paces the office, waiting for the papers to arrive back from the printers. His shoes click rhythmically on the polished hardwood floor. Lenny's first article is to appear on the front page. He is as nervous as an expectant father.

"Will you cut it out, Len? You're driving me *mishugena*."

Lenny perches on the edge of his desk. "Sorry, Moe. What time are they coming?"

Moe shakes his head. "Same time as always. Four o' clock. Any time now."

Lenny glances at the wall clock for the fortieth time. Four-ten. They're

late. He is crawling out of his skin with excitement. He lights another cigarette, jumps down from the desk, paces some more. He imagines his article
in print, sees how his name will look under the headline, when he hears
rumbling in the street below. The truck. He leaps into the hall and runs
down the stairs three at a time. The driver is unloading stacks of paper onto
his hand dolly. Lenny rips open the string holding the top bundle together.

"Hey," the driver swivels around. "Oh, hiya, Len. Thought it was those
damn kids again. Last week they pinched a full bundle while my back was
turned. Can you believe that? Brats probably sold them in the market at
half price." The driver turns back to his work of unloading.

Lenny grabs the top paper, scans it. His name looks odd in Yiddish,
but there it is, all the same. His first byline. "Nazis March into Soviet
Union," by Lenny Lapinsky. Lenny sits on a stack of papers and rereads
his article. It looks beautiful — the most gorgeous thing he's ever seen.
He is a real writer now. He looks up. Moe is standing beside him, reading
over his shoulder, grinning.

"Feels good, huh, Len?" Moe reaches for the paper, scans the article.
"Good work. I'm telling you, Len. You're a natural. Going to be a first rate
reporter. I'm real proud to have you on board. Come on. Let's go celebrate. Coffee and cheesecake on me." He throws his arm around Lenny's
shoulder to steer him down the street. Lenny reaches down and fills his
arms with a stack of papers. He can't wait to show his family.

Heat of the *Moment*
JUNE, 1941

"HEY KID." RUDY GREETS Sonny at the door of the gym. "Your pal
Johnny wants to spar with you today. But I want you both in headguards
and gum shields, all right? No injuries. You got a fight in two days, Sonny."

"Yeah, yeah. Whatever you say, Coach."

"And sparring gloves," Rudy adds. "I'm worried about that left hand of

yours." Sonny fractured a bone in his left hand a week ago, after a match
with Henry Young, a middleweight from Rochester who outweighed
Sonny by twenty pounds. It isn't completely healed and Rudy doesn't
want Sonny to take any chances.

Sonny's sparring partner, Johnny Mangiomi, lives in the next neighbourhood over from Sonny's, west of Ossington: Little Italy. They've fought
in Smokers together since they were kids. Sonny sees Johnny approach from
the other end of the gym, dressed in trunks and boxing boots.

"Hiya, Sonny. What do ya say? I got a fight tomorrow in Hamilton. I'm
up against Joe Hawkins. He's good, he's got a boxing style like you.
Charges at you hard and fast, like a bull. Can you help me out, pal?"

"Sure, Johnny. Let me get changed. Coach says we gotta wear shields
and guards."

Johnny follows Sonny into the locker room to get his sparring gear.
Both boxers wear the leather headguard and a bulky chest shield, which
always makes Sonny feel like a turtle in its shell.

It's a tough session. Johnny lacks Sonny's rapid-fire punch. His style is
different. He's a counter-puncher. He dodges and dances his way through
the opening rounds of a fight, saving his strength while wearing his
opponent down. Then he wallops the other guy with the hardest, meanest straight right; it's like getting smashed by a concrete brick. Johnny is
a master of the straight right. But Sonny holds his own with Johnny, beating away at him relentlessly with his short, quick blows. A left hook,
followed by a right. A left jab, then an uppercut with his right to the chin.
With Johnny it's all in his footwork, and that damn straight right of his.

"GOOD FIGHT," JOHNNY SAYS as they climb from the ring. "Wanna
grab a sandwich?"

"Naw. Gotta go see my manager. I'm going on tour next month.
Getting in shape for the championships in the spring."

"Oh yeah. You going?"

"Sure I am. All the way to Vancouver. I never been that far away."

"Me neither, 'cept maybe I will now that I got my conscription notice.
No way I'm going overseas though."

"Yeah. Me neither. They ain't called me up yet."

"You're only seventeen. Wait a few years."

Sonny is not a coward, but he has no intention of volunteering for duty overseas when, and if, the time comes. He knows he has a different calling. While other boys were hanging around the soda shop, or playing craps in the back alley or stickball in the streets, playing cranks or getting into trouble, Johnny and Sonny were punching bags in the gym, jumping rope and running three miles every morning in High Park. They were sparring and fighting other young boys in Smokers, waking up in the morning aching and bruised, and training through the pain. All that hard work is finally going to pay off. Sonny dreams of the first big purse he will bring home to his family. He pictures dumping the bills onto the kitchen table in front of his parents. He imagines their faces when he shows up with more money then they've ever seen. He sees himself picking it up and tossing it into the air, watching it float back to the table. He can't shatter that dream by throwing his life away in the stinking war. He can't do that to his parents either, not after all the sacrifices they made during the Depression. Sonny has no doubt he'd survive the war, even if he were sent into combat. No way he's gonna die on some lousy battlefield. But what if the war goes on for years? What if he's an old guy of twenty-five or thirty when he gets back? Good for nothing, except maybe coaching.

Johnny heaves open the heavy door that leads to the street. The brilliant sunshine flashes into their eyes; it is shocking after the dingy light inside the gym.

Loretta Mangiomi has been waiting for her brother outside the building for ten minutes, pacing back and forth under the athletic club awning to keep in the shade.

"Johnny!" she yells.

"Loretta. What's a matter? What are you doing here?"

"You gotta come with me to the market. Ma wants me to pick up ten pounds of potatoes. I need your help. I can't carry all that."

"Forget it, Loretta. I'm hungry. I gotta get something to eat,"

"Good. I'm hungry, too. Take me with you." She looks over at Sonny and bats her beautiful brown eyes at him. A force stronger than Johnny's hardest, meanest right uppercut swings from Loretta's eyes and pummels Sonny right where it hurts, in his heart, and somewhere deep in his lower belly. Loretta is a knockout, the most gorgeous girl he's ever seen. Dark Italian features like her brother, long dark hair, deep brown eyes, and a shapely figure that is finer than Betty Grable and Rita Hayworth put together. Sonny flashes his crooked grin, the one he's practised in the mirror.

"Hi," Loretta says. She takes note of Sonny's dimples. His strong jaw. Full lips. Crooked grin. His deep dark eyes. The little curl that droops over his forehead.

"Allow me to introduce myself." Sonny bows his head gallantly. "My name is Sonny Lapinsky, but soon I'll be known simply as The Champ."

"Not if I can help it," Johnny teases. "This is my sister Loretta."

"Charmed." Loretta sticks out one hand. Sonny takes it in his — the most beautiful hand in the world. His heart pounds in his chest. Sonny has dated lots of girls, but none has ever had such an enormous, instantaneous physical effect on him. Looking deep into Loretta's eyes, he lifts the hand to his mouth and kisses it, in the exact way he saw Clark Gable kiss Carole Lombard's hand in "No Man of Her Own." Johnny eyes Sonny suspiciously. Then he grabs his sister under one arm.

"Let's go, Loretta. Sonny's got a meeting with his manager. Ain't that right, Sonny?"

Sonny's eyes are still on Loretta. He could float away into her eyes and never come back. "Meeting? Ah, no meeting. Actually, I'm hungry too. I'll come and eat with you."

"No!" Johnny realizes he's almost shouting. "I mean, no you better not. I mean, remember your manager's waiting for you. You better get going." Johnny flashes Sonny a warning with his eyes. Sonny reads the message loud and clear. It says, *Stay away from my sister. Stick to your own kind. Leave her alone.* But Sonny knows he will never leave Loretta Mangiomi alone. Not now. Not ever.

"Right Johnny. I forgot," he says. To Loretta, Sonny says, "Nice to meet you, Loretta."

"Likewise." She places one hand on a voluptuous hip.

Sonny watches Loretta saunter down the street alongside her brother. She moves seductively from side to side as she walks. Sonny is aroused. He shoves his hands deep inside his pockets and arranges his trousers to hide his erection. He heads back in the direction of Checkie's office, thinking about Loretta the whole way and what it will feel like the first time he kisses her.

CHECKIE HAS INSTRUCTED Sonny to think about nothing but boxing. He's booked him onto amateur fight cards throughout the province, and next spring Sonny will fight in the Canadian Amateur Championships in Vancouver. Sonny stands a chance at winning the Welterweight Title. With that under his belt, Checkie plans to turn him professional and match him up with fighters all across the country and into New York State, "to build up your reputation." The final prize in two or three years will be a fight at Madison Square Garden. The purse for a fight at the Garden is 10,000 bucks. Even a prelim fight to warm up the crowd takes in that much. Checkie will take forty percent of Sonny's purse: Four thousand smackeroos. And this is just the beginning. His investment is finally going to pay off.

"Keep your mind on boxing, *boychick*," Checkie warns. "Boxing and nothing but."

But Sonny can't keep his mind off Loretta Maria Mangiomi. She is in his dreams at night, in his thoughts all day long. In his heart. And deeply entrenched in his body. It's driving him mad. Sonny knows where Johnny lives and finally a week after meeting Loretta, he works up the nerve to go there. He walks over to Johnny's neighbourhood and waits a block away from the house. Loretta will have to leave the house or return from somewhere, sometime. It's a brilliant June day. The sun shines in a cloudless blue sky. Sonny stands for a while waiting, but he's bored, so he paces half a block up, then back down, kicking at a rusty can. After two hours he's ready to give up when he sees Loretta walking down the street toward him. As beautiful in real life as she is in his dreams. She walks down the street alone, carrying a paper bag of groceries. Sonny heads toward her, hands shoved in his pockets. He waits until he is almost upon her. Then he looks up, feigns surprise. She stares at him, then smiles.

"Hey!" Sonny says. "Loretta. Hi. What brings you around here?"

Loretta smirks. She can see right through him. She cracks her chewing gum and points with her head. "I live right over there."

Sonny glances over. "Right there? What a coincidence. I was on my way to the uh ... store. Gotta pick up some items for my Ma. Oh, hey, can I carry your bag?"

"Sure." She hands the bag to Sonny. Their fingers touch. Heat radiates between them. Neither moves.

"So?" Sonny says, feeling more nervous than he ever has with a girl before. "You just live right over there?"

"Yeah. Right over there." Loretta is at a loss for words as well. She is almost as tall as Sonny. He is short for a man, she thinks, but so strong and handsome. His dark hair is slicked back, and she just loves the cute little curl that dangles over his forehead. His muscles are so developed he is practically busting out of his shirtsleeves.

Sonny glances at Loretta's house. "That's a nice-looking house."

She grins. "Thank you. I'll tell my father you said so."

"So, uh ... how about a soda, Loretta? With me," Sonny blurts out.

"Oh. Oh. No. I can't."

"Just a soda." He flashes his crooked grin.

"Well ..." Loretta glances over at her house.

"Just one little soda." He smiles wider.

Loretta flushes with excitement. She wants to go for a soda with Sonny Lapinsky more than she's ever wanted to do anything in her whole, entire sixteen years. But, her father would kill her. She's only allowed to go out with Italian boys. Catholic Italian boys. They have to be friends of the family. And they have to pick her up at her house, so her father can grill them about what they're going to make of themselves in the world. Even then, her older sister Gina has to come along as chaperone. "I can't, Sonny. I just can't." She grabs her sack of groceries from his arms and runs to her house.

Sonny watches her go.

THE NEXT DAY, after training, Sonny waits outside Loretta's house again. Loretta strolls down the street with her best friend, Ana. "Oh God."

"What's a matter Loretta?"

Loretta squeezes her friend's arm, whispers, "It's him."

"Who?"

"That boy I told you about."

"The Jewish boy?"

"Yeah."

"The boxer?"

"Yeah."

"Where?"

"Don't look." She squeezes Ana's arm hard.

"Then how am I supposed to see him?"

"He's right in front of my house."

"Oh." Ana leans forward, squints. They're three blocks from Loretta's house. She can just see the shape of a boy standing by the gutter. "How can you tell it's him?"

"It's him."

"What are you gonna do?"

"I don't know. What should I do?"

"Go for a soda."

"You think I should?"

"Sure."

"My father'll kill me."

"So? Don't tell him."

"Oh God."

"Do it, Loretta. Oh, he's cute." They are twenty feet from Sonny. He smiles his widest grin, removes his cap and bows at the waist.

"Afternoon, Loretta," He says.

"Sonny. You can't hang around outside my house."

"Well, I just happened to be in the neighbourhood."

"Again?"

"It's a nice neighbourhood."

Ana elbows Loretta in the ribs.

"Oh. This is my best friend Ana. This is Sonny, Johnny's friend. The boxer."

Ana sticks out her hand. Sonny holds the tips of her fingers and shakes vigorously. "Nice to meet you, Ana." He turns his gaze back to Loretta. "It sure is a lovely day, Loretta. Wouldn't you say so?" He's trying to act like the fancy gentlemen he sees in the picture shows. They always comment on the weather.

"Why, yes." Loretta attempts to be equally sophisticated. "It is lovely."

"Can I offer you two ladies a soda pop. Down at the confectionery?"

"Well …" Loretta says.

"We'd love to," Ana says. "Right Loretta?"

"Well …" Loretta figures, what harm could it do? Anyway, Ana's with her. It's not like she's going out with Sonny alone.

"What do you say, Loretta?" Sonny replaces his cap on his head and smiles that crooked grin that melts her heart.

"She says swell. Right Loretta?"

"Well … okay. Just for a … little while …"

"Swell." Sonny holds out both his arms. The girls each take one. Loretta can feel how strong his muscles are right through his shirt. They head down the street to the candy store.

TO SEE SONNY, Loretta has to lie to her family. Sometimes she says she is meeting Ana. Other times she says she is going for a walk, or shopping. They go to Chinatown, outside of both of their neighbourhoods. On the first date, Sonny is a perfect gentlemen. He buys sodas — chocolate for Loretta, strawberry for Ana. A Coca-Cola for himself. He brags about his boxing career while they listen to Ella Fitzgerald singing "Taking a Chance on Love." Sonny offers the girls cigarettes from his pack. Loretta, who doesn't smoke, declines, but Ana accepts. Despite his best efforts, Sonny finds it impossible to keep his eyes from Loretta's shapely body. Finally Ana leaves, whispering something in Loretta's ear before she goes. Sonny walks Loretta home. She leaves him several blocks from her house, just in case.

On the second date, Sonny puts his hands on Loretta's waist and kisses her. She throws her arms around his neck and kisses him back. He pulls her into an alley and they neck until their lips are sore. For the next few weeks they meet secretly. He takes her to the picture show in the east end of town. Sonny always chooses the back row. They miss most of the pictures. As soon as the lights fade down, they turn to each other. Loretta sticks her gum under her seat and they neck. Sonny uses the utmost restraint, although he longs to touch her. When Sonny takes Loretta home, they say goodbye in the alley behind the Chinese restaurant on Dundas Street, four blocks from her house. Sometimes they lean against the brick wall and neck for a long time before she pulls away, waves her cute little wave with one hand, and walks home by herself.

It is Loretta who tips the scales and encourages Sonny to take their ardour further. Ana has progressed from necking to petting with her boyfriend Nick, and Loretta isn't about to be left behind. She pushes her body against Sonny and pulls him tighter.

"Oh, baby doll," Sonny groans, his hands pressing against the small of her back.

Like Ana has suggested to her, Loretta pushes Sonny up against the wall and rubs her whole body against his. Sonny undoes the buttons on her blouse and reaches inside. He is surprised when she doesn't stop him. He touches the bare skin of her belly. She moans. Sonny's blood beats with passion. Loretta runs her fingers through his hair, kisses his face all over. Sonny is frantic with desire. He moves farther up and cups one breast, over her brassiere. "You're driving me crazy, Loretta." Boldly, he takes her hand and places it on the front of his trousers.

Loretta pulls her hand back and pushes against his chest. "No Sonny, not like this. Not here."

He lifts his head. Looks into her eyes. "Don't you want to?"

"Not on the street. It's dirty."

"Oh." He hadn't noticed. He aches with desire. He could take her right here, in the alley, if she'd let him.

"I want our first time to be … beautiful."

Sonny thinks, *hell, this is beautiful,* but he knows not to say it out loud.

"Somewhere romantic … you know … where we can be alone."

Sonny glances over his shoulder in both directions. "We're alone."

Loretta puts her hands on both hips. "In a bed, Sonny."

"A bed? How're we gonna do that?"

She glares at him and fishes in her purse for a piece of gum.

"All right." Sonny smoothes back his hair with his fingers. "I'll get us a bed. Don't worry."

"Somewhere romantic, Sonny. Like in the picture shows. I want our first time to be special."

"BORROW MY OFFICE? What for?" Checkie barely looks up from his paperwork.

"Well ..." Sonny isn't sure if he should tell the truth. "I just got ... uh ... someone I need to bring here."

"Someone? Who? What someone?"

"A person. What's the difference? We won't touch anything. Just a half an hour. Come on, Mr. Seigelman."

"He wants to bring someone here," Checkie says to the room. He stares at Sonny. The kid is nervous as a girl. A girl. That's it. He nods his head. "I get it," Checkie smirks. "You got a girl you want to bring here?"

Sonny smiles. "Yeah."

"A girl? Why the hell didn't you say so? Aw right. What the hell? I understand. You're almost eighteen."

"So I can use your office?"

"Yeah yeah. Only don't mess up the couch will you? I paid good money just last week to have the upholstery cleaned."

"Don't worry, Boss."

"Jeez. When did you grow up, kid? One day you were a little *pisher*. Now look at you. *Shtupping* broads on my office couch."

Sonny blushes. He stands. "Friday night. Okay? At nine?"

"Yeah yeah. Don't worry. I'll clear out."

"Thanks, Mr. Seigelman. Thanks." Sonny leans forward, grabs Checkie's hand and pumps it. Turns to leave.

"Hey, kid."

Sonny turns. "Yeah?"

"Don't forget to use a rubber. All right?"

"Right." Sonny runs out of Checkie's office. A rubber. Crap. He'd for-gotten about that. He'll have to stop at the drugstore. He'll go to the pharmacy by the athletic club. Mr. Berger at the drugstore in his neigh-bourhood knows Sonny's parents.

He flies down the street. He can't wait to tell Loretta.

YACOV AND MAX have become used to working without their car. Gasoline is so severely rationed that they have parked the old Model T up on bricks in the alley behind the house, for the duration. That's what everyone is saying these days: "For the duration." Every available resource is being pumped into the war effort. Ration books have been issued. Each family is allotted only a small portion of tea, sugar, flour, meat. Even with a coupon, there's no guarantee the stores will carry the items in question. Luxury items are impossible to find, items such as stockings, whiskey and chocolate. Since gasoline is so scarce, Max and Yacov are back to using the old pushcart. Sid pulls it along the street on their route.

In the last few weeks, Max has mysteriously arrived at work with silk stockings, bags of sugar, coffee, cigarettes and even Cuban cigars. He refuses to tell Yacov how he purchased caseloads of these rationed items. Customers snatch up the coveted products as fast as Max and Yacov can unpack them off the cart. Sales are booming.

What Yacov doesn't know is that this is all Sonny's doing. Checkie was driving him crazy.

"How's your Uncle Max?" he'd ask over and over, until Sonny couldn't stand it for one more second. He secretly arranged a meeting of the two men. Checkie and Max hadn't so much as acknowledged each other on the street since 1929. Checkie refuses to tell Sonny what happened between them, but Sonny figures it had something to do with money. But heck, thought Sonny, water's got to be under the bridge by now. One evening after dinner, Sonny dropped by Max's flat and invited him out for a drink.

"There's something I'd like to discuss with you, Uncle Max," Sonny said, his cap in his hand at the doorway. "That is, if you don't mind, Aunt Tess," he called to his aunt down the hall. She was in the kitchen cleaning up the supper dishes.

"Listen to him. Such a gentleman." Tess waved her dishtowel in Sonny's direction. "And so handsome. When did you get so handsome, Sonny?"

Sonny blew a kiss to his aunt.

"Where we going?" Max asked as they walked down the street.

"A little place I found over on the other side of Yonge Street. It's on me, Uncle Max."

Sonny had asked Checkie to arrive at nine o' clock, a good hour after he knew he would be settled in with Max. He didn't tell either one that the other would be there. He was prepared for anything.

Max and Sonny were on their second coffee when Checkie walked into the little greasy spoon on Yonge Street. He didn't see Max at first. Sonny had purposely positioned Max on the chair with his back to the door. When Checkie came around the table to greet Sonny, the two men saw each other. Max leaped to his feet.

"What the hell?" He glared at Sonny, then looked back at Checkie.

"What's the big idea, kid?" Checkie asked Sonny.

"That's it. I'm outa here." Max stood, plunked his hat on his head and made to leave. Sonny grabbed his arm. "Wait a minute, Uncle Max."

Max stopped. Kept his back turned.

"Look. If you want to be mad at anyone, be mad at me. I did this on purpose."

Max turned around. "What the hell?"

"Come on. How about we all sit down and discuss this calmly?" Sonny suggested.

"What for?" Max grumbled.

"Listen, I don't know what happened between you two, but you used to be pals."

"Yeah, until he double-crossed me!" Max shouted.

"Double-crossed you?" Checkie lunged forward, but Sonny stood between them.

"Listen." Sonny was angry. "I've had it with you two. Whatever happened, it's over. It was a long time ago, right?" He looked from one to the other and sensed a shifting. Max stared at his feet, head slightly turned. Checkie rubbed his forehead and the corners of his mouth tilted up, just a bit, edging toward a genuine smile. "Right?" Sonny repeated. Both men grudgingly agreed. "All right." Sonny moved out from between them. "Then I want you to shake hands and make up." No one moved. "Come on. Do it," he ordered. And a miracle happened. Max looked at the palm of his hand, then slowly, he stuck it forward, looking straight at Checkie. A big smile spread over Checkie's face as he clasped the hand of his former friend. They moved forward and hugged, slapping each other vigorously on the back. Then they sat down like civilized men, and had a drink together.

The next day Checkie called Max to his office. For a business proposition. Since then Max has been visiting his old pal every Monday and arriving back at work with boxes of rationed items.

"What about your cousin?" Checkie asks. "Did you tell him?"

Max winks. "Not yet." Max is planning on telling Yacov any day now. He's stalling because he knows Yacov won't approve. But Max is full of optimism. He is going to come out a winner after all.

The Honourable Thing
SEPTEMBER 1941

"IT'S SO QUIET around here." Sophie pulls out her sewing basket. "Sid's gone, Lenny's always at the *Zhurnal* office, or out somewhere with Moe, and Sonny's never home, travelling all over the place fighting ..."

"Well ..." Yacov says, glancing at Izzy, who, as usual, is in a dream world of his own, playing with a rusty toy car that must be fifteen years old. It had been Sid's or Sonny's once. "We still have one kid at home. And Sid's just around the corner. Besides, soon we'll be grandparents."

"What?" Sophie looks up. "What do you mean? Ruthie had another miscarriage."

Yacov shrugs. "I know. But they've been married over a year. They're healthy. I just figure any day now..."

"Grandparents. Oy." Sophie feels old for the first time. *I'm only forty-three*, she thinks.

But it is not Sid who will bring Sophie and Yacov their first grandchild after all.

"Are you sure?" Sonny asks Loretta, his heart expanding with a strange new feeling, a mixture of awe and terror. They are in the front seat of Sonny's new car, a 1940 deluxe-tone Studebaker with whitewall tires. It is one of the few cars on the road; Checkie can get gasoline above the rationed allowance. He wants his boy Sonny to feel and look like a winner. It'll bring him closer to being one. So he bought the car as a bonus, since Sonny's been winning every fight, and he provides Sonny with the gas. It's a beauty of a car, long-lined and sleek. A broad chrome stripe runs across the centre of the hood and down to the chrome bumper. A matching chrome stripe runs along each side, just above the door panels. The silver-plated grille hangs low over the bumper between the round headlights. The 1940 Studebaker Champion sells for $919 new. Checkie of course, picked it up wholesale from an associate for a mere $650.

A new song, "I Found a Million Dollar Baby," is playing on the RCA radio installed right in the dashboard.

"I'm sure." Loretta stares at her hands, nervous. She doesn't know how Sonny will respond.

"Well, I mean. How do you know?"

"Sonny …" Colour rises in Loretta's cheeks.

"Oh." Sonny knows little of the intricacies of women's bodies, other than vague notions and half-truths he's heard in athletic club locker rooms and read in dirty magazines.

"What are we gonna do, Sonny?" Loretta stares out the front windshield. Sonny turns and looks at her. So beautiful. She looks so scared. Like a little girl, six instead of sixteen. "My Papa's gonna kill you," she says.

"Oh God."

"Johnny's gonna kill you."

"Great."

"Dominic's really gonna murder you."

"Loretta …" Sonny reaches for the door handle and opens the door.

Tears spring to Loretta's eyes. At night in bed, she's been crying for the last month, hoping and waiting for her period to come. Her heart races. What's he doing? Is he running away? She watches as he gets out of the car, walks around the front and to the passenger-side door, opens it, drops to his knees. He takes her hand, his face serious, the love in his liquid brown eyes healing the pain in her heart. "Loretta … there's only one thing to do …" Sonny smiles, raising the dimples in his cheeks. "We'll get married."

"Oh Sonny." She throws her arms around his neck and lets out the breath she's been holding.

A stern voice on the radio announces, "Our fighting forces need, and must have, our all-out support. Freedom's cause must not be denied. Buy Victory Bonds now."

Behind Loretta's back, Sonny fumbles for the radio knob and switches it off. The realization of what he's just done to his life pounds in his ears.

"FOR CHRISSAKE," Checkie grumbles. Sonny sits across the desk from him.

"Yeah," agrees Sonny. "Bet you're surprised, huh?"

Checkie grabs a bottle of Scotch from his wet bar and pours them each a hefty shot. They down their drinks. He pours more. "For Chrissake," Checkie says again.

"Yeah."

"I told you to use rubbers!"

"I did."

"You did?"

"Well …"

"What?"

"Most of the time."

"Most of the time?"

"Yeah."

"Aw, Sonny …"

"Well, we forgot a couple times. You know. Heat of the moment."

"Heat of the moment?"

"Yeah."

Checkie raises a hand, like he's about to slap Sonny. "I'll give you heat of the moment."

"Sorry, Boss."

"You're sorry?"

Sonny sighs. "I'm in love with her."

"Thank God for small favours."

Sonny downs his drink.

"You gonna go through with it?"

"Yeah. Sure. But my father's gonna kill me."

"I could fix her up with a doctor-like. You know what I mean?" Checkie suggests hopefully. Better than letting the kid marry the girl. A married fighter loses his edge quicker.

"She's a Catholic."

"For Crissake."

They drink in silence for a moment.

"What about the championships?"

Sonny leans over the desk, his fists on its surface. "I'm going. Don't worry about that. I'm still going. Loretta won't mind. She knows this is important to me. She knows."

"All right. Don't get so excited. You're making me nervous."

Sonny leans back.

"Where you two gonna live?"

"I don't know. We'll rent a flat."

"Rent a flat? Never mind rent a flat. Leave that to me."

"Huh?"

Checkie laughs. "Sonny, I own five buildings. I'll get you a flat in one of them. Don't worry, no charge. On the house. Think of it as … a wedding present. Kensington or Parkdale, Casanova? Your choice."

"Kensington. Where else? Geez."

Checkie slaps the desk with one hand. "Done. I'll give you your new address later. Where you gonna get married?"

Sonny shrugs. "She wants a big Catholic wedding at a church, but I already told her to forget that. Can you imagine me in a church? She cried, big huge tears, just about broke my heart, but I pointed out the fact that her parents ain't gonna pay for a big church wedding if I'm the groom, and I ain't never heard of a rabbi who'd marry a Jew and a Catholic, so I told her we're going to a JP down at City Hall. Next week. You'll come and be a witness? Please, Boss. I don't know who else to ask."

"Yeah sure, Sonny. In fact, it would be my esteemed honour. I'll see if Lila will come. You know, she can help ... your girl. What's her name again?"

"Loretta."

"Loretta. With her makeup and all that women's business."

"Thanks Boss."

"Whatever. How far along is she?"

Sonny shrugs. "Huh? I mean, how do I know?"

"You don't know?"

"I never thought to ask."

Checkie shakes his head and refills their glasses.

AFTER THE WEDDING, Checkie offers to take the kids out for a fancy dinner.

"To celebrate-like," he says. "Right, Lila?"

"Great idea," Lila says, "I'm starved."

"That's nice," says Sonny, "but we better go and break the news. You know. To our families."

"Oh yeah, sure."

"Anyway," says Sonny. "It's Rosh Hashanah. Ain't you two going over to Lila's mother's?"

"She don't like me. That's the truth. Ain't it, Lila?"

"She just don't understand your profession, Shlomo."

Checkie's face turns red. "You gonna call me that? In front of the kids?"

"Excuse me. I forgot." Lila reaches in her purse for her compact. "You get used to a man. When I met him, he was Shlomo," she tells Loretta.

"Lila. I'm warning you."

"Then he makes a fortune. In six months. You never could believe it. He goes from rags to riches in no time. And changes his name. Checkie I should call him? What the hell kind of name is that? I ask you."

Loretta giggles.

"Sounds like a dog. A poodle or something. Don't you think, honey?"

"Sure it does." Loretta agrees with her new friend Lila.

"You see what I put up with?" Checkie asks Sonny. "Sixteen years I been with this girl."

"And I ain't got no ring to show for it." Lila holds up her left hand, wiggles her empty ring finger. "You should count your blessings, honey," she tells Loretta. "At least there are still some gentlemen left in the world."

"I asked her," Checkie shouts to the sky. "I asked her to marry me. As God is my witness Sonny, I asked her. You know what she says?"

"Do you see a ring on my finger?" Lila asks Loretta.

Loretta shakes her head.

"She says she can't marry me unless I go straight," Checkie continues. Sonny nods in sympathy.

"Straight she wants me to be. Can you believe that?"

"I don't know, Boss."

"She don't mind the dinners out. The fur coats I bought her. The diamonds. The jewels. She don't mind the swell apartment I set her up in on St. Clair Avenue. Where all the rich people live. British people, Sonny. You know, the kind what would spit in my face. She don't mind any of that. But Lila, she won't marry me — and for the record, I asked her forty-two times by now — she won't marry me unless I go straight. What the hell does she think I'm gonna do? Work in a bank? Dig ditches?"

"He's gonna wind up in jail," Lila tells Loretta. "What kind of a life is that for a lady? If I marry him, I'll end up visiting him behind bars. You're lucky. At least Sonny has an honest profession."

"You hear that, Sonny? She don't appreciate me."

"It's my wedding day, Boss. You two gotta fight on my wedding day?"

"He's right, Shlomo. There you go. Spoiling their big day. Loretta, allow me to apologize on Mr. Seigelman's behalf."

"The kids don't need an apology Lila. I need an apology."

"He's cute when he's mad. Ain't he, Loretta?"

Loretta shrugs.

"Come on, Checkie," she spits out his nickname with distaste. "Since we're not taking the kids out, let's go to my mother's."

"Your mother don't like me, Lila."

"It's a holiday. She'll pretend."

Checkie shrugs. "You kids gonna be okay?"

"Sure we are."

Checkie pulls a cigar from his pocket, stuffs it in his mouth. "You be careful, Sonny. All right?"

"Yeah. Sure, Boss."

"SHOULD WE GO SEE your parents first?" Sonny steers Loretta to his car, which is parked on the street outside City Hall.

Loretta sighs.

"What is it, Honey?"

She stops, turns to him. "Last night, I finally told my sister, Gina. She said, 'Don't bring him over.' She says it'll kill my mother. She's got a bad heart, you know? Gina asked me if you were cute. I told her you were more handsome than Tyrone Power and steamier than Robert Taylor."

"Yeah?" Sonny puts his arm around her shoulder.

"Gina wants to meet you. Anyway, I left a note for my mother and father before I left. Only I don't think we should go on over there now. Maybe give them some time to get used to the idea."

"Of you marrying a Jew, you mean?"

Loretta doesn't think they'll ever get used to it, but she doesn't tell Sonny. She can imagine her father screaming and yelling. Maybe Gina will talk some sense into him. "What about your folks?"

Sonny's lower lip sticks out, almost like a pout, only cuter. Loretta can't believe how handsome he is. "I'd like you to meet them. We'll go right on over there now. Okay? Come on. Get in the car." He opens the door for Loretta. She gets in. Sonny closes the door, leans into the window. "It's Rosh Hashanah you know?"

"What?"

"Jewish New Year."

"Oh."

"So there's gonna be a whole bunch of people there." He walks around to the driver's side, gets in. "Well, maybe that's a good thing. My Aunt Tessie's always liked me. Maybe it's better she's there. And my grandparents'll be there. My *Zayde* — that's Yiddish for grandfather — he's a swell guy. You know, he sticks up for me. You're gonna love him. And old Mr. Tepperman-the-boarder. My brother Sid and his wife. And Lenny and Izzy."

"So many brothers. I only have two and Johnny's gone now. They sent him to Halifax. Home defence or something."

This is not news to Sonny. Johnny paid him a little visit when he heard Sonny had knocked up his sister. Johnny was going to kill Sonny. He even had a knife stuffed in his sock, just in case. But in the end, he only roughed Sonny up a little. Pushed him against a brick wall. Sonny allowed Johnny to take a couple of swings at his chin. He didn't know what it'd be like to have a sister, but he felt equally protective of his brothers. Johnny had a right to stand up for Loretta. But they were square again now. He told Johnny he was going to do the honourable thing. And he had.

Sonny smiles at Loretta and puts the key in the ignition. As he starts up the car he thinks about how he barely had his own shoes growing up. Now he's got his own car, his own wife, a baby on the way and a promising career as a professional boxer. He's proud of himself, in spite of this unexpected situation with Loretta. He's a few months shy of eighteen and look how far he's already come.

Mourner's Kaddish
SEPTEMBER 23, 1941

AS THEY DO EVERY YEAR, Sophie and Yacov are having everyone over for dinner on Rosh Hashanah, the Jewish New Year. It is the year 5701 by the ancient Hebrew Calendar. The whole family is there: Sid and Ruthie; Lenny; Izzy of course; Sonny should be along any minute — he's been training all day at the athletic club; and Max, Tessie and their kids. Sophie's parents, Reuben and Channa are there. Louie Horowitz and his father, Sam, have attended the Lapinskys' Rosh Hashanah dinner for years — they have no family in Canada besides each other. Louie is overseas at a training base in England, but his father has gratefully accepted the invitation. He's even brought over a bottle of Manishevitz sweet red wine and a beef brisket he roasted the day before, using his late wife Esther's famous recipe. Max's boarder, old Mr. Tepperman, has been installed at the end of the table. It's crowded, but everyone is in a holiday mood. Only Sam is a little melancholy, worried about Louie.

"He's going to services in London. Jewish families invited the soldiers from the base," he says.

"London? I thought he went to Germany, to fight the *farkakta* Nazis," Mr. Tepperman says.

"Soon, Mr. Tepperman," Tess tells him.

"Vat's dat?" Mr. Tepperman yells.

"He's stationed in England," Tess yells close to his ear.

"I can't make out vat she's saying," he tells Sam, who sits to his left.

Sam nods his head and shrugs as if to say no one else can make out what she's saying either, so don't worry about it. This seems to satisfy Mr. Tepperman. He reaches for his prayer book, flips it open to page one, and begins humming to himself.

"I haven't heard from Louie. I don't know what's gonna be," Sam says wistfully.

"He'll be fine, Sam," Yacov reassures him. "The mail takes a long time to get here."

"Are they still bombing England?" Sophie's father, Reuben, asks. "Must be in ruins."

"They stopped, thank God. At least for now. That's what I read in the papers." Sam reaches for the schnapps, pours himself a glass. Louie's the only family he has. Other than his remaining relatives in Germany — a sister-in-law, a niece, a nephew. But he hasn't heard from them in more than three years. He fears the worst.

"Louie's gonna be okay." Lenny pats Sam on the arm. "Maybe they don't have much time to write letters."

"Maybe you're right, Lenny."

"Can you give me a hand?" Yacov asks Sam. "We'll bring up a table from downstairs." Happy for the distraction, Sam follows Yacov to Max and Tessie's flat on the first floor.

"Sophie, maybe you need a little help in the kitchen." Channa struggles up from the table, and teeters into the kitchen. "I could make my famous salad dressing. Everybody loves it. Ain't that right, Reuben?"

"From miles around, Channa," Reuben responds.

"What? Speak up, Reuben. Your father talks so quietly," she tells Sophie. "I swear to God. I can't hear a word he's saying."

"I know, Ma." Sophie gives her mother a smile. Channa's hearing is getting worse all the time. "Come on. Help me with the chicken. Do you think I should put it back in for a few more minutes?"

"What? The giblets? What did she say?" Channa asks Tessie.

The apartment smells savory, with the scent of roasted chicken, potatoes, chicken soup, giblets, onions and garlic. Through the open windows, a cool fall breeze blows. It's noisy in the apartment, with conversation and laughter.

The front door downstairs opens. Sid struggles inside with two kitchen chairs. Ruthie follows behind, a hot noodle *kugel* in her arms.

"Hiya, Pop," Sid says to Yacov.

"Only two chairs?"

"There's two more on the porch. Don't worry. I'll bring them right up."

"Where's your brother?"

"Who? Sonny?"

"Yeah, of course Sonny."

"How should I know?"

"Hurry up Sid," Ruthie pushes against him with her pan. "It's hot. I gotta put it down. My fingers ..."

"Okay. Okay." Sid starts up the stairs. Ruthie follows close behind.

"Is he still at the gym?" Yacov persists. "It's a holiday."

"I don't know why they had to send Louie all the way to England so fast," Sam says as he carries one end of the table from Max and Tessie's apartment. "They gave him two months of training. And boom. He was gone.

He's been there already almost two years. Why don't they send him home already?"

"Hi, Mr. Horowitz," Sid calls down from the top of the stairs. "Did you hear from Louie lately?"

Sam grimaces. "You know Louie. Not much of a writer."

Ruthie marches into the kitchen just as Sophie opens the oven. Heat permeates the room. It's the new gas range Yacov brought home. The gas is a miracle. No coal to light. You turn a switch, toss in a match and an even blue flame shoots up. Cooking is a dream. No more coal dust in the air, schlepping hunks of coal from the basement. The City pipes the gas right into the house. Modern technology. So convenient. Sophie wonders how she ever managed without it. She bends over to baste her roast chicken. Tessie lays out pieces of *gefilte* fish on a platter.

"I made *kugel*. My grandmother's recipe," Ruthie informs them.

Channa leans over, lifts up the foil on Ruthie's *kugel*. "Who made the *kugel?* Is it sweet? Or salty?"

"Sweet," Ruthie answers.

"What?"

"Sweet!" she says more loudly.

"Speak up, doll. I can't hear you."

Ruthie yells as loud as she can. "Sweet!"

"Oh," says Channa, disappointed. "I always make salty. With a little onion."

As the women prepare the food in the kitchen, Yacov and Sam struggle up the stairs with the table. It bumps against Yacov's knees. "Slow down," he orders.

"You want me to stop?" Sam asks.

"No. Just slow down. I can't see where I'm going. So fast he has to go?"

"Yacov!" Sophie scolds as they enter the apartment. "Your back. Sid, what is your father doing? Help him."

"I'm trying, Ma." Sid attempts to grab a corner of the table.

"Thank you," Sophie says. "Ruthie, can you bring the tablecloth?"

The door opens again and two sets of footsteps trudge up the stairs. Sonny, followed by Loretta, arrives at the top.

"Oh," Sophie says.

"Sonny?" Yacov says. "Who's the girl?"

"I didn't know you were bringing a friend," Sophie says. "Sid, run downstairs for an extra chair."

"There aren't any more chairs in our flat. We brought them all up," Tessie points out.

"It's okay," Sonny offers. "I don't need a chair."

"Don't be silly," Tess says. "Isn't there still a chair on the porch?"

"Sonny, you're all dressed up." Sonny is wearing a suit and tie, and Loretta is in a fancy white taffeta dress. They look as if they're on their way to a high school dance. Sophie's belly does a little flip. Something has happened. She can feel it.

"Ma." Sonny swallows hard. "We just got married. This is Loretta. My wife." The word feels odd in Sonny's throat.

The room is silent.

Sophie stares at her son, then at the pretty young girl beside him. "Married?"

"Yeah, Ma."

"You got married? You eloped?"

Sonny pokes one finger under his tight shirt collar, unfastens the top button. "Well … not exactly, Ma. We got married down at City Hall."

"Without a rabbi?"

Sonny nods.

"Why, Sonny? Why so sudden?" Sophie clutches the edge of a chair to keep from falling.

"Ma," Sonny says, ignoring her question, "say hello to Loretta."

"Loretta?" Sophie says tentatively. "That don't sound like a Jewish name."

"Well …"

"Well?"

"Well … Loretta's not Jewish."

"Not Jewish?"

"She's a *shiksa?*"

Sonny turns to Loretta. She's probably heard the word before, but he doesn't want her to be hurt.

Sophie sits heavily in the chair. "Sonny, I mean, why didn't you talk to us first?"

Sonny looks to Sid for help, but Sid doesn't have the answer. "It's complicated, Ma." A knot of fear tightens in Sonny's belly. He clutches Loretta's hand. Slowly Sonny turns toward Yacov to gauge his father's reaction. "Pop?"

Yacov stands. His lower lip is tight. His eyes are hard. He lifts one hand slowly, then bangs it down on the table. Dishes clatter. A wineglass tips over. Red wine soaks the white tablecloth, like blood. "No!" he shouts. "No!"

"Pop. Please ..." Sonny pleads, hands out in front of him.

"No!" Yacov slams his hand down again.

"Pop ..."

Yacov steels his eyes and looks at Sonny. "You wanna marry a *shiksa*? You can leave this house. Now!"

Sonny feels like he has just been kicked in the stomach. He almost falls over from the force of his father's rage. He was not expecting this. The family is not particularly observant. The boys all had bar mitzvahs, even Izzy had a bar mitzvah of sorts, but it's been years since Yacov has tried to get the boys to accompany him to Saturday-morning services. He rubs his belly, which feels knotted with anxiety.

The room is silent and tense.

"Pop ... come on ... it's not so bad ..." Sid interjects.

Yacov turns, glares at Sid. "You gonna start with me too?" he yells.

"No Pop." Sid lowers his eyes.

"East is east, and west is west," Yacov spits out.

"Pop, don't be mad at Sonny," Lenny bravely speaks up. Sonny's been protecting Lenny from bullies for years. The least he can do is protect Sonny now.

Yacov raises a hand as if to strike Lenny.

"We live in Canada, now. It's not the *shtetl*. It's not Russia," Lenny continues.

Sonny silently thanks his brother with his eyes. When did Lenny become brave?

"We stick to our own kind." Yacov bangs the table a third time.

"He's got a point," Max agrees.

"Shah. Keep out of it." Tessie nudges Max in the ribs.

"What did I say?"

"You will leave this house!" Yacov orders Sonny.

"Pop, come on, don't be like this." Sonny smiles at Loretta, a tight frightened grin. "He don't mean it," he tells her.

"Yes I do!"

Sonny gulps in a breath of air. He can't be banished from his family. They don't always agree, but they're his family. He didn't exactly think they'd be thrilled about him marrying a non-Jewish girl, but to disown him? To never see them again? He looks over at Izzy, who is trembling with fear. "Pa?" Sonny pleads, tears pushing at the back of his eyes, his throat closing in anguish.

"*Yis gadel v'yis kadash shmai raba.*" Yacov begins to recite the mourner's Kaddish, the prayer for the dead.

"Yacov, stop it," Sophie pleads.

"Pop. I'm not dead," insists Sonny, although he feels like dying.

"He's not dead Pa," Lenny implores.

"Dere's a war on. Boys are dying. Vat's Yacov doing?" asks Reuben.

"*V'yal ma de brach ki roo tai.*"

"I can't believe it," Sonny tells Loretta. "He's saying the mourner's Kaddish over me. Like I'm dead." It is taking every bit of strength Sonny has not to cry. He doesn't want to embarrass himself in front of Loretta.

"My son is dead!" Yacov shouts.

The words ricochet through Sonny's aching chest, striking his heart like shrapnel after an explosion.

"Pop, he's not dead," Sid says. "Don't say that."

"It's not the Middle Ages, Pop." Lenny shakes his head at the scene.

"Sonny. Sonny. Sonny?" Izzy shouts. He can feel the tension in the air.

"Yacov. Be reasonable," Reuben suggests.

"Stay out of it. *V'yam lich mal choo tay.* He's *my* son. *My* son! Not yours. What would you do if he was yours? Huh?" Yacov sways as he recites. "*V'yam lich mal choo tay. Bi chyay chon oovyomay chon. Uv hayay Di chal bais yisroel ba agala u beez man chareev. Vi yemroo amen.*"

"A-men," says Mr. Tepperman.

"What happened to Sonny?" Channa hasn't heard a word. "He looks upset. Sonny. *Tatelah.* What's a matter?"

Yacov stares hard at Sonny from the head of the table. "What are you waiting for? I said leave."

Sonny stares back at his father. He really means it.

"Sonny," Sid says. "Don't go."

"Ma?" Sonny asks.

She looks down.

"Ma?" Lenny can't believe his mother is going to do nothing.

Sonny wraps an arm around Loretta, steers her back down the stairs, and leaves his parents' home for the last time. His father's voice echoes in Sonny's heart as he closes the front door.

"Y'hay shma raba ... "

Deal with the Devil

SEPTEMBER 24, 1941

THE NEXT MORNING, the Lapinsky house is quiet and subdued. Sophie plunks a burnt piece of toast onto Yacov's plate. The house is so empty, she thinks. Only Lenny and Izzy are left. She says nothing, just serves up breakfast and sighs, over and over. Yacov ignores her and forces himself to eat the burnt toast. Gulps down a glass of tea, grabs his cap. He leans toward Sophie and tries to kiss her goodbye. She keeps her back to him.

"What?" he says. "What's this? Am I the bad guy? For a change?"

Sophie turns on the tap and noisily begins washing the breakfast dishes.

"Fine. If that's the way you want it." Yacov walks to the door. "I'm the bad guy. Fine," he shouts as he jerks the apartment door open.

"Pa's going," Izzy says quietly, frightened.

Lenny eats in silence, furious at his father for his old-country ways. Sonny probably got the girl in trouble, Lenny figures. Why else would he have married her like that? Suddenly at City Hall. At least he's a *mensch*, did the right thing by marrying her, instead of leaving her to deal with the problem on her own, like most of the guys in their neighbourhood have done. He's heard the stories, mostly from girls who were in trouble. It takes the two of them to tango, but once the girl is pregnant, the boy hightails it away from her as fast as he can. At least Sonny stuck by the girl. Lenny wonders what the girl's family thinks of her marrying a Jew. Has she also been disowned? Lenny doesn't know what he'd do if his parents threw him out.

On the way out, Yacov slammed the door harder than he had intended. He stands on the other side for a moment, wondering if he should go back and apologize. No, he decides. I am right. My son is dead. We have tradition. I came to this country, to the New World, but I won't turn my back on my father's traditions. And his father's before him. Yacov stomps down the steps to wait for Max. At the bottom of the stairs, Yacov's heart swells. *Sonny. My boy. Always the rebel. So strong. So stubborn.* Yacov feels tears in his eyes. He doesn't want Max to see him this way, so he roughly brushes them away with the back of his sleeve, takes a deep breath and steels himself. The downstairs flat door flings open. Max walks out, with a thousand-dollar smile across his face.

"Morning Yacov," he says enthusiastically.

"Yeah Yeah, come on. You're late," Yacov grumbles, then walks ahead to wipe at the fresh tears in his eyes.

Max catches up. "You want to talk about it?"

"No," Yacov snaps. "I don't want to talk about it. And don't ask again."

"Okay. Sheesh."

They walk in silence for a block or two. At College Street, Max turns right, while Yacov turns left.

Yacov stops. "Why are you going that way? We finished over by Harbord and Bathurst yesterday. Sid's meeting us with the cart. Did you forget?"

Max has a silly grin still on his face. "Nope."

"Then where you going?"

"To pick up our truck."

Yacov stares at his cousin. "Max, what are you talking about? We don't have a truck."

"Sure we do."

"What?"

"Come with me," Max says.

Yacov hesitates.

"Come on. Don't worry, Yacov. I phoned Sid. Told him to start ahead. We'll catch up with him later."

Max leads his cousin several blocks away. They stop outside an office building on College Street, in front of a battered, black pickup truck parked by the side of the road. The back of the truck has built-up plywood sides.

Max holds up a set of keys. "Come on. Get in." He goes around to the driver's side and hops in. Yacov waits until Max has started the engine. The ignition is electric. She starts up beautifully. Yacov jumps up into the passenger's seat.

With the increase in business because of his dealings with Checkie, Max decided to buy the truck. Checkie offered to sell him the used pickup truck for a good price. It's an old model, a 1936 Ford with wooden sides, but it runs. And Checkie has a way of obtaining gas. Max has avoided telling Yacov about his reunion with Checkie for as long as possible. But in order to expand in the ways he envisions, he can not hold out any longer. He steels himself for Yacov's anger.

Yacov sits sullenly. "I thought we agreed we weren't going to use the car until the war was over."

"We did."

"And so you go and buy a truck?"

"We need the truck, Yacov."

"What for?"

"That's what I'm going to show you."

"What are you talking about?"

"Look. We have the chance to make a lot of money for a change. Okay? Just stay calm, Yacov. That's all you gotta do. Is stay calm." The

truck backfires loudly. The springs are shot and the seat bounces errati-
cally whenever they hit a pothole or turn a corner.

"I'm calm. I'm calm. Don't worry. I'm plenty calm. Don't I look calm
to you?"

Max glances at Yacov. Forehead furrowed, lips pursed, neck sucked
into his shoulders. Looks like he's about to explode, or bust in two. "Sure
you do, Yacov," Max lies. He cranks the manual steering wheel hard, turns
into the back of Checkie's warehouse on Gerard Street and parks by the
loading dock. He opens his door. "Come on."

"Where are we?"

"You'll see."

Yacov follows Max, who raps on a steel door.

"Yeah?" a gruff voice answers.

"It's Joe," Max says.

"Joe?" Yacov stares hard at his cousin.

"Shhh."

"Hang on," the rough voice orders. There is the sound of many locks
being unbolted.

"No real names, okay?" Max says to Yacov.

The heavy metal door rattles open. From the inside Romeo cranks it
up with a squeaky manual pulley system and holds it open for Max and
Yacov. His jacket is open and Yacov notices a holster strapped around his
chest, with a gun hanging by the side of his rib cage. Romeo motions for
them to follow. Without a word he points to a skid with a dozen boxes.
Max motions to Yacov to help him with the boxes.

"Who's he?" Romeo asks Max.

"Oh ..." Max doesn't have a false name picked yet for Yacov, so on the
spot he says, "Jake."

"Jake?" Romeo cracks a slight smile.

"Jake?" Yacov repeats.

"Yeah."

"Joe and Jake?"

"Yeah."

"Whatever you say, Max," Romeo sneers.

"Joe."

"Yeah, that's what I said, Joe." Romeo snorts, amused, then stands with arms folded across his chest as Max and Yacov work.

They pick up box after box and carry them out to their truck.

"What is this?" Yacov whispers by the side of the truck.

"Shah, I'll tell you later."

They finish loading and leave the warehouse. Romeo locks up after them. Yacov stares at Max as they drive away.

"All right. Quit staring. I'll tell you now."

"Thank you." Yacov's anger seethes across the cab as they bounce along.

"You want to know what we just loaded in the truck?"

"Wouldn't you?"

"Tea, sugar, silk stockings."

"Tea? Stockings? You can't get these things. How did we get them? Whose warehouse is it?"

Max takes a deep breath.

"Max!" Yacov is agitated. He's close to striking his cousin.

Max turns, studies Yacov's face.

"Come on, Max. Tell me. If you're going to drag me into this, then at least you should tell me the truth."

Max sighs. "You're right."

"So *nu?*"

"Checkie Seigelman."

"What? *Vey iz mir.* Not again, Max. I thought you weren't ever going to speak to him again. After what happened."

Max shrugs. "That was a long time ago."

"A long time ago. What's the difference how long?"

"It was my fault anyway."

"What?"

"Look, Yacov, it's a business transaction. That's it. We buy the products from him and we sell it to the stores."

"Stores?"

"Yeah, stores. I'm tired of nickel-and-diming up and down the street. Yacov, we're taking this load right to the big department stores. And when we sell this we're buying more."

"The department stores will buy from us?"

"Sure. They can't get this stuff anywhere. Not with the war on."

"But how can they sell it? Nobody is supposed to even *have* this stuff."

Max shrugs. "They manage. They put it out a little at a time. That way nobody notices. How do I know what they do?"

"Max." Yacov tightly controls his anger. "You promised me."

"What?"

"Partners we are."

"Yeah. Partners."

"And so you go *again*, and make business deals behind my back?"

"All right, Yacov. Let's not make a big deal."

"Behind my back. With Checkie Seigelman. Again."

"Look, Yacov. I had to … act fast. You don't think there's plenty of other schmucks wouldn't jump at the chance?"

"So you couldn't discuss it with me?"

"Yacov." Max struggles for patience. "You're so …"

"What?"

Max shrugs. "Conservative."

"I'm conservative?" Yacov can't believe what Max is saying.

"I was afraid you wouldn't go along."

"You're right. I wouldn't."

"See?"

"Max, suppose we get caught?"

"We won't get caught. Don't worry. Seigelman has plenty of the right people on his payroll, see?"

Yacov's eyes are huge. "He pays the police?"

"Shhh."

"What? We're in a truck. No one can hear us." Yacov looks around.

"You shouldn't speak of such things out loud. That's all."

"I don't like this, Max." Yacov scratches his beard, nervously.

"You see?"

"What?"

"I knew you wouldn't. That's why I couldn't tell you before. You would have said no."

"What if I say no now?"

Max shrugs. "We're already in."

"Max."

"What?"

"Go to hell."

"Go to hell?"

"You heard me."

"Okay. I'll go to hell. In the meantime, I'm making us more money in one month than we made all last year."

Yacov turns to his cousin. "That much?"

"People will pay good money for these things." Max gestures to the back of the truck.

Yacov sighs. It would be nice to make some money for a change. They've struggled for so long. Years ago, before the Depression, Yacov and Max had a dream. They were going to open their own store. Maybe their dream might actually one day come true. "Tell me, Max. We really got silk stockings back there?"

"I think so."

"Maybe we could slip out one pair. For Sophie."

Max smiles. "Sure, Yacov. Good idea. Only …"

"What?"

"Maybe it's better you don't tell her exactly where we got it from?"

"Oh."

"What do you think?"

"I think you're right."

"Good. Settled."

Bacon and Egg Matza
SEPTEMBER 24, 1941

SONNY WAKES WITH a start. The sun is already up. He's overslept. He jerks upright and groggily looks around the strange bedroom in the new apartment. He and Loretta have no furniture yet, only a box spring and mattress he picked up wholesale from Checkie's vast warehouse. Their wedding night had been simple, which was fine with Sonny. Just the two of them, alone in their apartment, after Sonny's father kicked him out for good and said the mourner's Kaddish over him. He sucks back the pain in his heart; it is one more bruise to add to the others. He can take the punishment; he's trained for it. It feels weird if something doesn't hurt. He has to put on a brave face for Loretta's sake. Pretend to her and himself that his family will come around. *Of course they'd be shocked. They didn't even know we were dating. When the baby's born everything will be different. Their first grandchild. They couldn't turn away from their first grandchild.* Sonny tries hard to convince himself.

As he slowly wakes up, Sonny's heart floods with the memory of the visit to his family. Now, he can't go home, can't see his mother or Izzy. It's like the Christie Pits riot all over again. It's like what happened after Izzy's accident, when everyone hated him. Only worse. He rolls over onto his side, clutching his stomach, feeling everything all at once. He's happy to be away from the confines of his father's Old World attitudes, in his own apartment with his girl. But he is alone in the world now. An orphan. Responsible for a wife and a baby, and he's only seventeen.

"Sonny," Loretta calls from the kitchen. "There's coffee on."

Loretta. Her sweetness eases the pain. *It's me and her against the world. Soon we'll have a baby. A baby. My own family. Who needs a father? I'm going to be one myself.* Sonny smells meat cooking in the kitchen. His stomach rumbles. Loretta's small tabletop radio is playing. Sonny can hear Judy Garland belt out:

"When you're smiling, when you're smiling,
The whole world smiles with you.
When you're laughing, when you're laughing,
Then the sun comes shining through."

Taking Judy's advice, Sonny puts on a smile, and gets out of bed. He steps into his boxer shorts and trousers and walks into the kitchen, buckling his leather belt. Loretta is fully dressed, standing by the stove. He kisses her neck from behind.

"Good morning."

She giggles. "Careful, Sonny. I'll burn your breakfast."

He spins her around. "Who cares? I know what I want for breakfast." He kisses her passionately.

She kisses back. He pulls her toward the bedroom, slowly, gently. Loretta becomes lost in the sensation pulsing through her body. Sonny gently lowers the zipper on her dress. She feels the heat of his body against hers. Fat crackles in her frying pan. She pushes against his chest, laughing. "Sonny, breakfast. Go and get dressed." She goes back to the stove. He follows, wraps his arms around her waist from behind.

"What are you making?"

"Bacon and eggs."

"Bacon?" Sonny unwraps his arms, leans over and inspects the meat frying in the pan.

"Yeah."

"Loretta, I can't eat bacon." Never once in their courtshop did Sonny think about their cultural differences. In this moment those differences feel enormous.

"Why not? It's fresh."

"It's *trayf.*"

"What?"

"It's not kosher. I can't eat pig meat, Loretta. It's unclean."

"Don't be silly. It's fresh. I bought it this morning while you were sleeping. There's a butcher shop right down the street, on College."

"Loretta." Sonny smoothes back his hair. How to explain. "Uh ... listen,

I'm gonna be late. I'll explain it all later."

"Sonny. Aren't you going to eat? I made it special for you." She pouts.

"We'll talk about it later. Okay, baby?" He takes her in his arms, kisses her. She pulls away gently. "But Sonny, you gotta eat something."

"I'll grab a sandwich at the deli on my way to the gym." He leaves the kitchen and shuts the bathroom door behind him. "Bacon she makes me?" he complains to the ceiling.

Loretta hears the bath running. She stands with her back to the stove, spatula in hand, perplexed.

SONNY PUNCHES AT the heavy bag over and over, rapidly. Imagines it's his father's head. He loves his father, but it's hard to be dead when you're only seventeen. He may never see his mother or Izzy again. He can meet with Lenny and Sid on their own; his brothers know he's not dead. But Izzy's usually home, and he can't go back there. The thought of his mother brings tears to Sonny's eyes, and he punches harder to keep from crying.

Rudy watches from a few feet away. The kid is in fine form. His footwork is beautiful, his left jab perfect and his hard right uppercut practically knocks the bag off its chain. Rudy is proud of his achievement. When Sonny goes pro he'll have the talent to go far.

Checkie phoned Rudy first thing this morning to tell him about Sonny's hasty marriage.

"Aw nuts," Rudy said when Checkie told him the news. Someone should have taught Sonny about rubbers. "Hey, why didn't you just fix her up with a doctor. You know, take care of the problem?"

"Don't you think I thought of that, Rudy? You *putz*. She's a Catholic. You know how they are. Fire and brimstone. Can't kill the baby. All that crap."

"She's a Catholic?"

"Johnny Mangiomi's sister."

"Oy vey."

"Exactly."

"Does Johnny know?"

"He knows."

"How's he taking it?"

"He was ready to beat the crap outa Sonny for knocking up his sister, but I think he softened up after he heard Sonny did the … whatcha call it? Honourable thing. Anyway, Johnny's been called up for home defence. He shipped out to the army training camp in Borden two weeks ago. The kids have both been written off by their parents. Sonny's father said Kaddish, the whole bit. Just keep your eye on him, will you? He could crack under all the pressure. You know what I'm saying?"

"Yeah. Poor kid."

Rudy hopes the lucky bride is not the Queen Bee type. Sonny's career will require that he be on the road often. It's better when a fighter doesn't have a wife chained around his neck. Rudy figures the kid will never be as great as he was destined to be, now that he has a wife and a baby on the way. Still, he has to admit Sonny is looking sharp.

"All right, Sonny. That's enough," he shouts. Don't want the kid to hurt his hands on the bag. "Come on. We'll do some stretches now. Gotta keep your muscles limbered up."

"All right, Coach."

Visiting the Dead
OCTOBER TO DECEMBER, 1941

AFTER A DINNER OF Loretta's specialty, spaghetti and meatballs — Sonny took her to the kosher butcher shop in the market for the meat — someone knocks at the door.

Sonny opens it. "Aunt Tess!"

"Hiya, Sonny." Tessie glances over his shoulder into the small apartment.

Sonny checks the corridor behind her. "You're all by yourself?"

She shrugs. "Just me."

"How did you find us?"

Tess puts a hand on her hip. "Lila got your address for me, from Checkie."

"Oh." He'd forgotten Tess and Lila were friends. "Well, come on in, Aunt Tess."

Loretta comes up behind him, dishrag in hand. She vaguely remembers the woman in the doorway from her brief visit to Sonny's parents' house the day they were married.

"Loretta. This is Aunt Tess."

Loretta offers a limp hand for Tess to shake.

"What are we? Businessmen?" Tess grabs Loretta by the arms and kisses her on one cheek. "We're relatives now. Right?"

"Right," Sonny affirms.

Loretta apologizes, "We have nowhere to sit. Sorry ..."

"Aunt Tess, we haven't had a chance to get anything for the apartment."

Tessie looks around. Through the open door of the bedroom she can see a bed. The living room is empty. There are two hard wooden chairs and no table in the small dining room. It's a shame. If Sonny had married a Jewish girl, there would have been a big wedding. There would have been presents, to give the kids a start in life. They'd have dishes and cutlery, candlesticks, maybe even a table with matching chairs. Now, they're going to have to make it on their own. Everything they own, Sonny will have to work for. "Why don't we walk down the street to the deli," Tess suggests. "My treat. I wanna talk to you kids."

INSIDE THE UNITED BAKERY Dairy Restaurant they order tea with lemon, and poppyseed cake. Loretta is nervous, but Sonny is thrilled with the visit. Tessie is the first person from the family to stop by since they've been married. Even Sid hasn't made the effort yet. But here's Auntie Tess, sitting across from Sonny and Loretta. This proves he's not dead after all. *You can stop reciting the mourner's Kaddish over me, Pop. Good old Auntie Tess is here to resurrect me from the dead.*

The bakery is filled with smells of pumpernickel bread, honey cake, cinnamon buns, blueberry pie and fresh coffee percolating. They are sitting in a booth with plush red leather seats. A bowl of sugar cubes is prominent on the table, an ashtray beside it. It's a noisy restaurant. The waitresses shout their orders over the counter and customers talk and laugh loudly.

"Your father will come around," Tessie tells Sonny in between bites of cake. She has come on a mission, full of purpose.

Sonny swallows hard. "How do you know?"

"I've known your father a long time now. Believe me. He didn't accept me when Max and I were first married."

"He didn't? How come, Aunt Tess? I didn't know that."

She opens her purse, finds her cigarettes, holds out the pack. Loretta doesn't smoke. Sonny's not supposed to — he's in training — but he slides one between his lips and leans over when Tess pulls out her lighter.

"I'm only half-Jewish."

"What?" This is news Sonny has never heard before.

"That's right." Tess blows smoke rings, watches them float to the ceiling. "My father was Jewish. My mother is Irish."

"She is?"

"Sonny. Didn't you ever think it was strange that no one from my family ever comes around the house?"

Sonny shrugs. "I guess I never thought about it."

"I never really knew my father. He came over from Russia and got a job at the O'Keefe plant, took a room in my grandfather's rooming house. That's where he met my mother. He only married her because she was pregnant with me."

"Izzat right?" Sonny glances at Loretta.

"Sure it is, Sonny," Tessie continues. "After my youngest sister was born, he took a powder and we ain't never heard from him since. Maybe he's dead now. Maybe he went back to Russia. Who knows?" Tessie's eyes are hard.

"What was his name?"

"Baruch Rosenthal. He named me Tessie. I think it was after his mother. What a name for a nice Jewish Catholic girl, huh? Tessie Rosenthal. So, naturally when Max met me, he thought I was all Jewish. With a name like that …"

"When did you tell him the truth?"

Tessie winks at Loretta. "After we were married. You know how men are."

Loretta nods.

"Was he mad?" Sonny asks.

"Are you kidding? Your Uncle Max is crazy about me. It's your father who had a problem with it."

"Good old Pop," Sonny says sarcastically.

"Listen Sonny. He means well. He loves your mother. He works hard. He loves you too."

Sonny grunts.

"He does, Sonny. You'll see. He'll come around. He's just …"

"Pig-headed?"

"Traditional," Tess says. "That's it. He's got what you might call Old Country ways. He acts sometimes like he's still over there."

"Yeah. That's for sure." Sonny smiles at Loretta and takes her hand under the table.

"Tell us about your mother." Loretta leans toward Tess. Behind her, someone yells loudly in Yiddish for the waitress.

Tess shrugs. "Not much to tell, sweetie. She still lives on Sackville. Over in Cabbagetown. That's where I grew up. That's right. Don't look so surprised. I was raised over there. The poorest section of the city. After my father left, she was with another man. Clive." She spits the name out bitterly. "Bastard. Pardon my language. When my mother was working night shift he tried to … take advantage of me one night … so I kicked him in his private parts if you know what I mean, and ran to my grandmother's house. Remember that, Honey," Tessie advises Loretta, "if a man ever gives you trouble. It's their one weak spot. It worked. He left me alone. After that, I never got along so good with my mother and I started to go my own way. I met Checkie Seigelman when I was a young girl. Oh, not like you're thinking. I was upset one night on account of this no-good boyfriend who dumped me, and it was raining, and I was standing right outside Checkie's pool hall, crying, and he came along. I'll never forget it. He offered me his hanky and asked me to come inside. I told him which lake to jump into, of course. I could tell what he thought of me. But I had him all wrong. See? His girl Lila. Yeah, they were an item back then. She was inside and he said she'd take care of me, on account of I was so upset. And that's how I met Lila."

"Does my mother know?" Sonny asks.

"What?"

"Well … that you're only sorta half-Jewish, Aunt Tess."

"Course she does."

"And she doesn't care?"

Tess tosses her head from side to side. "I think she did at first. Your mother's …"

Sonny laughs. "I know … kinda traditional."

"Yeah. That's right. But you know, we're good friends. Almost like sisters now."

"My ma doesn't have any real sisters. Just two brothers," Sonny tells Loretta.

"So you see? You just give your parents a little time, Sonny."

"I don't know."

"What?"

"Well, it's different with you, Aunt Tess. I'm their son. You know? Pop's pretty worked up."

"I know. Listen, kids. You know, you can always come to me. Right?"

"Sure, Aunt Tess."

"Thank you, Ma'am."

"Please. Call me Aunt Tess, Loretta."

Loretta smiles, shyly.

"Hey," Tess calls to a waiter. "How about some more hot water over here. Huh?" She leans in toward Loretta, speaks in a loud voice so the waiter overhears. "I'm telling you. Lousy service they got in here these days. Next time, maybe we'll go down the street to the Eppes Essen. Better service they have there. You can get a little hot water when you need it."

AFTER WEEKS OF NAGGING Sid to invite Sonny and his new wife over for dinner, Ruthie takes matters into her own hands. She wants to meet her new sister-in-law. She knows Sonny is busy training, but it's only right to introduce herself to Loretta. She gets up early one morning and bakes a nice honey cake. When it has cooled, she wraps it in a paper bag and tells Sid that she's going to walk to Sonny's apartment, just four blocks away.

"Don't mix in," Sid warns her.

"Who's mixing? She's family now, Sid. It's only right. You haven't even seen your own brother in a month. Imagine how scared he must be."

"I didn't tell him to marry an Italian girl," Sid says more self-right-eously than he truly feels.

"There's such a thing as compassion," Ruthie responds severely, piercing Sid with the look in her eye. She's right. He shrinks back. Ruthie is the most compassionate person he knows. He feels ashamed. Truth be told, he would like to go with her, but he's supposed to meet his father and Uncle Max. They have a big delivery this morning. A load of tea and sugar just came in. They never let Sid go with them to the warehouse for the pickups. But he always helps deliver the goods to the department stores. Sid has been trying to figure out what's going on, but he doesn't want to offend his father and uncle. One day soon, he's going to follow them to the warehouse and find out for himself.

At the house on Palmerston, Ruthie spots a directory on the porch. The big old house used to be a mansion owned by a rich family when it was built before the turn of the century. Even before the Depression, the large houses on the stately street were subdivided into apartments and flats. There is no sign of Sonny's name on the directory, but one apartment is blank: apartment four. Ruthie tries the front door. Open. She walks up to the third floor and knocks on apartment number four. Loretta opens the door. She's just starting to show. Ruthie figures she must be in her fourth month. Ruthie feels a pang of jealousy, but she stuffs the feeling deep down inside.

"Yes?" Loretta doesn't recognize the woman standing in the hall, holding a baking pan.

"Loretta?"

"Yes?"

Ruthie sticks out one hand. "I'm Ruthie."

Loretta shakes the hand but looks puzzled.

"Your sister-in-law. My husband, Sid, is Sonny's brother."

"Oh. Oh." Loretta is flustered, unsure what to do.

"I guess you don't remember me."

Loretta shakes her head.

"I was there. At Sonny's parents' house. On Rosh Hashanah."

"Oh. I …" Loretta glances behind her. "I didn't know you were coming."

"I thought it was time to meet you, so …"

"Oh."

"I figured I'd drop by."

"Oh. I'm sorry … come in." Loretta steps away from the door and lets Ruthie walk past.

Ruthie is surprised to see that the apartment is almost completely bare. When Ruthie and Sid were married, Sid's father and uncle bought them a dining room set, her parents paid for their bed, and from other relatives they got dishes, cups, saucers, curtains, even a bit of cash to use how they wanted. Looking around she realizes for the first time that Sonny and Loretta are completely on their own.

"We haven't had a chance to get a thing for the apartment," Loretta apologizes, her hands resting on her slightly extended belly. "I don't even have a place for us to sit."

"There are two good chairs," Ruthie points out.

"Yes, but…"

"I'm sure you'll get more things in time. Look, I brought a nice honey cake."

"Oh, thank you. Let me make some tea." Ruthie seems nice, thinks Loretta.

"That would be lovely."

Ruthie waits while Loretta fumbles with a saucepan to boil water — the newlyweds don't have a kettle yet. Loretta takes two cups down from the cupboard; they're the only two cups they have. Ruthie makes a mental note to buy Loretta a wedding present. Maybe a teakettle, or some dishes. She sits on one of the hard kitchen chairs and waits for Loretta to finish making the tea. The poor girl is nervous. No wonder, after the way Sid's parents treated her. Ruthie wanted to speak to her then, to follow Sonny and Loretta out. To welcome her into the family. But she didn't want to anger her in-laws. At least she can make up for it now. Ruthie intends to sit with Loretta until they get to know each other. Even if it takes the entire day.

LENNY HAS NOT SEEN his friend Ted in a while. He misses the conversation, the interesting people Ted introduces him to, and the poetry readings, the plays, the art. He walks the ten blocks to Ted's apartment on Grace Street, runs up the stairs to the second floor, and knocks on Ted's door. No answer. He tries the knob. It's open, so Lenny walks inside.

"Ted?" His voice echoes through the bare rooms.

Lenny's shoes clack on the hardwood floor as he walks through the empty apartment. Everything is gone: the furniture, the paintings, the plants, the books. In the bedroom closet Lenny finds a discarded shoe. Just one.

He can't believe Ted would leave without at least saying goodbye. Did he move across town? Or leave the city altogether? He is sore at Ted, but he doesn't want to lose him forever. Lenny leans against a wall, and slides to the floor. He sits there for a long time, thinking.

After a while, it's growing dark inside the apartment. Lenny gets to his feet, and quietly leaves. He runs into Ted's neighbour as he's closing the front door of the building. She's an elderly woman who peers at him suspiciously.

"Do you know when Mr. Cornwall moved out?" Lenny asks her.

"Two weeks ago. About time."

"Well, where did he go?"

"How do I know? Jail maybe," she says as she pulls her dog along.

"What?"

She stares at Lenny. "This is a nice building. We don't want your kind around here."

Lenny has no idea what she's talking about. Does she mean Jews? Why would Ted be in jail? Doesn't make any sense. Lenny rushes to the library.

Miss Johnson, the morning librarian, smiles at Lenny sweetly. "He resigned a month ago. He said he was moving to the West Coast."

"But why?" Lenny is perspiring. He's having a hard time making sense of all this. Why didn't Ted tell him he was leaving? He counts back to the last time he saw his friend. A little over a month ago. Maybe Ted hadn't known he was going to move yet.

"I don't know. He went with his friend."

"Friend?"

"I believe his name is James."

Lenny is stricken. He's not exactly sure why he is feeling such a loss; he hadn't been getting along with Ted lately anyway. But it feels like a part of him has been wrenched away.

"Don't worry. Mr. Hedgewick, our new evening librarian, is very knowledgeable. I'm sure he'll be able to assist you with your research as well as Mr. Cornwall."

Lenny doesn't wait for her to finish. He staggers out of the library and into the air, feeling lost and entirely alone.

After the Virgin
MAY TO JUNE, 1942

IN LATE MAY, Sonny is packing for the Canadian championships in Vancouver. Loretta is overdue to give birth.

There's a huge lump in Sonny's throat. "Come on, Loretta," he says as he tosses five pair of boxer shorts into his duffle bag. She has been crying, pleading with him not to go. "Geez, I've been training for this for eight years, since I was a little kid. This is all I ever wanted, Loretta. When I was a kid, I didn't play outside with the other kids. I trained. Every spare second I was at the gym or running in front of Rudy's car. Working hard, for this moment. I gotta go, Loretta. I gotta win the championship. I can't help it that your time is coming now."

"Please Sonny, don't go now. I need you." Loretta lowers herself onto the edge of the bed. It's not so easy; her balance is off.

"Aw baby. Come on. Don't be like that. You know what this means to our future. Now come on, quit crying. I got a guy lined up to drive you to the hospital when your time comes. Romeo. He works for Checkie. Here's his number." He fishes in his pocket for a crumpled piece of paper, hands it to his wife. "Just call him, he'll be over in a flash."

Loretta doesn't want one of Sonny's cronies from the gym to drive her. She wants her husband. Why doesn't he understand?

He stuffs a couple of white T-shirts into his bag.

"Sonny, I'm scared …" The truth is she's terrified. She can't even call her own mother to help. She hasn't spoken to her mother since the wedding, although she's secretly met with her sister, Gina.

Sonny sits beside her on the bed, drapes an arm around her shoulder, pulls her close. "Baby, I'm sorry I gotta go away. But … I can't drop out now. This is too important, Loretta. You understand, don't you? I mean, what good would I be at the hospital anyway? I'd faint at the sight of blood."

"You see blood all the time, in the ring."

"Yeah, but it's not your blood, Sweetheart. In the hospital I'd just be pacing in the waiting room, smoking a cigar."

Loretta sniffles softly against his chest.

"See? I knew you understood. It's gonna be all right, honey. The doctor'll take good care of you. Anyway, maybe it won't happen until I get back. Huh? Come on." He lifts her chin. "Give us a smile. Huh?"

Loretta smiles for Sonny, but inside her heart is breaking. If he really loved her, he wouldn't go.

LORETTA'S WATER BREAKS one week later while Sonny is having his first pre-fight rubdown. Instead of calling Romeo, Loretta calls Ruthie, who comes calling for her with Sid, in the truck. Sid lied to his father, said there was an emergency with his friend Ralph Shapiro. Sid and Ruthie drive Loretta to the hospital.

"All right, sweetie. I'm here." Ruthie helps her sister-in-law through the hospital doors. "I'm staying with you the whole time. Go on. Squeeze my hand. You can squeeze harder. It's okay."

Loretta sniffles and smiles weakly. Ruthie is the kindest person she has ever known.

With Ruthie by her side, Loretta gives birth to a baby girl — seven pounds, two ounces. She names her Mary after the Virgin, and decides to baptize the child before Sonny gets home. They had agreed that it would be best to have no religion in the house.

"No baptism, no circumcision. No nothing," Sonny said. "We don't need that religious crap."

Loretta had agreed, but the moment Mary is born, Loretta knows she cannot go through with their plans. It wouldn't be fair to the child to deprive her of a proper baptismal ceremony.

Loretta's sister, Gina, and her friend Ana attend the baptismal. Gina begged her mother to come along, but to keep peace with her husband, Loretta's mother declined. Loretta is heartbroken.

"Mama says bring the baby over when Papa's at work," Gina tells Loretta.

SONNY DOES NOT do as well at the championships as he had hoped. He wins a few bouts but overall in the welterweight division, he comes in at fifth place. And he didn't even get to see much of Vancouver because it rained the whole goddamned time. Rudy claims there are mountains in Vancouver, but the thick grey clouds obscure them from view, and Sonny thinks Rudy is lying. He is thoroughly depressed by the time they leave. He feels defeated, angry and cheated. If his father hadn't disowned him, he'd have been able to concentrate better. He'd have won like he always does. On the train ride back across the country, Sonny replays each and every fight in his mind, trying to figure out how he could have done better. He talks endlessly about his mistakes to Rudy, who sits across from him in the club car. The train rhythmically jostles and bumps along the track.

"Listen, Sonny. You did good. Don't you get it? It was your first shot. You're only eighteen. We didn't expect you to win. You did fine, kid. Just fine. Next year, we go back, and bam. You take 'em by storm, see?"

"Fifth place, Rudy. How could I do so bad?"

Rudy pulls a cigarette from his pack of Players Navy Cuts on the table between them, sticks it between his lips, lights it, inhales and exhales deeply.

SONNY ARRIVES HOME with flowers. He doesn't feel like the champ any more, now that he's lost the championships. Loretta sits on the new living-room couch she purchased without him. It's covered in plastic to protect the upholstery. She is feeding the baby formula from a bottle. Sonny walks in, bends down on one knee, lays the flowers down. He can smell the sweet baby smell of his daughter. She sucks hungrily from the rubber nipple.

"Loretta. Oh my God." Sonny looks down at the bundle in Loretta's arms and the frost over his heart melts.

"Meet your daughter, Sonny."

Sonny reaches over and touches the baby's chin tenderly with one finger. "Hi little baby. God, Loretta, she's a knockout."

"Whadja expect?"

"What are we gonna call her?"

"I already named her. She's called Mary."

"Mary?" Such a *goyisha* name?

"After the Virgin," Loretta says matter-of-factly.

Sonny looks at his wife suspiciously. Has she gone off her rocker? The Virgin? He stands. "I mean, can't we talk about this a little? Maybe something a little less ..." he wants to say Christian, but holds his tongue.

"It's too late, Sonny. She's already been baptized." Loretta removes the bottle from the baby's mouth, drapes a clean cloth over her shoulder and lifts the baby onto it to burp.

"Hold it. Hold it. Wait a minute, sweetheart. We agreed, right? No religious hocus-pocus. Right?"

Loretta says nothing. She just shrugs and pats the baby's bottom, rocking her slightly.

"Oh boy." Sonny sits down beside his wife on the crinkly plastic of the new couch. "Where did this couch come from?"

The baby burps. A little drool of spit-up drips onto Loretta's shoulder.

"Sonny. You've been gone two and a half weeks. I needed a chesterfield."

"Don't worry. I was planning on getting you one. Geez."

"Well, you took too long. I needed it now." She lowers the baby back onto her lap and sticks the bottle into her mouth.

"How did you get it?"

"Sid brought it over. We're buying it on payments. You gotta pay him a dollar fifty a week. Ruthie got it all arranged."

"Ruthie?"

"Yeah, Ruthie. She helped with everything. Including the birth of your daughter," Loretta says with ice in her voice. The baby fusses. Loretta removes the bottle, raises the baby back to her shoulder and sways her body from side to side.

"What are you so sore about?"

Loretta glares at Sonny.

"All right, all right. That was nice of her. Why are you looking at me like that?"

"Why haven't we gone for a visit?"

"What?"

"To Sid and Ruthie's. She had to come over here by herself just to meet me."

"That's it? That's what you're mad about? I'm sorry. I didn't know you wanted to go over so bad. Look, we'll go over soon. Okay. How's that?"

Sonny pushes off the couch, bends down on one knee in front of Loretta, bows his head and smiles at her with his crooked grin, the one that makes her laugh and breaks her heart.

"Sonny …"

"Loretta."

"Oh Sonny." She opens her arms. "I missed you so much." He moves in toward her, kisses her. She throws one arm around his neck; the other remains clutched around the baby. The passion that has always been between them surfaces. They kiss hungrily.

"Sonny, the baby. Be careful," Loretta giggles.

"Oh." He pulls back.

"It's time for her nap anyway." Loretta stands, with the baby in her arms. Hand in hand, she and Sonny walk to the bedroom."

The Weaker Sex
JUNE 1942

SOPHIE WANDERS INTO the boys' bedroom. It's getting on in the afternoon and she's waiting for Izzy to return from Tanenbaum's grocery store. She should run to the market herself and pick up something to cook for supper, but she feels melancholy. Standing on tiptoes, she retrieves her scrapbook from the top shelf in the closet, where she hides it from her husband. She sits on the edge of Izzy's bed and opens it to page one. Sonny is in the newspapers so often, this is her fourth scrapbook. Even if she can't see him, at least she keeps up with his life. Yesterday afternoon she pasted in several articles about Sonny's trip to Vancouver. She's worried about him. The paper says he came in fifth in the championships. She knows Sonny will be hard on himself for not winning. She wishes she could phone him. She misses having the boys at home. She's glad at least Izzy lives at home — will always do so, until she and Yacov are gone. She supposes Sid will take care of him then. She can always count on Sid to be the steady one. Not like the other boys. Well, Lenny's steady, doing well working for the Yiddish paper. That's something. But will he ever get married? Who knows? Maybe he'll be a bachelor all his life. He doesn't seem interested in girls, even yet. And, well, Sonny has his important career — some career: beating other boys up. *Feh.* Sophie will never understand such a thing if she lives to be a hundred. She's proud of Sonny's fame, but the sport itself baffles her. She closes the scrapbook and replaces it on the shelf. Anyway, as long as he's happy. Oy. Sophie wonders if Sonny is happy. Did he really want to marry the girl? Or had he felt trapped? Well, he did the honourable thing. She has respect for that. That's the one thing her stubborn husband doesn't understand: the woman's point of view. All he can think about is the faith. He goes on and on. "Marrying outside of our faith." Drives her crazy.

"East is east and west is west," Yacov shouts endlessly, whenever she brings up Sonny. "And never will they meet."

His other favourite is "Blood is thicker than water," and he recites it as if he himself invented the phrase.

Sophie has heard stories. She's heard about other neighbourhood boys who weren't exactly as honourable as her Sonny. Michael Cooper, her friend Ida's eldest boy, just to name one example, got a *shiksa* pregnant and denied all responsibility. The girl's father came to the Cooper's door begging the boy to marry his daughter. And as far as Sophie heard,

Michael made like he'd heard the girl had been with other boys, so how's
he to know he's responsible? Right to her father's face. Sophie has heard
that excuse before. *Feh.* That's a *mensch?* Leaving a poor girl in the lurch?
When it was time for the fun, it took the two of them. It's easy for the boy
to walk away. But the girl? Can she walk away? And then there's poor little
Sarah Feinberg. Also in the family way. She pointed her finger at Ralph
Shapiro, one of Sid's friends. He used the same excuse.

Naturally, Sophie laid into Sid about that.

"Ma, take it easy," Sid said. "It wasn't me."

"Well, he's your friend, isn't he? Can't you talk some sense into him. It
isn't right. The poor girl. What's she gonna do now. Huh? Answer me
that, Sid?"

"Okay Ma. I'll talk to Ralph."

Did Ralph do anything about it? He sent the girl money. Tried to fix
her up with a doctor who would get rid of the baby. Some doctor. Poor
Sarah Feinberg was sent away to stay with an aunt in New York. Who's
gonna marry her now? A young girl with a baby and no father? *Feh.* At
least her Sonny wasn't a deserter. Of course, Sophie wishes he had found
a nice Jewish girl. But at least he took responsibility for the girl he got in
trouble. Not a lot of young men his age could say that. Oy. But try and get
that through Yacov's head. Like talking to a wall.

From the floor, Sophie scoops up Izzy's discarded jersey, folds it and
opens the dresser drawer. Inside, she finds a photograph of the whole family, taken a few years earlier, before Sid was married, before Sonny left. They
look raggedy, but happy, and together. Sophie holds the photograph to her
heart. Her eyes fill. She sits on Izzy's bed, tears running down her cheeks.

Yacov won't allow Izzy to work with Sonny any more, so Izzy has a new
job, given him by his mother. His task is to stand in line outside Tanenbaum's
grocery store with the family ration book. With clear instructions from
Sophie, he can manage the job. Often the queue lasts for hours. At various
times throughout the day Mr. Tanenbaum sticks his head out and announces
that he has received a case of a rationed item — butter, or tea. Those fortunate enough to have the time to stand in the line will be the first to purchase
the coveted items — that is, if they have the appropriate coupon in their

book. Of course, a great deal of coupon swapping occurs. But that is no business of Mr. Tanenbaum's. As long as the customer can provide a coupon for the rationed item, he doesn't care how they get it. It's almost like the Depression again, only this time people have the money, stores just don't have the goods. With the tough times so recently in everyone's memory, it isn't all that difficult to find creative ways to get along with less.

FOR DINNER SOPHIE has baked a meatloaf, with potatoes and carrots. Strange how everything turns out. Now there's only the four of them at home and they can afford meat. A few years earlier she'd have killed for a pound of ground beef to feed her kids. Half a pound even. The kids were half-starved in those days, making do with soup and bread. Meat on Friday nights if they were lucky. It was enough to break a mother's heart.

Her despair is still with her when Yacov walks in the door.

"Oh boy, does that smell great," Yacov says, hanging his hat and jacket on a hook in the hallway. "Where's Izzy?"

"Waiting in line at Tanenbaum's. I had a coupon for sugar." She sighs deeply.

"What's wrong?"

"Nothing."

"Sophie. Something's wrong. I know when something's wrong. And something's wrong right now."

"Nothing's wrong. Sit down. Make yourself at home."

Yacov takes the bottle of seltzer from on top of the fridge to the kitchen table and pours himself a glass. He takes a long drink and sits at the table.

"If you weren't so stubborn …" Sophie begins, then trails off.

"Okay. Now we're getting somewhere. If I wasn't so stubborn …?"

"Oy." Sophie sighs a long, deep, guilt-entrenched sigh, the kind of sigh that could make a grown man cry.

Yacov spritzes more seltzer into his glass.

"Maybe I should have married Saul Weinstock. Maybe he wouldn't have been so stubborn."

"That's it!" Yacov bangs a heavy hand on the table, just as the front door opens and Izzy runs up the stairs to their flat.

"That's it!" Yacov shouts again.

Izzy stops at the top of the steps, lowers his head.

"Yacov, stop it," admonishes Sophie. "You're scaring Izzy. Izzelah, come on. Come inside." She holds out open arms. Izzy moves forward, leans down into her embrace. "Don't worry about your father. He's just a stubborn old man."

"Old? I'm old? When did I become old? I happen to be younger than you by six months."

"Stop it!" Sophie warns. Izzy shrinks away. "Never say that again!"

Yacov stands and holds his hands out, worried. He's never seen his wife like this. Is she going through the change of life? "All right, Sophie. I'm sorry. I apologize. I'll never say it again. I promise. I'm sorry. I forgot you're sensitive about that. Just calm down. Izzy, go wash up for dinner. Don't worry about your mother. She's a little upset is all."

Izzy slinks nervously to the bathroom.

Yacov approaches his wife, carefully. "Tell me what's wrong."

Sophie turns her back to him. If he doesn't understand by now, why should she tell him?

"Sophie?"

"What's the difference?"

"What's the difference? Plenty of difference. I want to know. Please tell me."

"You don't care."

"Of course I care."

"No, you don't."

"Sophie, please. I care."

"If you cared, you would know."

"How can I know if you won't tell me?"

"You already know."

"I already know?

"Yes. You know." She shakes a finger in his face.

"Oy." Yacov slumps back down at the table. He thinks hard.

"It's about our children."

"What about our children?"

She turns to face him. Her eyes flame with anger. "We don't speak to all of our children, do we, Yacov?"

"Oh." He nods his head, up and down. "So that's what this is about?"

"Yacov, please. It's enough already. I miss Sonny."

He bangs the table hard. "No! *Yis gadal v'yis kaddash shmai raba.*"

"Oy. If the whole world were as stubborn as you, no one would talk to anyone."

"No Sophie. It's not right. We didn't raise him to marry a *shiksa.*"

"Yacov, what's done is done."

"He didn't have to do it."

"There's worse things he could do."

"*V'yal ma de brach ki roo tai.*" Yacov rocks back and forth at the table, like a rabbi on the Day of Atonement.

To the ceiling she says, "You see? Stubborn. The most stubborn man in the world and I had to marry him. I could have married Saul Weinstock."

"You want Saul Weinstock? You can have him. I'll get him on the phone for you." Yacov jumps up, grabs his hat and coat and runs down the stairs and out the door.

Sophie pulls open the kitchen window. "Good!" she yells to Yacov as he flees down the street. "Get him on the phone then. Because I'd really like to talk to him. I bet he wouldn't be so stubborn."

She pulls her head back in and slams the window shut. She knows her husband will eat his dinner with Manny and the bachelors at the deli. After she's made such a nice meatloaf. Stubborn man. What is she going to do with him?

LENNY SEEMS DOWN in the dumps when he comes home a bit later. Sophie has noticed he hasn't been going out as much as he did before. He used to go to poetry readings and art shows all the time, but she hasn't heard him mention such things in a while. She eats dinner with the two boys. Izzy is always happy, God bless him. Sophie approaches her other son delicately.

"You're worried about something?" she asks Lenny.

Lenny looks up from his dinner. How can he talk about things he doesn't understand himself? Sophie never approved of his friendship with Ted. He can't see how she'll be sympathetic now. Except for Moe, Lenny doesn't really have any other friends, and Moe's really his boss more than a friend, even though Lenny sometimes tags along when Moe goes to Zionist meetings or lectures put on by the Communist Party. He fakes a smile and shakes his head.

"I'm okay."

Sophie knows that he is not, but she can't force him to talk. "Have some more meatloaf." She cuts him another slice. At least she can do that.

IN THE MORNING, Sophie's anger at Yacov has not diffused. She says nothing to her husband while she serves his breakfast — hot porridge and a hard-boiled egg. She addresses only Izzy. Lenny left the house early for a staff meeting at the *Zhurnal.*

"It looks like rain today, Izzy, so you'll do me a favour? Before you go out you'll put on your rubbers. All right, darling?"

"Rubbers." Izzy smiles.

"Goodbye, Sophie." Yacov says, slipping into his cotton jacket and pausing at the top of the stairs.

She says nothing.

"I'm going to work now," Yacov continues.

"So go. Who's stopping you?"

"That's the way you want to be about it? Fine." He plops his hat on his head.

"It's up to you."

"It's up to me?"

"You heard me."

Yacov shakes his head, begins walking down the stairs. "Me she calls stubborn," he tells God. "You want to know who's stubborn? I'll tell you who's stubborn." He pulls open the door and waits for Max on the front porch.

"Stubborn!" Sophie calls down. "Eat up, Izzy. You want some more?"

AFTER IZZY HAS LEFT for Tanenbaum's, this time for flour if he can get it, Sophie spreads a bedsheet on the bed. Into it she gathers up the laundry, pulls the four corners into the middle and ties the ends. She picks up the bundle and a cup of Lux soap flakes and trudges down the stairs.

"Tessie," she calls from the bottom of the stairs. "You home?"

"I'm home, Sophie. I'm home." Tessie saunters to the front door, cigarette dangling from her mouth.

"I came to do a load."

"Fine."

A month before, Max and Yacov brought home an electric washing machine, with a built-in wringer for the families to share — another bonus from dealing with Seigelman. There is more room in Max and Tessie's flat, so the washer is kept in their large kitchen. No more washing by hand with a scrub board in the sink. The washer is a fantastic luxury. Tessie is not the housekeeper that Sophie is. She's more haphazard and lackadaisical, and her flat is messy, the sink overflowing with dishes, ashtrays filled with butts. But there's a joyful life to the apartment. Drawings by her children are tacked to every wall, a jigsaw puzzle halfway done lies on the table, cookies are baking in the oven, photos of movie stars clipped from magazines are pinned to the walls, newspapers and books are scattered about, children's toys dominate every available surface. It's a relaxed environment — messy, but cozy.

Tessie leans against the kitchen door frame and smokes while Sophie loads her laundry into the round tub of the machine. She attaches the hose to the kitchen faucet and watches as the tub fills with water.

"So? How's everything?" Tessie asks.

"How should it be? It's nice to have a little money for a change."

"It's so quiet with the older boys away."

"Is it ever. When they were little, I dreamed of quiet. Now … *feh*. What I wouldn't give for a little noise. You're lucky, Tess. You've got two girls. Girls stay with their mothers. Boys … well, boys go away."

"Lenny's still home. Sid's still close by."

"Sure, but he's married now. He has Ruthie. He doesn't need his old mother."

"He doesn't visit?"

"He visits plenty. I'm only saying it's not the same." Sophie dumps the cup of soap flakes into the tub and switches the machine on. The tub swivels from side to side, and the water bubbles up. A modern miracle. Does all the work for her. A *michaya*. She closes the lid, turns to face Tessie.

"You want some tea?" Tessie asks.

"Sure. Why not?"

Tessie is also feeling out of sorts. Times are changing for the better, but even good change is an adjustment. Her kids are still at home, but they're all in school during the day, and some days she doesn't know what to do with herself.

Tessie fills the kettle with water, switches on a burner on the gas stove. The breakfast dishes are still on the table. Sophie moves a bowl out of her way and sits.

"Tessie, tell me the truth. What do you think?"

"About what?" Tessie leans against the counter, puffing on her cigarette.

"Doesn't it seem a little strange to you?"

"What's strange?"

"Well …" Sophie shrugs. "First the boys start bringing home tea and sugar and stockings — all the things you can't get because of the war. Then they buy a truck. Where are they getting the gasoline? No one else can get gasoline. But our husbands can get it. And the new stoves. The washing machine?"

Tessie takes a long drag on her cigarette, inhales, blows out the smoke in a steady thick stream, turns around, runs cold water over the butt, tosses it in the metal garbage can in the corner. *Poor Sophie,* she thinks. *So naive.* Would it be better for Sophie to remain in the dark? Or should she tell her the truth? What she figured out herself, and through conversations with Lila?

"Tess," Lila had said, with frustration in her voice. The two friends were having tea out, in a cafeteria on Queen Street. "Checkie can get anything. He has ways."

"Oh."

"Look, honey. Don't worry. It's business. Your Max is making a nice living finally. Isn't he?"

Tessie nodded.

"So? What's to complain? Who's getting hurt? Checkie told me the merchandise he buys wholesale is goods that were, what's that word? I know … confiscated by the bank. On account of the companies couldn't

pay their bills. You see, Tess? It's all on the up and up. It's just a little …
what's that word Checkie uses? I know … unorthodox. That's it."

"Unorthodox."

"It's business, Tess."

Tessie wasn't born yesterday. Lila could use all the euphemisms in the
book, but Tessie understood the truth immediately. She didn't grown up
in Cabbagetown for nothing. She saw. She listened. She understood.
Unorthodox my ass, thought Tessie. Just a fancy word for stolen goods.
Red-hot items. Who Checkie stole from, Tessie didn't know. Whoever it
was probably deserved it. Probably *goniffs* themselves, like the big department stores. Put their prices up so high ordinary people could only gawk
at their merchandise and fantasize. And those snotty credit managers
would never give someone like Tessie credit. So? For all she cared, they
could *gai in drerd arein*. She was with Lila on this one.

"Sophie," Tess says, pouring the tea. "It's nothing to worry about. It's
business." She decides to use Lila's terminology.

"Business?" Sophie adds a lump of sugar to her tea.

"Sure. They buy this stuff wholesale. Better than wholesale. Wholesale
on wholesale. It's goods that have been … confiscated … on account of
the companies couldn't pay their bills."

"Confiscated? By who?"

"Who knows? The banks, I guess."

Sophie sips her tea. It seems to make sense. But something just doesn't
ring true. Even the banks can't get their hands on gasoline.

"Sure, Sophie," reiterates Tessie. "Nothing to worry about. It's all on
the up and up."

"You're sure?"

"Course I'm sure. Would you like a piece of sponge cake? From the
Harbord Bakery. It's fresh."

"If it's fresh, of course." *All on the up and up?* Where does Tessie get
these expressions? The other topic she wants to bring up is more delicate,
but who else would understand, if not Tessie? "Oy," Sophie sighs.

Tessie plunks down two plates of sponge cake, sits across from Sophie, lights another cigarette, holds the pack open. "What is it, Sophie? There's something else?"

"I don't know." Sophie accepts a cigarette.

Tess leans over with the lighter. "It'll help to talk a little. Come on."

"It's Yacov."

"So? What is it this time?"

"It's about Sonny."

"Oh. Still?"

"Uh-huh."

"Oy."

"I don't know what to do, Tess."

Tessie tilts back her head, blows smoke rings through her tongue. "What do you want to do?"

"Want? I want my family back together. It's a mess."

"So? What's the problem?"

"The problem? You know the problem. The walls are paper thin. You must have heard. The problem is Yacov. Such a stubborn man. He won't give in. Sonny is dead. Sonny is dead. To Yacov it's a closed book."

"Sophie." Tessie leans forward. "In my experience, men are weak."

"Sure. So?"

"You know that."

Sophie frowns, bounces her head from side to side, in partial agreement.

"Weak. Without us, what are they? Oh, they like to pretend they've got the world in their control. Why? Because they go out and make a little money? You think that's so hard? I was making money when I was a teenager …"

Sophie looks hard at Tessie, surprised at this news.

"… but that's another story. All I'm saying is, making money is easy. Is it so easy to bear children? To raise them? To keep a house?"

Sophie glances around at the disarray. She would like to point out that Tessie's not so good at number three, but she holds her tongue.

"Those are the hard things in life. Remember what it was like just a few years ago, when we had to make supper out of thin air? You remember, Sophie. Like magic, somehow, out of nothing we managed. Right?

Of course right. Because, I don't care what they say ..." She leans forward, her voice rising. "Women are not the weaker sex. You agree? Of course you agree, you're a woman. It's the men who are weak. Tell me the truth, Sophie. Who runs your household?"

"Well ..."

"You of course. Right? Of course right. Does Yacov make the decisions ...?"

"Well ..."

"Of course he doesn't. You just let him think he does. Right? The trick is to do what needs to be done, and let him think it was his idea."

"But how?"

"Easy, Sophie. You just do it. You want to see Sonny? Go see him."

Sophie's eye brim with tears.

"You want to meet your granddaughter?"

The tears fall down Sophie's face. "What about Yacov?"

"What about him? You don't need his permission to meet your grand-daughter. Believe me. A stubborn man is just waiting for his wife to make the move. Then he can blame you for it. So? What do you care about that? Pride *shmide*. Only men worry about silly things like pride. Meanwhile, you can bring everyone back together. Now, come on, eat your sponge cake. Soon, my kids will be home for lunch and your laundry will be ready to hang on the line. Here. Have some more tea." Tessie fills Sophie's cup with strong black tea.

Sophie considers Tessie's advice. She's never lied to Yacov before. It would feel strange to do so now. Sophie thought Yacov would cool down and welcome Sonny back into the family after the baby was born. How can they have a grandchild they've never met? But still, Sophie doesn't relish the idea of sneaking around behind Yacov's back, no matter how much her heart aches to see Sonny and to meet her granddaughter. No, she longs to bring her family back together properly, with no lying. It's true that she could walk to Sonny's apartment right now and pay him a visit, no matter what her husband has to say about it. She just isn't sure she can bring herself to do that to Yacov.

BOOK THREE

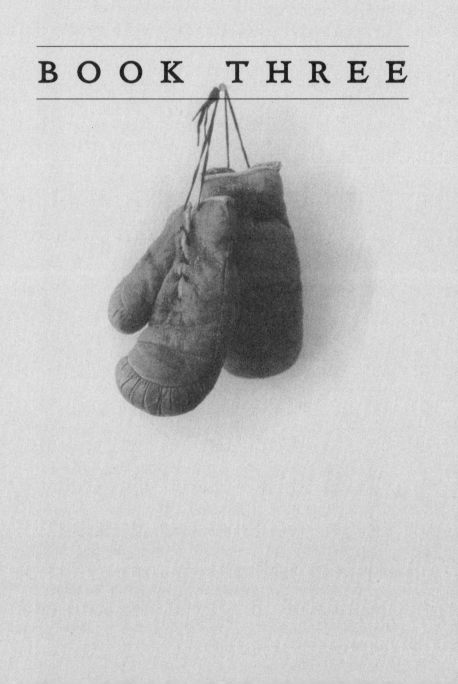

I WAS BORN in the spring of 1945, while my father was overseas fighting with the First Canadian Army, which was pushing its way through the Rhineland as the Germans headed for defeat. All over North America, maternity wards must have been teeming with expectant mothers and wailing newborns. I was among the first wave of the baby boomers. The moment I drew my first breath, my father was sitting in a wet, muddy trench somewhere in Holland. I didn't meet him until I was almost a year old. According to the *Toronto Daily Star* in 1945, the classic film "Imitation of Life" with Claudette Colbert was released, as was "The Body Snatcher" with Boris Karloff. You could sit down to a fresh whole lobster at the Savarin Restaurant for one dollar, there were long lineups of women desperate for stockings outside hosiery shops on Bloor street, people were buying Victory Bonds to "help bring our boys home," Russian assault forces were smashing Berlin's defence zone, Shirley Temple was delighting audiences along with Ginger Rogers and Joseph Cotton in "I'll Be Seeing you." A brand new spring-loaded, drop-back chesterfield could be had for $19.95 and a chest of drawers was selling for $5.95. And finally, after six years of war, reports of the atrocities committed in Nazi concentration camps were beginning to find their way into Toronto's newspapers, as the United States Third Army continued to liberate the survivors, and the British Second army stormed into Hamburg.

I don't have many early memories of my father, because even after the war he was never home. He was always touring somewhere, boxing his way all over New York State and across the Eastern Seaboard. He seemed to come home only for short periods, sometimes with eyes swollen shut,

KAREN X. TULCHINSKY

and bruises all over his chest and back, his broken nose held together with white tape. When I was small, I thought all fathers went away and came home beaten to a pulp. It's not that he was losing. When I was little, he was working his way up to becoming a top middleweight contender and he was winning most of his fights. The bruises, the broken blood vessels, the busted nose, sprained wrist and dislocated knuckles simply came with the territory of being a professional boxer, the way a mechanic can never quite get the grease out of his fingernails, or an accountant will eventually develop a stooped shoulder or poor eyesight. My father made his living getting his brains bashed in. He did a lot of bashing himself, of course, but even when he's winning, a boxer will take an enormous amount of blows to the body and the head. He's just more conditioned than the rest of us to deal with the punishment.

Although I didn't see my father often, from my childhood I do remember three things with extreme clarity. The look of disappointment on my father's face when it was clear I was more interested in spending my time in libraries than athletic clubs. That he slapped me across the face, yelling, "I'll give you something to cry about. You're a man. Men don't cry," when I ran home in tears after being picked on by the class bully when I was seven years old. And that he came close to reciting the mourner's Kaddish over me, when at the age of twenty-four, six months after discovering I was gay, I revealed the news to him.

I'm a history professor at Simon Fraser University in Vancouver. I wrote my thesis on immigrant communities in Canada in the first half of the twentieth century, a subject near and dear to my heart, I suppose, because I am the offspring of such communities. Two to be exact, though I hardly fit the bill of what was expected of me. I was supposed to marry young like my parents, like my brother and sister, have a brood of unruly children, settle down and raise them. Perhaps I'm cut from the same the cloth as my Uncle Lenny, whom I never met. He was a bachelor until the day he died. I've seen photos of Uncle Lenny: a dapper, handsome man. He was thin, almost dainty, and even though his family was poor, he dressed elegantly. There's one photo taken when he would have been nineteen. He'd just started his first job as a journalist. He's wearing a black pin-striped double-breasted suit. The pleats on his trousers are pressed just so and he sports a silk tie with a classic design, a tie I'd kill for now, the kind you'd find in vintage shops with a hundred-dollar price tag. His fedora sits on his head at a striking angle. He has a pencil thin moustache. His tie clip is a thin silver chain, almost like a mini-necklace that fastens at the buttonhole and hangs over the tie. It's not so much the suit — everyone wore suits back then. It's not even the necklace, or the moustache. It's the look in his eye. Hard to describe exactly; it's just a sixth sense I have. He has a certain soft glint in the eye, a slight ironic curl of the lip. It's the way his hands are neatly folded, his nails immaculately mani-cured. I just think if Uncle Lenny had been born twenty years later, perhaps he would have been gay.

My grandmother, *Bubbe* Sophie, has told me Uncle Lenny had a best buddy during the war, a man named Charlie. They were inseparable. They took care of each other overseas. They were planning to start a business together once the war was over. There's a photo of Charlie and Uncle Lenny taken in Aldershot, the training camp in England. They're striking in their Canadian Armed Forces uniforms. Charlie was tall, blond and handsome in a rugged, masculine way. A real butch — just the type of man I usually go for. Lenny was thin and slight, yet gorgeous, with a movie-star quality about him. He had beautiful full lips, a sculpted jaw with a cleft in the chin and soft brown eyes with long lashes. In the photo, they're barely touch-ing. Charlie's elbow rests on Lenny's shoulder, in a buddy kind of way, but the look in Uncle Lenny's eye is unquestionably the look of love. Romantic love. Undying devotion. I know the look. I've worn it myself once or twice, although never quite as intensely as Uncle Lenny in the photo. I doubt he ever acted on his feelings, but who knows? For the biography, I'm trying to find a war veteran to interview. I'd like to find out if there were gay rela-tionships among the soldiers overseas. It's a tricky question to ask, especially of veterans, who are all in their eighties or nineties. You don't just come out and ask an eighty-five-year-old war veteran if he knew any homosexuals when he was in the army. Not unless you want to upset an old man. I've written to the Canadian Lesbian and Gay Archives in Toronto, requesting any information or leads they might have on gays in World

War II. So far, all they've turned up are postwar articles on the subject. But I believe if I persevere I shall find something of relevance. A letter perhaps, a photo, or the names of soldiers dishonourably discharged.

I'm not trying to rewrite history. God knows, as a historian, the very thought offends me. The official family story is that Lenny was a bachelor, a man who just hadn't found the right woman, but once he did, he'd marry her, settle down and raise a family like everybody else. But the look in Uncle Lenny's eyes in the photo as he gazes upon Charlie disputes the family story. As a gay man, my *gaydar* is infinitely refined. I can spot a homosexual from a hundred paces, from halfway across the world, from sixty years into the past, from the faded image on a grainy old black-and-white snapshot. I could be wrong. God knows, I have been before. But I don't think so. I just wish Uncle Lenny was still around. Then I could ask him myself. Believe me, coming out in 1969 was nowhere near as easy as it is today, and as far as I know, in my family I'm still the only one. But if Uncle Lenny was around when I was coming out, perhaps he could have made my path just a little easier. Can you imagine my plight? Being half-Italian, half-Jewish, born at a time when intermarriage was uncommon and being a little light in the loafers, even though your dad is a world-famous middleweight boxing champion? I mean, what would you do?

If it hadn't been for Stonewall and the start of the gay liberation movement, hippies and *peace, love and grooviness*, I don't know if I would ever have come out. Perhaps I'd have been like Uncle Lenny. A dapper dresser, a perennial bachelor. A permanent closet case. I'd date a woman once or twice a year, bring her to family weddings and bar mitzvahs, to prove to the family how straight I was. But deep inside I'd be dying a little bit every day. Maybe I'd visit the parks, or the baths, for a quick release. Anonymous sex with strangers. But I'd never admit to being gay. Never know the pleasures of a relationship. I'd lie to my family my whole life about who I really was. As hard as it was to come out when I did in 1969, my heart breaks when I wonder if Uncle Lenny knew he was gay in 1940, when gay meant merry, and queer meant deviant, and you would lose your job, your home, your family, even your freedom for being queer.

The forties — when people were buying Victory Bonds, collecting scrap metal, sending their sons off to war in faraway places with foreign-sounding names, and a funny little man with a funny little moustache and a horrifying, harrowing agenda was systematically murdering eleven million people.

HISTORY REPEATS ITSELF

Waiting to Beat Hitler
JUNE 1942

LENNY IS SURPRISED to see Moe already in the office when he arrives early, ready to begin his sixth in a series of articles about the rapid advancement of the Nazis farther east into Russia. Last month, there was good news. The Russians won several major battles, including the recapture of key villages near Staraya, Russia. He's eager to write an update. Lenny stops in the doorway, a bad feeling in his stomach from the look of dread on Moe's face.

"Sit down, Lenny," Moe says gently.

"What is it?"

Moe sighs, lights his pipe. "I'm sorry, Len. It's not my decision."

"What?" Lenny's stomach churns. He reaches for his cigarettes, lights one.

"Mr. Bloom phoned me late last night."

"Oh." The publisher.

"His nephew needs a job."

"Nephew?"

"Wants to be a reporter."

"Oh." Lenny feels as if he's been pushed off a ledge. He's hurtling to the pavement, with nothing to break his fall but cold hard concrete.

"I'm sorry Len. I went to bat for you. Told Mr. Bloom you're already trained, why bring in a new man? Told him you're a first-rate writer, which you are by the way. I tried, Len. I really tried." Poor Moe looks devastated.

"It's okay, Moe." It's not okay. But it's not Moe's fault.

"I'm sorry, Len."

Lenny's throat closes. The bile rises. He's going to throw up. He pushes open the office door.

"Mr. Bloom's the publisher, Len. He calls the shots."

The bitterness repeats in Lenny's throat. He races from Moe's office.

"Lenny?"

Lenny rushes down the stairs, out to the street, and makes it to the back alley, where he leans against the wall and vomits. What's he going to do now? There's no point in trying any of the other newspapers. The *Star* is the most liberal. If they wouldn't hire him, the others aren't going to. He can't go back to schlepping up and down the streets, collecting debts for his father. Lenny wipes his mouth with his handkerchief and leaves the alley. In a fog, he walks.

"Hey Lenny. What'sa matter with you? You walked right by me!"

Lenny looks up. "Sonny!" They don't see each other much any more, although Lenny has been to visit a couple of times since the baby was born a few weeks ago. He just doesn't mention it to Yacov or Sophie.

"What's wrong? You look terrible."

"Got laid off."

"Already? Geez. That's awful. I'm sorry, Lenny."

"Yeah." Lenny notices a huge recruiting sign on the building behind Sonny. It shows a group of soldiers marching behind a huge traffic signal. *Stop! Waiting to beat Hitler?* the sign reads, *Go! Enlist now.*

Lenny stares at the sign. His heart beats quickly. *Enlist now. Beat Hitler.*

"Lenny? I said, what are you gonna do now?" Sonny asks.

"Maybe I'll enlist," Lenny says.

"What? Enlist? You?" Sonny laughs at the thought of Lenny in the army.

"Why not?" Lenny is offended.

"Well, Lenny. I mean, come on. You're just not the type. That's all."

"Oh yeah?"

"Listen Lenny, I gotta go. I'm late. I got a fight tonight. I'll see you later. Why don't you come over on Sunday. You should see the baby more. She's your niece, after all."

"We'll see if I'm the type," Lenny says after Sonny is out of earshot. Anything's got to be better than door-to-door peddling. Lenny heads toward the large recruiting centre on Front Street.

THE WHOLE FAMILY escorts Lenny to the Canadian National Exhibition grounds where he is to report for basic training. For the first two months he'll be right in the city. Then he'll either be shipped to Halifax for home defence, or overseas to Britain. When he enlisted, Lenny signed the form for voluntary active duty overseas. He could be sent anywhere. Yacov has mixed feelings about sending a son to the war. He would like the war in Europe to end as swiftly as possible, God knows; he's worried enough about his family in Russia. But does he have to sacrifice one of his boys? And Lenny of all people?

Sid is jealous. It should have been him. He was ready to fight. Seeing Lenny in his Private's uniform, Sid can taste it. He's already had several letters from Louie Horowitz. Louie is a Private in the Royal Regiment of Canada, stationed in Aldershot, where he is learning basic tactics and battle drill. Any day now, his unit will be shipped to the front, or be engaged in battle when Hitler invades Britain. How Sid longs to be there too. And he is worried about his brother. Lenny can't even fist-fight, never mind hold a gun. What the hell kind of army is it that turns down a guy like him, but takes his brother-the-bookworm?

Izzy doesn't understand where his brother Lenny is going, but he's fascinated by the uniform. Lenny lets Izzy wear his Private's cap until it's time to go inside the base.

Sophie is a mess. Up until the last minute she has hoped for a miracle. She hates the war that is taking away her Lenny. She fears she will never see him again. How will Lenny cope in the army world? Sophie wishes she could change the world. If she were in charge, there would be no wars. Young boys would not be wrenched from their homes to carry guns and shoot bullets at other young boys in faraway countries. Why do men persist in waging wars so that mothers have to see their sons off to tragic fates? Sophie is not educated, but she can see from reading the newspaper that wars are waged by rich old men who send poor young men to fight for them. Why don't the politicians fight their own wars? Why must she send her son?

"Did you pack your wool socks?" Sophie's eyes fill with tears. She promised herself she wouldn't cry, but it's hopeless. She can't stop herself.

"Yeah Ma, I got the socks."

Through the CNE gates, soldiers enter and exit. A company in formation marches by, their legs stepping in time to the sergeant's call, unloaded rifles slung over their shoulders. It's time for Lenny to report. He leans down and embraces his mother. She sobs openly onto his shoulder. Yacov strokes her back.

"I love you, Ma. I'll write every week. Anyway, I'll get four days' leave before they send me out of the city. Who knows? Maybe I'll end up in Halifax or somewhere." Lenny pulls away, removes his wedge cap from Izzy's head and places it on his own, tilted at a striking angle. Sid shakes Lenny's hand solemnly. Yacov hugs his son. Finally Lenny pulls away, smiles at his family one last time and enters the gates.

Sophie clutches Izzy as they watch Lenny go. At least Izzy will never be sent to war. When Lenny passes through the steel gate to the CNE training ground, a piece of Sophie's heart breaks off and enters with him. She covers her mouth with her hand as he walks off. She has a bad feeling. She spits on the ground fiercely to ward off the evil eye.

SONNY SAID HIS GOODBYES to Lenny the day before. He is worried about Lenny. He's been protecting his brother since they were little, beating up the bullies who picked on Lenny, who called him a sissy and a fairy boy just because he likes to read and was never good in sports. Who's going to protect him now? If they send Lenny to England, maybe Sid could write to Louie Horowitz, see if he can watch out for him. For the last week, Sonny has been teaching Lenny basic boxing moves: how to dodge and hit; how to jab with the left, then punch hard with the right. Well, Lenny is left-handed, so in his case they tried it the other way around. But either way, it's hopeless. Lenny can't punch his way out of a goddamned paper bag. His wrists are weak, and he is slow. Sonny just shook his head, and stuffed his feelings deep down inside where he didn't have to deal with them, but all week long, when he looked at Lenny he knew he was looking at a dead man.

"Remember," Sonny advised, "Keep your chin down, and your fists up. Always cover your face with your fists. Oh, and watch your opponent through the eyebrows. You got it? The eyebrows. That way, you'll keep your chin down."

"Chin down." Lenny lowered his chin. "Eyebrows. Got it, Sonny. Thanks." Sonny hopes to God Lenny remembers.

The War Effort
JUNE 10, 1942

SID GULPS THE REST of his coffee, kisses Ruthie and grabs his hat.

"Don't forget your lunch." Ruthie hands Sid a brown paper bag, with two smoked-meat sandwiches, three apples, a banana, two kosher dill pickles and a large slice of honey cake. A big man, Sid burns a lot of energy during the workday. He smiles, puts one hand on her belly protectively. Ruthie is ten weeks pregnant. It's their fourth try. Ruthie has had one false alarm and two miscarriages already. For the first time in weeks, she has no morning sickness. She's a little worried, but who knows? Maybe it comes and goes. She has an appointment with Dr. Grossman later in the week. She'll have to remember to ask him.

"See you at dinner, Ruthie." Sid blows a kiss and closes the apartment door behind him.

Sid and Ruthie's apartment is spotless. Ruthie throws all of her boundless energy into being a good housewife. Sid works so hard, she thinks, it's the least she can do. She clears Sid's breakfast dishes into the sink and checks in the icebox. There's a nice piece of chicken she can roast for dinner and yesterday Sid brought home five pounds of potatoes and a special treat — strawberries, which she'll bake into a pie.

Sid meets his father and Max at the corner of Harbord and Manning. Yacov tells Sid to come collecting with him; Max has to pick up some tea they have a wholesale line on. Max has promised never to take Sid along to Checkie's warehouse. Yacov doesn't want his son involved in anything illegal. As Max starts up the truck and lumbers down the street, Sid and Yacov walk down Manning. They have quite a few customers on the street, and will spend the morning walking door to door, collecting payments.

"If only I could find out some news," Yacov says to Sid. He is terrified for his family in Tiraspol. Every day he reads in the newspapers of the German advance across Russia. Surely their town is occupied.

"Maybe they'll buy their way out. Rachel's husband is a butcher, right Pa? I heard people can bribe their way across the border."

"Maybe Lenny will end up over there. Maybe he'll find out what's what."

"Maybe, Pa." Sid still can't picture Lenny as a soldier.

AT LUNCH, YACOV MEETS Max at Manny's Delicatessen. Sid begs off, borrows the truck. He has Ruthie's bagged lunch from home. Besides, he promised to help Izzy today.

Izzy has become patriotic. On the big radio in the front room he hears about the war effort on the news. People are being urged to collect scraps of metal and rubber to donate to the effort. These materials will be used in the construction of weapons and ammunition for the Allied forces. Sophie tries to keep Izzy occupied by standing in queues at the store, but there are only so many hours to be filled waiting to buy sugar and tea. Anyway, lately Yacov has been able to buy most rationed items from Seigelman. "An old business associate," he tells Sophie. So there really is no need for Izzy to spend so much time standing in line. After Izzy heard about the scrap-metal drive, he began to roam the city, searching in the alleys, ditches, ravines, in abandoned buildings and backyards, for pieces of scrap metal. He drags Yacov's old pushcart around, and fills it with discarded tin cans, old steel bumpers from cars, bicycle frames, heating ducts, plumbing pipes. When his cart is full he rolls it home and dumps his haul into the backyard.

Sid parks the truck in the back lane, opens the gate and enters the backyard. Izzy is sifting through his pile of junk. He has learned how to separate out the copper from the steel. Tin cans go in one pile. Hubcaps in another. Sorting is a task well suited to Izzy's capabilities. He grins when he spots Sid.

"Lots of good stuff this time?" Sid asks.

Izzy holds up a piece of copper piping. "Look, Sid."

Together they load Izzy's haul into the back of the truck. Sid will drop off half to the war-effort collection site. The other half he sells to his buddy Ralph Shapiro, who, true to his word, runs a scrap-metal yard, "Sharpiro's Scrap." Every cent Sid takes in goes into a bank account in Izzy's name. Sid is determined to provide for Izzy after their parents are gone. It's his responsibility. Sid can't ever forget that Izzy could have had a normal life, if only Sid had been more careful.

Every morning Sid prays that this time Ruthie's pregnancy will work out. He can't understand why they've had so much trouble. They're both young, both healthy. He knows he'd be such a good father. He wants to have four or five kids. Maybe even six or seven.

Obstacle
JUNE 10, 1942

LENNY LAPINSKY WAS supposed to be a Private in the Royal Regiment of Canada, the same regiment as Louie Horowitz, but a clerical error lands him in the Royal Hamilton Light Infantry. This regiment is comprised mostly of Hamilton and Dundas boys, but once Lenny is there, the army decides to leave him there. It doesn't make a difference to Lenny, really. One Company looks the same as the next from where he sits. He soon finds there is, however, a slight yet crucial difference. The Royal Regiment of Canada is made up mostly of men from Toronto, and so there are a few Jewish boys in each company, whereas the Royal Hamilton is practically free of Jews. Most of the boys are good old British stock. They fondly call the regiment "The Rileys," from its initials, RHLI.

Basic training begins at 0600 after a hearty breakfast of porridge, toast, scrambled eggs, sausages and hash browns. In the noisy mess hall, the men sit at long, narrow tables, crammed in elbow to elbow, to chow down on soggy overcooked food. The din of hundreds of men talking at once is thunderous. Most are between the ages of eighteen and twenty-six, and many are away from home for the first time, living in close quarters, eating, shaving, showering and sleeping together in long rows of double-decker bunks in what used to be animal barns at the Canadian National Exhibition. The floors have been doused liberally with strong disinfectant, but underneath, the scent of horse and cow manure lingers. The men are constantly finding little bits of hay everywhere. The walls were treated years ago with creosote, and that, along with the pine oil that was also used in an attempt to mask the animal smells, invades their senses.

The mess hall reeks of grease, onions, cigarette smoke, weak coffee and the sweat of crowded men. Lenny soaks up the all-male atmosphere. The food is dreadful, but the excitement of being part of something important is infectious. Lenny digs into his scrambled eggs, even tastes a bit of the sausage on his tray — he's never eaten unkosher food before. It's not bad, though a bit salty for his tastes. He soon becomes popular when the other men find out he gives his bacon and ham away to whoever is lucky enough to sit beside him at breakfast.

The army has constructed an obstacle course on the CNE grounds. Lenny falls into formation with his section at exactly 0600. His green wool uniform is hot under the blazing summer sun. Even so early in the morning, Lenny can feel drops of sweat forming under his arms and at the back of his neck. A loud, foul-mouthed sergeant rattles off names in a roll call. Eyes forward, standing at attention, feet together, arms stiff at sides, stomach in, chest out, the soldiers answer, one by one.

"Lapinsky, Leonard, Private."

"Yes sir."

"Williams, John, Private."

"Yes sir."

They are twelve men to each company, four companies in a battalion, three battalions in a brigade. Roll call goes on forever. Lenny is supremely

bored. If he'd known the army was all about standing at attention, calling out names, chin in the air and "yessir" this and "nosir" that, he
never would have enlisted. Makes peddling door to door look like a
dream job.

The Sergeant marches the men to an obstacle course. "Not a picnic,
men," he assures them. "No weapons training, no drills, no lunch, no
water, no nothing until you successfully complete the course. In its
entirety. Understood, men?"

"Yessir!"

Each man is given a knapsack filled with rocks, weighing in at exactly
fifty pounds, and an unloaded rifle with a shoulder strap. First they are to
climb a metal structure twenty feet off the ground. Easy enough for
Lenny, even with the fifty pound knapsack on his back, rifle slung over
one shoulder, tin helmet on head. At the top, they are to run across metal
beams, gun in hand. Lenny dances gracefully on top, while others in his
section struggle to maintain their balance.

Charles Geoffrey Bain Jr. of Queen Street East in the Beaches is right
behind Lenny. He enlisted in the Royal Hamilton Light Infantry because
his maternal grandfather, Charles Andrew Ralston II, had served with the
Rileys in the Boer War from 1900-1902 and risen to the rank of Lieutenant-
Colonel by war's end, eventually commanding a battalion of his own. In
the Great War, he was promoted to Brigadier and was in charge of a full
brigade. When Charlie was about to enlist, his mother insisted he sign up
with her father's regiment.

Charlie entered the Rileys in May of 1942 at the age of twenty-three as
Lance Corporal, just one step above a Private. His grandfather wouldn't
look him in the eye.

"Should have made him a Sergeant at least," Grandfather grumbled.

Upon his departure, Charlie's father said, "Keep your helmet on, son.
And … write to your mother. She'll be worried." Then they shook hands.

No one accompanied Charlie to the CNE grounds for basic training.
He said goodbye to his mother and sister on the porch of their home in
the Balmy Beach area of Toronto, then Charlie slung his duffle bag over
one shoulder and caught the Queen streetcar on his own.

Charlie climbs the structure with no problem, but with the sack and rifle he finds balancing on the thin beams close to impossible. He walks a few feet, teetering, then stops at the first crossbar to catch his rapidly failing balance. He glances ahead and notices how the man in front of him, Private Lapinsky, runs across like a ballet dancer, with ease and grace. Mesmerized, Charlie stands still, until the next man bumps into him.

"Come on, move, buddy."

"Sorry." Charlie lumbers slowly forward.

At the end of the structure, they are to climb back down and crawl on their bellies across a field. For Lenny, this is a piece of cake. Lenny can make himself as thin as a garter snake slithering across a beach. He's way out in front.

After the field is another metal structure. Must be thirty feet high, at least, thinks Lenny. The object is to get to the top of the structure and then swing on a rope down to sandbags below. To get to the top they must climb a single rope. There is one knot at the bottom and that's it. The rope itself is raised six and a half feet off the ground. Lenny is five foot eight. He stands at the starting line, runs like the others to the rope, jumps with one hand raised, grabs the end of the rope all right, but can't pull himself up to climb. He dangles from the rope, legs kicking, until his arm gives out and he drops to the ground.

Charlie has caught up. He watches Lenny plunge to the ground in defeat. The Sergeant marches over, screams in Lenny's face.

"Again, Private!"

"Yessir!"

"Come on. Move! Jerry's waiting for you at the top."

"Yessir!"

"With a loaded gun."

"Yessir!"

"You're dead, Soldier."

"Yessir!"

Lenny runs back to the starting point. Charlie smiles encouragingly. A spot deep inside Lenny's heart flips over. He grins back at the handsome blond man with the sky-blue eyes. A comrade-in-arms. Two guys in the same predicament. Lenny faces front, concentrates on the rope. Takes a breath. Runs. Leaps. Misses. Falls to the ground with a thud.

The Sergeant is beside him, leaning over.

"Again, Private!"

"Yessir!"

"On the double."

"Yessir!"

Lenny runs back to the starting point.

"Don't lose your momentum."

"What?" Lenny turns around. The blue-eyed man smiles at him.

"Momentum. That's all it is."

"Oh. Right. Thanks."

Lenny faces front. His heart pounds with unfamiliar longing. It's a bright warm sensation that begins in his chest, somewhere above his heart, then spreads like wildfire though his body. He'd like to look at the blue-eyed man again, but instead he stares at the rope. Momentum. He runs. Leaps. Grabs. Misses. Falls flat on his back.

"Okay, Private. Sit this one out."

"Yessir." From Lenny's prone position the sergeant looks bigger and meaner than ever.

"After the other men have gone. You go again."

"Yessir."

"Until you make it."

"Yessir."

"To the top."

"Yessir."

"Even if it takes all night."

"Yessir."

"Are you a man!"

"Yessir."

"Or a mouse."

"Nosir."

"We'll see about that, Private Lapinsky."

"Yessir."

"Get up. And join the back of the line."

"Yessir."

Lenny scrambles to his feet and runs to the back of the line. Charlie Bain winks at him as he passes. Lenny wants to die. He's not sure if it's from happiness, fatigue or humiliation.

Charlie's up next. He runs, leaps and effortlessly grabs the rope. With his strong arms he pulls himself up to the top in record time. Charlie was a quarterback on his high school football team, and a track and field star. He's climbed a thousand ropes; a hundred thousand. He could climb a rope from here to Germany, empty his rifle of bullets, kill a couple hundred Nazis, then climb all the way back again in time for lunch and not be winded. Charlie straggles behind after he's been dismissed for lunch and watches poor Lenny grow increasingly fatigued as the Sergeant pushes him to his limit.

"Again, Private!"

Some of the other guys have gathered to watch. Someone yells, "Powder Puff" at Lenny.

But you should have seen him dancing across the beams, Charlie thinks. He wants to shout this. *He was like liquid fire. Lightning. He could dance across a loaded minefield and not be blown up. You guys should have seen it.* Charlie keeps silent and watches, patiently. That's the kind of guy he is: slow, methodical, plodding, patient.

After lunch, Lenny is still trying. The sergeant has left him alone to practise. Lenny is exhausted and hungry. And determined. He stands at the starting position. Runs. Leaps. Misses. Falls onto his back. Lies there, staring at the sky.

"Momentum," Charlie says.

"What?" Lenny leaps to his feet, startled. "Oh. I didn't hear you coming." It's the handsome blond boy.

"Sorry. Didn't mean to scare you."

Lenny attempts a weak smile. He wonders if the sergeant sent this boy to check up on him. He walks back to the starting line, his muscles aching.

"Momentum." Charlie says again, following Lenny.

"Momentum." Lenny repeats, but he doesn't get it.

"Watch." Charlie gently shoves Lenny out of the way, and stands at the starting place. "You keep stopping at the crucial moment."

"Crucial moment?"

"Watch." Charlie perches at the starting position on the balls of his feet, concentrates on the end of the rope, starts off running, gaining speed, then leaps, grabs, grabs, grabs, grabs, grabs, all the way to the top without stopping for even a breath. At the top, he holds his hands up above his head and sucks in air, gasping for breath, triumphant. Momentum.

Momentum. Lenny gets it: Don't let up. Use the speed gathered to carry you to the top. Don't stop until you get there.

"Momentum!" Charlie screams from the top of the metal structure.

Lenny nods. He copies Charlie exactly. He stands in position. He concentrates on the rope. He takes off, runs, gains speed, reaches for the rope and grabs, grabs, grabs, sucks in a breath, stops mid-climb. Looking up he sees there's a long way to go. He loses steam, hangs there, breathes. His arms feel heavy. He tries to climb higher. His body is too heavy. His muscles ache. He's slipping. Slipping. He slides down the rope, burning his hand. Drops into the sand, onto his back. Defeated.

"No!" Charlie screams from the top. "Momentum."

Lenny lies on his back, mortified. Why doesn't the handsome boy just go away and leave him alone? Before he was just a failure. Now he is a failure with an audience. A beautiful audience. This guy is as bad as Sonny — a perfect graceful athlete. Lenny just wants to die.

Charlie smiles, watching the dancer from the top. Charlie is a born teacher, an eldest son, used to helping his younger brother Richard along. He climbs down and stands above Lenny, one hand outstretched. "Again."

Lenny looks up into the sky-blue eyes, takes the hand and allows Charlie to help him to his feet.

"Again," Charlie says gently.

Lenny cannot refuse. He feels perfect trust and his belly turns over. He runs back to the starting position.

The next fourteen tries, he fails. Maybe they'll just give him an honourable discharge, he thinks. He tried. Even a dishonourable discharge.

Who cares? As long as he doesn't have to climb this stupid rope again.

"Take a break," Charlie recommends. "Walk around. Loosen up your muscles. Shake it out." He demonstrates the technique with his hands. "Take a breath."

"Look," says Lenny to the blue eyes. "I just can't do it."

"You can do it."

"No."

The blue eyes bore their warmth into Lenny's heart. "You can do it." Charlie says it with such conviction, Lenny almost begins to believe it. Almost.

"I ... don't think ..."

"Don't think. Just watch."

Charlie goes to the starting position. Stares at the rope. Concentrates. Runs. Gains speed. Faster. Faster. Faster. Leaps. And grabs. Grabs, grabs, grabs, grabs, all the way to the top, without stopping. Lenny watches in awe. And finally, he gets it. In his heart. In his body. In his soul.

"You can do it," Charlie shouts down, breathless. The wind rushes through his hair. He looks like a perfect Greek god.

You can do it echoes through Lenny's confused heart. *You can do it. I believe in you.* Charlie doesn't say this part out loud. But Lenny hears it just the same: *I believe in you.* If such a perfect specimen of manhood believes in me, he thinks, then goddamnit ... I can do it.

Lenny stands at the starting line. He doesn't notice the other guys who have gathered after lunch by the side of the course to watch. He concentrates, obliterating everything in the entire world except the rope and Blue Eyes, who waits for him on top. If Lenny can only get to him. Concentrate. Concentrate. Lenny lifts off. Runs. Runs. Gains speed. Speed. More speed. Leaps. Grabs the rope and grabs, grabs, grabs, grabs, grabs, all the way to the top, without pausing for breath, for fear, for fatigue or anything. Just grabs grabs grabs to the top, adrenalin sweetening the ache in his muscles, grab, grab, pull, pull, until in a split second Lenny is standing beside Blue Eyes, panting for breath, exuberant with endorphins, adrenalin and love. A cheer rises from below. Lenny looks down. All of Company B, including the Sarge, are gathered below, watching and cheering him on. Lenny smiles with triumph.

"Momentum," says Blue Eyes. Then, "Charlie. Charlie Bain." He sticks out a hand. Lenny clasps the hand. It is cool and strong and soft.

"Lenny."

See, Sonny? I did it. What do you think of that? For the first time in Lenny's life, he has faith in the abilities of his body.

AT THE END OF JUNE 1942, Lenny's company is going overseas. He is granted four days' leave. Lenny arrives home in the afternoon.

"Ma!" he calls as he takes the stairs two at a time.

Sophie is in the kitchen, koshering a chicken with salt for dinner. She drops the chicken in the sink at the sound of his voice. "Lenny. Oh my God." She runs into her sweet boy's arms. "Lenny. You're home."

"Four days' leave."

"Only four days." Her heart sinks.

"Shhh." Lenny hugs her tight.

ON LENNY'S LAST NIGHT HOME, Sophie invites Tess, Max and their kids; Reuben and Channa; Sid and Ruthie; and Sam Horowitz for dinner.

"All the way over to England?" Tessie says. She doesn't remember the boys growing up, never mind being in a war. Thank God she has girls, and Morris, well, he's only eight years old. Surely to God the war will be over before he comes of age. She feels sorry for Sophie. First Lenny, and Sonny's sure to follow. She can see Sid's pain at being rejected, but thank God, at least he won't get shot up on some European beach or field. *Feh* to all of Europe as far as Tessie is concerned.

"It's a training camp, in England. Then I could be sent anywhere," Lenny answers.

"Anywhere?" Yacov is surprised. "Not to Germany I hope?" The newspaper reports for years have informed the Lapinskys that to be a Jew in Germany in 1942 is certain death. Even a Canadian-born Jew, Yacov supposes.

"I don't know, Pa. France, I guess. Maybe Italy."

"I wish you were staying home, Lenny. Who needs the army? Maybe you could get another job, stay home by your family, help me around the house," suggests Sophie.

"Ma ... stop."

"Well, I think it's exciting." Tessie saves the moment. "Imagine — our Lenny a hero."

"Well ... not a hero, Aunt Tess. Just one of the guys."

"Over there in England ... a handsome boy like you ... I bet you'll have lots of girlfriends ..."

"Well ..." Lenny isn't really thinking about girls.

"A girl? What girl?" Sophie is alarmed. Are there Jewish girls in England?

"I'm not going to look for a girl. I'm doing a job."

"A handsome boy like you ...?" Tessie touches Lenny's face. He has filled out since he's been training at the CNE.

The blood rises in Lenny's cheeks.

"Sure, Lenny's gonna come home with a wife or two," Max teases.

"Only two?" Yacov joins in.

"Stop it." Sophie plunks a plate of chicken in the middle of the table. She's a bundle of nerves. She has a bad feeling about Lenny going off to war. She's a mother, so of course she's worried for her boy. But Sophie also trusts her instincts, her deep inner knowing. She is terrified for her son. "Supper's ready," she says.

"I love you, Ma." Lenny throws one arm over Sophie's shoulder and kisses her cheek.

Sophie tries to hold back the tears, but the force of her fear is too heavy. It pushes out of her eyes, rolls down her cheeks. "Oh Lenny."

"Shhh. Ma. Come on. Be happy."

Yacov opens a bottle of Manishevitz sweet red wine. Sid fetches glasses. Yacov can hear an announcer on the radio reporting that "Sugar ration is now half a pound per week per person."

Max winks discreetly at Yacov. Just two days ago, they were able to procure six caseloads of sugar. People will be clamouring for it.

Sitting Ducks
JULY AND AUGUST, 1942

ONCE HE'S STATIONED at the training base in Aldershot, England, Lenny runs into Louie Horowitz. Louie's been thirty miles southwest of London, at the military station called Hampshire, training with the Royal Regiment of Canada since December of 1939. Two and a half years. A lifetime ago.

Two Canadian divisions, including Louie's, have been held in England all through the threat of a German invasion across the Channel. It has been clear for some time that Hitler's plan to invade Britain is not going to happen. There has been nothing much for the officers to do with the Canadians, except keep them training. The soldiers have done ten-mile marches, bayonet and rifle training, target practise, landing-craft training. They are in top shape and are bored and frustrated. They left their homes to fight Nazis and so far the only fights they've had have been among themselves. The Canadian soldiers may speak English, but culturally they are strangers in a strange land. Some of them are as young as eighteen, away from home for the first time. The Canadians are in awe of British pubs. There are no such places in conservative, dry, Protestant Ontario. The young men do not hold their liquor well. They have been known to annoy the British citizens with their unruly behaviour. Their commanders realize that something will have to be done with the restless Canadians. And soon.

Louie Horowitz is thrilled to see someone from home, after all this time. "You look good, Lenny," he says, standing back to take a proper look. "You filled out."

"Yeah. Not so skinny any more. Bet the guys wouldn't recognize me."

"The army'll do that to you. Geez, I never expected to see you over here."

"Well ..."

"Sure am glad to see you, though. How's your folks? Have you seen my Pa?"

"Yeah. Oh, here." Lenny fishes in his tunic pocket for the letter Sam Horowitz sent with him for Louie.

Louie recognizes his father's handwriting and tucks the letter inside his pocket. He'll read it later, when he's off duty. "Thanks, Lenny. How's Sid?"

"Sid's good. You know he married Ruthie?"

"I know. He wrote me. Any kids yet?"

"Not yet."

Behind them, an army supply truck, camouflaged with brown netting, heads for the main gates, rumbling under the weight of its load. Louie leans in and whispers, "Guess you heard the rumours, huh?"

"Yeah, but no one knows where we're going."

"France. That's what I heard. A frontal assault on the beach."

"France?"

"Gotta be a beach. Why else have we been rehearsing landing on the beaches over here?"

"Gee. Guess you're right, Louie."

"I heard it'll be any day now." Louie holds up an invisible rifle, sights his target. "I'm going to kill as many Jerries as I can. They killed my uncle in Germany, you know. Sent him to a labour camp. No one knows what happened to my aunt or cousins."

"I know, Louie."

"Ack ack ack ack ack." Louie splays invisible machine-gun fire over invisible German soldiers. They fall over dead, clutching their miserable murderous Nazi bellies in agony.

Lenny doesn't mind the training base, even though the barracks, which date back to mid-Victorian days, are uncomfortable by Canadian standards, mostly because they have no central heating. They are as drafty as the Lapinskys' cold-water flat on Clinton Street was, and at least at home they had a coal furnace in the basement. Here the barracks are heated by scattered open fireplaces, and although the soldiers' rations of coal are much larger than the rations given to the native Britons who haven't grown up with central heating and are accustomed to the chill, at night it's cold in the drafty barracks. Much of the time, Lenny curses his decision to enlist. He's never been so uncomfortable, so sore, so humiliated by his lack of physical prowess in his life.

Over time, though, things begin to shift for Powder Puff Lapinsky. Perhaps it's the twenty-mile marches all over the English countryside, carrying fifty-pound rucksacks on his back. Perhaps it's learning to scale obstacles, clear minefields, embark and disembark in freezing ocean water, first from mock landing crafts, then from real boats. Perhaps it's crawling under piercing barbed wire, scaling up cliffs, pulling his aching body up ropes, scrambling up rock faces. Perhaps it's being screamed at by superior officers, running on drills, a Sten gun over his shoulder, heavy rucksack on his back, smaller pack strapped on his chest, hitting the dirt on command, rolling under wire obstacles, climbing over steel structures. Perhaps it is all of the above, but somehow over the months of training, gentle sweet tender Powder Puff Lapinsky becomes a soldier: hard, fit, prepared, disciplined, brave and strong. Ready for combat.

IN JULY OF 1942 the troops know something is up, although they are told nothing. The men have received lectures on security and strict unit censorship is put into effect. They engage in amphibious training on England's beaches. They are taught to embark and disembark from assault landing craft, to use toggle ropes, to scale perpendicular cliffs and get their weapons ready for action. They learn how to land under smoke. They are trained in speed marches. They tramp the roads of the Isle of Wight in battledress until they can march eleven miles in two hours. They engage in training designed to increase their stamina and ability. They practise fighting with bayonets, firing on the run and from the hip, crossing rivers in freezing water. In the day they march all over England with eighty-pound packs. At night, they use stunted spades to dig slit trenches, six foot long by thirty inches wide by four feet deep, to sleep in. They are in peak physical condition, every single man in the Royal Hamilton Light Infantry. Even Powder Puff Lapinsky.

AT 0300 ON AUGUST 19, 1942, ships carrying Toronto's Royal Regiment of Canada, the Royal Hamilton Light Infantry, the South Saskatchewan

Regiment, the Queen's Own Cameron Highlanders, les Fusiliers Mont-
Royal, and other Canadian companies leave England for Dieppe. Among
the Canadians are two British regiments and fifty men from the U.S.
Rangers. They have rehearsed. Trained. Practised. And rehearsed again.
The troops are ready to give the Jerries hell. At 0430, Private Louie Jacob
Horowitz of the Royal Regiment of Canada stands in the middle of his
landing craft, three rows from the front, with his section of soldiers. Each
soldier is clutching his Sten gun, tin helmet fastened tightly around his
chin, twenty-four hours of emergency rations, canteen, knife and kit bag
affixed to his belt. K rations and tin mess kits are in their packs. Around
their middle, they wear inflatable canvas life jackets nicknamed "Mae
Wests." They carry extra ammo for their Stens in cotton ammo bags slung
over one shoulder. In their deep left trouser pockets they hold cigarettes,
chocolate, two grenades each, and Sten mags. In a shoulder pouch they
carry an escape kit, containing French money, silk handkerchiefs printed
with maps of Germany and France, a compass and a tiny file. Hanging
from the back of their packs, the men carry stunted spades for digging
the slit trenches that may save their lives or for digging graves to bury
their comrades. Thirty-five men to a landing craft, they stand shoulder to
shoulder in three rows.

The vessel sides are metal and seven feet high. The infantrymen
packed tightly inside can't see over the sides or the front. If they could,
they'd see that the water near the shore is littered with huge sharp metal
obstacles, that the beach is booby-trapped with coils of barbed wire, and
that above the seawall, well-dug into the cliffs in trenches, protected by
foot-thick concrete pillboxes and armed with machine guns and heavy
artillery, the Germans are waiting for them, have in fact been expecting
an Allied amphibious assault on this particular beach for weeks.

Something's been bothering Louie. Unlike a month ago, when they
were loaded onto landing craft for the same mission, which was later
aborted due to bad weather, they are carrying identification. Last month
they were stripped of everything but their dogtags in case of capture. This
time, they're carrying ID, personal letters and photos. Their commanding officers are even bringing along plans for the raid in plastic bags,

stuffed in their packs. Something about this seems wrong to Louie, but he's just a Private. They didn't ask for his opinion.

The men are bobbing in the choppy waters of the English Channel, eight miles off the coast of France, when the landing craft is slowly lowered over the side of the Royal Navy carrier, chains buckling from the weight. The weather is not cooperating. The waves are high and the wind is fierce. The small boat pitches and weaves off course. The five-foot-high waves toss the boat as if it were a toy. Water crashes overboard, soaking the men, some of whom are seasick and vomit onto the floor, spattering their own boots. The Royal regiments are supposed to land before dawn on the beach called Puys, code-named Blue Beach, under cover of darkness. They are counting on the element of surprise. The beach is heavily dug in with German defence. Their objective: to take the beach and secure the town.

A bitter taste rises in Louie's mouth. He's not scared. It's just nerves, natural under the circumstances. His shoulders bump and knock into his best buddies, Private Jeremy Simpson and Private Patrick McCaffrey, both Toronto boys from the east side of town. They've been training, eating and sleeping together for almost three years. Back home they'd never have met, being from different communities, but here they know each other like brothers. They are prepared to risk their lives for one another. The boat rises and falls with the waves. On its descent, water splashes inside, over their heads. Louie is soaked from the waist up. His feet are wet. Even his legs are slightly damp. Under his helmet, his head would be dry, except he's perspiring. Drenched inside his tunic pocket is the letter from his father. And the other note in his father's handwriting. He found it in his uniform when he first tried it on. "God Bless You." He couldn't figure out how his father got it into his uniform. How could Sam know which uniform would be assigned to Louie? Then he heard that three out of ten other guys in his division found the same note in their pocket, same handwriting. He knew his father was working part-time at the uniform factory. Now it made sense. Thanks, Pop. Louie had never realized his dad was sentimental. Growing up just the two of them, it was a male household. Not exactly filled with motherly hugs or words of affection.

God knows how many of these notes his father has stuffed into the uniforms he has sewed. It gives Louie an unusual sense of security to know there were guys all around him with a note from his dad in their tunic pockets. Jeremy found a note in his pocket. Patrick didn't, but then to make him feel better, Louie forged a note in his dad's handwriting and snuck it into Patrick's trouser pocket one day. Patrick couldn't understand why he hadn't noticed it before, but he was glad it was there all the same. A devout Catholic, Patrick feels protected by Sam Horowitz's sentimental note. As long as he holds onto the note, he knows he is going to survive.

Their landing craft slows, then stops. Louie is in the middle of the vessel and can't see anything. From above, he can hear the roar of aircraft, but he's not sure if it's German Messerschmitts or British Spitfires. He can hear the clank of the grappling irons as the toggle ropes let down the front ramp. The major yells for the men to disembark. Machine-gun fire rattles, shells explode like canons on the rocky beach, men scream in agony and die. The men at the front of Louie's boat are mowed down in seconds. Bullets rip through them as if they are made of dough. Blood pours from open wounds. Everything is suddenly loud and chaotic all at once: bombs bursting, gunfire ripping, water spraying, smoke, men shouting and screaming. The major yells again. "Go go go go go!" Beside Louie, Patrick fishes inside his mouth, removes his false teeth, stashes them in a pocket of his tunic beside his "God Bless You" note. He promised his mother he would take them out when fighting. False teeth are expensive. Not so easy to replace.

"Go, go, go!" The major repeats. Louie's stomach turns and his bowels feel loose, as if he has to go to the bathroom. The men at the front of the boat lean heavily backward, dying or dead. Louie, Patrick and Jeremy have to push the bodies of their comrades out of the way to disembark. They leap into the chest-high water, pulled dangerously down by the weight of their gear and the wet wool of their uniforms. Some guys lose their guns on impact, the heavy metal weapons sinking like stones to the bottom of the rocky ocean. Helplessly, they dive down, grasping. Louie, Patrick and Jeremy wade slowly to shore, rifles held with stiff arms high above their heads. The water is freezing. They shiver involuntarily. From dug-in positions on the cliffs above, the enemy bombards them with shells, mortars, grenades, anti-tank artillery and machine-gun fire. They are sitting ducks. The men slog through the water as fast as they can. All around Louie, guys are being hit. He hears the bullets ricochet off the water's surface, ping against the steel of helmets, silently slice through flesh. Inches away, a guy is hit, slips down into the icy water. On his other side a shell bursts, water sprays high in the air, a soldier in his regiment is ripped in two, flies up, then lands hard into the water in pieces. Screams. Moans. Grunts. Blood spreads in the water, deep red. "Go go go go go," the Major yells, relentless. Louie tries not to look to the side, only straight ahead, at their objective. Jeremy and Patrick are still on either side of him, guns raised, ducking and dodging fire, plodding through the water.

The survivors of B Company miraculously make it to the beach, but it is booby-trapped with coils of barbed wire. Designated teams dressed in leather jackets throw themselves onto the wire and act as human carpets while other men walk over them. The men on the bottom endure the pain, as their trousers are ripped to shreds and the wire begins to tear at their skin. Their fingers and palms where they hold onto the wire are quickly cut to ribbons, dripping with blood. Louie runs over the human carpet on the barbed wire onto the rocky beach, readies his gun into position, aims up at the high cliffs where the enemy is dug in. His finger is on the cold trigger, ready to fire. He's going to kill as many Jerries as he can, avenge his uncle in Germany who was killed by Nazis just for being a teacher, avenge his grandfather, his aunt, his nieces and nephews, make the world safe for democracy and freedom. The roar of the high-velocity shell sounds a few seconds after it explodes by his side, like an after-thought. Louie's tin helmet falls to one side as he pitches forward and slams down hard, face first, onto the slick shingled beach. He doesn't feel much. His nose hurts. Probably broke it on the fall. He doesn't think he's been hit. Just knocked over by the force.

He glances to his left. Patrick is lying beside him, groaning. Patrick's hands are blown to bits. He has just a thumb on his right hand; the other hand is completely gone. Blood pours from his open wrist and there is blood gushing from a wound to his chest.

"Louie."

"Yeah, Patrick?"

"Go in my pocket and fetch my teeth. Please. I don't wanna die without my teeth."

"You're not going to die, Pat. You'll be fine."

"Please Louie. I promised my Ma ..."

Irritated, Louie musters all the strength he can find. His stomach aches something fierce. He glances down and sees that his intestines are spilling out of his belly from a huge gaping wound. He pushes them back inside with one hand, holds them in place best he can, then he reaches into Patrick's pocket with bloody fingers, feels the hard porcelain of false teeth.

"Got them."

A shell bursts on the beach inches from Louie's head, splaying the round stones and water up in the air. All over the beach, men are screaming and dying. Overhead, aircraft engines howl. Machine-gun fire keeps up a continual lethal rhythm. Rat tat tat tat tat tat. There's the shrill cry of mortar shells falling to earth, the rumble of rocks giving way down cliff's edge. The smell of blood, smoke, saltwater, fear and death.

Louie shoves Patrick's teeth inside the blue stiff lips. Patrick is already dead, so it's hard for Louie to get the teeth properly in place. Patrick is being no help at all. Louie gives up, turns his attention to his open belly. The stony beach beneath him is deep red-black with his blood. It has a sweet smell. He needs a medic. He's going to have one helluva scar. Right across his belly. Geez. That'll sure impress the guys. He wonders what Sid will think.

Louie's other buddy, Jeremy, has no right leg. It's simply vanished. Jeremy lies on one side, staring at the blank space where his right leg used to be. Blood pours from the open wound, forming a large red-black puddle on the rocks. There is a gash in the side of his head. Shrapnel wound. A piece of metal protrudes from below his ear; he looks like a lopsided Frankenstein.

"Sid?" Louie says.

"What? No, it's Jeremy. Louie. Oh my God, Louie." Jeremy has noticed that Louie's guts are blown to bits. There's a big hole in the middle of his stomach. Shot clean through.

Louie can't focus. Where the hell is Sid? He was just here. The pain in his gut is unbearable. He is halfway unconscious.

"Oh Louie. Oh crap. Help! Somebody! Stretcher! Here!" Jeremy screams loud, but his voice is muffled under the shells, bombs, grenades, machine-gun fire, boats, planes, screams of dying and wounded men. Jeremy's shouts fade underneath it all.

"Sid? Let's get outa here," Louie suggests, through thick, bloody lips. He is blind. Can't see. Is it sand? Has he been hit in the eyes? Are his eyes closed? "Mama?"

"Son?"

Louie opens his eyes. He can see. It's a miracle. He focuses. It takes a minute. He knows the face. Captain John Foote, the Catholic padre with the Rileys — Lenny's regiment. Everyone knows Captain Foote. He made it a point in Aldershot to meet as many of the troops as time permitted. And before they left England they bowed their heads as he prayed for their safety. Then the Catholic boys took communion.

"Yessir." Louie's words are slurred. He's not sure where he is. At Manny's Delicatessen? In the back of his Pa's tailor shop? Sewing a pant cuff? Going over the books for his Pa? Maybe it's the Christie Pits riot again, and his head is being bashed. With a baseball bat. A merciful wooden bat. A headache. A bruise, and in the morning good as new. Louie turns his head to one side and vomits into the sand.

"What's your name, soldier?"

"Name?"

"Would you like last rites, son?"

"Last?"

"Rites? Are you Catholic, soldier? Protestant?"

"No." Louie looks past the padre and sees his mother. She's standing on the beach, half in and half out of the water, wearing a bright yellow dress, with beautiful flowers in her long dark hair. Red poppies. He hasn't seen her since he was ten years old. Before she died. Her smile penetrates Louie's heart. "Mama?"

"Yes, Lazar." She calls him by his Yiddish name. "*Tatelah.* Come to Mama."

"Mama?"

"Soldier?" The padre touches Louie's forehead. He's burning with fever.

"Come, my darling. I'll take care of you. Come to your Mama." She holds out her warm, generous arms. Louie folds himself into her soft embrace. Feels the warmth of her bosom. So full. So soft. Not angular and hard, like Papa. Not at all. Not like a hard rocky beach. More like a soft, sweet pillow. A *michaya*. An unexpected pleasure. Mama.

"You're of the Hebrew faith?"

"Yessir."

The padre strokes Louie's forehead, brushes the bloody hair from his face. "It's the same God, son." He begins last rites. In Latin. Sounds like Greek to Louie. Almost like Hebrew. His mother smiles, happy to see her baby after all this time.

"Come *Tatelah*."

"Yes, Mama."

"The Father, the Son, and the Holy Ghost."

"Come, Louie."

"Mama."

The padre closes the Hebrew soldier's eyes for the last time. A shell bursts to his left. He hits the dust. The groaning of Private Jeremy John Simpson calls to the padre.

He crawls over. The soldier's leg has been blown right off. He's losing blood rapidly.

"What's your name, son?"

"Louie?"

"Would you like last rites, soldier?"

"No, sir. I'm fine, sir. Our objective is to hold the beach, sir. Oh." Jeremy looks around, distraught. "I've lost my gun, sir. Where's my gun?"

"It's okay, son. I'll find it for you."

"Our objective, sir … ."

"Yes …" gently the padre covers Jeremy's body with his own, as the shells burst around them.

"If you could just help me up, sir."

"Certainly, soldier. In a minute …"

"My leg! I can't feel it."

"You're gonna be fine, soldier. Look into my eyes, son."

"My leg!"

"My eyes, son."

Jeremy stares hard into the padre's eyes. He hears the excruciating roar of another shell. Captain Foote covers Jeremy with his body. As the bombs burst, as machine-gun fire rips on all sides, as Allied and enemy aircraft tear through the sky, Jeremy dies under the warm embrace of the padre. Captain Foote blocks his ears to the screams. His men need him. He can't hear the screams. He sees only the men. He closes Private Jeremy Simpson's eyes and crawls on his belly to the next casualty.

Boys With No Heads
THIRTY MINUTES LATER

LENNY'S COMPANY OF THE Royal Hamilton Light Infantry bob in their landing craft, scheduled to hit the main beach half an hour after Louie's Royal regiments. From the boat they can't see much. Only those at the bow can see the beach, behind smoke. But they know that something is terribly wrong. The buildings sheltering German defence are standing. They expected to see only rubble from the Royal Air Force bombings of the previous night, which were supposed to crush the German defence on the beach. This was supposed to be a breeze. Involving more than 6,000 men of the combined forces — infantrymen, air and naval support. They were going to surprise the Germans before sunrise, take as many prisoners as possible, destroy specific targets of the German stronghold, then fall back across the channel later in the day. A quick and dirty raid, to show the Germans their strength.

But everything is still standing. Even the windows in the buildings are intact. They can see a rocky beach backed by a high concrete seawall. An ominous castle overlooks the beach and the cliffs are dotted with caves.

Major Christopher Brentwall, commanding officer of the Rileys' D Company, is concerned. There are lots of great spots along that cliff for German defence positions. Overlooking the beach like that. High on the cliffs. The Jerries would be watching his landing craft heading to shore. With binoculars, his boat could easily be sighted and the Germans have superior field glasses. Major Brentwall is deeply concerned. Is he leading his men on a suicide mission?

Lenny stands in the back beside Lance Corporal Charlie Bain and Private William Spiggot. The men are excited. Finally, after all the months of training, they are going to see some action. Lenny's heart pounds in his chest. Perspiration gathers in his thick brown hair inside his tin helmet and drips down the sides of his face and the back of his neck. He's not sure he will be able to actually kill another man. *Even a lousy stinking fascist Kraut.* Not if he has to look into the man's eyes. Lenny keeps this thought to himself. It's not the sort of thing you tell your buddies just before going into battle.

Their boat has drifted behind the others. They are going to be late. The sun is rising. The Royal regiments, Louie's battalion, should have secured the beach at Puys by now. The Rileys' job is to clear the main beach, code-named White Beach. It should be a breeze. They should be back in England in time for supper, telling each other battle stories. They've been promised an extra rum ration this evening when they get home.

The boat has stopped. The landing ramp drops down. Machine-gun fire rips across the vessel and on all sides. The order is given to disembark. "Move it! Move it!" Lenny nods at Charlie as they follow their company down the ramp, into waist-high water. They wade as fast as they can to shore, feeling the ping of gunfire hitting the water all around them. They are luckier than the Royal regiments. They make it pretty much intact through the water and onto the beach. The barbed wire has been flattened by the earlier troops. Following Major Brentwall, they run like hell. Their objective is to knock out enemy positions, including a hotel, a post office, Gestapo headquarters and a casino. Lenny can see the casino up ahead, a stucco, three-storey building about 250 feet long, already partly demolished by the Germans. Machine-gun fire from the upper windows strafes the company, shattering rocks, echoing up through the soles of Lenny's feet to his chest, which thumps so rapidly he's sure he's going to have a heart attack. Mortar and machine-gun fire from above is intense and accurate. The soldier beside Lenny, Private Benjamin Boulton, is hit in the leg and goes down. Lenny clutches Ben around the waist, is dragging him along when a second shot rips through Private Boulton's abdomen and he falls to the pebbled beach.

The major yells for them to run faster. Lenny leans Ben against the cliff face, where he hopes he'll be safe until the medics come, then he follows in the dash to the building, where the soldiers flatten themselves against the wall as mortar shells burst around them. His back smashed against the brick, Lenny glances back down at the beach for the first time. The ground is littered with dead and dying Allied soldiers. He sees a Canadian landing craft that has been blown apart. Severed body parts of an entire platoon are piled inside the shattered boat, on top of exploded weapons; the boat is filled with blood and guts. The stench of death rises in the air. It looks like most of the men in the Royal regiment are casualties. Lenny can see that they never had a chance, never even stepped off the boat before they were mowed down. He is sure he is going to die here. Scattered about the beach, with broken treads and stuck in anti-tank ditches, are dozens of the British Churchill tanks that were supposed to provide the infantry with support. Lenny notices that one has been burned from inside. Its driver's charred body dangles over one edge of the small round entry hole, as if still trying to escape. From one tank, which is stuck at a forty-five-degree angle in a ditch, its tracks busted and falling off, an injured gunner fires toward the German defences on the cliff. Lying in a heap under the cliff face are scores of dead Royal regiment soldiers. Hit by artillery fire, they are limbless and headless. Lenny sees a boot with a foot still inside, a severed head and arms lying about. One corpse is a torso and head only, everything below the navel blown off, intestines trailing from the open wound in a deep puddle of blood. Lenny stares, the horror of it registering in his brain.

The major gives the order to advance farther inside the casino. Lenny is paralyzed with fear. He stands stiffly, his hands clutching his rifle so tightly, his circulation is being cut off.

"Lenny!" Charlie shouts, his face an inch away from Lenny's.

"Oh God."

"Lenny. Come on."

"No hands, or legs …"

Charlie hauls back one hand and slaps Lenny across the face, hard as he can. "Come on, damn it. You wanna die here?!" He grabs Lenny by one arm and roughly pushes him forward. Lenny breathes and runs with his friend. They look round the doorway inside the casino. He sees an ornate lobby leading out to gaming rooms. Directly in front, men from their company are exchanging gunfire with a small platoon of Jerries. Charlie aims his gun and sprays machine-gun fire. Lenny snaps into automatic, as he was trained to do, and pulls the trigger. Rage rises in him. He wants revenge, for all the dead men on the beach. He fires with a fury. He sees Germans falling. There's a scream directly beside him. He glances, keeps shooting. Private Spiggot clutches his chest and falls to the ground.

"Bill's been hit!"

Charlie and Lenny grab Private Spiggot under his arms, drag him forward. Another stray bullet catches Spiggot, tearing off half his scalp, exposing his brain, grey and soft. The Major screams to leave him, he's dead. Nothing they can do for him now. Shocked, Lenny and Charlie drop their buddy's arms. His body crumples to the floor in a heap, blood and brains oozing from the hole in his head. Bile rises in Lenny's throat. He vomits quickly onto the floor. Wipes his mouth, carries on.

The Major signals for them to move forward and they scramble into the next room, where they are met with fire from the retreating Germans. Room by room they inch their way through the casino, easily overrunning the small group of Germans protecting the building. Lenny figures Jerry wasn't expecting them to get this far; they've left the casino vulnerable. Lenny and Charlie follow the Major out into the streets. A mortar shell explodes the second their feet hit the cobblestones. The Major and three others are blown sky-high. Their bodies land in bits and pieces. A forearm here. A foot there. An empty tin helmet. Charlie, Lenny, and the remaining men of their company hit the deck, then scramble on bellies to the edge of a wall, where they take turns sniping at the Germans who are dug into narrow slit trenches above them on the cliff's edge.

"It's no use," Charlie says. As Lance Corporal, he's now the commanding officer. "Withdraw," he orders, tossing a grenade to give them a few seconds, then he dashes back the way they came, with Lenny hot on his heels, through the casino, outside to the beach, where they discover that a full withdrawal has been ordered. They run for the water, where under a smokescreen from the carriers, battered landing boats wait to take the survivors to the ships that will carry them back to England. Lenny follows Charlie, stumbling over the dead and wounded. The beach is hell. Pieces of men's bodies, severed limbs, are strewn all over the sand. The dead are washing ashore. The water is red with their blood as the tide goes out. The sweet sticky scent of blood and burning flesh catches in Lenny's throat. If there was anything left in his stomach, he would vomit again. Fires burn in disabled Allied tanks. Smoke obliterates everything. Lenny splashes through the water like a madman, and though he doesn't know it, he runs right past the body of Private Louie Jacob Horowitz, who lies in a pool of blood, his guts now free of the confines of his abdomen.

The relentless roar of shells bursting, planes buzzing overhead and machine-gun fire merges in a thunderous cacophony of noise. Lenny and Charlie wade into the ocean waist-deep, and slog their way to a landing craft. They embark quickly, as they had practised in England. Lenny feels the relief of British steel under his feet. Men from a variety of Canadian regiments, along with several British soldiers, crowd the boat to dangerously full. The landing ramp is raised. Ocean water sloshes over the top, soaking them, stinging saltwater on their wounds. The motor chugs full-steam ahead. Lenny notices a sharp sudden pain in his hand. The tip of one finger has been shot off. Blood pours down his wrist. He didn't even notice the hit. It momentarily shocks him, then he realizes it's nothing. A fingertip he can live without. Could have been much worse. He's seen what becomes of boys with no heads. He passed by quite a few on his way back to the water. Boys without arms, legs and torsos. Above in the sky, the roar of aircraft. The sweet sound of the boat's motor carrying them to safety. Lenny clamps a wet handkerchief tightly around the wounded finger. He checks Charlie, who seems to be all in one piece, except for a deep gash on one cheek. They are covered in nicks and scrapes on their faces and hands, from the shattered bits of stone thrown from the force of shells bursting. Lenny and Charlie look into one another's eyes, two men sharing an experience that can find no words. Well, maybe one word: Horror. There's no room to sit in the crowded boat, so the soldiers lean against each other, holding each other up, rocking with the waves. No one says a word.

Miscarriage of Justice
NOVEMBER 1942

RUTHIE FINISHES WASHING the last breakfast plate and puts it in the drainer to dry. She reaches for the dishtowel and a cramp sears her abdomen. She clutches her belly and leans forward. Drops of blood splatter the tile floor. Something is ripping her insides apart. She reaches for the phone.

In his office a few hours later, Dr. Grossman tells Ruthie and Sid the miscarriage was inevitable.

"Sometimes it's for the best," he tries to reassure a stricken Ruthie. "Sometimes in a case like this the baby wouldn't have survived."

"What was wrong with him?" Sid asks, his eyes wet with tears, his hand on Ruthie's back.

"I can't really say, but a miscarriage at five months means something was wrong. God has a way of taking care of these things. The body too. Believe me, Ruthie, a stillborn baby is worse."

"Stillborn?" Ruthie is dazed. She imagines giving birth to a dead baby and her eyes flood with tears again.

"I'm prescribing iron tablets, extra bed rest, and for the pain, an analgesic powder. You take it with water."

Dr. Grossman writes a prescription. Sid brushes roughly at his eyes. Ruthie stares straight ahead, in shock. The pain in her heart is far worse than the pain in her uterus. This is her third miscarriage and this time she was so sure she would carry to term. She had begun singing to the baby, getting it used to her voice. She thought she'd felt it kick once or twice. She was sure she could feel it growing inside of her. Now, the baby has been torn mercilessly from her womb. No amount of medicine will soothe the pain. Ruthie knows she would be such a good mother. Why is this happening to her?

Ruthie was almost five months along, but she feels the same grief as if she'd buried a child. Over the next few weeks, she has to force herself out of bed in the mornings. Once awake, she can't stop crying. Every time she sees a woman pushing a baby carriage, the hole in her heart aches. She's barely managed to cook a decent meal since the miscarriage, relying on food Sophie has been bringing over. But it's not fair to Sid, who has to go to work even though he feels like God has forsaken him too. Finally, Ruthie drags herself from the apartment to the market, where she picks up some potatoes, carrots and onions to go with the chicken Sid brought home yesterday. She's going to fix a nice dinner tonight if it kills her. She trudges up the stairs to their third-floor apartment with her cloth shopping bag, turns the corner and is surprised to see Sam Horowitz standing by her apartment door, leaning against the wall, hat in his hand. He looks pale and exhausted.

"Mr. Horowitz?" Ruthie leans toward him.

He looks up at her slowly. His face is a picture of anguish. He raises one hand. In it is a crumpled telegram.

"Mr. Horowitz? What is it?" Ruthie's heart pounds. She knows what the telegram says, doesn't have to read it. She can see it in his face. There's no other look like it.

He shoves the telegram toward her. His hand shakes. Gently, she pries it from his grasp and smoothes out the thin paper. It's from the Department of National Defence, addressed to Mr. Sam Horowitz, of Manning Avenue, Toronto, Ontario.

REGRET TO ADVISE THAT YOUR SON HOROWITZ, LOUIS JACOB,
PRIVATE, IS REPORTED KILLED IN ACTIVE SERVICE OVERSEAS,
IN DIEPPE, FRANCE, ON AUGUST NINETEEN, NINETEEN
HUNDRED FORTY-TWO STOP LETTER FOLLOWS

"Oh, Mr. Horowitz. Oh. Terrible news. I'm so sorry. Please, come inside. I'll make tea. Sid will be home soon."

"No." He snatches the telegram from her grasp and staggers down the hall, grief-stricken. Ruthie watches helplessly.

SID SLUMPS ON THE living room couch, head in his hands.

"Oh God. What did it say?" His big brown eyes fill with tears. He removes his glasses, loosens his tie, fishes in his pocket for his white cotton handkerchief.

"He was killed in action. In France. I forget what it said. Dipper. Or somewhere like that."

"Dieppe?" Sid had read about the terrible military blunder. The Canadian troops' first entry into active battle was a slaughterhouse. Everything went wrong. There were over three thousand causalities, out of five thousand men. He was praying Louie would be one of the survivors, but a part of him knew that his friend had fallen. He'd had a dream on the day it happened. Louie had come to him in sleep. He was smiling. His face was bloody from battle, but he was happy in the dream. As if he'd come to reassure Sid.

"Yes. That's it." Ruthie remembers now. "Dieppe."

"Oh my God." Sid leans forward, elbows on knees, head in hands, his glasses dangling from two fingers. If Sid had been accepted into the army, he'd have been on that beach with Louie. Ruthie might be sitting here today reading a telegram about his death.

"Oh Sid. He was your best friend." She sits beside him on the couch, runs her hand over his tear-stained cheek.

Sid stands abruptly, grabs his hat from the coffee table. "I better go see Mr. Horowitz. Louie was his only son. He has no one now."

"Should I come with you?" Ruthie asks.

"I better go alone." Sid stumbles outside in a daze.

Called Up

MARCH 1944

SONNY'S NOTICE FROM the Department of Defence arrives near the beginning of 1944. Loretta holds it out in front of her, hands shaking. They both know what the letter says. She'd been praying that Sonny wouldn't get called up, that the war would end before he had to go. Now she will be all alone with the baby and she is terrified.

Sonny rips open the letter. He is to report for training at the Canadian National Exhibition grounds in twenty-one days. The end of April.

"Geez." Sonny tosses the letter onto the table. "Just a few blocks downtown."

"But after that they could send you anywhere, right Sonny?"

"Home defence only. They can't ship me overseas unless I volunteer for active duty. And I ain't gonna volunteer, Loretta. Don't worry."

"But they could send you anywhere in Canada."

"I guess."

"It's a big country, Sonny." They could send him all the way to Vancouver, or Halifax. It's a long journey by train or bus. How will she manage with Sonny gone? They sit in silence side by side on the couch for a while. The baby is sleeping in her crib in the bedroom.

Sonny is thinking about his family. Besides Aunt Tess, bless her heart, and Lenny and Sid, he hasn't seen anyone since he married Loretta. He knows his father won't see him, but he wants to see his mother and Izzy. He's tried to see Izzy since he was banished, but it's tricky. Izzy is always with one of his parents. What if Sonny gets sent to Halifax or Vancouver, or somewhere far from home? What if the Nazis attack? Or the Japanese?

There are dangers involved. Even in home defence. He's got to see his mother and Izzy once more before he goes.

Sonny waits until he is sure his father will be at work. Then he walks the four blocks to his old neighbourhood.

IT'S A BLUSTERY MARCH morning, but Izzy stands faithfully in the queue at Tanenbaum's Grocery. He has been there for two hours. Sophie asked him to try and get some tea. They haven't been able to buy any in more than two weeks, despite their ration coupon for a pound of tea. Even through his mysterious "business associate," Yacov hasn't been able to buy any tea lately. Sophie has been reusing the same old tea leaves. Yacov hasn't complained as the tea becomes weaker and weaker, but Sophie can only stretch the meagre leaves so far. Besides, waiting in line gives Izzy something to do. A mission. He feels as if he's contributing.

Mr. Tanenbaum sticks his head out the door of his shop and announces that he's just received a shipment of sugar.

"Please keep the line in an orderly fashion," he adds, a little nervous. He read in the newspaper that last week at O'Malley's, a small grocery store on Bloor Street, there was a fight between two young men over the last pound of sugar. Nobody was seriously hurt, but the police had to be called and an entire display of packaged wheat germ was knocked over in the altercation. Tanenbaum prays that nothing like that happens in his store.

Izzy holds his place in the line. He is supposed to buy tea. He doesn't know what to do. Mama didn't say anything about sugar. Just tea. He will just have to wait until Mr. Tanenbaum calls tea. His feet are freezing, but he doesn't want to go home without the tea, so he waits in his spot. A dry snow begins to fall, swirling with a brisk wind. Izzy hops from one foot to the other to keep warm.

On College Street, a streecar rumbles past, metal wheels screeching on the tracks as the driver brakes at the bus stop. The back door hisses, then swings open as passengers disembark, stepping over dirty grey-brown snowbanks at the curb. Izzy watches with interest as the breadman steers his white horse to the right of the streetcar tracks and up and over the curb. His wagon wheels slip and slide dangerously on the icy road. The horse clip clops along as a black car swerves, honking its horn noisily as it speeds by. The breadman pulls back the reins on the horse to steady her. She has a black blinder on either side of her face to keep her from getting spooked. Izzy puts a hand on either side of his face to see what the world would look like through blinders. The trees along College Street are barren. Izzy looks through the branches of a tree to the pale blue sky and decides the cloud behind looks like a giant loaf of bread. He realizes he's hungry. His stomach growls angrily. He already ate the piece of bread his mother gave him on the way out of the house.

Three teenage boys arrive and shove into the line in front of Izzy.

"Hey," Izzy says.

The boys turn around and face him. They are a year or two older, not much bigger but years smarter and buckets meaner. "What'sa matter retard? Got a problem?" one boy says, moving right up so that his nose is in Izzy's face.

"I was here," Izzy says quietly.

The boys laugh. "Ya hear that guys? The retard says he was here." He turns back to Izzy, grabs the collar of his jacket. "So what are ya going to do about it, Retard?"

Izzy doesn't know what he is going to do about it. His eyes well up with tears. Behind him in the line stands an old woman, who shakes her head, but says nothing.

"Huh?" the bully challenges, his hand still grasping Izzy by the jacket. "I said what are ya gonna do about it?"

"He's gonna pop you one in the kisser," answers a young man's voice from behind them. The boy lets go of Izzy, wheels around.

"Sonny!" shouts Izzy. "Sonny, Sonny, Sonny."

The boys back away, scared out of their minds. Everyone knows Sonny "The Charger" Lapinsky, the boxer. His picture's in the newspaper all the time.

Sonny grabs the bully by his jacket and picks him up, right off his feet. "That's my brother you're bothering," he tells the bully. The kid's two friends run off down the street.

"I didn't know. I'm sorry," the bully sputters.

"You think that makes you a big man? Picking on a guy who's defenceless?"

"No Sir."

"What?"

"No Sir."

"No Sir, what?"

"No Sir, it doesn't make me a big man," the bully squeaks.

"That's right." Sonny thrusts the boy against the brick wall of the building, so that the back of his head bangs against the wall. "You know what it makes you? It makes you a yellow coward." He drops the kid to the ground. "If I ever see you so much as breathe on my brother, I'm gonna personally send you to the moon." Sonny holds his right fist menacingly in the bully's face. "Now go on. Scram." The kid cowers against the wall, afraid to make a move. "Go on. Beat it," Sonny repeats. The kid squeezes past Sonny and runs down the street in the direction of his friends, slipping once on an ice patch, then scrambling to his feet and running off. Sonny turns his attention to Izzy. He can't believe how big he's grown in the past year and half. At fifteen, Izzy is two inches taller than Sonny, and big-boned like Sid.

"You all right, buddy?"

Izzy nods. His lips are blue, his cheeks bright red. Sonny wonders how long his brother has been standing in line.

Suddenly he grabs Sonny in a bear hug. "Sonny. You were gone."

"Izzy. Take it easy. You're gonna crush me. Geez." Sonny smiles, flattered with Izzy's enthusiasm. "I missed you, too. I wanted to come and see you, but Pop's mad at me."

"I know," agrees Izzy. "Pop's very mad."

"Yeah? What does he say?" Now Sonny's a little scared to go home.

"Pop's mad."

Sonny nods. He's not going to get any more news out of Izzy. It's now or never. And his father will be at work. No way he's going into the army without seeing his mother one more time. "Come on, I'll take you home."

"Gotta get tea," Izzy pleads, afraid to leave without completing his mission.

"It's okay, Iz. They don't have any tea today. You try again tomorrow. Come on, your feet must be freezing." Sonny throws an arm around his brother and leads him out of the line.

Izzy remembers how cold his feet are and looks down. "Oh yeah," he says, happy to be alongside Sonny. They clomp along the hard frozen ground as snow floats down, collecting on their caps and shoulders. The biting chill of the wind brings tears to Sonny's eyes. He reaches over and flips Izzy's collar up around his neck. Sonny feels sick inside. What would have happened to Izzy if he hadn't come along?

THE FRONT DOOR of his parents' house is never locked. Sonny pushes open the door. Izzy flies inside and up the stairs.

"Sonny's home, Sonny's home, Sonny's home," he announces, running into the kitchen. Sonny climbs the stairs to the apartment and stops at the top. Sophie is kneeling on the floor, a bucket of soapy water by her side, scrub brush in her hand. She's not paying attention to Izzy, who often thinks he sees Sonny walking down the street. It's just wishful thinking. Sophie hums along with a Lux soap suds commercial playing on the radio, as she scrubs the hardwood floor by hand. Sonny watches her for a moment. She looks tired, but beautiful as always. Behind her, a load of damp laundry is piled in its basket, waiting to be hung on the line.

"Hi Ma," Sonny says gently, not wanting to scare her.

Sophie looks up. "Oh," she says and drops the brush into the bucket. She stands up, holds out her arms. Sonny moves forward and embraces his mother.

"Oh Sonny." Tears gather in Sophie's eyes and fall down her cheeks.

"Ma," he pulls away. "I'm going into the army."

Sophie's hand flies to her mouth. "Oh no."

"Don't worry Ma. I'm staying in the country. Home defence. I'm not even leaving the city yet. I have to report for training at the Exhibition Grounds. But that's it, so far."

"Home defence?"

"Yeah, you know — they'll send me to Vancouver, or maybe Halifax.

Maybe even stay right here. Or end up on a farm in Saskatchewan, or somewhere. Guarding the cows." He flashes his mother his trademark grin.

"Oh." She is relieved. That doesn't sound too dangerous. She hasn't heard from Lenny in a while. He's over there somewhere. England, last she heard. She can't even imagine him holding a gun, or throwing a bomb. The curse of sons. Sophie fishes in the sleeve of her sweater for the cotton handkerchief, one of Yacov's she uses to wipe her face.

"So, I wanted to say good-bye, to you and Izzy."

"Your father's at work."

"I know, Ma. I came now on purpose. Pop don't want to see me."

She sighs. "You should only give him some more time, Sonny. That's all. A little more time he needs."

"No, Ma. I don't think more time will help." Sonny's voice breaks.

Sophie smiles faintly. "Believe me, Shmuel. I've known your father a little longer than you. Stubborn he is, but … .in time …"

"Ma. You heard what he said. I'm dead to him. He said Kaddish. I did the worse thing."

"The worse thing it isn't."

"To him it's the worse thing."

Sophie nods. She doesn't approve of mixed marriages either, but Sonny is still her child. She can't disown him.

"Tell me about her, Sonny. Your wife. What's she like? And the baby?"

"Really Ma? You really want to know?"

"I just asked, didn't I? Come on, sit down. I'll make us some tea. A little weak, but hot."

"I don't think …"

"Don't worry. Your father won't be home for hours. Please, Sonny. Sit with us for a while before you go."

"OK, Ma." Sonny grabs the blackened teakettle, fills it with water from the faucet.

"Tell me about the baby." Sophie sets the silver samovar onto the table. The overused tea leaves float on the inch of cold water in its glass bottom.

LATER, SONNY EMBRACES his mother at the front door.

"Do you have a warm coat, Sonny?" Sophie asks as Sonny turns to leave.

"Ma, I'll be in uniform. The army will give me everything. A jacket and a woollen greatcoat."

"Oh, of course. All right. Well, don't forget to wear it, then."

"I won't. So long, Ma." Sonny steps off the porch, then turns back to face her. "I'll write you. I'll send the letters to Sid's place. Ruthie can bring them over when Pa's at work. Okay?"

"Okay. *Zy Gezunt,* Sonny." Be well.

"Bye Ma. Come on big guy. Walk me down the street," he says to Izzy.

"Okay Ma?" Izzy asks.

"Go on. Walk your brother home. Go see his new apartment, Izzy."

"Really Ma?" Sonny is touched.

Sophie nods. "I love you, sweetheart."

"I love you, Ma." There's a huge lump in Sonny's throat. He swallows hard. "Come on, Iz. Race you to the corner."

Sophie watches as the boys run down the street. Sonny is still a boy, barely a young man, and already he has the responsibilities of a husband and father. She hopes he can cope. There is a brisk winter chill in the air. She shivers, then she turns and walks slowly back up the stairs, to finish the laundry. She'll have to hang the damp clothes to dry in the kitchen, on a string suspended over the stove.

LORETTA IS SULLEN as she watches Sonny pack his army-issue duffle bag. Even the baby seems upset, lying in her crib and fussing.

"Come on, Loretta. Don't be sad. You know I got no choice. Anyway it's only for a few months."

She throws her arms around Sonny, pushes her face into that sweet spot, between his neck and shoulders, where she feels safe and protected, where he smells like shaving cream and Ivory soap and his own scent. "I know, Sonny. I just don't want you to go. How am I gonna manage without you?"

"I'll send you money every week, and Ruthie'll help out." He kisses her cheek. "Come on, Loretta, don't cry." He pulls her tightly to him, his arms around the small of her back, protectively.

"I'm scared. What if something happens to you?"

"I'll be fine. I promise."

Sonny pulls his young wife down onto the bed and they make love with a desperation, like two people who know they may never see each other again or that when they do, everything will be entirely different.

Zombies

APRIL 1944, TORONTO

FOR SONNY, TRAINING CAMP is a breeze. The obstacle course, the rope-climbing that had given Lenny such a hard time, is child's play to Sonny. He enters the campgrounds at the Canadian National Exhibition in peak physical condition. Compared to his usual training, the athletics expected of Sonny here are different, but easy as pie. Sonny is used to lying on his back having a hard medicine ball slammed into his abdomen. He can run ten miles, twenty miles a day, all day if you want, and not be winded. He can jump rope for hours and never miss a beat. You can punch him in the gut and hurt your hand. He can dodge any fist, roll under it like nothing and counter with a hard uppercut or a straight right, toss a combination faster than machine-gun fire. He can carry the fifty-pound sack, the rifle, extra ammo, and dart through tires spread out on the ground, go back to the start and do it again. With ease. He can climb the rope in twenty seconds. He could do it with one hand tied behind his back if he had to. Sonny can do everything the army asks him to do, effortlessly. He is promoted to Lance Corporal after the first month and put in charge of training the men. Getting them into shape. What a joke. Four weeks and he's already a Corporal.

Sonny doesn't really care what stripe they sew onto his arm. He doesn't care what task they assign him to. He doesn't even mind the tasteless grub served in huge communal mess buildings. He doesn't notice the barnyard smells of the barracks or the crowded conditions of the washrooms.

He just wants to get the hell out of here. He wants to serve his mandatory three months and get back to his boxing career. Three months is a long time to be away from Rudy and his training regime, so to keep in boxing condition, Sonny wakes early every morning and runs through camp before breakfast. He jumps rope, does his push-ups and sit-ups, and stretches while the other guys are still in bed. He seeks out and finds a couple of other amateur boxers and in their off-duty hours, they spar to keep in condition. He doesn't want to go soft in the army.

Sonny and the other soldiers serving their mandatory conscription duties at home are nicknamed "Zombies" by the men who've volunteered for active duty. "Zombies" are scorned by the boys ready to risk their lives overseas. Some are shamed by the stigma into signing up. Others, like Sonny, couldn't care less what the other guys call him. No way he's volunteering for overseas duty. His brother Lenny's over there doing the patriotic thing. That's enough for one family. Besides, what did England ever do for him? Sonny's got a wife and a baby and a career to get back to. Let those other *schmucks* get their heads blown off on some stinking battlefield over there. *Go ahead and call me anything you want,* he thinks. *Doesn't bother me. Soon, you'll all be calling me Champ.*

The Company of **Men**
APRIL TO JULY, 1944
ALDERSHOT, ENGLAND

AFTER THE RAID ON DIEPPE, the surviving soldiers of the Royal Hamilton Light Infantry are stationed back at the Hampshire Military Base in Aldershot to regroup. The most seriously wounded were sent home as soon as they could travel. They were followed by the moderately wounded. Men who left limbs or other vital body parts on the beach in France were, of course, honourably discharged. And the men who came back crazy, the ones who couldn't shake the sound of enemy aircraft buzzing in their brain, shells exploding by their sides, or the sight of their best buddy blown apart in front of their eyes, they too were put on a freighter to Halifax. The others, those with minor wounds, the survivors, are sent back to the base in England for more training.

Throughout 1943, training intensifies for Lenny and the other Canadians in England. They scale obstacles, clear minefields, embark and disembark as they did before Dieppe, this time in Bracklesham Bay on England's south coast. They crawl under wire, jump into cold water, grab for ropes, pull themselves up rocks while waves crash one hundred feet below. They are being prepared this time, for all possibilities. All conditions. They are being readied for a second coordinated attack on occupied France. By the spring of 1944, almost three million soldiers, Americans, Canadians, British, Australians and New Zealanders, are training in the English countryside.

To remember Dieppe, the men are given more demanding and realistic training

To forget Dieppe, the men are given frequent leave. In London's many pubs they drink warm, wartime, watered-down British ale, with local girls sitting on their knees, who later, in drafty flats and rooming houses, will lie beneath them. Lenny drinks the watery ale but is seldom seen fraternizing with girls. He prefers the company of men. A specific man to be exact: Lance Corporal Charles Geoffrey Bain Jr. Charlie loves his buddy Lenny like a brother, especially after Dieppe, but Charlie also loves girls. All girls. Any girl. And girls love Charlie. His sky-blue eyes, and blond boyish hair, broad shoulders, perfect smile, athletic body and Corporal's stripes attract all the prettiest girls in the tavern. When Charlie and Lenny go together to the pub, more often than not Lenny ends up sitting alone nursing an ale, while Charlie is off with his latest English lass. The girls, having lived through the bombing of London, are well-versed in living in the moment. Later they could be dead. They spent most of the summer of 1940 in the underground tube, growing slowly used to the constant rumble and explosions during the London blitz, then after the bombing stopped, dashing home to find their homes in rubble, or their Mummies and Da's, their sisters and brothers, dead, or missing, or maimed. They know how precarious life can be. One second you could be walking home from your shift at the armaments factory, the next you could be buried alive under a pile of Victorian or even Edwardian bricks. The girls of London don't require a uniform to be in the front lines. They have been there. And back. By the spring of 1944, the deepest desire of every young English girl is to get the bloody hell out of England. To be engaged to a Canadian would be grand. Charlie has his share of invitations. Even Lenny is constantly propositioned. Being a virgin and not particularly aroused, he politely declines, although he has many times bought a few rounds with his army pay, delighted by the conversation. In his unusual way, he charms the girls with his lack of lust for them and the are relieved to enjoy the company of a man who doesn't only want one thing from them. The girls nickname him Cary Grant, because he is witty and a gentleman to boot. Then Charlie returns and together they make their way back home.

IN ALDERSHOT IN THE EARLY SUMMER, new recruits pour into the base every day. These boys are fresh-faced and ready for action. They can't wait to be sent to the front. Unlike the Dieppe veterans, they are sure that death is something that will happen to others — not themselves or their friends. Lenny would like to inform them otherwise, but there's no use. He knows they wouldn't listen.

June 5, 1944

Dear Ma, Pop and Izzy,

I'm in the same place I was last time I wrote. I'm not allowed to say any more, but I know you'll figure it out. We've been here a long time. Something is going to change soon. We can all feel it, but secrecy is of the utmost, so we at the bottom — I'm still just a Private — know nothing really. But everyone figures we're going back. And this time we're going to beat the Nazis. Don't worry. This time we'll win.

I feel like my whole life is ready to bloom. I've grown up and become a man since I've been here. I have had lots of time to think these last months. I have so much I'd like to tell you, but

somehow writing my thoughts on paper isn't enough. When I get
home I know opportunities will be there for me. Things I couldn't
do before, I can do now. That's all for now because we've been
told to hit the hay early. Something's up for the morning I think.

Your loving son, Lenny

Lenny stuffs the letter into an envelope and addresses it. Sitting beside
him on the ground outside the barracks is Charlie, who is also finishing
a letter to his folks back home in Toronto. Lenny slips two cigarettes
from his pack, lights both, hands one to Charlie, who looks up from his
writing and smiles as he accepts the cigarette. They've been kept out of
battle since Dieppe. Training and preparing. Dismantling and cleaning
their guns. Getting through inspection. Dismantling and cleaning them
again. Shining their shoes. Darning their socks. They've been marched
on ten-, twenty- and thirty-mile hikes throughout the English countryside. Marched until their feet no longer bleed, callused as they are, and
their army boots need replacing. They practise crossing the River Trent.
They learn how to get across stretches of deep, clinging mud when they
leave their assault boats at low tide. The River Trent has plenty of mud
and they sink waist deep into it and have to be pulled free with ropes.
They train wading chest-high in freezing water, with heavy equipment,
holding their guns high above their heads. They're assaulted with blank
bullets and strafed with blank mortar shells to get them used to loud
sounds. The Sarge screams at them. *Go go go go go!* when they stall.

Other Canadian regiments have been involved in the Italian campaign, but their battalion is being held in reserve for something big.
They've been training intensively, just like before Dieppe, only more
fiercely, with better equipment, and more efficient planning. They've
practised landing on a beach, slithering on bellies across sand, how to
stop snipers, how to keep from being hit while running forward. The
army has developed new specially designed armoured fighting vehicles:
flail tanks to clear paths through minefields; the amphibian "Alligator," a
tank that can float in deep waters and drive on land; upgraded landing
craft that will better protect the infantry on their way to shore.

Charlie thinks they're going back to France, maybe even Dieppe again, but no one knows for sure. The troops are kept in the dark until the moment they're shipped out. Lenny watches Charlie write while he smokes. Strange. Even as they are about to go back to battle, Lenny feels a sense of peace he's never felt before.

July 16, 1944

Dear Ma, Pop and Izzy,

I guess you've read in the papers by now all about D-Day and the invasion of Normandy. I wasn't there, so don't worry. Our company is being held back for some other mission, although I don't know what yet. And even if I did, I couldn't tell you. The Jerries have spies everywhere. There might even be some in Toronto at the post office who could go through my letters to you. Makes you think, doesn't it?

My best pal Charlie and I are going into business together when we get home. I don't know what exactly yet, but I've got plenty of ideas and Charlie's got money back home. Plus I've got $107 in my pay packet right now, and if I'm here for another year I'll have $243. Maybe I'll even go to college. Wouldn't that be swell? It would sure be nice to see everybody. It feels like I've been in England forever. In a way, I guess I have.

I've enclosed a photograph of me and Charlie, taken on the training base. You can see I'm fine and healthy, so don't worry about me. I know you'll worry anyways, but I promise I'll make it back home to you. I have so many plans for my future. I just have to come home.

Your loving son,
Lenny

Lenny folds the letter in perfect quarters and carefully places it inside his kit bag. Tomorrow, he'll drop it off to be mailed.

JULY 17, 0500. Sergeant James Miller enters Lenny's barracks, switches on the overhead light and wakes the company. The men are told to dress quickly in battledress and report to the mess tent, where they are fed a hearty hot breakfast.

"Eat. Even if you're not hungry," the sergeant warns. "Could be the last hot grub you get for a while."

Lenny's stomach is tied up in knots. Flashes of the beach at Dieppe pass though his mind. The severed bodies, dead and dying boys strewn over the beach, the screams, the noise, the godforsaken infernal racket of shells and machine-gun fire, the planes, tanks. Rumbling. Exploding. Dive-bombing. He can hear it all inside his head. It's the sound that sticks with you, even more than the gruesome and bloody sights. Or the smell of burning flesh and flowing blood. The scrambled eggs taste like lead, but he forces down as much as he can.

At 0630, they are sailing across the Channel back to France. On the lower deck, Lenny's company is briefed on their objectives. The Allies have command of all of the Normandy coastline and are now pushing their way through the German defence in France. Lenny's company of Rileys are part of the 2ND Canadian Corps. Their commander, Lieutenant-Colonel John Rockingham, known affectionately as Rocky, is tough, determined and loved by his men. "Rocky's Rileys," they call themselves. Some, like Lenny and Charlie, are Dieppe veterans, hardened experienced soldiers now. Others are new reinforcements, inexperienced but fresh and excited about finally being in action. They are trucked to the front lines, the town of Caen. German anti-tank guns and mortars control the area south of Caen. The country there is open, with a series of low ridges that rise as high as three hundred metres near Falaise. From the ridges, German mortar fire has been pulverizing the advancing Canadians.

0300 JULY 19. Lenny falls in line with Charlie by his side. They're in battle-dress, tin helmets strapped under their chins; fifty-pound backpack carrying extra ammo, grenades, K rations on their backs; the smaller canvas ammo pack strapped to their chests; kit bag, square meal tin, metal cup, and canteen of water dangling from leather waist belts. Bren guns slung over their shoulders. Their company is advancing on the hamlet of Verrieres, a German strongpoint. German defences have no shortage of mortar shells, and the Allies discovered in the early part of July that daylight advance was suicide. So they leave under cover of full darkness, using "Artificial Moonlight," searchlights bounced off the clouds to provide enough light to move out. Just outside Verrieres, Rocky gives the signal. The company charges on the town, surprising the Germans, chasing them out with seventeen-pounder anti-tank guns, portable mortar artillery and machine-gun fire. The village cleared of Germans, the Rileys dig in, positioning anti-tank artillery in strategic defensive positions. Lenny and Charlie are part of an infantry platoon positioned on a ridge, looking down.

The fighting continues all through the day. The Germans return and counterattack. It's going to be a fight to hang on to the village. The Rileys are rotated into front-line positions every couple of hours. There is no hot food, just K rations. Lenny was a bundle of nerves at first — the shelling and all the noise took him back to Dieppe — but now he has reached a rhythm, a calm. He could do this all day if he had to. And he will have to. At 2230 Lenny and Charlie are relieved, ordered back for grub and rest. On their bellies they slither, until it is safe to stand.

"Cold bully beef, my favourite." Charlie sticks his fork into the canned meat, smells it with suspicion. Also in their square tin Compo-boxes they find cold steamed pudding, hard tack and a cup of repulsive powdered tea. They sit on the ground, their backs leaning against an armoured supply truck. They can hear the pounding shells and machine-gun fire from the front. The smell of smoke and gunpowder is thick.

"Are you kidding?" Lenny jokes, "men are dying for this beef." Lenny tastes his with the tip of his tongue. It's rather revolting, but his stomach is rumbling.

The hilarity strikes them. They laugh as if Lenny has just said the funniest thing either has ever heard.

"Actually," says Lenny, taking a bite, "my father would kill me for eating this." He takes a small, tentative bite.

"Why?" Charlie digs in, ravenous. It's not so bad. When you're really hungry.

"It's not kosher." Lenny chews slowly. It's a little on the salty side.

"What?" Charlie polishes his beef off in two more bites, wishes there was more.

"Long story. Sometime I'll explain it." Lenny tries the hard tack. Better. Like a thick biscuit.

"Oh, a Jewish thing, huh?" The pudding reminds Charlie of his mother's cooking. Bland but soothing.

"Yeah. We've got a lot of rules."

"Not as many as the Catholics, I bet." Charlie eyes Lenny's uneaten bully beef.

"Probably more."

"You know … you're the first Jew I've ever known," Charlie admits.

"Oh yeah?"

"I used to hate you."

"Me?"

"Well … not you. Jews."

"Why?"

"I don't know. When I was fifteen …" Charlie stops, not sure he should go on. He doesn't want his best friend Lenny to be hurt. And frankly, Charlie is ashamed of the truth.

"What?"

"Don't get mad, Lenny. Okay?"

"Okay. What?"

Charlie lowers his voice, embarrassed. "I joined the Swastika Club."

"You did?"

"Only for a couple of months. I didn't even know what it was, at first. Not until the riots."

"The riots? At Christie Pits? You were there?"

Charlie sighs. "Yeah."

"Me, too." Lenny sits up straight. Another connection between them.

"Wasn't everybody?" Charlie smiles.

"I guess." Lenny smiles back.

They eat in silence.

"I'm sorry, Lenny."

"It's okay." Lenny thinks about Izzy whenever anyone mentions the riots, but Charlie doesn't know about Izzy. The story is too long. Where would Lenny start? He'll tell Charlie some other time. After the war. When they're home again.

"I didn't even know what a swastika was when I joined."

"Don't worry."

"I was just a kid."

"It's okay, Charlie. You didn't know."

"A stupid kid."

Lenny smiles. He wants to say, *It's okay, Charlie. You're my best friend. I love you.* But men don't say that. Not to each other. Lenny reaches over and punches Charlie on the arm. Charlie punches back. *I love you too, pal.*

They curl up to sleep side by side underneath the supply truck. Safer under there than in the open. Unless the truck takes a hit to the fuel tank. Then they'd go up in flames in seconds. Exhausted, they nod off to a serenade of artillery fire.

0500, July 20, the sergeant wakes them. Time to relieve the men on the front line. The Rileys still have a hold on Verrieres, but the Germans won't let up. Morning grub is thick lumpy oatmeal, with lots of sugar, and watery powdered milk. Lenny and Charlie are issued grenades, which they stuff in pockets, and ammunition to add to their cloth packs. They check their guns, strap them over their shoulders, load up with extra ammo and grenades — you can never have too many — and walk toward the front, past the thick green hedgerows, planted one thousand years ago as a windbreak around the French farms.

"First thing I'm gonna do when I get home," Charlie says.

"What?"

"Have a long hot bath. I haven't felt clean since we got to England. How about you?"

"A pastrami-on-rye at Manny's."

"Who's Manny?"

"Manny's Deli. On College Street … I'll take you there when we get back. Manny's the greatest. And it's the best smoked meat in the country."

The sniper fire comes out of nowhere, entrenched deep inside the roadside hedge, lacing a stream of bullets across Charlie's body. Instinctively, Lenny hits the dirt, as they've been trained to do, his rifle off the shoulder and in his hand. He shoots in the direction of the sniper. Ack ack ack ack ack. Lenny sprays his rifle empty, adrenalin pumping. He reaches for more ammo. The sniping has stopped.

"Crap." He turns to Charlie, who lies prone on his back. "Charlie! Oh no. No. No, no, no. No! Don't do this to me, Charlie." Lenny takes Charlie under both arms, and drags him to the edge of a ridge, under cover, slides to a sitting position and holds Charlie in his arms. Charlie opens his eyes, sees Lenny, smiles.

"It doesn't hurt." Blood drips from the corner of Charlie's mouth.

"Medic!" Lenny screams, his voice lost beneath the explosion of mortar fire. He rips open Charlie's tunic. Buttons fly. One hits his face. There is blood everywhere. He wipes the blood aside with his bare hand, counts three bullet holes at least, across Charlie's belly, and one dangerously close to his heart. Blood streams out, forms a puddle on Charlie's chest. Doesn't look good.

"Take this ..." Charlie's weak hand clutches the silver cross around his neck. "My mother's ... take it."

"Come on, Charlie. Hang on. You're gonna make it. We're going into business together, back home. Remember? What kind of business?" Lenny prompts, smoothing the damp hair over Charlie's feverish forehead.

"Business?" Charlie feels hot. Burning up. What's Lenny talking about? He's tired. So tired. *Just need to close my eyes. Just for a minute.*

"Charlie! No! Open your eyes, damn it!"

Charlie snaps his eyes back open, under order.

"That's it. Hang on, buddy. You're going to be okay." Lenny clutches Charlie tightly to him, grips an edge of his tunic, rocking him like a mother with her baby. Oh Charlie. Sweet baby blue eyes. My Charlie. From the bottom of his heart, Lenny begins to hum the sad sweet melody of a swing song, one of his favourites that played on the radio a few years ago. He used to sing it in the kitchen with his mother. The words come to Lenny now. He sings gently to Charlie.

"*I'll be seeing you, in all the old familiar places,*
That this heart of mine embraces, all day through,
In that small café,
The park across the way,
The children's carousel,
The chestnut trees, the wishing well,
I'll be seeing you, in every lovely summer's day."

Lenny sings until his throat is raw, his arm muscles cramped, and Charlie lies still, cold, and quite dead in Lenny's tender embrace.

"Private Lapinsky?"

Lenny looks up into the eyes of Sherman Jackson, his Company Sergeant Major. Then he looks down at Charlie, gently closes his lifeless eyes, lovingly lowers him to the ground.

"What happened?"

Lenny ignores the question. Isn't it fucking obvious? He relieves the Sergeant Major of the trench shovel that dangles from the back of his pack. Lenny jams the spade into the dry earth with a deep and profound rage. Sergeant Major Jackson stands back, watching. He's been overseas since the beginning of the war, has miraculously survived some of the bloodiest battles. He knows grief when he sees it. Private Lapinsky is drenched in heartache. Sergeant-Major Jackson considers helping Lapinsky, but maybe it's better to let him do this alone. Still he feels he should stand by, keep an eye on Lapinsky. He's seen guys lose their minds completely after their best buddy buys it. And these two were exceptionally close.

Every shovelful of dirt is the heart of a stinking Nazi. Lenny strikes, pounds, pulverizes his enemy as he digs a grave for his friend. His buddy. His Charlie. Hot tears of rage and sorrow roll down his cheeks. It's a shallow grave. But that's all there's time for. Lenny has something else he must do. He allows Sergeant-Major Jackson to help position Charlie in the grave. Lenny removes the silver cross from Charlie's neck, puts it around his own, where it nestles against his Star of David. He straps Charlie's kit bag around his own waist, relieves him of his ammunition, gun and grenades. At the graveside, Lenny recites the mourner's Kaddish, swaying and keening like a rabbi on the Day of Atonement. Charlie should have the Christian prayers said over him, but Lenny doesn't know how. And he's not about to let Sergeant-Major Jackson do the honours.

Yisgadal v'yis kadash shmai raba ...

Above, Allied aircraft roar by, dropping bombs somewhere over the front lines.

When Charlie is properly covered with dirt, and the hastily thrown together wooden cross bearing his name, rank and serial number is planted, Lenny calmly walks toward the front, with both machine-guns, and all the extra ammo.

"Private Lapinsky?" the Sergeant Major calls after him, alarmed, but there's no time to follow.

Lenny doesn't bother slithering on his belly to the front. He is a man possessed. He will not be struck down by sniper fire. No matter how many German snipers are hiding in the hedgerows, none of their fire will touch Lenny. He is protected. He has a job to do. For Charlie. His love. *Olev hashalom.* May he rest in peace.

LENNY ARRIVES AT THE FRONT LINES just in the nick of time. An entire platoon of his company is pinned down by a counterattacking panzer division. Heavy machine-gun and artillery fire rains relentlessly across the narrow space between the armies, as mortar shells explode all around. A German tank methodically belches its ammo at the Canadians. Entirely without fear, possessed only of a profound rage, Lenny runs gracefully forward, past the astonished faces of his pinned-down company, right toward the German tank. Pulling the pin with his teeth, he tosses the first grenade at the tank, followed by a second which miraculously slips right inside the small view hole, blowing the tank and its occupants to smithereens in a beautiful light show. Without missing a beat, Lenny hollers a deranged battle cry, an ancient howl that echoes through the bowels of the German soldiers. The crazy Canadian charges solo onto his enemies, like David unto Goliath, spraying machine-gun fire madly off in all directions, instantly killing at least four Germans and wounding several others, before his own body is laced with bullets and he drops to the ground.

His company uses the diversion to their fullest advantage. They charge forward, blasting the other two German tanks and beating back the Jerry riflemen to reclaim the ground they lost earlier in the day.

Lenny sees the boots of his comrades run by. *Charlie was right. It doesn't hurt. Doesn't hurt at all. I'm sorry Mama. I tried to make it home. I tried my best. I wish you could have met Charlie. He was a swell guy. You would have loved him. Mama. I'll find you in the morning sun and when the night is new, I'll be looking at the moon, but I'll be seeing you.*

Blood Brothers
JULY AND AUGUST, 1944

THE TELEGRAM SLIPS from Sophie's grasp. Her knees give out and she falls hard to the floor, landing in a strange sitting position, her back to the wall.

"Mama?" Izzy is frightened to his core. He flies downstairs in a panic to find Auntie Tess. "Auntie! Auntie! Auntie!"

"SHE'S RESTING," Tess informs Yacov, when he rushes in the door.

"The telegram," he demands.

His hands tremble. Such a callous, cold message. Lenny was a person. A boy. Their son. Not a private. *Regret to inform you. Lapinsky, Leonard, Chaim, Private. Killed in action. Active duty. France.* This isn't his son. Lapinsky, Leonard, Private. The hammering in Yacov's chest drowns out the cry that spills from his throat. He sits down at the table, head in hands, and sobs.

Tessie stands behind, one hand on his shoulder.

"Papa?" Izzy doesn't know what's going on. He has never seen his father cry.

"Izzelah," Tessie says, teary-eyed, "go and find your brother Sid. Go on. Hurry."

LANCE CORPORAL SONNY LAPINSKY is ordered to report to the Sergeant. He leaves his supper tray at his place at the long wooden table and follows Private Joe Mazario to the Staff Sergeant's office.

"At ease, Corporal." Staff-Sergeant James Galloway hates the Zombies. Bunch of disrespectful slackers, the whole lot of them. Cowards. Too concerned with their own yellow hides to fight for their country. Still, he reserves his judgement this time, on account of the news this poor sucker's about to hear.

Sonny stands at ease, trying to wipe the smirk from his face. He hasn't grown used to all the saluting and standing at attention he's required to do in the army, finds it ridiculous, grown men playing a big dumb game. Like large little boys.

"Sit down, Corporal."

"Yessir!" He sits in the chair opposite the Sergeant's desk. The Sergeant leaves the room. Sonny looks around, bored. Why'd they have to call him out during dinner? The only halfway decent meal they ever get around here. Tonight it was some kind of unidentified meat, with potatoes and half-dead vegetables. Beans maybe, or peas. Apple pie for dessert. The door opens and when Sonny looks up it's not the sergeant, it's his brother. He jumps to his feet.

"Sid! What the hell? What's wrong? Is it Loretta? The baby?"

Sid's eyes are red and bloodshot. Looks like he hasn't slept in weeks. "No, Sonny. Sit down."

"Has something happened to Izzy?" Sonny sits. A huge lump forms in the base of his throat and sits there, strangling him from the inside.

"It's Lenny ..." Sid's voice cracks.

"Lenny?"

There's nothing to do but just say it. "He's dead." Sid still can't believe it. The words sound so strange and unreal when he speaks them out loud.

"No."

"In France. He was a hero, they said."

"Killed by Krauts?" Sonny leaps to his feet again. Feels like he's been kicked in the stomach, the wind knocked out of him.

"Yeah. In Normandy, we think."

"Damn them." Sonny smashes his fist into the wall, breaking a hole right through the plaster.

"Sonny, you better stop that. I mean …"

Sonny punches the wall with one hand then the other. He can't stop. Grief churns in his heart and spreads throughout his body, a white hot hurricane of feelings. Shock, denial, anger, guilt and pain. He punches until he's done considerable damage and the Sergeant has run back into the room.

"Corporal! At ease!" Sergeant Galloway commands. He hates the sight of emotion. Give him good old drill duty any day over this.

Sonny charges forward, grabs the sergeant by the lapels, like he's going to slug him. Only instead he says, "Sir, I want to volunteer for active duty overseas."

In an even tone, the Sergeant says, "Corporal you'll take your hands off me, at once."

Sonny looks down, realizes what he's done, drops his hands, steps back, and salutes. "Sorry, Sir. Forgot where I was. Sir. I'd like to volunteer for active duty, Sir. Where do I sign? Sir."

"Sonny …" Sid begs, "don't …"

"Corporal, are you sure you wouldn't like to think about it? For a few days?"

"With all due respect, Sir, I would not. I'd like to volunteer for active duty." Sonny repeats.

The Sergeant sighs. "Very well." He opens a file drawer and pulls out a form.

"Sonny … maybe you'd better wait …"

"Shuttup, Sid. I know what I'm doing."

The Sergeant places the form in front of Sonny. He signs his name violently, as if signing with the blood of his brother Lenny.

THE *SHIVA* IS DOWNSTAIRS in Tessie and Max's apartment. The funeral was at the Shaarea Tzedec Synagogue, where the boys had their bar mitzvahs. It was a funeral without a body. They don't know where Lenny is buried and won't find out until after the war. Sophie moves as if on automatic. Her head feels shrouded in heavy gauze. Her heart is covered in a much thicker material. Steel perhaps. Or stone. If it weren't for the covering, she would not be able to crawl out of bed in the morning and shuffle downstairs to sit on a low stool in Tessie's living room, while relatives and friends pass through the house, while the men gather in the morning and the evening to say the prayers, while Tessie or her mother or Ruthie force her to drink a little tea, eat a little something, even just a piece of sponge cake. Somewhere under the layers is Sophie's heart, which lies as broken and bleeding as Lenny's body on the battlefield. If the protective covering was not in its place around her heart, she would be nothing but searing hot pain. She can't look at Yacov. It's all his fault. If he hadn't sent Sonny away, Lenny wouldn't have died. Bad luck brings more bad luck.

Yacov has armour of his own. He will mourn Lenny by hating the world. He never trusted anyone outside his family before, anyway. Now he has all the more reason to fear the world. It has taken away his child. Dear sweet Lenny, of all people. The army sent a nice letter. He was a hero, their Lenny. He lost his life saving a group of twenty other soldiers who were pinned down by enemy fire. He gave his life for them. Yacov hopes their parents are happy. He lost his son so they could have theirs. The army sent an award posthumously. In a purple velvet box. A cross. The Victoria Cross. A big honour, he's told. With a letter signed by the Prime Minister. He'd have preferred if they'd sent back his son.

LANCE CORPORAL SONNY LAPINSKY is given one week's leave to sit shiva with his family, and see his wife, before he is shipped out with the next set of reinforcements to England for training, and later to the front. There have been heavy casualties as the Allies fight for the liberation of France. All available men are needed. Yesterday if not sooner.

"But I can't go to the shiva," Sonny tells Sid, who picks him up in the truck at the CNE gates. "I'm dead. Remember?"

"Sonny … I think under the circumstances …"

"... No! I'm not going. Not while *he's* there."

"Okay okay Sonny. At least go and see Ma."

"Only if he's not there."

Stubborn to the core. *Just like Pa,* Sid thinks. "Okay, I'll phone you when the coast is clear. Pa goes out in the mornings every day for a long walk."

"Fine."

LORETTA OPENS THE apartment door to find Sonny standing there in his uniform. She throws herself into his arms. Her beautiful soft embrace brings forth Sonny's tears for his brother Lenny.

Loretta kisses the tears that fall from his eyes. She takes his hand, leads him inside.

Sonny wipes his face with the back of his sleeve, embarrassed by his tears, but Loretta understands.

"Come and sit down. I'll make tea."

"Do we have any whiskey, Loretta?"

After a stiff drink, he tells her his other news.

"No, Sonny. You can't. They won't let you. You have a wife and a baby."

"They know that, Loretta. They know everything about me."

"So they can't let you go."

"They need men over there. They'll take anybody who signs up."

Now it's Loretta's turn to cry. "But why, Sonny? You said you wouldn't go. You said ..."

"I have to go now, Loretta. Don't you get it?"

She folds her arms across her chest, stares at him.

"For Lenny."

"What about me? And the baby?"

"Don't worry. I'll be back."

"Oh Sonny." She can't stay mad at him. Especially not now. Her heart is breaking for him. She knows how she would feel if anything like this happened to her brother Johnny. She throws her arms around her husband's neck and pulls him close. He nestles his face against her soft breasts; the safest place in the world. She strokes his hair. He raises his head up, kisses her neck, seizes her lips in a passionate kiss.

"Loretta …"

"Sonny …"

"The baby?"

"In her crib. Come on." Loretta takes him by the hand and leads him to the bedroom.

TESSIE ANSWERS THE DOOR. Her hand flies over her heart at the sight of the young man in uniform. "May I help you?"

The young man checks the name on the package he holds. "Mrs. Yacov Lapinsky?"

"She's not well, at the moment. Can I help you?"

"Package for her." The man hands it to Tessie. "You have to sign for it, ma'am." He holds out a clipboard, hands her a pen.

Tessie sits with Sophie on the front-room sofa as they open the package. On the top is an official-looking note that reads, "Personal effects of Private Leonard Chaim Lapinsky, Royal Hamilton Light Infantry." Sophie can't do it. She shoves the box into Tessie's lap. Tess reaches in. She finds a small burlap bag, Lenny's kit bag. She opens it.

She pulls up a chain with Lenny's Star of David. No, wait. Two chains, intermingled, tangled together. Strange. One is a silver cross. What would Lenny be doing with a cross? Maybe it belongs to another young soldier and it got mixed in by mistake. There is a package of cigarettes, slightly bent, a Ronson lighter, a pen, and a letter, neatly folded in quarters. Sophie watches out of the corner of one eye, dying to touch the precious package, but scared of the intensity of her grief. Tessie gently places the Star of David in Sophie's hands. Sophie raises the Mogen David to her lips, kisses it.

"Oh Lenny." The stone around Sophie's heart cracks, just enough to let some feelings out.

"There's a letter, sweetie. Do you want me to read it?"

Sophie takes a breath, nods through her tears, clutches the Mogen David tightly.

Tessie opens the letter. A black and white photograph falls out. Lenny and another soldier, in uniform, smiling. Sophie clutches the photo over her heart. "It's dated July 16," Tessie says. Four days before Lenny died.

"Dear Ma, Pop and Izzy," Tessie reads.

More cracks open over Sophie's heart. "Go on." she says.

Tessie continues. "I guess you've read in the papers by now all about D-Day and the invasion of Normandy. I wasn't there, so don't worry. Our company is being held back for some other mission, although I don't know what yet. And even if I did, I couldn't tell you. The Jerries have spies everywhere. There might even be some in Toronto at the post office who could go through my letters to you. Makes you think, doesn't it?"

Sophie's armour drops away completely. Tessie stops, puts the letter down. Sophie crumples into her arms, sobbing.

"That's it, Sophie. Let it out. Let it all out."

Now that Sophie has begun to cry, she knows she will never stop.

Something Bigger
AUGUST 1944 TO MAY 1945

SONNY IS AMONG THE FIRST of the new recruits to be sent to France. There have been heavy losses over the summer, especially in the infantry, which has had a casualty rate of seventy-five percent. Corporals are in short supply and trained men are needed. Sonny is classified as officially trained and battle-ready with a company of the Royal Regiment of Canada, which has experienced its heaviest losses since Dieppe in the push across France. With his company, Sonny sets sail across the English Channel at the end of August.

Sonny and the other new soldiers join the men who have been fighting, a convoy of the 2nd Canadian Division. The veterans are exhausted, dirty and battle-weary. The fight for the Forêt de la Londe has cost the regiment 149 casualties, thirty of them fatal, including several officers. Along with forty-eight fresh reinforcements, Sonny arrives on August 30, 1944 and is trucked into Lachapelle, where his regiment has withdrawn for a brief rest after heavy fighting. It's a cloudy day, rainy with only occasional breaks. The men are treated to a bath parade for the first time in days, a pleasure to the veterans who've been in battle for more than a month, and put on R & R for the rest of the day. The enemy has withdrawn across the Seine. Sonny is raring to fight. He doesn't need any of the mandatory rest. He notices how fatigued the veterans are. They all look thin and tired and grey and, ironically, a little like zombies.

A few days later, the Royal regiment rolls into the freshly liberated city of Rouen to a glorious welcome from the French civilians. Columns of tanks, trucks and converted tanks known as "Kangaroos," filled with soldiers, pass by the tearful, jubilant townspeople. Women and children stuff flowers into tanks, girls run up and kiss the Allied soldiers, men with tears of joy hand them bottles of victory wine and cigarettes.

Sonny is shocked to see women, children and old people in the midst of the ruins of the city. He'd never really thought about it before, but he'd had a vague notion of there being nothing over here but Nazis and Allied soldiers. It hadn't occurred to him that the townspeople would have nowhere else to go and simply endured the bombing of their homes, burying their dead when the shelling stopped, carrying on with life in the middle of a war as best as they could. Houses are shattered from Allied and German bombing; whole blocks have been reduced to rubble.

A beautiful, voluptuous French girl kisses Sonny on the lips. He smiles, and feels like the fraud that he is. He hasn't done anything brave. Not yet. He doesn't have any idea how broken up some of the men in his division feel as they pass through the town that is only forty miles from the Canadian disaster of Dieppe. Survivors of the 1942 fiasco are haunted by memories of the massacre two years earlier. They wonder every day why they survived while other men were obliterated.

Sonny's regiment continues through the beautiful, if war-littered, countryside beyond Rouen. The newly liberated French people have already built temporary bridges across anti-tank ditches left only the day before by the hastily retreating Germans, to allow easier passage for the Allied vehicles. Still green to battle, Sonny can't get used to the sight of German corpses, dead and bloated cattle, carcasses of burnt-out vehicles and artillery, both Allied and German, littered everywhere. The French population in every town and village they pass through treat the Canadian liberators like heroes. They are thrown fresh-cut flowers as their convoy rumbles through town. They are offered wine and brandy. Civilians jump onto their jeeps and Sherman tanks, cheering as the 2nd Division creeps forward.

Sonny uneasily receives benefits he hasn't earned. And even though the French folks don't realize what a fraud he is, Sonny knows the difference. He doesn't deserve their admiration. He hasn't done anything. Not yet. But maybe he came too late? Maybe it's all over now? His heart rages with anger over Lenny. He just wants to have a crack at some Nazis, not sit like a loafer on a Sherman tank while French girls kiss him and men give him cigarettes and wine he hasn't worked for.

THE TWENTY-FIVE VETERANS of Dieppe in the Royal regiments figure they are not going to be able to take the town without one helluva fight. All units are briefed for the battle. There will be heavy air cover — British, Canadian and American. Warships will be mobilized to shell the port. The British and Canadian naval forces will be on hand. The French Resistance has been mobilized to conduct small yet important acts of sabotage. The Belgian underground has also been duly notified. Meanwhile Germany is suffering major loses in the Soviet Union and this is eating up its precious resources. The German defence in France is considerably weaker than it was only two years ago. This will be an all-out combined operation: Land, air and sea. No chances this time. While the veterans of Dieppe are scared to the soles of their blistered feet, Sonny has no idea what could await him. Sounds like a piece of cake to him. And it is. On the morning of September 2, two years after the first raid, the Allies march into Dieppe with no opposition. The Germans are gone — they fled during the night. French civilians pour into the streets to greet the Canadian division, and ply them with more wine and flowers. The tank on which Sonny rides is mobbed by happy liberated people, who pull soldiers from their vehicles and lead them to the cafés, feed them wine and bread and cheese. This overseas mission is nothing but a whole lot of celebrating, thinks Sonny. In a café, a beautiful young French girl claims

Sonny as her personal prize, feeding him, filling his wineglass, lighting his cigarette. He can't understand a word she says, but she sure is beautiful. He accepts her kindness. What else can he do?

On the shingled beach of Puys where Louie Horowitz died, and where the Royal regiment lost hundreds of other men, there is a memorial plaque honouring their fallen comrades. Sonny is chosen to be among a small burial party. They thoroughly search the area of Forêt de la Londe. Most of his battalion's dead were buried by locals long before, but they find several bodies and take them back to the small military cemetery at St. Ouen-du-Tilleul. The badly decomposed bodies are Sonny's first brush with the horrors of war.

ON SEPTEMBER 3, 1944, the soldiers of the 2nd Canadian Division march in formation through the streets of Dieppe, in tribute to the men who gave their lives in the raid two years earlier. Out of respect for Louie Horowitz, Sonny goes to the cemetery, and says the mourner's Kaddish, although he doesn't see any graves marked with a Star of David, only crosses. Lots of them. White wooden crosses. He stands by another soldier's grave — he has to stand somewhere — and recites the words his father said over him. This time, though, there is a body. He's just not sure exactly where.

Sonny wishes he knew where Lenny was buried. As he recites the age-old prayer, his tears well up for his lost brother. Lenny, who could have been a writer, a schoolteacher, maybe even a scholar. A hero. Sonny vows to kill some Nazis before he is through.

SONNY'S COMPANY IS RECALLED to England. Besides Sonny and a handful of other reinforcements, the men have been in heavy combat in France for three months. They are given a well-deserved rest — a week's leave in London. Then back to Aldershot for specialized training. Sonny reports to his company Sergeant Major and requests a transfer.

"I'd like to fight some Nazis, Sir!" Sonny shouts, military-style.

"You'll do what you're told, Corporal."

"Yes Sir. But Sir … please … that is … how's about I replace some other guy who's awful tired. See, I'm fresh, Sir. Plus I'm a fighter, Sir."

Staff-Sergeant Nicholas Billington looks up at the young corporal for the first time. "A fighter, you say?"

"Boxer, sir. Welterweight. Sir!"

"Swell. Why don't you put on your gloves and take a swing at some Nazis in their panzer tanks, huh?"

"Excuse me, sir?"

"Corporal. This is the army. You go where we tell you to go, understood?"

"Yes, sir," Sonny says bitterly.

"We don't care what you want to do. This is a war, soldier. Understood?"

Through clenched teeth. "Yes sir."

"Your orders are to go on leave. Are they not, Corporal?"

"Yes, sir … but …"

"Then go to London. Get laid. Drink until you're sick. Have a good time, Corporal. That's an order."

"Yes sir."

The guilt is killing Sonny. He came here to avenge his brother's death. Why won't the army let him?

In the end, though, Sonny finds it easy to follow the Sergeant's orders. In London there are pubs, where you can sit like a civilized person with a pint of ale — unlike Ontario, where drinking in public is illegal. And there are plenty of British girls who throw themselves at Sonny. He is one of the more attractive boys, and a corporal to boot. For the first few days he resists their attentions. For Loretta's sake. And the baby. He's a married man, after all. By the third day Sonny gets caught up in the patriotic spirit around him. He follows Gynne Somebody back to a dingy bed-sitting room, where they have tepid sex, not as good as the passionate sex he has with Loretta, but Gynne is right here right now and Loretta is a million miles away. And anyway, he might get hit by a bomb at any second, so why deprive himself of the pleasure? The next girl, Lindy or Linda, is much more passionate. Sonny actually has a good time with her. He never really remembers the third girl's name, or the fifth. Was there a fourth?

WHEN SONNY RETURNS to the base at Aldershot there are two letters
waiting for him. He opens the letter from Loretta first. Holy cripes. She's
pregnant again. So soon?

The second is from Checkie. It is brief.

> Are you outa your fucking mind? What the fuck do you think
> you're doing, schmuck? I had a fight tour all set up for you. Putz.
> I got half a mind to come over there myself and bust you in two.
> Except I ain't as stupid as you to go over there and have bombs
> dropped on my fucking head.

Checkie's letter makes Sonny laugh. Loretta's makes him want to cry.
He's made a big mistake coming over here. The stupid army is not going
to let him get near any Nazis. Loretta's pregnant and he's throwing his
boxing career down the toilet. What was he thinking?

He reports to the Sergeant and begs to be discharged. "On account of
my wife's pregnant and we already got a little baby."

"Sorry, Corporal. You're being sent to the front."

"Sir?"

"Orders just came down. You're going to the Scheldt."

"The what?"

"Get your battle gear ready, son. You're going back up."

THE AMERICAN ARMY has taken the Belgian city of Antwerp from
German hands, but the Germans still hold all approaches to the port. The
First Canadian Army has been assigned the task of clearing the German
defences. Antwerp is on the Scheldt River, fifty miles from the sea. The
peninsula of South Beveland and Walcheren Island are comprised of
low-lying fields and meadows, below sea level. The water is held back by
fifteen-foot-high dikes, on top of which the Germans are heavily
entrenched in defensive positions. The land is completely flat, with a net-
work of canals and ditches and areas that are permanently flooded. The
fields are open with no cover. It is onto this flooded flat land, into thigh-
deep mud, that Sonny's company is deposited in early October.

Sonny can't remember ever being this cold, or this wet. The rain is incessant. In places, the water is chest-high. On shorter men like Sonny, it rises as high as the neck at times. The damp goes right through his bones. For weeks, the soldiers live in these muddy conditions, never having the chance to dry out their feet, or get warm. They have rot in every conceivable body part. Between their toes, under the arms, around their balls and assholes, between their fingers, behind the knees and elbows, even on their eyelids and behind their ears. They are truly in hell, though it is not burning like the Catholics have been taught. It is cold and wet and mouldy. Delivering hot food is impossible. They eat "compo-box" rations, cold bully beef, hard tack and cold powdered tea. It barely fills their stomachs, and does nothing to soothe their souls or calm their frayed nerves. The fighting is hard and Sonny's company suffers heavy casualties. The Germans are too far away to be seen, so the Allied soldiers shoot in the general direction of the blasting, duck, and hope for the best.

As hastily trained as he was, Sonny and the other reinforcements are not well-versed in weapon handling, field craft or regimental discipline. In the one quick month of training Sonny was given in England before he was shipped across the Channel, he'd received only three hours on the Sten machine pistol, the Bren gun and grenades, of which he'd thrown exactly three before being considered battle ready. There was no range practise, no instruction in field craft, no target recognition and very little information on the German army. Most of the time Sonny doesn't have a clue what he's doing. He keeps his head low. Common sense will teach you that, he thinks. He sticks his gun over the top of whatever trench he happens to be sitting in, and squeezes the trigger. For all he knows, he's shooting blanks, or aiming at his own regiment. So far, no one's complained.

It's a rifleman's battle — a steady continuous struggle. There are perils every step of the way. Sloshing through water, sometimes up to their chests, an infantryman could step on a mine; pushing aside the body of a dead enemy might trigger a booby trap; innocent piles of hay might conceal a German panzer tank; going through barbed wire sometimes trips a silent alarm.

Slowly and steadily, the Allies push the Germans back. Now that he's here, Sonny longs to be back in France liberating civilians, being showered with gifts and wine and women. In this cold muddy hell, shooting at an invisible enemy, he feels like the real war is passing him by. The others feel it too. So far, he hasn't seen a single German. Warfare isn't anything like boxing, where your opponent is inches from you, where you can see the effect you have on him, can feel your fist pounding his body, taste victory up close. Warfare is all about taking orders, learning how to say "yes sir," digging the best and safest trench — four feet long, thirty inches wide, six feet deep, like a grave — keeping your head low, and your wits about you, finding ways to keep your feet and crotch as dry as possible even in a swamp, remembering to swallow the pills to stave off dysentery and typhoid, nineteenth-century diseases that flourish in these conditions. It's about finding a best buddy and taking care of each other. Surviving. Trying somehow in the midst of insanity to remember you used to be a *mensch*. A civilized person.

Private Harry Wishman is Sonny's best buddy. Harry has been overseas since 1941. He used to be a Riley, before they transferred him to reinforce the Royal regiment, which was badly in need of experienced men. He's one of the few Canadian survivors of Dieppe. He lost the hearing in his left ear after a shell blew up his Captain, who was standing right beside him. He could have gone home, a legitimate injury, and according to regulations he should have been honourably discharged. But Harry begged his commander to be allowed to stay and fight. He wants revenge on the Jerries who killed his captain. And the Royals needed experienced men, so his papers are fudged. You don't really need to hear a hundred percent to be a good soldier and Harry has ten times more training than the new recruits. His right ear works fine. He'll never play the piano again, but Harry can dig a slit trench faster than anyone in his unit, can hit his mark nine times out of ten and has a sixth sense about the enemy. Harry claims you can smell the Germans. They use a different kind of soap. If you pay attention you notice the difference. Saved his life more than once. His new Captain would rather have ten Harrys with bad hearing than most of the newbies, who don't really know their elbows from their assholes.

"Your brother was a great soldier." Harry passes a damp cigarette to Sonny, as they lie in a muddy ditch, rifles at the ready, although there has been a lull in fire for the past hour or so. A much-needed respite.

Sonny takes a deep drag from the cigarette.

"He went berserk after Charlie bought it."

"Charlie?"

"Charlie Bain. Lenny and Charlie were like this." Harry twines the fingers of both hands together.

"He went berserk?" Sonny wriggles his toes inside his boots. He has to remember to move his feet every few minutes or they'll seize up, from the damp. He has newspaper wedged between his toes in a feeble attempt to keep them dry. They burn from the rot. But it's the itching that really drives him crazy.

"He had no fear. None. He had Charlie's gun and his own, one in each hand, and he charged at a Jerry tank that had us pinned down for over an hour. I saw him, out of the corner of my eye."

"Lenny? My brother? Are you sure?" Sonny can't picture it. He sees Lenny trying to hit a ball in a stickball game on their street, and striking out every time, throwing the ball underhanded, like a girl. He remembers Lenny reading books, going to the library all the time. He had no interest in sports, could never climb a tree. He was always getting picked on. Sonny had to bail him out of fights two, three times a week. He can maybe picture Lenny digging a slit trench, or driving an army truck, working in the mess tent, being a medic maybe, carrying a stretcher. But a rifleman? He can't see Lenny here at all.

"Yeah, your brother. Lenny. He charged in like I said, a gun in each hand, then he starts throwing grenades. Must have thrown a dozen in the space of a minute." Here's where the truth begins to bend a little, and in the retelling of the story, Harry embellishes, turning it into a legend. "Course I couldn't see so good, from where I was lying. The Jerries hadn't let up their fire on us. Then one of Lenny's grenades shot right through the tank's view hole and exploded, killing all the Jerries inside. Then he shot ten or twelve more. That's when we moved forward. I didn't see what happened to your brother. They got him with machine-gun

fire. He saved a whole platoon. Gave us an opening to charge on the
Jerries. Who knows what would have happened if he hadn't gone berserk
like that? You should be proud, Sonny. Your brother's a hero. I owe
Lenny my life."

Sonny is proud. He's damn proud. He lights another cigarette to hide
the tears welling up in his eyes.

Harry sees, but says nothing. He'd be choked up too, if it was his
brother.

FURIOUS, PISSING, DRENCHING rain again. No tank support. It is
impossible for vehicles to advance in the thick mud. The infantry inches
forward in the muck. Crouch, crawl, stumble a few feet, a few yards, chip-
ping away at a defence that holds tight, well-armed and entrenched.
Living in temporary, wet, muddy, cold slit trenches, moving forward,
digging new trenches every two days, sometimes taking over trenches left
by retreating Germans. The men in Sonny's company are wet, dirty,
bearded, hungry and tired. It is difficult for Sonny to remember what he
is doing here. Except he wouldn't have it any other way. It's a deep inner
knowing. Nothing tangible. Just a sense that he is a part of something
big. And important. Even here in the stinking muck, rotting as he is. Even
though he hasn't a clue where in the world he is. Holland? As abstract in
his mind as Africa. Or the moon. He always pictured Holland as sunny,
with happy people in wooden shoes, women with blonde hair curling up
at the ends, smiling farmers, dairy cows, with lots of tulips. Bright red
and yellow with green stems. Strange, since the only colour he sees
around him is brown. Mud and muck. And pissing grey rain.

Two months later, in December, Sonny remembers the mud fondly.
His unit has been moved to take up new positions in the Rhine, as the
Allies push through Holland. The company has taken over abandoned
farmhouses, and while it sure beats the hell out of the muddy ditches of
the fall, the temperature has dropped to well below freezing. They can't
use the wood stoves inside the houses. The smoke would give away their
positions. So they bundle up in woollen coats and pace the floor to keep
warm. They sleep clustered up like bears hibernating, sharing whatever

body heat they have to offer. They are issued extra blankets and a daily rum ration, but even still, Sonny trembles from the bitter cold. Can't get warm. Especially at night. The landscape is bleak and adds to their depression. Trees blown apart by shells, bloated cattle corpses rotting, craters in the mud, farmhouses with great holes in the sides, fields torn up, metal debris scattered everywhere.

Fortunately, there is a lull in the action as the weather grows colder and there is time finally to properly train the newer recruits. After four months of active duty, they are given infantry training and are, at least, in theory, ready for action. Sonny is lucky, having attached himself to a veteran like Harry who briefs him on the most important things: how to dig in, how to stay dry, how to move silently in the dark. They discover abandoned German bunkers and are astonished by the German precision. The concrete blocks, which were used to hide heavy artillery, anti-tank and anti-aircraft guns, were made to simulate civilian dwellings, with bricks, doors, windows, even lace curtains.

They are moved again, this time to newly captured trenches. Sonny wishes he was back in the unheated farmhouse. There is snow on the ground. The enemy is sometimes as close as 400 yards. They remain in their trenches all day, with little chance for movement without being seen. He and Harry still share a trench. They do little else but watch, wait, and occasionally exchange fire. They eat twice a day: once in the morning, once at night. They pass the food from dugout to dugout. Cold compo rations: scarce, unidentifiable meat, overcooked grey vegetables and some sort of pie, all mixed together in the middle of the square tin container. Hold their piss until after dark. Unless it's an emergency, and then they pee into a bottle and empty it later, under cover of darkness. Learned that from experience. After a guy or two poked their pecker over the top of the trench and got it shot off.

On New Year's Eve, both sides serenade each other with flares and mortar shells. For a noisy few minutes, the sky is bright with the flash of flares and tracers. The next morning they are surprised by scores of German aircraft flying overhead, heading for an attack on Allied airfields in Holland and Belgium.

Nineteen forty-five begins for Sonny in a frozen trench. It's one of the coldest winters Western Europe has seen in decades. Major Earnest McCabe arrives with bottles of Calvados, a fiery apple brandy from Normandy. Bottles are passed from trench to trench, enough for a couple of decent shots for each man. Sonny savors the warm liquid as it spreads through his chest, the first time he's felt anything resembling warmth in months.

An hour later, he's freezing again. His fingers stick to the cold metal of his rifle. He raises it periodically above the trench and shoots in the general direction of the Germans.

Finally, all ranks are issued snowsuits — white uniforms, excellently camouflaged against the snow, but noisy. They rustle with every step and can't be worn on patrols for fear of giving away their positions. At least when he's back in his trench, and in the white snowsuit, he's something close to warm. Not quite, but close.

Toronto
JANUARY 2, 1945

WHEN RUTHIE COMES HOME from her daily trip to the market, she finds a pregnant Loretta sitting on her stoop with Mary fidgeting in her lap. Shivering. It is colder than usual this January.

"Loretta, honey. What happened? Come on. Let's go inside. You must be freezing. I'll make tea." Ruthie puts one arm around her sister-in-law's waist as they climb the stairs.

"I'm going crazy, Ruthie. On my own with a baby and pregnant again. My mother would help, but I still can't go over there. My father won't let me."

Ruthie pats Loretta on the arm. "Come on. Let's go inside. We'll figure it out together."

When Sid comes home from work later, Loretta is lying down on the sofa. Mary sits on the floor, playing with a stack of canning jar lids Ruthie put down for her.

"Shhh," Ruthie says, pointing to the sleeping Loretta, taking Sid's hand and leading him to the bedroom to talk. She figured everything out that afternoon. There is a two-bedroom apartment available next door. Now that Sid is making good money, they can afford it, and Sonny sends money home to Loretta from his army pay. Letting Loretta move in with them is the only decent thing to do. The poor girl has no one else to turn to. Sid feels awkward about the idea, but he knows his Ruthie. She has a heart of gold and is as stubborn as they come. He knows there is no point in arguing with her. Anyway, Sonny will be back home in a couple of months. Everyone knows the war is almost over. It's only temporary.

"That's fine, Ruthie," Sid says. "When do we move?"

Ruthie throws her arms around Sid's neck. He is such a sweet man. If only she could give him a child.

LORETTA GOES INTO LABOUR three months later, once more with Ruthie by her side and her husband halfway around the world. It's a boy. Seven pounds, two ounces. Healthy and big. She names him Moses, the most Jewish name she can think of. His middle name will be Nino, after her father, even though it looks like he'll never actually meet his grandson, the way things are going. On Moses' first night of life, Loretta weeps. She's worried that Sonny will die in the war and the baby will never meet his father. Not even once.

The Netherlands
JANUARY 15, 1945

IN HOLLAND IN THE SECOND HALF of January, there is heavy snow and bright clear skies. Just like a January day in Toronto, Sonny thinks. They replace the oil in their weapons with kerosene, which will not freeze and jam the gears. By the end of the month, the temperature drops to five degrees Fahrenheit, the damp chilling their bones. Sonny and Harry sense that something is going to change soon. Senior officers have been driving up to the front to strategize. Every day they hear the rumble of armour as tanks assemble. During the night of February 7, they huddle in their slit trench as waves of Allied bombers roar overhead for hours. They can hear the explosions as the pilots hit their targets — German defences still dug into the Dutch towns of Kleve and Goch. They can feel the vibrations through their bones, but they experience no fear, more like exhilaration at the Germans getting clobbered. In the trenches they've been given orders to maintain strict silence. Every ten minutes there's a short lull in the bombing to give the Jerries a chance to fire back and reveal their positions, but the Allied bombing has been so thorough there is very little reply.

The infantry advance begins at 10:30 p.m., but Sonny's regiment is ordered to stay put. Within hours, German prisoners are escorted past Sonny and Harry by the Royal Welsh Fusiliers, another Canadian regiment. Sonny sees his first Nazi up close. He climbs out of his trench to look the POW in the eye. Dressed in camouflage green with a long wool coat, no helmet, long hair of battle falling in his face, the Jerry is only a little taller than Sonny. The propaganda for so many years that the Germans are a superior race is false. Sonny could clobber this guy with one hand tied behind his back. He's not even Aryan blond. His hair and eyes are as dark as Sonny's.

IN MARCH, SONNY'S REGIMENT is trucked to a new position in the Reichswald Forest. They take over abandoned log cabins and dugouts left behind by the retreating Germans. The weather has finally turned. It is something resembling warm. They stay put for two weeks. There's no fighting. It's heaven. They are not wet or cold. Their crotch rot heals. They catch up on badly needed sleep. They spend their days training, resting, even playing baseball and soccer. Sonny entertains his buddies sparring with a private from Hamilton, an amateur boxer, in his platoon. Sonny could knock out the private in thirty seconds, but he chooses to dance around, put on a good show for the guys. Besides, he doesn't want to hurt the poor guy.

By mid-April they are working their way through the Dutch city of Groningen, flushing out Germans and Dutch collaborators house by house, flat by flat. It's a tedious, gruesome detail. You creep up to a door, open it, toss in a grenade, flatten against the wall, try not to puke while the Jerries inside scream and die. Run past their corpses to the next door, do it all over again. It takes four days to secure the city.

They are moved again, farther north to protect the left flank of the 30th British Corps. As they pass through Holland, they are greeted by elated citizens. Part of Sonny's regiment goes on to cross the border into Germany, where the war is not quite over. Sonny's platoon remains behind in Holland as part of the rearguard. The weather is finally warm and sunny.

Mail is delivered to the troops. There's a letter from Loretta. She had the baby, a boy. Both are fine. But she's lonely.

"She named him Moses," Sonny tells Harry.

"A fine name."

They share a shot of rum from their rations.

"*Mazel tov*," says Harry, knocking back his shot. "You were smart to get married before the war," he says sadly. "Me? I got no one waiting for me. Just my mother and two sisters."

ON V-E DAY, MAY 8, 1945, Sonny reads the great news in the *Maple Leaf* army newspaper that has been delivered with food, cigarettes and chocolate.

"KAPUT," reads the bold headline. Hitler is dead. Germany has signed an unconditional surrender. Sonny is going home without ever shooting a single Nazi.

BOOK FOUR

Notes on The Biography of Sonny Lapinsky
by Moses Nino Lapinsky, Ph.D.

MAY 30, 2003, VANCOUVER, B.C.

MY PARENTS' MARRIAGE began to fall apart after my father came home from the war. Almost immediately he got back into touring around Ontario and New York, boxing any opponent his manager Checkie Seigelman could match him with. My mother hated being left alone all the time. She was vocal about her displeasure, being, as we say nowadays, a bit of a drama queen. She could make scenes better than any queen I've ever known. It was something that drove my father crazy. He was always more emotionally steady, even though he fought for a living.

My mother became pregnant with my brother Frankie shortly after my father came home from the war. I was just over a year old, and Mary was four. They were a fertile combination, Loretta and Sonny, in their early years together. Mom used to say he only had to look at her and she'd become pregnant. My father never really got out of the habit of adultery after his time overseas, when women were throwing themselves at his feet. Once home, as an up-and-coming young boxer on the circuit, in a different town every night, women kept dropping in his path. He couldn't think of a reason not to climb on top of them, as long as they were there. A woman in every port.

My mother sniffed it out eventually, but rather than confront him, she kept it to herself for a long time, letting it eat away slowly at whatever foundation was left in their rocky relationship. As for my father, nothing was more important than getting to the top, having a chance at the world middleweight title. Not his wife, not his children who barely knew the man we called Daddy, certainly not the women with whom he had affairs. He'd lost two precious years of his boxing career in the army. Now he had to make up for lost time. Nothing would stand in the way of Sonny's desire to win the crown.

Postwar Canada was booming. Men were returning from overseas, or from home defence across the country. Munitions plants were shutting down. Wartime production of aircraft was being converted to the manufacture of commercial airplanes. Automobiles were in great demand, as were electric ranges, refrigerators, radios, phonographs, bicycles, and other material luxuries of middle-class life, so factory jobs were plentiful, but only for men as women were laid off and ushered back into the kitchen. The baby boom had begun in earnest. In 1946, with all the returning soldiers and newlyweds out on their own for the first time, apartments were scarce. Those available for rent were snatched up instantly. The Attorney General of Ontario vowed to end liquor-law hypocrisy. Cocktail bars were finally on their way into Ontario. Thousands of Japanese Canadians were returning to their homeland, including their Canadian-born children, under a repatriation program. The stage play "Oklahoma" was playing at the Royal Alexandra, Paul Robeson was performing at the Coliseum, and an Addison table-top radio, with a five tube circuit, styled in rich brown plastic, was going for $29.95. Men's striped flannelette pyjamas were $3.95, imported gabardine suits were $75 at the May company, and you could furnish your dining room with a seven-piece dinette suite for $169.

There's a photograph or two of my father in his corporal's uniform. In one, a group shot taken at the CNE training camp, Sonny holds up his fists in the boxer's stance, while his buddies show off their rifles and army-issue knives. There's one taken in France. I found it after he'd died, in a shoebox filled with other photos, playing cards with naked women on the back, five thousand U.S. dollars in cash (I gave the money to my mother), a couple of yellowed, frayed newspaper clippings, mostly about his Middleweight Title bouts, and surprisingly, an accordion-style photo holder filled with pictures of my sister Mary, my brother Frankie, my mother and me. The war picture is one I'm sure my mother has never seen. In it, a French girl has her arms tightly around my father's shoulders, her face buried in his neck. It's obvious from the way they are touching that they've been lovers, at least for one night. My father looks terribly young, strong, brave and terrified, all at the same time.

I remember asking my dad about the war a couple of times growing up. He was never eager to talk about it.

"There should never be a war in your lifetime, Moses," he'd say. "There are no winners in war. Only losers."

Once when I was around six, my parents had stayed at home with us kids on New Year's Eve to ring in 1951. Rudy, Dad's trainer, stopped by with his date, Delilah. Uncle Sid and Aunt Ruthie dropped by early in the evening. Even Checkie, Dad's manager, and his girlfriend Lila showed up with a bottle of Scotch for my dad and Coca-Cola and chocolate bars for us kids. The grown-ups were drinking champagne. I remember because I even got a sip from my father's cup. It was bitter on my tongue but I drank it anyway to prove I was a man. Later, after everyone left, we were watching Guy Lombardo on our brand new Westinghouse black and white TV, when the show was interrupted for a news flash on a recent battle in the war in Korea. The news was graphic. An entire platoon of American soldiers were killed in the fighting, some as young as eighteen. My father became pensive. He got up and switched the television off. We listened quietly as he spoke.

He told us a story. It happened near the end of the war. He was sharing a trench with his friend, Harry Wishman. It had been a long day of fighting. They were wet and cold. It was March, and a winter chill was still in the air. But there was optimism amongst the troops. The Russians were pulverizing the Germans on the eastern front. The Americans were bombing the hell out of Germany. The Allies were pushing their way through western Europe, gaining ground every day. It wouldn't be long now. You could feel it in the air. C rations were passed around at dinnertime, and my father and Harry took turns covering their position while the other ate. Suddenly another soldier scurried over the lip of their trench and tumbled inside. He was from another unit, the Regina Rifle Regiment. He wasn't more than eighteen years old. He'd been hit running a message to his field commander. There was a gaping wound across his chest. He was dying. There were tears in my father's eyes as he told the story, and I remember being frightened, because I'd never seen him cry before, and because I could picture the injured soldier, bloody and hurt. He held the boy, whose name was Daniel, in his arms, like a mother would hold her child and he sang him a Yiddish song, one his mother used to sing to him, as the boy died in his arms. Daniel was engaged back home in Regina to a girl named Margaret, his high school sweetheart, a girl he would never see again, who would hear about his death only when the Western Union Telegram boy cycled up to his mother's door with the dreaded news. I felt so grown up, listening quietly as my father told the story. When he was done, he went to the cupboard and poured himself a large shot of Scotch and downed it in one gulp. He let me stay up late that night, sitting beside him, even after my sister and brother went to sleep and my mother had retired to their bedroom. There were no more stories that night. We just sat there together, quietly in the dark, while he sipped his Scotch and smoked. It was the closest I'd ever felt to him.

Back in 1946, my father had returned from overseas the same man who'd gone away — a tortured, talented boxer. To the untrained eye, he hadn't changed a bit. But it wasn't true. War had taught him several things. He learned how to stay dry while sitting in knee-deep mud, and that foxhole buddies have more intimate relationships than men and women could ever hope for. He learned that war is insane. Unlike boxing, nobody wins a war. He learned to despise mashed potatoes, tinned bully beef and imitation powdered tea. He knew that if he survived the war, he would succeed in his goal to be Middleweight Champ of the world, because any punishment he would take in the ring would be a piece of cake compared to war. When he handed in his army-issue Bren rifle at the end of his tour of duty, he vowed to never touch a firearm again — a promise he kept. He knew that guns were for killing. They really had no other purpose, no matter what the gun enthusiasts had to say. Even though my father was never really sure if he actually killed anyone in the war, having mostly shot across long empty fields (perhaps he killed the occasional rat among the many feasting on the corpses that lay on spent battlefields), it still made him sick to think he may have killed a man. No matter how much revenge he wanted to exact for the death of his brother Lenny when he volunteered to go overseas, once there, in the midst of the horror, he lost his appetite for murder. Boxing was a fair fight. War was a crapshoot.

And although he wasn't to realize it for another eight years, while he was overseas, sitting in his muddy trenches, shooting blind at an unseen enemy, my father learned how to forgive.

PEACE TIME

Embraceable You
MARCH 1946

SONNY ARRIVES HOME in March of 1946, in time for Moses' first birthday. He arrives by train from Montreal, by way of Halifax, by way of England, by way of Holland and the Rhineland. After the news reports started coming in of the piles of corpses, the walking dead, the gas chambers, crematoriums, torture and murder of six million Jews inside the German concentration camps, Sonny was glad his regiment was not among the camp liberators. It's a sight he wouldn't have wanted to see firsthand. Any one of the prisoners could have been a relative from Russia: his father's sister, nephews or niece. If circumstances had been different, it could have been him. Strong and tough as he is, Sonny doesn't think he'd have had the stomach to witness the horror.

Walking home from Union Station, he observes how nothing much has changed in the time he's been gone, and yet everything looks completely different. Compared with Europe, Toronto is clean and shiny and new — innocent, childlike and fresh. Sonny has grown used to the sight of bombed-out buildings and piles of rubble, dead and dying men, orphaned children, poor peasants wandering the streets with all their worldly possessions wrapped up in tiny bundles, men missing an arm or a leg, parades of displaced persons and prisoners of war. Back home there are few signs that there has even been a war on. He passes by other men still in uniform who nod at him, and he notices Victory Bond posters and billboards, but otherwise there is practically no evidence of war. It's as if he'd been sent to an entirely different world.

Toronto seems to have prospered in his absence. Gone are the empty storefronts that were common during the Depression, and people sitting on front lawns with their furniture thrown into the street. The people he passes are well dressed and well fed. There is the hustle and bustle of people on their way to work, people who have somewhere important to go. He hears the sound of radios spilling from open windows, big-band music and swing. There are more cars on the road than ever before, large, solid and shining new. And there are fewer horses and buggies. Even the neighbourhood milkman, old Mr. Robinson, has switched to a motorized truck. Men are dressed in double-breasted pin stripped suits, with wide ties and big-brimmed fedoras. Women wear sleek skirts with shoulder-padded blazers and feminine versions of the fedora. Department store billboards advertise a wealth of material possessions for sale: electric ice-boxes and ranges, automatic washing machines, radios, phonographs, electric toasters, coffee percolators and scores of other modern conveniences.

Sonny walks to Sid's apartment, half an hour away from Union Station. He needs the time to get used to being back. When he finally arrives, he runs up the stairs two at a time to the third floor. He listens at the door for a moment before knocking. He can hear a baby crying; must be the son he's never met. Moses. He's glad that with their second child, Loretta picked a Jewish name, but if he'd been home when the baby was born, he'd have suggested they name the baby after one of his deceased relatives, as is the custom, Lenny perhaps, or Berel maybe, a male version of Bayla, his grandmother who died many years ago in Russia. From inside, he hears women's voices, talking and laughing. An upbeat song plays on the radio. He recognizes the tune, Judy Garland singing "Embraceable You."

> "Embrace me, my sweet embraceable you,
> Embrace me, my irreplaceable you ..."

His cap in his hand, he knocks lightly.

"I'll go," says Loretta. Inside, Ruthie stirs a pot over the stove. Moses sits on a blanket stacking wooden blocks. Little Mary plays nearby with a baby doll. Loretta swings open the apartment door. She stares at Sonny. He'd wired ahead that he was on his way, that he'd be home sometime this week, but she didn't know it would be today. Her heart stops. He is so handsome in his uniform, but he looks weary and his eyes are so sad.

"Sonny," she murmurs as flings herself into his arms. Sonny buries his face in her neck. Their bodies fit just so. Loretta's arms are wrapped around Sonny's neck. His are around her waist. The chemistry between them is as strong as ever. She takes his face in her hands and kisses him all over, thanking God for returning him to her, thanking him for coming home and in one piece. Ruthie turns off the stove, puts on her hat and coat, bundles up the baby in a snowsuit, helps Mary into her little red overcoat, hat and mittens, and leads the toddler to the door.

"I'll take the kids out for a walk," she says, squeezing past Sonny. "Welcome home, Sonny. Sid will be happy to see you."

"The kids," Sonny remembers. "Let me see you." He bends down, scoops Mary up in his arms. She cringes, unsure exactly who this man is. Sonny kisses the top of her head, leans toward Ruthie and kisses the baby's cheek, then puts Mary back down. She clutches at her Auntie Ruthie's legs and peers at the man shyly.

Loretta says, "It's your Papa, honey." To Sonny, she says, "Don't worry, she's shy. In a few days ..."

"Sure, I know," he says, disguising the hurt. "I've been gone a long time."

"Come on, Mary," Ruthie says. "We'll be back in an hour," she tells Loretta.

When the door closes behind Ruthie, Sonny stares at Loretta. She looks a little older, but more beautiful. Not like a girl any more, but like a woman. Voluptuous. Sexy. Loretta touches Sonny's face, coarse with stubble. He also looks different. Fit and strong and calm. His nervous energy has been tamed. He's a different man than the man who left.

"Sonny ..."

"Loretta ..."

"Shhh." She puts one finger on his lips, pulls him closer, caresses his head. He is back, and that's all she cares about. Sonny nuzzles her neck, taking in her sweet scent. He presses against her, wanting her. He lifts his head, looks into her eyes and kisses her. She kisses him back passionately, running her fingers through his thick hair. She takes his hand and leads him to the back bedroom where she has been sleeping with the children while he has been gone. With the desperation of lovers who have been apart far too long, they rip their clothes off and clutch at each other.

"WHAT WAS IT LIKE?" Loretta asks later, lying in his arms, sharing a cigarette.

He takes the cigarette from her fingers, sucks in a deep draw, kisses her head, so glad to be home. In clean sheets, in the arms of his wife. "It's cold."

"Cold?"

"And dirty. You can never get clean. And it's wet."

She reaches up and strokes his face.

"Boring sometimes."

"Boring?"

"I spent I don't know how many hours, days, crouching in a trench, just listening and waiting."

"For what, Sonny?"

"Everything. The enemy. Orders. Food. Cigarettes. Water. Warm clothes. You wait for everything in the army. And sometimes ..."

"What?"

"It's ... terrifying. Bombs bursting ... just a few feet away. Only by the grace of God ... the guy beside you takes a hit. You wonder why you were so lucky. You watch him bleed, hold him in your arms, like a brother, screaming for the medics who never come. They're too busy. Or already dead. Or they can't hear you. I was Mama to ... I don't know how many guys."

"Mama?"

"That's what happens when you're dying. You want your mama."

"Oh Sonny. It must have been terrible."

"I did all right."

"You came home to me."

"I love you, Loretta."

"Let me take care of you now." She pulls him down onto her breasts, holds him tightly and softly.

The pain, the terror, the horror that has been lodged in Sonny's throat loosens, then bursts free and he cries in Loretta's arms. He cries for all the boys he watched die. For all the maimed children and women in France and Holland. For the muddy days, and the freezing nights he spent in a hole, or a ditch, or a swamp, or somebody else's cold, ruined, abandoned home. For the countryside in Europe that is now destroyed. For his own mother, whom he missed. For the father who has forsaken him. For his sweet brother Izzy who will never be a man because of what Sonny did so many years ago. And most of all for his brother Lenny. The hero. *Olev hashalom.*

THE NEXT DAY, Sonny takes the streetcar to Checkie's office, dressed in his uniform. He doesn't have to wear it. He is fully discharged from the army and can dress in civvies if he wants to, but Sonny enjoys travelling around the city in his sharp Royal Regiment of Canada Corporal's uniform. Men nod at him, women smile, children look at him in awe. Like he's a hero. He rides the streetcar for free. His Studebaker has been up on blocks for the duration. He'll have to put it back on the road later this week.

"Sonny." Checkie smiles broadly, stands and walks around to the front of his desk as Sonny enters his office. "*Mishugena.* You're back. So what did you prove? Did you prove something?"

"No."

"See? I coulda told you that. War is for fools. There's nothing there. Except death. And suffering. And dirt."

"You're right, Mr. Seigelman."

Checkie smiles. "Cut it out with the Mr. Seigelman. You're a grown man. You've been to war. Call me Checkie now. Aw right?"

Sonny smiles. "Sure, Checkie."

Checkie puffs on his cigar, studies Sonny. "What am I doing? Come 'ere, kid." He grabs Sonny in a big bear hug, lifting him off the ground for a moment before releasing him. "Let me see you. Everything okay?"

"Yeah sure. I'm fine. Everything's fine. Not even a scratch."

"Good."

"Well, I had lice for a while. And crotch rot. And a terrible cold. And the shakes. But I did all right."

"Lice?"

"Don't worry. I've been deloused about ten times. They won't let you back in the country until you're clean."

"That's disgusting."

"That's war."

"Aw right. Never mind that. Sit down. Let me get you a drink. Scotch?"

"Yeah sure, Scotch. That's great. Christ, haven't had Scotch in two years. Just army-issue rum, watery British ale, and homemade French brandy."

At the wet bar in the corner of his office Checkie pours Sonny a drink, and one for himself. "You look good in uniform. Are you still supposed to wear it?"

"I don't have to. Just got used to it."

"You're okay? Really?" He looks his fighter over for damage.

"Couple of close scrapes. That's all. I did a lot better than most. Lost a little weight is all. Don't even ask about the food over there." He rubs his flat belly.

"Listen. I'm sorry about your brother. That's a damn shame." Checkie slugs back his scotch.

"Yeah."

"I heard he was some kind of hero."

"They awarded him the Victoria Cross. Can you beat that?"

"A cross? They couldn't have made it a Star of David maybe? I'm just kidding." He laughs. "That's fantastic. What an honour."

Sonny knocks back his Scotch. A bright sun streams through the slats in the venetian blinds. Outside horns honk, a streetcar rolls by on its tracks. It's noisy outside the window on Queen Street, but it's peacetime noise. No bombs dropping. No shells bursting. No machine-gun fire.

No screams of agony, or shouts of orders. Just good old regular city sounds. Pedestrians and civilians. He's glad to be home.

"Listen, kid, I've been working out a few things for you since you've been gone."

"Good." Sonny sits taller in his chair. "'Cause I'm ready. I'm in good shape. And I'm ready to get back to work. I want to go pro, Checkie."

"I know. I know. My whachacallit? Sentiments exactly. I'm thinking of getting you on a ticket down at Maple Leaf Gardens."

"Aw Checkie, I want to go to New York. I want some real action, real money. I got a wife and two kids now to support, you know."

"Yeah, I know." Checkie shakes his head. "What's a matter with you? You never heard of rubbers?"

"Don't you start on me about that. Listen, I want to fight at Madison Square Garden. Can you get me on a card there? Or what?"

Checkie sighs. "Sure, sure Sonny. Just hold your horses. You've been away for a while. I can't just snap my fingers. You gotta build up your name again right here, then we'll see."

Sonny slaps the armrest of his chair. "Never mind that crap, Boss. Just get me there."

"Aw right, aw right. Jeez Sonny. I can see how much your manners have improved since being over there in Krautland."

"Holland."

"Whatever. Listen, we'll start with Maple Leaf Gardens. The purse is decent, plus I can get you some action on the side. You can make more that way anyway. Then I'll start working on New York."

Sonny punches the air. "That's better. That's what I like to hear. How soon?"

"I don't know, Sonny. Calm down. If we go to New York, we do it right."

"Whadya mean?"

"We go on tour. Not just the Garden. We go all over New York State first. Build up your name over there, like. Get you a whachacallit? A reputation, see? Then we finish at the Garden. By then your name'll have been in the papers and we'll get a real crowd. You'll start getting known over there. How's that sound, Champ?"

"That sounds fine, Boss. Just fine."

Checkie pours more Scotch. They both sip on their drinks for a long moment. Checkie studies Sonny over his glass. "So, what about the wife? And the kids? What's she gonna say about you going on tour? You know it could be four, five weeks at a time."

"You let me worry about Loretta, okay? Don't worry about it. Just get me the fights."

"How is she anyway?"

"She's good. She's fine."

"So things are working out okay?"

"Yeah, sure."

"Okay. Good. That's good, Sonny. She's a nice girl."

"Yeah."

"Come on. Let me buy you some lunch. What do you say?"

"Yeah sure, okay. But nothing with mashed potatoes, or white bread and margarine. In the army, every hot meal comes with godamn mashed potatoes with gravy all over it. And the cold rations always have hard-tack bread and white margarine. Don't even ask about salted meat. Jeez Boss, I've had enough *trayf* to last me a lifetime. Goddamn meat and mashed potatoes. And goddamn gravy on everything."

"Don't worry. We're going to Shopsowitz's. Bet it's been a long time since you had a pastrami on rye, huh Sonny?"

"Too long." Sonny drains the rest of his Scotch then follows Checkie out of the office.

SONNY MOVES HIS WIFE and kids back into a flat in one of Checkie's houses on Manning Avenue, south of Harbord. Loretta is thrilled to have her husband back and to have her own apartment again, after living with Sid and Ruthie all that time. She throws herself into her children, her husband and their home, trying out new recipes she learns from Ruthie, making curtains for the kitchen and living room windows. Sonny goes back into training. Every morning Rudy picks up Sonny and they drive out to High Park. Rudy drives behind as Sonny runs three miles to get his legs into shape — just as they did when Sonny was a kid. He's out of shape after sitting in trenches for two years — he's easily winded and his legs ache. After breakfast, they go to the Cecil Street Athletic Club for Sonny's gym work. Rudy puts him back to square one, working on the heavy and light bags, jumping rope, lifting barbells, working with the medicine ball, before he matches Sonny with sparring partners. Sonny is impatient to get back into the ring.

"Come on, Rudy."

"One step at a time, Sonny. You're soft. What the hell did you do over there?"

"Sat in a lot of trenches. Laid down in others."

"One step at a time, kid."

AFTER SONNY'S BEEN HOME more than two weeks, he's dying to see his mother. He waits for a Monday when he knows his father will be at work. As he rounds the corner, he sees Sophie on the front porch shaking out a rug. It's unseasonably warm for March, and she's wearing only a thin sweater over her cotton dress.

Sophie stops suddenly. She can't believe her eyes. It's her Sonny walking down the street toward her. A miracle. She'd heard from Sid that Sonny was back. She just couldn't allow herself to believe it until this moment. He looks good. Healthy. All in one piece. Thank God. She isn't sure, but he seems to have grown a little taller. Many times while Sonny was away, Sophie wanted to visit Loretta, especially when she heard from Sid there was a new baby, Moses. Two grandchildren Sophie still hadn't met. But she just couldn't work up the courage to defy Yacov and she knew she'd feel awkward dropping in on Sonny's wife, a woman she'd barely met once.

Sonny smiles at his mother.

"Hi, Ma."

"Sonny." They embrace. Sophie's heart heals just a little. At least Sonny came home, alive and well. "Are you all right? Everything's all right?"

"I'm fine."

"Oh Sonny. Thank God." She pulls him close, clutches him to her. "Thank God."

"Where's Izzy?"

Reluctantly, Sophie releases him. "Out collecting scrap. For the war effort."

Sonny smiles. "The war's over."

"Try telling your brother that. He doesn't have much else to do."

"Is he okay?"

"You'll wait a while. See for yourself. He'll be home soon."

"What about Pop?"

"He won't be home until supper. Sit." Sophie sits on the porch, reaches in her apron pocket for her cigarettes. Sonny sits beside her, accepts a cigarette, though he's not supposed to. In the army he smoked all the time, as much as possible, for the nerves, also to cover the stench of decaying bodies and dead cattle that lay about in all the fields, bloated and slowly decomposing. But Rudy doesn't like his fighters to smoke. Bad for the lungs. Sonny's trying to cut down, but it's not easy.

"You got any pictures?" asks Sophie.

"Huh?"

"Of your kids."

"Oh. Sure." Sonny smiles, thrilled that his mother wants to see. He pulls his wallet out of his back pocket, flips it open. He has a long plastic accordion-style photo holder, crammed with pictures of Loretta and the kids.

Sophie takes one end and scours the photos. "Your wife is pretty. I remember that."

"Yeah, Ma. She's a knockout. Ain't she? And that's Mary. And this is Moses."

Sophie's heart expands at the sight of her grandchildren. "They look exactly like you as a baby. Both of them."

"You think?"

"Sure they do. Oh Sonny." Her eyes fill with tears.

"You want to meet them, Ma?"

Sophie nods slowly. "They're my grandchildren, aren't they?" She wipes her tears with her handkerchief, blows her nose.

"You mean it, Ma?"

"As soon as Izzy gets home, we'll go."

LORETTA IS FLUSTERED by the unexpected visit from her mother-in-law. She wanted everything to be just right when they finally met. As it is, when Sonny, Izzy and Sophie arrive, a pot of rice is boiling over on the stove, the sink is filled with dishes, the highchair is covered in Moses' baby food, Loretta is in the bedroom dressing Moses, and Mary is having a tantrum in the corner of the kitchen.

"Hey, hey, hey." Sonny picks Mary up. "What's a matter with you?"

Mary wails something unintelligible, through her sobs.

"What? Loretta!" he hollers.

Loretta walks into the kitchen, Moses over her shoulder, her hair disheveled, a stained apron tied around her waist, baby puke on her dress. "Oh." Loretta stops in the doorway.

"There you are. Loretta, this is my mother."

Loretta glares at Sonny, tries to push her unruly hair back off her face. "You should have told me, Sonny. Everything's a mess." She feels ashamed.

"I remember what it's like with babies. Loretta, I'm just happy to meet you." Sophie puts her hands on Loretta's shoulder, leans in and hugs her daughter-in-law. "I'm so sorry it's taken this long." Tears well up in Sophie's eyes. It is her turn to feel ashamed. They're just kids, Loretta and Sonny. Loretta can't be more than nineteen. Maybe twenty. With two babies. Why has she waited this long to meet her grandchildren? "Let me see the baby." She reaches out for Moses and takes him in her arms, nuzzles him against her neck. He has that fresh sweet baby smell. It's been so long since Sophie's held a baby. His tiny little hand clutches her thumb. Mary stops crying and from the safety of her father's shoulder, peeks at the strange lady.

"Come on. Let's sit down, everybody. All right?" Sonny says.

They sit on the crinkly plastic of the sofa. Dominating the living room is a playpen, filled with toys. There are no pictures on the walls, no rug, no furniture besides the sofa, a coffee table and a radio. On the floor is a stack of old newspapers, mostly turned to the sports section. Sonny glances at

Loretta, who smiles through her fear. What if Sonny's mother thinks she's a bad wife? If only she'd known there were coming. She could have tidied up, baked cookies, made tea. On Sophie's shoulder, Moses begins to cry.

"His diaper needs changing," Loretta reaches for him.

"Let me do it," Sophie volunteers.

"No. I mean, you're a guest." Loretta doesn't want her mother-in-law to see the bedroom, which is in even more disarray. The bed's not made, Sonny's pyjamas and her nightgown are strewn across the bed, the laundry from yesterday has not been put away. It sits in piles on top of the dresser.

"Don't be silly," Sophie insists, hugging her grandson against her bosom tightly, heading for the bedroom.

OVER DINNER, Yacov asks Sophie how her day was.

"Fine," she says.

"Sonny's house," Izzy pipes up, between mouthfuls of chicken.

Sophie cringes.

Yacov stiffens at the sound of his son's name, and looks over at Sophie.

"He's back? You saw him?"

Sophie places the serving bowl of vegetables on the table. "Look, Yacov. We have two grandchildren, whether you like it or not. I wanted to meet my grandchildren. What's so terrible?"

"What's so terrible?" Yacov yells. Izzy flinches. "What's so terrible? You think it's fine that he married a *shiksa*? Suddenly, now everything is fine?"

"No. I don't think it's fine. Of course, I wish he'd found a Jewish girl. But Yacov, he didn't. All right? He didn't. How long are you going to keep this up? We lost one son, Yacov. Not two."

"How long? I tell you how long? For as long as he's married to a *shiksa*."

"You have two beautiful grandchildren."

"No!"

"He was in the war."

"No."

"Oy, so stubborn," Sophie says to the ceiling.

Yacov stands abruptly, scraping his chair against the floor.

"Where you going?"

"For a walk."

Yacov grabs his jacket and hat and flees down the stairs and out the door. It's cooler now as the sun slips behind the horizon. There is a brisk breeze. It might even snow later tonight. He turns up his collar and marches down the street, stomping hard on the pavement.

Grandchildren he has yet? Most days, he tries not to think about Sonny. It's too painful. He made up his mind, and that's it. Done. Finished. He doesn't want to be reminded of it again. Why does Sonny have to be so stubborn? There are plenty of Jewish girls in the neighbourhood. He could have married one of them. Then he'd have Jewish grandchildren. According to Jewish law, the mother determines whether or not the children are Jewish. The mother in this case is Catholic. So the kids aren't Jewish. How can he be the grandfather to kids who aren't Jewish? That's it. Plain and simple. But why does he feel so bad inside, then? Why does Sophie make him out to be the bad guy? Because he is bad. He feels terrible about the dealings he and Max have with Checkie Seigelman — buying goods he knows are stolen from God-knows-where-or-who? He feels ashamed. And trapped. Every day he asks God for forgiveness. He is just trying to support his wife and family. The Depression years are still fresh in his mind. He doesn't ever want to be that poor again. Every day Yacov tells himself he will continue to deal with Seigelman just one more day. Then he will get out and be an honest businessman, buy from honest manufacturers. Here he is, a middle-aged man, buying from a *goniff*. Maybe that's why Sonny turned out bad. It is his fault, after all. What did Sonny do that was so wrong? Who is he hurting? Maybe no one. But, he married against Jewish law. *If everybody marries outside the faith, then where will we all be?* No. He can't forgive. He can't forget. He said Kaddish over Shmuel. And that's it.

The Contender
JULY TO SEPTEMBER, 1946

SONNY CRAMS HIS extra socks and boxer shorts into his duffle bag. Rudy has already packed up his road equipment and ring trunks, robe, boots, gloves, mouthguard, athletic supporter, towels, gauze, tape and first-aid supplies. Loretta hovers in the bedroom doorway with Moses balanced on one hip, smoking a cigarette with the other hand, a habit she took up during Sonny's absence. There's another heat wave on. Every summer it's the same thing. The apartment is baking.

"I don't see why you have to go all the way to New York. There's plenty of places to fight right here at home," Loretta says. *Like right here in this bedroom with me,* she thinks, but doesn't say out loud. It seems to Loretta that since Sonny's been home, all they do is fight.

Sonny takes a deep breath. He is tired of explaining. "I already told you, Loretta. It's a road tour. I'm fighting all over New York State. To build up my reputation."

"How long you gonna be gone this time, Sonny?" Loretta puffs at her cigarette. Sonny just got home, it seems, from the war. And now he's leaving her again? Little Mary wanders into the room and leans on her mother's legs.

"Six weeks, Loretta. I already told you that part, too."

"And what am I supposed to do while you're gone for six weeks?"

"How the hell should I know? Do whatever you usually do, Loretta." She moves closer to him and softens her tone of voice. "Don't go. Please."

"I have to go. I won't make it big staying here at home. It's that simple. After this tour, Checkie's gonna try and get me into the Garden and that's when the money'll start rolling in, Loretta. We won't have to live like this." He sweeps his arms around their humble apartment. "You can have diamonds and furs, Baby. But I can't get on a good fight card until I drag my ass around New York State, building up my name. *Farshtaist?*"

"Stop talking in Jewish, Sonny. You know I don't understand," she snaps.

Even to her own ears, she sounds shrill. She hadn't meant to. She's just scared. And lonely. And hot.

"One word, Loretta. *Farshtaist.* You know what it means. Jesus."

"And don't use the Lord's name in vain."

"Huh?"

"Not in front of the children."

"Loretta," Sonny warns, "don't start with that Jesus stuff again."

"Why not? I'm a Catholic, ain't I?"

"Aw geez, Loretta." Sonny sits on the edge of the bed. *Don't remind me.*

"And what's going to be after this, Sonny? Chicago? Detroit? California? You'll come home from this and then you'll be off to fight somewhere else. Won't you?"

"This is what I do, Sweetheart. You knew it when you married me." With the back of his hand, he wipes sweat from the sides of his face.

"I didn't know you'd never be home."

"Look." He glances at his watch, a Timex with a silver-plated flexible band. Rudy will be by any time to pick him up. "I gotta go downstairs. We'll talk about it when I get home. All right?" He stands, zips his bag, grabs the handles. He kisses the top of Mary's and then Moses' head, moves to kiss Loretta. She pulls back. He sighs, shakes his head and walks past her.

Inside, Loretta is proud of Sonny. He's on his way to becoming famous and successful. She wants him to succeed. But when he goes away, she's lonely. And for the past few weeks, her hormones have been off kilter. She feels everything so deeply. Everything feels immense and insurmountable. If Sonny goes away again, Loretta's not sure she can cope with it all. She's not angry with Sonny. She's scared. Since they've been married, it seems that all he does is go away.

"I won't be here when you get back, Sonny." Loretta surprises herself. She wasn't planning to say that at all.

He stops in the doorway. "Aw Loretta. Don't do this to me. This is not a good time. I have to go."

"That's fine, Sonny. You go. Just don't expect to find me here when you get back."

Sonny hesitates. He hears the honk of Rudy's Ford. "Damn it, Loretta."

"Sonny. I said watch your language in front of the kids."

"All right. Geez."

Rudy honks again.

"I gotta go."

"So go."

"Baby. Come on. Don't be sore." He approaches her. She glares at him, even as her eyes fill with tears. "I love you, baby," he says, "You know that."

Loretta throws her free arm around his neck. "Oh Sonny. I miss you."

"I'm right here, baby."

"But you're going."

"Just a few weeks ..." He kisses her neck.

Heavy footsteps clomp their way up the stairs. There's a knock at the door. Sonny breaks free. He smiles his crooked grin and reaches again for his duffle bag. "Bye kids. See you in a couple weeks."

"Sonny ..."

"What is it Loretta?" Sonny asks impatiently.

The tears flow. "I went to see Dr. Grossman yesterday."

"What? What's a matter? Something wrong with you? Or Moses? Mary? What?"

Loretta takes a deep breath. "I'm pregnant."

"Again?"

She nods.

There's another knock at the door, harder this time.

"Why didn't you tell me? Jesus. Just hang on."

Sonny leaves the bedroom, walks through the living room to the apartment door, and flings it open. The doorknob hits the wall behind.

"Come on, Sonny. Time to hit the road."

Loretta has followed Sonny to the door, Moses still on her hip, Mary trailing behind her mother.

"Oh, hiya Loretta. Hi kids."

Mary hides behind her mother's leg. "Say hi to Uncle Rudy, Mary."

"You set?" Rudy asks Sonny.

"Hold your horses, Rudy. Take a load off." He gestures to the sofa.

"Okay. But we should get going." Rudy checks the time on his watch.

"Just gimme a minute." Sonny turns to Loretta, puts his arms around her. "Are you sure?"

She nods.

"Okay, baby. Listen. It's good, right?"

She sniffs. "I guess."

"Sure it is, baby. Hey Rudy, guess what? Loretta's, you know ... knocked up."

"Again?"

"Sonny, have some class," admonishes Loretta.

"What?"

"Knocked up," Loretta mimics.

"*Mazel tov*," says Rudy. He stands. "Listen, we really gotta go, Sonny."

"Sure, go ahead Sonny. Don't keep Rudy waiting." Anger surges through Loretta. "He's more important to you than me."

"Aw Loretta, don't be like that."

"Maybe I should wait in the car," offers Rudy. He shuffles closer to the door.

"You're making this very hard, Loretta," accuses Sonny.

"Oh. So it's all my fault?"

"That's not what I said. Look, Sweetheart. You're upset. You're tired." *You're crazy*, he wants to say. *Was she this crazy last time she was pregnant?* Sonny tries to remember. "Look, I'll call you long-distance, okay? And we'll talk about it then." Sonny leans over to kiss Loretta. She offers only a cheek, which he pecks.

"Loretta ..."

"Go, Sonny. Rudy's waiting." She pushes him forward.

Sonny's gut turns over. It's not how he wants to leave. But he reaches for his jacket and cap and follows Rudy out.

Loretta removes one shoe and hurls it against the closed door.

"Mama," Mary clutches her mother's leg. Moses starts to cry.

IN BUFFALO SONNY WINS his fight by decision. In Utica, he knocks out his opponent in the third round. In Syracuse, he wins by a knockout in the sixth. In Albany Sonny knocks out the contender, a local favourite, in fifty-five seconds. He hadn't meant to. Rudy always drummed it into his head to take it easy. Go slow. People don't want to pay for a fight that's over in sixty seconds. They want to see blood. Even if he knows in the first few seconds he can take down his opponent, he is trained to back off, take a few hits, box around the ring, give and take for a few rounds, sweat, dance, bleed, then go in for the kill. Audiences love that, Rudy has told him again and again. They love a turn-around fight, where they think a guy's going to get clobbered, then he rises from the dead to beat the crap out of the one who seems to be winning.

"It gets good press," Rudy tells Sonny. "That's what we want."

"I thought I'm supposed to win. I want a crack at the title."

"Course you're supposed to win, you putz. But you gotta put on a good show. *Farshtaist*?"

"Yeah yeah."

"That's what people remember. That's what they're paying for."

But in Albany the contender is finished before he even starts. Washed up. Too old. Rick Jones. Guy must be over thirty-five, Sonny decides. It's kind of pathetic. No way Sonny's gonna be fighting when he's thirty-five. At twenty-two, Sonny is in his physical prime. His first punch tosses Jones to the floor and he stays down for a six-count. It's all over thirty seconds after he drags himself back up.

They drive through the Catskill Mountains, and stop for a special exhibition bout at a new Jewish resort called Kaplan's. It's more of a gag than anything. There's a professional fighter booked against Sonny for an evening bout. But for the afternoon, Sonny is scheduled to dance around the ring with any hotel guest who wants to take a crack at the Canadian champ. The owner, Morty Kaplan, is a crony of Checkie Seigelman. Checkie figures, "It's kinda like a whatchacallit ... publicity stunt. See? Anyways, they're all a bunch of *alta cockers* and *pishers*. And you're one of their own. They like to see a nice Jewish boy make good. Don't forget to wear the robe with the Jewish star and your name on the back. I want them to remember your name."

"Aw boss, I can't do that. It's embarrassing. I'm a pro."

"Yeah, and that's why you're gonna do it, Sonny. Trust me. It's worth its weight in gold. Free publicity. Every person there's gonna remember your name. Next time you pass through their town, they're gonna bring ten of their friends to your fight. Sometimes we all gotta do things we don't like, okay boychick?" Checkie grabs the flesh on each side of Sonny's face and squeezes hard.

"Yeah, okay. Okay. Ouch."

"Just don't hurt anybody. You got that? Just dance around, make 'em feel good. Let 'em hit you once or twice. Defence only. You got that, boychick?"

"Yeah, I know. Whatja think? I'd slug a little kid, or something?"

"Just be careful, that's all."

They're staying at Kaplan's for the weekend. Rudy and Sonny share a two-room cabin, with a washroom, screen door and its own porch. Meals are taken in the big communal dining room. Everyone wants to sit by the boxer from Canada, so Sonny has to keep moving tables. There's more food being plunked on the tables than Sonny's ever seen in one place before. Smoked meat, cabbage rolls covered in tomato sauce, *verenishkas*, *kishka*, potato *latkes*, chopped liver, coleslaw, dill pickles, beef *knishes*, fresh rye bread, roast beef, roast chicken, salads, chicken soup, cabbage borscht, split-pea soup. And desserts: cherry cheesecake, sponge cake, honey cake, apple pie, blueberry pie, ice cream in three different flavours with chocolate sauce and sprinkles. In the army Sonny would have killed for such food. But he can't eat most of it. On his fight-schedule diet, he eats lots of steak and salad. Rudy lets him have one piece of bread with each meal. Dessert is out of the question.

After breakfast — Rudy restricts Sonny to poached eggs, toast, oatmeal and tea, although on the menu there are also pancakes, smoked meat, kosher sausages, French toast, steak, fried liver, cheese omelettes and twelve different brands of cold cereal — they wander around the resort grounds. The Catskill Mountains are pretty and the resort is surrounded by towering evergreen trees, maples and majestic oaks. There are outdoor activities everywhere. On the lawn, a young dance instructor is teaching a crowd of fat old men dressed in flowered bathing trunks and matching cabaña shirts and middle-aged women in summer shifts, a few with purses slung over their arms, straw sunhats on their heads and horn-rimmed sunglasses on their noses, how to dance the rumba. Arms outstretched, they follow the instructor.

"And a one and a two, a one and a two. That's right Mrs. Schwartz, kick your foot," the young instructor prods, a huge smile on his amused face.

Rudy and Sonny try not to laugh.

On a porch, at portable bridge tables, there are two serious poker games in progress. The middle-aged men sit four to a table, in short pants and white undershirts, cigars clamped between their lips, cups of strong coffee laced with whiskey snuck from a hip flask when their wives are not looking.

Four elderly men play pinochle for pennies at the next table.

"Dat's twenty-tree cents you owe me, Eli," a white-haired man tells his friend.

"Vat are you talking about? You lost dat round, Yankel."

By the lake, Rudy and Sonny watch youngsters swim. A teenaged camp counsellor rushes by in shorts and a Kaplan's T-shirt, clipboard in hand, blowing on her whistle. Sonny watches the curve of her thigh as she dashes past with a gaggle of young children.

In the afternoon Sonny performs the sideshow. He dutifully boxes around the ring with twelve-year-old boys and balding, fifty-year-old men with paunches. He easily deflects their slow attempts to hit him and once in a while he lets a guy connect with his chest, or upper arm. A little boy of ten has natural talent. Sonny keeps the kid in the ring for extra long and shows him some technique. The real fight is scheduled for seven o' clock that evening.

The resort has set out chairs on all four sides of the rented boxing ring installed in the middle of a large green lawn. Every guest in the hotel attends the fight. Sonny warms up in the hotel gym, shadow-boxing before the fight. When Rudy leads him into the ring, a cheer resounds. He recognizes some of the boys and men he pretend-boxed with in the afternoon, sitting proudly up front. Some pat him on the back as he passes. Others point him out to their parents, their wives. Dutifully, he smiles, acts like their best friend. They beam back at him. As he crosses the front row to the ring, he notices a beautiful older woman, with long dark hair

and intense dark eyes, staring and smiling seductively at him. He holds
her gaze for a moment, then climbs into the ring.

The fight is close. His opponent, Dave Malkin, is good — a professional
middleweight from the Bronx. But Sonny is five years younger, a lot faster
and hungrier to win. They box all the way to the eighth round, and then
Sonny goes in for the kill, knocking out Malkin and winning the fight. The
referee holds his arm up in the victory salute. Sonny keeps his eye on the
beautiful woman in the front row, as he climbs out the ring and is mobbed
by boys and men for autographs.

She is waiting for him, after he has showered and changed into a double-
breasted suit, no tie, shirt collar spread out on his lapels.

"Go for a walk?" she suggests as Sonny steps outside his cabin. The
screen door clatters shut.

"Well, hello there." Sonny is a little surprised by her forward approach.

Wordlessly, she takes his arm and leads him to a footpath. "I'm
Myrna," she says.

"Hello, Myrna. Cigarette?" He holds out his pack as she takes one. He
stops and faces her to light it. They look deep into each other's eyes. She
licks her lips and moves closer. Sonny leans over. She flings her arms
around his neck and they kiss passionately.

"Atta boy, Champ." An older man slaps Sonny hard on the back,
laughing as he passes them on the path.

Sonny pulls away, grabs Myrna's hand and leads her back inside his
cabin.

Myrna leaves several hours later to look for her husband, a much older
man who is in the diamond trade. She freshens her lipstick on Sonny's
porch before heading on her way.

SONNY BARELY REMEMBERS the next three towns, but he wins every
fight. They pass through New York and cross the border for a bout in
New Jersey; then Staten Island; Great Neck; Connecticut; and then finally
Brooklyn and the Bronx. After the Catskills and Myrna, Sonny makes a
regular habit of indulging in the pleasures tossed his way. In every town
there are women throwing themselves at him.

"Sex is death for a fighter, Sonny," Rudy warns. "You gotta abstain when you're fighting."

"Why? I'm winning, ain't I?"

"Yeah sure, but it saps your strength."

"I got plenty of strength."

Rudy shakes his head. "Checkie ain't gonna like this."

"Aw come on, Rudy. You don't have to tell him."

"Yeah, I do."

"Maybe in my case, sex is, you know, kinda like a good thing."

"I don't know, Sonny."

"You don't change things around when you're on a winning streak, Rudy, you said so yourself. If it's working, keep doing it."

"Wise guy."

"Well, it's working, ain't it?"

"I guess so."

"Thanks, Rudy."

"Just don't ask me to straight-out lie for you. That's all."

"You're a pal, Rudy."

"Especially to Loretta."

Sonny feels stung. He says nothing.

"Anyway, Checkie's meeting us in Brooklyn tomorrow afternoon. He wants to be here for your last couple of fights."

BY THE TIME Sonny reaches Brooklyn in late August, his reputation has preceded him. The papers call him "The next Middleweight Champ," "The Hebrew Jake La Motta," "The Canadian Charger," "The Next Max Baer." It's even more than Checkie has dreamed of. His plan is working just fine. The press is eating right out of his hands and Sonny's never been in finer form.

"It's because of being in the war," Sonny tells Rudy.

"How do you mean?"

"Concentration I guess."

"Yeah?"

"And something else …" Sonny can't quite pinpoint it. It has to do with Lenny. That's as far as he can take the thought. When he's in the ring he's doing it for Lenny. It's so easy. He doesn't even think of himself. Doesn't notice the pain of being hit in the same spot repeatedly. Doesn't feel the fatigue, sore muscles, the blows to the head. His opponent's gloves bounce off Sonny. He's invulnerable. Like Superman. It's almost like Lenny is protecting him from the grave and no harm can come to him. He wins every single fight on the tour. If Lenny could run onto a battlefield alone, and save an entire platoon against a Panzer attack, then Sonny can stand in a ring and take any punishment any fighter can dish out, and barely feel a thing. This morning when he checked out the *Times*, he found himself on the cover of the sports page, plus there was a small item about his fight right on the front page. Of the *New York* Fucking *Times*. How's that for a ghetto boy?

"What are you talking about?" Rudy unpacks his shaving kit and tosses it on the dresser of their hotel room.

"I don't know. I can't lose. That's all. I just know I can't lose."

"Atta boy."

CHECKIE ARRIVES IN BROOKLYN in time for Sonny's pre-fight steak, sits across from him in the restaurant booth.

"So? *Nu*? I got news for you boychick."

Sonny looks up from his dinner.

Checkie grins. "I got you on a card at the Garden."

Sonny drops his fork. "The Garden?"

Checkie nods.

"*The* Garden?"

"There's more than one, maybe?"

"You're not pulling a fast one, are you Checkie?"

"Would I do that?"

Sonny leans forward. "When?"

"December. After this tour you're coming home and training hard. 'Cause if you win the fight at the Garden, you're on your way to being a contender. How do you like that?"

"For the title?"

"What else?"

"The middleweight title?"

"Are you a middleweight?" Checkie asks sarcastically.

"Yeah, sure."

"Of course the Middleweight title, you nut. Get him," he says to Rudy.

Rudy nods and smiles broadly. His boy is headed for the title.

IN SEPTEMBER, a week after Sonny comes back to Toronto from his successful summer tour of New York, Loretta leaves the kids with their grandmother and walks directly to Ruthie's. On their phonograph, Ruthie is playing a seventy-eight album from the hit Broadway musical, Finian's Rainbow, "Old Devil Moon."

"Come on in, honey. I'll make some tea." Ruthie holds open the door for her sister-in-law. "Where's the kids?"

"With Sophie. Can you believe it?"

"*Mazel tov*, Loretta. That means congratulations."

"I know."

Ruthie gives Loretta a little hug. "I've also got news."

"Good news?"

"The best. I'm expecting again. And I think it's going to work out this time. I'm already in my third month and Dr. Grossman says everything looks good. I just have to take it easy. No heavy lifting. Extra rest."

"*Mazel tov*, Ruthie." Loretta leans over and returns the hug. "That is wonderful. Does anyone else know?"

"Just Sid. I don't want to say anything yet. Maybe it'll bring bad luck."

"I won't tell a soul." She's not showing yet, so Loretta doesn't say a word about her own pregnancy. Ruthie's had such a hard time, three miscarriages, and Loretta gets pregnant every time Sonny so much as looks at her. She doesn't want Ruthie to feel bad. Plenty of time to tell her later, and what if Ruthie miscarries again? For the sake of her sweet sister-in-law, Loretta sincerely hopes not.

"I'm so happy." The tea kettle whistles on the stove. Ruthie takes it off the burner, pours boiling water into a china pot. "And Sid is ecstatic.

We've been waiting so long." She opens the kitchen cupboard for teacups and saucers.

There's a second or two of static from the record, then the next song begins to play. Ruthie only vaguely pays attention to the words, as she opens the icebox for milk. The music swells for the chorus.

"When I am not near the girl that I love,
I love the girl I'm near."

Loretta leans her head in her hands and makes a strange sound. Laughing? What's funny? Ruthie glances over and realizes that Loretta is not laughing, she's crying. She sits beside Loretta, strokes her back. "Honey? What is it? Loretta?"

Loretta gives an agonized wail. "Oh Ruthie ... Sonny's cheating on me."

"Oh, Sweetheart. That's terrible. How do you know?"

Loretta abruptly quits crying and looks Ruthie in the eye, silently. A woman knows.

Dreams
OCTOBER 30, 1946

MAX LAPINSKY SHAKES HANDS with Hymie Goldberg and hands him two hundred dollars cash to cover first and last month's rent. Inside the empty storefront on College near Spadina he counts out the twenties, one by one, into Hymie's open palm. Yacov and Max have been working toward this moment for twenty-five years. They are both in a state of shock. This is a scene they have played inside their heads many times, especially during the lean days of the Depression. It's hard to believe it's actually happening. Their dream has come true. They are both afraid to breathe, in case the vision goes away. The store smells of strong cleanser. Mr. Goldberg had it cleaned just yesterday after the last tenant left. The windows are covered in a white soapy mixture that's been smeared on to block the view inside. Yacov perches nervously beside Max as they read the rental agreement. Sid stands behind, reading over Max's shoulder.

"I'm sure you gentlemen will find everything in order," Hymie Goldberg says impatiently, cash in his pocket, his brown felt fedora already back on his head. "If you'll just sign the lease at the bottom …"

"Oh sure," says Max. "We'll read it later. You must be busy."

"Hold on, Uncle Max." Sid reaches for the document. "I think we should read before we sign."

"What's a matter? You think I'd cheat you?" Goldberg snaps.

"Take it easy, Hymie," Max placates. "You know how the young people are these days."

"Nothing personal, Mr. Goldberg," Sid adjusts his glasses. "I just think we should read before we sign. If you're in a hurry, we can hang onto the lease and drop it off to you later."

Goldberg eyes Sid. He is offended. On the other hand, he has to admire the young man. A good head for business. He'd never sign a document without reading the fine print. "All right. Sure. No problem. If I'm out you can leave it with my secretary." Goldberg heads for the door. He reaches into his pocket. "Oh, here." He tosses a set of keys to Max.

They clink in Max's palm.

"Uh, Mr. Goldberg, we'll need a receipt for the rent," Sid says, buttoning his double-breasted suit jacket. Sid is in his element. He has trained his whole life to be a businessman. Now here they are, on the crest of a new wave in their lives. And Ruthie is pregnant. He feels hopeful. This time it's got to work out.

"What a guy." Hymie shakes a fist in the air, "Everything's gotta be on paper nowadays? Whatever happened to a gentleman's agreement? All right. All right. I'll have my secretary write you up a receipt. *Ich vais nicht.*" He opens the door, shaking his head. "Young people," he mutters, closing the door behind him.

Max looks at Yacov, then at Sid.

He tosses the keys high into the air and catches them. Then he tosses them to Yacov. "Huh? What do you say, Yacov? We did it!" He takes long strides down the linoleum floor, walking from one end of the store to the other, feeling the pride of ownership. His shoes echo in the empty space. The corner of College and Spadina — the absolute perfect location. The grand opening will be on December 1, just in time for Christmas shoppers. They have a month to fill the store with shelving and merchandise. The three men are going to be equal partners in the business. Their wives are going to help pull the store together. Tessie has wonderful ideas for decorating, Sophie wants a hand in ordering, and Ruthie, a whiz with numbers, is going to do the bookkeeping. Now, instead of operating out of the back of the truck and selling to department stores that make most of the profit, the partners will sell retail. It is to be the first bargain store in the neighbourhood. A revolution in retail — small household items and clothing bought for a song and sold inexpensively. Cash only. No credit. All sales final. No refunds. No fancy displays or expensive counters. Just solid bargains, wall to wall. They smile at one another, filled with hope. Prosperity is just around the corner. For the first time in many years, they can actually feel it.

It's a bittersweet moment for Yacov. Sophie is still, well, delicate. Since Lenny's death.

"Money isn't everything," she said to him last night.

"I know, Sophie."

"No you don't."

"What are you talking? I know."

"Go to your store, Yacov. That's more important than your family."

"It's all for my family." These days he can't say the right thing to Sophie, no matter how hard he tries.

November 1946

TO MAKE SURE that Sonny is in perfect condition, Checkie books him a fight every two weeks leading up to his engagement at Madison Square Garden on December 12, when he'll meet Joey Ricardo, another

up-and-coming middleweight. Ricardo grew up in the Bronx and has
the support of the New York media, so Sonny is going to have to work
extra hard to win the fight. There's already talk of Ricardo challanging the
current middleweight champ, "Tiny" Dave Johnson, for the world title. If
Sonny knocks out Ricardo, he'll be on his way to being a contender.
There's a lot riding on the bout.

In between fighting every two weeks to keep his edge, Sonny undergoes
the hardest training of his life. Roadwork, gym work, sparring and
absolutely no fooling around. That means no booze, no women, home
and in bed every night by nine o' clock, and every morsel of food that goes
into Sonny's mouth is monitored by Rudy. Sonny is up every morning at
five, runs six miles, then eats a chunk of cheese with milk, showers and
goes back to sleep for an hour. When Sonny wakes, he eats a high-protein
breakfast of half a dozen eggs with lean smoked meat, toast and porridge.
Then Rudy puts Sonny through his paces in the gym: pounding the heavy
bag for strength, working on the speed bag for rhythm, jumping rope for
coordination and punishing exercises with the medicine ball.

Rudy made a special trip to Chicago to watch Ricardo fight and to
study his style. Ricardo is a counter-puncher. He bides his time, keeping
his defence up, waiting for his opponent to make a mistake, then he
moves in with a smashing right uppercut to the jaw. His usual pattern is
to KO his opponent by the sixth or seventh round. He stays sharp because
he covers his face at all times and rarely takes a hit to the jaw. His Achilles
heel, notes Rudy, is his size. He is taller than Sonny by three inches, and
bulkier, which means two things: one, his punch packs a wallop, and two,
he is slow. Rudy realizes that Sonny will have to work on his defence. As
long as he doesn't take too many hits from Ricardo, Sonny can wear him
down, tire him out and then go in for the kill.

Rudy hires every Toronto fighter he can find with a style like Ricardo's.
The closest he finds, ironically, is Sonny's old pal and brother-in-law,
Johnny Mangiomi, one of the best counter-punchers around. In the
locker room, Sonny is lacing his boots when Johnny walks in.

"So you beat me to a bout at the Garden," Johnnie says, dumping his
gym bag on the bench.

Sonny claps Johnny on the shoulder in greeting. "You gotta go on tour in New York, Johnny. You can't get there from here."

"I know. Tell Angela that. She don't like it when I travel." Johnny slips off his shirt, hangs it on a hook in his locker.

Sonny can't believe his brother-in-law. "You gonna let your wife tell you what to do?"

Johnny rummages in his duffle bag for his boxing trunks. "It ain't like that, Sonny. She gets lonely."

Sonny knows that Loretta gets lonely when he's gone. But he can't let that stand in his way. Once he wins the crown he won't have to travel so much. And they'll be rich. He'll be able to take off all the time he wants to spend with his wife and kids. Plenty of time for that later. Right now, Sonny will do whatever it takes to get where he's going. He takes a look at Johnny and knows his brother-in-law will never make it to the Garden the way he's going. You have to make sacrifices to achieve greatness.

"Did Rudy tell you the drill?" Sonny shifts the conversation back to the task at hand — their sparring session.

"Yeah," says Johnny, slipping into his trunks. "He wants you to build up your stamina, so I'm supposed to box you around the ring without ever letting you find an opening."

"Right."

"And I'm supposed to clobber you as much as I can with my hard straight right, so you get used to a hard punch from a heavier guy."

"Good. See you out there." Sonny grabs his gloves and roll of white tape and heads out to the gym to find Rudy.

LATER, WHEN SONNY gets home, he finds Loretta in the kitchen, preparing a three-pound steak for Sonny, with a huge green salad — as ordered by Rudy. In the oven, a lasagna bakes for Loretta and the kids. Before Sonny has a chance to hang up his coat, Mary and Moses run to their daddy, throw themselves against his legs.

"Daddy, read me a story," Mary holds up a picture book.

"Up, Daddy," Moses stretches his arms upward, hoping Sonny will pick him up.

"Leave your father alone, kids," Loretta calls from the kitchen. "He just walked in the door."

"It's okay. Come 'ere you." Sonny snatches each child in an arm and picks them up. The kids giggle with delight. Sonny plops down onto the sofa, with the kids on his belly, and lets them tickle him until he is out of breath from laughing.

Loretta watches from the kitchen doorway, wiping her hands on a dishtowel. This is the happiest she has ever been in her marriage to Sonny. On his strict training schedule, he is home for dinner every night by six o' clock. After the kids are put to bed, Sonny has a long hot bath, while Loretta massages his back. They are in bed every night by nine. And Sonny has been out of town only twice since he got home from his New York tour, and only for a night or two — once in September, when he fought a match in Ottawa, and once in October when he spent one night in Guelph after a fight. The new baby will be born in the spring. By then, who knows? Sonny may get his chance at the world title. He's promised Loretta that as soon as he's won the middleweight crown, he's going to take some time off to spend with her and the kids. She hasn't forgotten that Sonny betrayed her by going around with other women in New York. But he seems to have settled down now. And Loretta can't help it. She loves Sonny. She can't imagine her life without him. She decided not to confront him on his affairs with other women. What good would that do? Anyway, he may have had a few girls on the road, but he always comes home to her.

December 1, 1946

YACOV SLURPS DOWN the rest of his tea and stands up. He is so nervous he can barely eat breakfast. The grand opening of Lenny's House of Bargains is in three hours, and there is still much to do.

"You go ahead," Sophie tells him. "I'll come by a bit later with Izzy." She's having one of her good days. The opening of the store has been good for her — it's something happy to think about. Takes her mind off the pain. It was Sophie's idea to name the store after Lenny, as a way of keeping his memory alive. In a place of honour, near the front door, hangs a framed photograph of Lenny in his Private's uniform, taken the day he entered the CNE training ground. His Victoria Cross is set out in a glass display case by the cash register. Customers to Lenny's House of Bargains will know who Lenny Lapinsky was, and that he was a hero.

"All right. How do I look?" Yacov poses.

Last week, Yacov and Max purchased new double-breasted suits for the opening. They want to look like successful businessmen. Sid already has a nice suit. He accompanied then on their visit to Sam Horowitz, to make sure they picked a style currently in fashion. Yacov hasn't bought a new suit in years. He was still wearing a three-piece woollen suit with a vest he'd bought before the Depression. He wanted to keep it, but Sophie insisted he throw it out. The cuffs were threadbare, the material on the lapels had worn right through and Sophie had replaced the buttons so many times, she couldn't remember any more which were the originals.

Max wanted to do something special for the grand opening, something memorable. Sid came up with the idea. They borrowed a roulette wheel from Checkie Seigelman, just for the day. And over the usual numbers on the wheel, they pasted signs that read, "10% off," "20% off," or "half price." The wheel is perched beside the cash register. Each time a customer buys an item, Sid will spin the wheel. Whatever it lands on, that's the discount the customer gets. Of course, the wheel is rigged. It will never land on half price, although it will slow down and appear to almost stop there. Most of the time it will land on "5% off" or "10% off." One of the "20% off" spots can be hit once in a while. That way they won't lose too much, and the novelty is bound to bring in the folks and encourage them to buy something on opening day.

Sid is already in the store, setting up the wheel, when Max and Yacov arrive together. They have spent the past month painting, installing shelves, having the store name painted in the front window and on the awning. The store still smells vaguely of fresh paint and sawdust. The merchandise is mostly bought from Checkie at cut-rate prices. Most of it is of suspicious origins. Yacov doesn't feel good about it at all. He argued with Max. If they're going to open the store, why not do it right? Max figures no one will ever know and why shouldn't they make a better profit? Still, he agrees they shouldn't tell Sid the whole story. No sense pulling him into it. Max promises Yacov that they will only start out this way.

"Once we're in the black, that's it," he promises. "We'll buy from a legitimate wholesaler. Okay?"

"Good. Fine. Terrific."

The store shelves are filled with kitchen items — dishes, pots and pans, cutlery — and other household items such as light bulbs, hardware, and ready-to-wear clothing for men, women and children. It is a store where people can buy almost anything, not unlike general stores in smaller towns, but in a larger setting at discount prices. Although Yacov is uneasy, Max is in his element. This is the moment he's been waiting for: He's a respectable businessman, with his own store. He was up late the night before, walking around, checking out every inch of the store, making sure everything was just so.

Sid is excited too. He's never done anything but work with his father and his uncle. The move to a store seems like a natural progression to him. He has a good head for business, and he has modern ideas that he brings daily to Max and Yacov. Sid knows that one day he will run the store by himself, in many years. Maybe with his sons. If he ever has any. In the meantime, he is happy to continue working with his father and uncle.

By ten o'clock Sophie arrives with Izzy. She walks around the store, admiring everything. Tess arrives a few moments later with her kids. She also tours the shop, adjusting a shelf here, a dress there. Ruthie has been there all morning, helping Sid set up.

At exactly noon they open the doors. People stream inside. It is a curiosity: a bargain store, with so many different items in one place. Soon people are lined up at the cash register as Sid makes a big deal of spinning the roulette wheel. More people pour in.

Sid tried to talk Sonny into coming to the opening. He figured their father would be in such a good mood, he'd forgive Sonny and welcome him back to the family. Sonny flat-out refused.

"Forget it, Sid. It won't work. You don't get it."

"Why don't you give it a try?" Sid pushed.

"You don't know what you're talking about. Besides, I'll be out of town. Got a rematch with Jake Fisher, in Rochester. He's a light heavy-weight. A tough fighter. And Rudy's got me on a strict training schedule for my fight at the Garden. I ain't got the time to fool around."

Ruthie tells Loretta to come and bring the kids, but Loretta doesn't think it is right. Even though Sophie now regularly visits Sonny and Loretta and has even occasionally invited Loretta to bring the kids over during the day when Yacov has been at work, she has never properly met her father-in-law. Her curiosity gets the better of her, though, and since Sonny is out of town, Loretta walks down College Street, kids in tow, where she peers through the front shop window, but does not go inside.

Checkie waits until later in the afternoon to make his appearance. He has Romeo drive right up to the front doors. Romeo carries a case of champagne that Checkie ceremoniously pops open, pours into glasses he has rented for the momentous occasion and begins handing out to cus-tomers. Sophie is more than a little disconcerted at the sight of Checkie Seigelman. She never trusted him. She has no idea of his involvement in the store, and his cocky attitude worries her. He acts as if he has a stake in the business. She glances at Yacov warily. He avoids her eye. He hadn't been expecting Seigelman at the opening. Although he reluctantly agreed to continue buying from Seigelman, he prefers not to deal with him so directly. He glares at Max, who shrugs. On top of being a *goniff*, Checkie Seigelman is the person Yacov holds responsible for his rift with Sonny. If Seigelman hadn't taken Sonny into the boxing world, he'd never have met that Italian girl and made her pregnant.

Most of all, Yacov holds Seigelman responsible for his and Max's money troubles during the Depression. If Checkie hadn't pulled Max into the stock market, they would have had their hard-earned nest egg to get them through the lean years. Yacov holds Seigelman responsible for everything. That terrible day burns in his memory. Seeing Checkie Seigelman in Lenny's House of Bargains brings it all back to Yacov with frightening clarity.

Tuesday, October 29, 1929

MAX AND CHECKIE paced back and forth at the curb outside the Toronto Stock Exchange. Behind them was a crowd of men, many of whom were also pacing. Checkie's broker was inside. The news was bleak. Prices had plunged the week before, had recovered slightly, but now were dropping steadily even though it was only nine in the morning.

"Just tell him to sell," Max said for the fortieth time in five minutes.

Checkie grinned and put a reassuring arm around Max's shoulder, smoke from his cigar wafting into Max's face. "Relax, Max. He knows what he's doing. I told him if it drops too low, sell fast. Otherwise it's better to shvitz it out. You get my meaning? That's the stock market. It's like a craps game, Maxie. You can't pull out just 'cause you lose a few rounds. Later on you'd kick yourself. If you'd stuck it out you would have come out ahead. *Farshtaist?*"

"Yeah, I *farshtaist*," Max said nervously, removing his cap, anxiously smoothing back his hair with his hands. "I'm sunk. I'm cooked. I'm finished. Checkie, do me a favour? Call your guy out here. I wanna sell. While I still got something to sell."

"All right, Maxie. All right. He'll be outside as soon as he can to let us know the uh ... the uh ... whachacallit ... the uh ... the present situation." Checkie tugged his fourteen-karat gold watch from his vest pocket, snapped open the lid.

"Can't you call him out?" Max struggled out from under Checkie's arm.

"Who do I look like?" Checkie replaced his pocket watch, adjusted the chain, which was slung through the buttonhole of his vest. "The King of England? You're a funny guy, Maxie. Call him out. Yeah sure, and maybe I can get elected Prime Minister too. That's a good one." He removed his white straw boater, tipped back his head and laughed loudly from deep in his belly, then he stuffed his cigar between his lips and puffed.

Max felt his stomach drop to his feet. He was perspiring, even though there was a chill in the air. Ten years of savings have gone down the stock-market drain — the money he and Yacov had been religiously saving since 1913 when they first arrived in Toronto, in an account at the Bank of Montreal. Twenty percent of whatever they took in each week was deposited in the account. Rain or shine. On good weeks and bad. Even when it meant they had to do without. All to fulfill their dream of open-ing a store, and getting out of the peddling business. Yacov didn't know Max had withdrawn their savings. Didn't know he'd invested in stocks. Max kicked himself for taking such a risk. The signs were on the wall weeks ago. He'd almost pulled out. Checkie had said the same thing then: "The market goes down, everybody sells cheap, then it goes back up. And the poor bastards who sold low jump outa windows all over Bay Street. But, if you got *chutzpah*, like me, and you stick it out and hang on, in the end you win out. You see Maxie? While all the other schmucks are selling cheap, I'm buying what they're selling. Then the market goes back up and I'm laughing outa my ears. Come on boychick. Relax. Trust me."

By noon Checkie's broker emerged, a small wiry man in his early for-ties, his face whiter than the concrete of the curb. The news was not good. Panic was the order of the day at the TSE, the Montreal Stock Exchange and the New York Stock Exchange. People were bailing out, unloading tens of thousands of shares at rock-bottom prices. Still, he recommended to Checkie and Max to hang on.

"It's a slight dip," he assured them, pushing his wire-framed glasses back up on his nose.

"Dip?" screamed Max, frantic with worry. "You call that a dip? That's not a dip. It's a plunge. It's a crash. A disaster. I don't feel so good." He sank down on the curb, his head in his hands. He noticed Checkie was decked out in new, genuine-leather, Italian-made shoes, covered in clean, white spats.

Later they called it "Black Tuesday." Before the morning was out, Max's uneducated prediction came true. The stock market did indeed crash. It plummeted from the top of the highest skyscraper, dragging with it the economy of the entire world, free-falling hundreds of feet and splattering on the newly paved roads of America. And somewhere on the bottom of the heap of splattered humanity was Max Lapinsky of Clinton Street in Toronto, formerly Moishe Lapinsky of the town of Tiraspol in Russia. Max was wiped out. Ruined. Finished. Kaput. And he had brought an unwilling and unknowing Yacov to the bottom along with him.

When Max heard the final news he walked the streets of downtown Toronto, fire burning up his *kishkes*, churning and brewing. What was he going to do now? What was he going to tell Yacov? Checkie's broker finally sold Max's stock at one 'o clock. His original investment of two hundred and sixty-seven dollars had shot up to eleven hundred and fifty-three the week before the decline, and had bottomed out at four dollars and forty-three cents. Four bucks. That's all he had after the broker sold his pitiful shares.

IT WAS CHECKIE who had pulled Max into the game. One day only four months earlier, Max was shooting pool with Checkie when he had asked Max where he kept his money.

"In a bank," Max had answered, leaning over the table to knock the five ball into the corner pocket.

Checkie laughed so hard he choked.

"What?" Max straightened up.

"You got any stocks? Or bonds?" Checkie asked once he stopped laughing.

Max had heard about guys making fortunes on the stock market, and he was intrigued, but he honestly knew nothing about buying stocks, and the newspaper confused him even more. Securities, commodities, blue chips, brokers. He didn't know what any of it meant. His family in Russia hadn't even known how to use a bank. He thought he was modern to have a savings account.

"No stocks. No bonds." Max rubbed blue chalk onto the tip of his pool cue.

Checkie threw a heavy arm over Max's shoulder. "Maxie. Maxie. You'll never get anywhere if you keep your dough in a bank."

"They pay five percent interest on my savings." Max moved out from under Checkie's grasp. Eyed the table to set up his next shot.

"Five percent?" Checkie shouted incredulously. "Five percent?"

"Yeah." Max leaned over, sunk the nine ball into the side pocket.

"Max, how long are you gonna keep on schlepping up and down the street, selling *shmates* to housewives? Huh? Don't you wanna make something of yourself?"

"Sure I do." Max missed his next shot. "I got ideas."

"Oh yeah? What ideas?"

"Plans. I got plans."

"What plans, Max?"

Max reached for his glass of beer. "A store."

"A store?"

"Yeah. With my cousin, Yacov. We're planning to open a bargain store. Right on College Street."

"A bargain store?"

"Yeah."

Checkie pursed his lips together. Nodded. "Not bad. A bargain store. I can see it."

"Yeah?"

"Sure. But Maxie, you're gonna need uh ... whachacallit ... capital. Am I right?"

"Sure."

"So? That's what I'm talking about." Checkie leaned forward over the table, and hit the cue ball hard. It ricocheted off the side and clacked precisely against the two ball, sinking it.

Checkie insisted he could double Max's money in a couple of months. So Max withdrew his savings. He handed two hundred and sixty-seven dollars to Checkie, who assured him he had the best broker in town. Max stopped by Checkie's pool hall on Queen Street often to inquire how his money was doing. The news at first was spectacular. Max couldn't believe it.

Checkie was smiling. He opened the daily *Mail and Empire* and flipped through the pages to the financial section to show Max. He located various company names listed on the stock analysis page.

"See? Montgomery Ward. Right here. Everyone calls it Monkey Ward," he informed Max smugly; he was a man in the know. "You bought twenty shares at nine bucks each last week. Today your shares are worth twenty-two. And my broker bought you thirty shares of Canadian Marconi for four bits last week, now up to twelve-eighty each. How's that boychick? I already made you a bundle. Now, that's," he accentuated each word carefully, stabbing his cigar in the air as he spoke, "how to make your dough work for you. See?"

Max was thrilled. At this rate of growth, he'd have enough money to open the store and give up the door-to-door business in a couple more months. It couldn't be soon enough. The summer was dragging on, and the heat was killing Max. He decided against telling Yacov about the stock market. He knew his cousin was too much of a greenhorn to understand. But look at how quickly their money was growing. In a few more months, he would sell his shares at a huge profit and they could open up their business. Yacov would never need to know. Max began seriously scouting for a suitable storefront to rent, while he waited to become rich.

"AW, DON'T TAKE IT so hard," Checkie tried to soothe Max on Black Tuesday. "This'll blow over. Then you can start all over. Remember last month? Everything tripled in no time. Remember that?"

Max walked away.

"Hey Maxie. Come on. Don't be sore."

But Max was sore. He was very sore. He was hurting in the worst way. He wanted to kill Checkie Seigelman. He rued the day he'd met the man. Checkie could be calm because he hadn't lost everything. The money he had in the market represented only a small portion of his business affairs. He owned the pool hall, with a bookmaking operation in the backroom, ran a wholesaling warehouse with goods of questionable origin. And he was in the loans business. Unofficial-like. Checkie had his finger in several pies. But for Max, this was it, the sum total of his achievements in Canada. He thought all that day of climbing to the top floor of the TSE and throwing himself out the window. At least he would go in an instant, instead of facing a slow, painful decline. But he couldn't do that to Tessie. What would she do without him? There was nothing to do but face the truth.

AT FIRST YACOV didn't believe Max. They were a few blocks from home on Harbord Street. Max had asked Yacov to go for a walk. He had something to tell him.

"Come on, Max. We don't play the stock market. But I read about it. Boy, some poor schmucks lost everything."

Max didn't say anything. Just stood before Yacov, cap in his hand, shuffling from one foot to the other. Yacov studied his cousin.

"What are you trying to tell me, Max?"

Max shuffled some more.

"Max?"

Max shrugged. "You should have seen it. In one week I tripled our money…"

"Max, you didn't."

"We couldn't lose."

"Moishe…" Yacov used his cousin's Yiddish name, his hands unconsciously balled into fists by his sides.

"Yacov, at the rate we were saving it was gonna take two more years at least before we could open the store…"

"Moishe. You didn't?" Yacov brought his hands up to his face.

"You should have seen it, Yacov." Max peered at Yacov, trying to see his face beyond his hands. "Yacov?"

Slowly, Yacov lowered his hands, rage and confusion clouding his mind. He glared at Max hard and long, his body stiff, tight, his face like stone. Max wished Yacov would scream or hit him. Anything to break the tension. But Yacov simply turned his back on his cousin and slowly walked away. Max absorbed the weight of Yacov's anger inside his belly, which was turning over with anxiety.

"Yacov …" Max called. But Yacov kept walking.

WHEN YACOV ARRIVED HOME he found Sophie standing in front of the kitchen sink, washing clothes on a scrub board, the sleeves of her print housedress up above her elbows. A lock of her hair had escaped from her bun and was out of place, loose over her forehead. Slumped at the kitchen table, he told her the news. He was embarrassed to tell her

Max had played the market without his knowledge, so he didn't tell her that part. It made him feel weak. And when he thought about it, he realized he was weak. He'd grown so used to following while Max led, it was their way of life. When did it start? How long had they been doing things that way? He was so ashamed of his failure, he led his wife to believe the two cousins had gambled their money together. That felt like the lesser of two crimes. This way he was foolish, but at least he was a man.

"You what?" Sophie yelled, removing her hands from the sudsy water, turning to her husband. "I don't understand."

Yacov scratched the back of his neck.

Sophie wiped her wet hands on her apron and tucked the stray hair back under the clip. "What about the store? We've been scrimping and saving for years, putting every last penny in the bank so you and Max could open the bargain store."

"Well …"

"It's gone? All of it?" Sophie couldn't understand how so much money could disappear.

"Sophie … it's not so bad." Yacov didn't know what to say. There wasn't anything he could say.

"Not so bad? Not so bad, he says," she yelled to the ceiling. "Tell that to your children when they're starving."

"Sophie. No one's gonna starve," he said, but he wasn't sure it was true. Izzy was an infant, Sid was nine, Lenny seven, and Sonny was five. Four growing boys to feed. And nothing in the bank.

"How do you know? Are you the one who has to make dinner out of nothing? Out of thin air?"

"Sophie. Please stop yelling."

"I haven't even begun to yell, Yacov." She turned her back on her husband, reached into the sink and furiously scoured a cotton shirt up and down over the glass ribs of the washboard.

WHEN MAX STEPPED in his door a few minutes later, Tessie had news of her own. She dashed into his arms. "Oh Max. It's wonderful. We're going to have a baby," she said, kissing his face. Their first child. Max's heart sank and exploded at the same time. He wanted children, but the timing couldn't have been worse. On the exact day he lost his money. How could he support a family now? How could he save for the store with another mouth to feed? He hadn't the heart to tell Tessie the news. Not just then. She was so happy. Max tucked away his own worries and smiled broadly. The ultimate salesman. Picked his wife up in his arms and spun her around the room. From the kitchen the soft sounds of music flowed from the radio. A news reporter interrupted the music with a special bulletin. "Prices came tumbling down in the greatest crash of all at the opening of the stock markets today," he announced. "And what took hours to accomplish on Thursday was accomplished in minutes this afternoon," he continued. Max wanted to listen to the report, but didn't want Tessie to hear. He walked quickly into the kitchen and turned the dial until he found music.

"Let me call you sweetheart,
I'm in love with you,
Let me hear you whisper that you love me too ... "

"Hey Baby Doll," Max said to his wife, who had followed him into the kitchen. "I'm taking you out tonight. To celebrate."

"You mean it, Maxie?"

"Sure, Sweetheart. Why don't you go on and get yourself all dolled up. I gotta go upstairs for a minute. Something I forgot to tell Yacov. Business."

"Can't it wait, Max?"

"No. No. It can't wait ... I uh ... it's important, see? Something that can't wait. You understand, Tess. I'll be right back, Doll. You go ahead and get changed. Back in a flash." He blew her a kiss off the edge of his fingertips.

She tilted her head, frowned at Max.

"Be right back, Gorgeous."

Tessie watched him back away toward the stairs, a bundle of nerves. *He's probably excited because I'm expecting,* Tessie figured. She turned toward the bedroom, wondering if she should wear her red dress, or the green.

UPSTAIRS, MAX DRAGGED YACOV toward the bathroom, the only unoccupied room in the flat. Sophie shook her head as Max passed her in the kitchen, but she said nothing. Yacov's kids were sprawled throughout the apartment.

Yacov closed the lid on the toilet and sat, crossed his arms over his chest, glared at his cousin.

Max leaned against the wall, jammed both hands in his pockets, then took them back out, held them in front of his body. "Listen …" he whispered, conscious of Sophie in the next room. "I know you're sore … you have every right to be … I know … it's all my fault … I shouldn't have done it … but Yacov … just you wait … I'm gonna turn this here thing around … you shoulda seen it. Oh boy." Max moved his weight from one foot to the other. "I'm telling you … in one week I tripled our money … tripled it. You shoulda seen it."

Yacov shook his head. "*Our* money, Max," he said quietly, his dark eyes burning a hole through Max's chest. "*Our* money. Not yours. *Ours.*"

"Yeah, yeah. Our money. I know. I know. But listen Yacov … just have a little faith in me. I'll turn this here thing around. In no time. You'll see …"

" … Max …" Yacov rose, his face inches from Max's.

"Yeah. What?"

"When were you going to tell me?" He asked quietly, his voice tightly controlled.

"Tell you? Well … you know … I was just about to."

"You were about to tell me?"

"Yeah. Sure I was."

"Why not before?"

Max shrugged with his hands. "I didn't think you'd understand, see?"

"Why? Am I stupid, Max?"

"That's not what I'm saying."

"Then what are you saying?"

Max shifted uneasily, reached into his shirt pocket for his package of Chesterfields. "Look, Yacov … all I'm saying is …"

"What?"

Max held out the pack. Yacov slipped a cigarette out, placed it between his lips. Max struck a wooden match on the wall. "Yacov … it was a sure bet …"

"Gambling? Is that what you were doing with our money?" Yacov leaned his cigarette forward into the flame.

The match burned down, licked the edge of Max's finger. He dropped it. "Ouch. No. That's not what I mean …"

"So? What then?" Yacov inhaled deeply, blew smoke into Max's face.

Max slid out a cigarette, stuffed it between his lips. "I'm sick of walking door-to-door. Aren't you sick of it? *Schlepping* up and down the street. Day after day. Knocking on doors." He grabbed the cigarette with thumb and forefinger, pointing it at Yacov as he spoke. "Bothering people. Doors slammed in my face. For what? A few lousy cents. We couldn't lose, Yacov. It looked so easy. Guys were making fortunes, see? I figured we'd be able to open the store. Like we always talked about. I knew we could make a killing in no time …"

"… without me."

"Yacov … don't …"

"Without me?"

Max lit his cigarette. "I'm sorry."

"He's sorry," Yacov said to the ceiling.

"I'm sorry. I was wrong. All right?"

Yacov grunted, sat back down. Stared hard at Max, puffed on his cigarette, scratched the back of his neck.

Max waited, watched Yacov, smoothed back his hair. Smoked.

"You'll promise me something, Max?" Yacov finally said.

"Sure, Yacov. Anything." Max leaned forward.

"Never again. *Farshtaist?* We're partners aren't we?"

"Absolutely. Never again. Next time, we're in on it together." Max held out one hand.

Yacov stared at his cousin, then slowly raised his hand.

Max clasped their hands together in a tight grip, as if to repair their broken bond. He grinned in relief. "All right. Good. So? I'll see you in the morning?"

"Where else would I go?"

"Good. All right. Eight o' clock?"

"Don't we always meet at eight o' clock?"

"Good. Fine." Max reached for the handle, swung open the door, plastered an artificial grin on his face and went downstairs to his wife.

IT HAS TAKEN MAX and Yacov sixteen years to recover the lost money, to save enough to finally open the store. It is now, as they say, water under the bridge, but Yacov can never forget. He has, in his way, forgiven his cousin Max. But he cannot forget. And he cannot forgive Checkie Seigelman.

So on December 1, 1946, when Checkie approaches Yacov with a glass of champagne, Yacov turns his back, prefers to help a customer. Seigelman takes the hint, saunters over to Max, who accepts the drink, even clinks his glass with the one in the gangster's hand. Yacov gets back to work. People pour into the store in droves. It's a beautiful sight. On a day like this, even Seigelman can't ruin Yacov's pleasure.

Later, after closing, the partners count receipts, sipping the rest of the champagne. Ruthie sits by the cash with her hand-cranked adding machine and enters numbers that Sid calls out, a long white tape snaking onto the floor by her feet. The opening has been a roaring success. Sid keeps one hand protectively on Ruthie's shoulder. She's into her second trimester, Dr. Grossman said. So far, so good. Maybe things are looking up finally.

But Sid and Ruthie's happiness is cut like a knife through the heart later that night, when Ruthie wakes with excruciating cramps.

"Sid," she nudges him awake, as she pulls the blanket aside to see the blood she knows will be there. She seems to get pregnant successfully enough. Why can't she carry to term?

The Holy Shrine

DECEMBER 12, 1946

MADISON SQUARE GARDEN, NEW YORK, NEW YORK

IN THE LOCKER ROOM, backstage at Madison Square Garden, Rudy tapes Sonny's hands. "Remember what I told you," Rudy grills Sonny. "Guard my face with my right. Wait for an opening. Tire him out. Then charge." Sonny recites the mantra Rudy's been drumming into his head every day for months. He is in peak condition. Rested, ready and pumped for this fight. Earlier in the afternoon, he weighed in at his heaviest weight ever, 152 pounds of solid muscle, and he met Joey Ricardo for the first time. Ricardo weighed in at 165. Sonny could see right away that Rudy was right. Ricardo may have the extra weight behind his punch, but his reflexes are slower. Sonny tested it out at weigh-in by tossing an apple to Ricardo suddenly. Ricardo missed.

"It's time, Sonny," Rudy says, checking the lacing on Sonny's gloves once more, before draping the blue robe over Sonny's shoulders. Checkie had ordered the silk robe especially for this fight. On the back is a white Star of David, and Sonny's name embroidered in gold thread.

Sonny follows Rudy down the long, narrow hallway toward the arena. Even back here, he can hear the din of the crowd. Checkie reported a few minutes earlier that the gate recorded sixty thousand people in the stands — a huge crowd, considering it's not even a title bout.

A minute later, Sonny slips through the ropes and into the coveted ring, the holy shrine of boxing, Madison Square Garden, New York, New York. The ring itself is no different from any other ring Sonny has fought in, although the stadium is much larger. It's the meaning behind this particular venue that is huge. This fight will take Sonny one large step up the ladder of his success. Everyone knows if he wins this fight, it's only a matter of time before he'll get his chance against Tiny Johnson for the middleweight title.

Checkie figures it'll happen within a year. "By 1948 at the latest," he predicted.

In his corner, Rudy removes Sonny's robe and slips his mouthguard into place. Sonny dances in place to keep his muscles warm until the referee calls the boxers to the centre to receive their instructions.

The bell rings for the first round and Sonny charges toward Ricardo. With Rudy's strategy repeating itself in his mind, Sonny keeps his right fist up, guarding his face as he dances Ricardo around the ring. Ricardo swings with a left hook. Sonny sees it coming and dodges the punch. Ricardo hits air and loses his balance slightly. Sonny sees that Ricardo's left cheek is wide open and he throws his right fist, landing hard against Ricardo's face, opening a cut over his lip and knocking him back against the ropes. The audience leaps to its feet. The television announcers go wild. It's only the first few seconds of the first round and already there is blood.

By round four, Ricardo is slowing down, while Sonny has only taken a couple of jabs to the body. Sonny keeps up Rudy's pre-fight plan. Relentlessly, Sonny dances his opponent around the ring, keeping his face covered, never letting up. Seconds before the end of the round, Ricardo changes strategy, surprising Sonny with a left hook, followed by a straight right that catches Sonny under the jaw, knocking him to the canvas. He's down for a count of three when the bell rings and the referee backs Ricardo to his corner. Sonny pulls himself up and drops onto his bench.

"You dropped your right hand," Rudy warns, while sponging Sonny's face with cool water. "Keep your guard up. Be patient. Wait for your opening."

Sonny shakes his head to clear it. Rudy's damn right. Ricardo's punch is the hardest Sonny's ever taken. He can't afford to take too many hits like that. The bell rings for round five. Sonny searches deep inside and finds what he needs: his rage and his heart for fighting. The powerful anger he's used since he was a boy to win in the ring. He decides to finish this thing off. In his signature style, Sonny charges to the centre of the ring and faster than Ricardo can react, Sonny throws out a combination: two left hooks and Ricardo drops his right fist, giving Sonny the opening he needs. He slams Ricardo, with all his strength and the magnitude of his heart, with a right uppercut. Sonny can tell he's hit his mark. Ricardo flies back and slams onto the canvas. The crowd shouts in excitement. The referee begins the count. 1-2-3. Sonny hovers in a neutral corner, waiting. Ricardo struggles to his feet on the count of seven. But Sonny knows he's won. He charges forward again and to trick Ricardo, Sonny starts with a right jab, a left hook, and bam. Plows him again with his right.

The audience is back on its feet as the referee counts all the way to ten. Sonny has won. A knockout in the fifth round. Rudy leaps into the ring, raises Sonny's arm high in the air in victory. The crowd screams its appreciation. Through the racket, Sonny hears a television announcer predict that Sonny "The Charger" Lapinsky will be a middleweight contender sometime next year.

Mourning Has Broken
FEBRUARY 1947, TORONTO

SOPHIE HOVERS NERVOUSLY at the kitchen sink, peeling carrots and potatoes for a stew. Yacov is slow this morning, lingering at the table, having a second cup of tea, leisurely reading the morning paper. Usually, he's gone already to the store by this time in the morning.

"Hurry up and finish. You're late," Sophie tells him.

"What's the hurry? Sid opens up in the morning now."

"So? Doesn't he need your help? It's a big store."

"I had a bad night. I sent Izzy ahead to help Sid."

Sophie drops the potato peeler in the sink, and sits across from her husband. He is acting strange this morning. "What's a matter?"

"Dreams."

"What kind of dreams?"

"What's the difference? They were bad ones."

"I'm your wife. Tell me your dream."

Yacov hesitates. Sophie waits. "About Lenny."

"Oh." The wound in Sophie's broken heart slips open. Her chest is one big hole, stitched together so hastily and so loose after Lenny died, it's easily unravelled.

"What did he say?"

"I don't remember."

"So tell me what you remember."

"He was a little boy in the dream."

Sophie presses her palm over the hole in her heart.

"He was running down the street. With Sonny, who was also a little boy."

The thread slips free completely. Two large pieces of her heart drop to the bottom of her belly.

"And that's it." Yacov's eyes mirror Sophie's pain.

She can't look at him. "That's it?" Sophie sips her tea, wills the warm liquid to slide down her throat and spread into her chest to fill up the empty space where her heart used to be.

"That's all I remember."

They sit in silence, each alone with their own private pain. Sometimes when Sophie looks at her husband all she sees is a shattered family, one actually dead son, one pretend-one, another who will never grow up, and another who can't seem to have any sons of his own. And she has to look away.

Sophie and Yacov are so preoccupied with their respective grief that they don't hear the door downstairs open and close. They don't hear Loretta plodding her way up the stairs with the children until she is on the top step. "I'm sorry," she calls out to Sophie. "I'm a little late. Moses threw up just as we were leav … oh." She sees Yacov.

"Oy," Sophie leaps up to greet Loretta, her eyes hard on Yacov's, begging him silently to behave. He stands slowly. Loretta waits at the top of the stairs, Moses clutching her left hand, Mary behind, carefully climbing, one step at a time, holding tight to her mother's right hand.

They stare at one another for a long silent moment. Yacov looks at the children. The little boy looks exactly like Sonny at that age. The girl must be four years old. Loretta's belly is big. She must be eight months pregnant.

What is she doing here? He glares at his wife. "Hurry up. You'll be late," he mimics.

"Yacov …" she warns.

"I'm going to work. Excuse me, miss." Yacov grabs his hat and coat, eases past Loretta and down the stairs. He closes the door quietly. A man in perfect control of his raging emotions.

"Oh, boy." Loretta grimaces. "I'm sorry …"

"Never mind. He's old and stubborn. And ridiculous. Come on. Sit down. I'll make tea." She picks up her grandson. "Hello, Moses. Hello, sweetheart. How's my big boy?"

Loretta sits at the table and Mary stands by her legs. Sophie bends and kisses the top of Mary's head. "Hello, sweetheart." Mary pushes shyly against her mother.

"It's your grandma, honey," Loretta tells her. "Remember?"

"Oh." Mary stares at Sophie, trying to figure out what a grandmother is.

Sophie fills the kettle with water, puts it on the front burner, lights the element. Blue flames lick the bottom of the kettle. "Does Sonny know you're here?"

Loretta tosses her head from side to side. "He's young and stubborn."

Sophie nods. "That's what I thought. They're too much alike."

"Are they?"

"That's the problem right there." Sophie helps Moses out of his snow-suit. He giggles when she tickles his belly. "How are you feeling, Loretta?"

"My back's killing me."

"It happens."

YACOV STOMPS HIS WAY down Clinton. His grandchildren. The little boy's eyes dark and brooding, so like Sonny's. The pretty little girl. He's a grandfather. A *zayde*. He's been a grandfather technically for four years, but he doesn't think of himself that way. How can he? His son is dead. How can he have grandchildren from a dead son? The boy looks exactly like Sonny when he was little. And a little like Yacov's own brother, Shmuel. Sweet little Shmuel. Thinking of Shmuel, Yacov can smell the dusty roads of Tiraspol even now, all these years later. Hear the pounding of horse hooves. See his brother's crumpled little body. So peaceful. So dead. All his fault. Tears slide down Yacov's cheeks, and he barely notices people staring at him as they pass. He imagines what Sonny would look like now. It's been five long years. He heard that Sonny had gone overseas. He didn't want to know. He overhead Max asking Sid about it. Of course, Sonny's name is in the papers in the sports section all the time these days. Once Yacov caught a glimpse of his picture in the *Star*, but he couldn't bear to look. He crumpled it up. Threw it away.

He feels prickly and ashamed. The children are so innocent. How can he be mad at them? He wanted to hold them and kiss them. He almost reached out. But he couldn't. There is such a thing as Tradition, he reminds himself, grinding his teeth as he tromps forward. A cold wind prickles the back of his neck. Somewhere deep inside, even through his stubborn pride, he can feel something almost resembling forgiveness beginning to take shape. But it's going to take some time. Like a rusty screw, it's stuck in place. It's going to take a long time to slowly work itself loose. But maybe … maybe he can start with his grandchildren. How could it hurt? Yacov suspects even God would understand.

On College Street, Yacov stops in front of Lenny's House of Bargains. There's a line of shoppers, even in the bitter cold weather, already waiting for the doors to open. Since the beginning, the store has been packed every day. They're making more money than Yacov ever dreamed possible. His dream has come true. He is blessed. Why then, does he wake every day with a heart full of lead?

BOOK FIVE

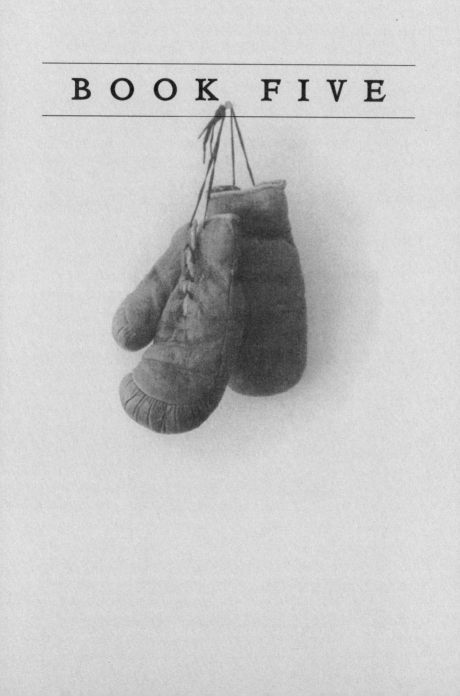

Notes on *The Biography of Sonny Lapinsky*
by Moses Nino Lapinsky, Ph.D.
JUNE 15, 2003, VANCOUVER, B.C.

─────────────

I'VE REALIZED AS I research his biography that my father lived a large part of his life shrouded in guilt — all because of one small error in judgement he made as a boy. Even if, in the end, after many long years, my grandfather forgave him, I don't think my father ever forgave himself. It's tragic really, because my father's actions at the Christie Pits riot did not arise from selfishness. Rather, he saw it as a community act, to protect his family and his neighbourhood. His actions triggered an avalanche, which smothered his family in a sorrow I don't believe they ever recovered from.

I didn't meet my grandfather, *Zayde* Yacov, until I was almost two years old. Of course, I was too young to remember our initial meeting, but I do remember my mother taking me and Mary to visit our grandmother, *Bubbe* Sophie, and *Zayde* Yacov would be there. I remember how different he was from my father. Sonny liked to roughhouse with us. He'd wrestle us to the floor, tickle us until we couldn't catch our breath. In later years, when Frankie and I were in elementary school, our father would teach us how to box. Frankie, a natural athlete, excelled in weaving and dodging, left hooks and right uppercuts. I tried my best, was a good student and learned all the moves, but I was never fast enough, could never punch hard enough.

Unlike Dad, *Zayde* was a storyteller. I remember sitting beside him on the living room sofa, fascinated with his stories of the ruby necklace that he lost in the Dniester River while being smuggled out of Russia, of how he had to sleep in the bottom of a dry well for seven days while hiding from the Russian police, how he walked across Romania and through

Germany to Hamburg, then got on a boat all by himself for a long voyage across the Atlantic Ocean at the age of fifteen, to land in Halifax, then make his way to Toronto, without a word of English. Out of my siblings, I was the most interested in my grandfather's tales. I remember also that these were secret visits. My mother instructed us not to mention our visits to my father. At the time, it didn't strike me as odd. It's just the way things were. We were told by my mother that knowledge of the visits with *Zayde* would upset our father. It wasn't until much later, when I was grown up, and my father and grandfather had reconciled their differences, that I realized how awful the situation was for everyone.

It also has become clear to me, the more I've delved into my father's life, that my *Zayde*'s anger toward my father began long before Sonny married my mother. Outwardly, *Zayde* Yacov had a perfectly good reason — at least in his mind — to disown Sonny: he married outside the faith. Inwardly, though, I believe he had never forgiven Sonny for letting Izzy get hurt at the Christie Pits riot in 1933. I'm not a psychiatrist, I'm a historian, so my observations as to *Zayde* Yacov's emotional state are purely hypothetical, but I believe that he could not see his way clear to forgive Sonny for letting Izzy get hurt, because he had not yet forgiven himself for letting his own little brother Shmuel be murdered in the pogrom of 1913. The circumstances had too many parallels. When my grandfather looked at Sonny, he saw himself. When Izzy was hurt in 1933, *Zayde* was emotionally transported to his own youth, when he failed his brother.

The year 1933 was a difficult one. People were out of work and desperately poor. There was no end in sight as more and more people were laid off and businesses went under. There were no safety nets, no medical insurance, no welfare, no pension. No food banks. No relief at all. You sank or you swam on your own. If you were lucky you had a close family, and you took care of each other as best you could. So if your brother got laid off, then evicted when he couldn't pay his rent, you'd take in him and his wife and kids, even if they were sleeping in the hallway and thirteen people were sharing one bathroom. At least they had a roof over their heads. Otherwise, they'd be in the streets.

The world was both terrifying and terribly innocent in 1933. Scanning Toronto's newspapers of that year, I find that "42nd Street" was playing at the Uptown, George Raft was appearing in person at The Imperial, Baby Yack of the Elm Street Athletic Club was duking it out with Sammy Fier of the YMHA, cotton shirts were going for $1.29 each, you could have a three-piece suit dry cleaned at Varsity Cleaners for ninety-five cents and buy a floor lamp for $5.95. You could read that Nazis had cut out the eyes of a Jewish lawyer in Berlin before killing him. That in the first year of Hitler's chancellery, Jews in Germany were being downgraded to second-class citizenry. There was a motion in the Ontario Legislature to allow the sales of beer and wine in hotels. You could buy a brand new coal stove for $21.95, an Electrohome Mixmaster for $3.95, Maxwell House coffee had more flavour because it came in a Vita-fresh pack. In Germany, Aryans with Jewish escorts would be punished. You could buy fifty bushels of coal for nine dollars, and if you wanted comfort, you got behind the wheel of a Buick with its new improved draft ventilation. Clark Gable and Carole Lombard were starring in "No Man of Her Own," and you could purchase a ten-tube Super Heterodyne Westinghouse Columaire Radio with compact shielded chassis, silent tuning and dual-range speakers for $4.75 down and $6 a week. A roll of waxed paper was 19 cents and at Bitterfeld, near Berlin, groups of Nazis forced the closing of Jewish market stalls and ordered the proprietors out. Silk nylons were 50 cents, you could get a dozen eggs for 19 cents, sugar was 99 cents for a twenty-pound bag, beef was going for 6 cents a pound, a Gurney three-burner gas range could be had for $18.95, all Jewish merchants in Annaberg, Germany were arrested, a bank robbery in Markham, Ontario yielded the robbers the princely sum of two thousand dollars. In Breslau, Hitlerites attacked a Jewish shoe dealer, dragged him out of his store, ripped off his coat and the suspenders from his trousers, and forced him to run half-naked through the town, and in Berlin, a group of distinguished Jews were found murdered by Nazis, after being stripped naked, chained, beaten with steel rods and burned with cigarettes.

My father was nine years old in 1933. During the Depression, his family was desperately poor. I remember how, in later years, my *Bubbe*

Sophie would talk about the Depression with a sense almost of nostalgia, oddly enough. She proudly told stories of how she could make a whole pot of soup out of two chicken bones, a couple of onions and sheer determination to feed her growing family. I remember being ten, twelve, fourteen and being constantly hungry. And we had lots of food. I only had to ask and my mother would open the fridge and make me something to eat. My father was not so lucky. When he was that age, he was slowly training himself for his career as a boxer, and doing so on Depression rations of watery soup and day-old bread.

When I read the newspaper accounts of the day of the Christie Pits riot, they astound me. Such a paradox of innocence and evil all on the same pages. On that day, Hitler was savagely enacting his plan to annihilate the Jews of Europe, all across Canada people were starving, young men were riding the rails, Prairie people were living in tent cities, city folks were being evicted and sleeping in the streets, yet nobody carried guns, you didn't have to lock your doors at night, you knew all your neighbours by name and people watched out for each other.

My father, in many ways, was one of those lucky people who knew what he wanted at a young age. From the first time he'd seen local legend Sammy Luftspring fight at the athletic club, Sonny was struck with boxing fever. Watching Sammy Luftspring from the back row, where he sat with his older brother Sid, my father could see every move, every dodge, every punch. He understood instinctively what the boxers were doing. Natural talent, I guess; an affinity for the sport. He knew from that moment on what he wanted to do, and he spent the next couple of years getting himself in condition and finding a manager. At the age of nine. I'm astounded when I think of it. I don't remember being so responsible that young, or even thinking much beyond tomorrow. I suppose times were different back then and children grew up faster.

The events of the world in 1933 were bigger than nine-year-old Sonny Lapinsky. Whether he was conscious of it or not, on August 16, 1933, my father was symbolically fighting an enemy thousands of miles away. Physically he was battling British Canadian boys from the Beaches draped in homemade swastikas, but emotionally he was battling Hitler.

While Canadians like to pretend we knew nothing of Nazi atrocities until after the war, the truth is that newspapers across the country were publishing graphic accounts and reproducing photographs of Nazi brutality against Jews in Germany as early as January of 1933. When the Swastika Club began its campaign and Toronto's Jewish youth fought back, they were fighting for their people in Germany who could not do so themselves, upon fear (and reality) of death. Every swing my father took at the Swazis (as his gang called them) was a blow against Hitler and a statement of pride. It was saying (though of course, he did not know it at the time) that Jews did not walk into the gas chambers like sheep to the slaughter. In some parts of the world, we fought back, and did so bravely. I doubt my father ever consciously analyzed the symbolism of his actions, that fateful day in the summer of '33. I only hope that, in his heart at least, he understood.

RIOT IN CHRISTIE PITS

A Multi Millionaire
JUNE 7, 1933
KENSINGTON MARKET, TORONTO

SONNY LAPINSKY PUSHES the thin sheet down to his feet. He is naked except for undershorts. In the narrow bed beside him, his brother Lenny, who is always cold, sleeps in cotton pyjamas, his side of the sheet wrapped tightly around his torso up to his chest. In the other bed, Sid snores loudly, sweating, his covers pushed completely off. Little Izzy is crammed up beside the wall next to Sid. He is flapping his arms around on the bed, deep in the middle of a bad dream.

Sonny opens his eyes and sits up in bed. It is hot. The air is still in the crowded, stuffy, second-storey room. The tiny window is propped open a few inches with a stick of wood. Sonny has always been an early riser, likes the quiet of morning before everyone else is awake. He tosses on a T-shirt, short pants, shoes, tweed cap. Silently he creeps downstairs, pulls the heavy wooden front door toward him, slips outside and around the side of the house to the backyard. He raises one hand over his forehead to shield himself from the bright rays of the morning sun. Birds nestled in the depths of the backyard apple tree chirp. The chickens in the next yard run around squawking and pecking at each other. Mrs. Pincinni, the old grandmother next door, is already up sitting on her rocker on the back porch. Sonny waves to Mrs. Pincinni as he passes. She mutters in Italian.

"Morning, Mrs. Pincinni," Sonny recites sweetly. Mrs. Pincinni doesn't speak a word of English. Sonny could say anything he wanted and it wouldn't matter. He thinks of all the rude comments he could make, but restrains himself. What if she really *does* understand English?

Sonny is short for his age, but he's strong. The muscles in his chest and arms are developed and defined. Since the beginning of the spring, he has exercised every morning without fail. He started with twenty-five push-ups, and twenty-five sit-ups, but he quickly worked his way up to a hundred sit-ups and now he is up to forty-five push-ups. After the exercises, he lifts weights. He doesn't have real barbells, just an assortment of rocks of different sizes, which he clutches and lifts, sometimes from the chest up above his head, other times from the ground to his waist. Sonny is dying to get into a real gym and learn how to lift proper weights, but he is too young. Besides, the family has no money for luxuries. They have barely enough to keep a roof over their heads and food on the table, his mother says.

"Twenty-five, twenty-six, twenty-seven." Sonny lies flat on his back on the crabgrass, hands clasped behind his head. The lawn smells fresh and is damp from the morning dew. His feet are wedged under the bottom of the rotting wooden fence that separates their narrow yard from the Pincinnis'. He lifts his body from the waist up. His elbows have to touch his knees for it to count. Then down and up. Down and up. "Twenty-eight, twenty-nine, thirty," he grunts softly.

From the window above, Lenny watches his younger brother. He admires Sonny's discipline and determination, although the repetitive nature of physical activity seems tedious and trite to Lenny. He doesn't see how Sonny can do the same routine every single day.

The feather pillow hits Lenny squarely across the back.

"Hey," he whips around. His older brother Sid grins, sitting up in bed.

"Get away from the window, will you, Lenny? You're blocking the breeze."

Lenny tosses the pillow back at Sid. "What breeze?"

Five-year-old Izzy giggles, stands on the bed, picks up his pillow and throws it toward Lenny. It flies a few feet, then lands softly on the floor. "Throw it back, Lenny." Izzy says.

Sid tackles Izzy around the waist, picks him up. "Come on little guy, I'm hungry. Let's go see what's for breakfast."

Izzy howls in glee as Sid heaves him up on his shoulders and heads for the doorway. At thirteen, Sid is almost as tall as his father, and broad-shouldered.

"I'm the king of the castle," Izzy proclaims from his perch.

"Hey, you guys," Lenny says, "get some clothes on first. You know Ma hates it when we walk around half-naked."

"It's so hot," Sid complains.

"Yeah, too hot," Izzy agrees.

Lenny grabs discarded T-shirts and knickerbockers from the night before and tosses them. The clothes land on Sid's head. Izzy squeals in delight at the sight of his big brother's face covered in a T-shirt. Sid puts Izzy on the floor and shakes his head, knocking the clothes off.

"All right, all right. Come on Izzy, let's get dressed." Sid picks up Izzy, places him on the bed, holds his little brother's short pants out, for Izzy. The pants, handed down from older brother to younger, have been patched already in three places.

"I can do it myself," Izzy tells Sid.

"I forgot." Sid leaves Izzy to dress while he attempts the same, then realizes he has Izzy's tiny undershirt, instead of his own, and switches them.

IN THE KITCHEN, Sophie Lapinsky sets out a loaf of black pumpernickel bread she baked the day before yesterday. There's nothing to put on the bread, but there is a small piece of hard cheese in the icebox. She crumples up a piece of yesterday's newspaper, tosses it inside the belly of the blackened, cast-iron coal stove, lights a match to start a fire. On such a warm morning she'd rather not heat up the flat, but she needs to boil water for tea. A curl of grey smoke escapes as she closes the front hatch. She opens the icebox. The ice block from the day before has melted away already. The water tray is full. Not much point in buying ice in summer. Slowly, she slides the tray from its grooves, dumps the water into the kitchen sink, replaces the empty tray. There is just enough milk for morning tea, if she takes hers without. Her husband takes his tea black, but the boys like a little milk. There isn't much in the icebox, except the cheese, a few pieces of herring, some pickles wrapped in wax paper, and a compote she will serve after dinner. Sophie sighs, shuts the icebox and rests for a moment, leaning against the kitchen window, fanning herself with a makeshift newspaper fan.

She switches on the RCA floor radio, which stands in a corner of the kitchen. "Paper Moon" is playing. Sophie sings along.

"Say it's only a paper moon,
Shining over a cardboard sea,
But it wouldn't be make believe
If you believed in me ..."

Sophie adores music. When she was a girl, her best friend Minnie Rosen's family had a piano. Minnie knew how to play and she taught Sophie. The girls would sit for hours playing and singing the latest songs, read from sheet music Minnie's mother bought for them. They especially loved songs from Broadway musicals. Cole Porter. Ira and George Gershwin. Rogers and Hart. Irving Berlin. Yacov has promised to buy her a piano one day. He bought the radio in 1928, when times were good. Sophie dreads the day one of the radio tubes blows. They couldn't afford to replace it and, these days, listening to music shows is the greatest pleasure in her life.

With a cloth, Sophie wipes at the grime that collects on the windowsill from cooking and heating the house with coal. She makes a mental note to ask her husband to clean out the coal cellar. She's been nagging him for more than a month to take care of it. They won't be using the furnace again until winter.

The kitchen window faces east and the morning sun shines brightly inside the apartment. Perspiration gathers in Sophie's armpits and under her breasts. A faint dusting of grit floats in the air and settles on her skin. Outside on the street she sees Sam Gershman and his son Joe trudging toward College Street, carrying small brown paper bags and a Thermos. Both father and son were laid off weeks ago from jobs in the needle trade. Every morning, Sophie sees them walk by. She knows from Sam's wife, Rose, that the men spend all day looking for work. On many afternoons, Sophie spots them returning. She can tell by the looks on their faces that every day it's the same story. No one is hiring. How much longer will they be able to manage? The younger son, Jake, sells newspapers on the corner, from early in the morning until late in the evening. On that he supports the entire family.

Yacov, dressed for work in dark trousers, and a short-sleeved white cotton shirt, sneaks up behind Sophie, kisses the back of her neck, then sits at the head of the table. She breaks off a piece of black bread and sets it on her husband's plate.

"Eat. You'll be late," she says.

"So? What's the news?" Yacov chews on his dry bread. She brightens when he asks. Sophie stands by the window every morning, watching the neighbourhood. From this activity and her pipeline of friends, she knows exactly what's going on with in their neighbourhood. It gives her pleasure to report the news.

She glances toward the old charred kettle perched on top of the stove — the water's not quite boiled yet — then turns to look out the window at the empty street, as if conjuring up the images. "Sam and Joe are still looking for work. Ida Cooper's taking in sewing now, because Abe took a cut in pay to keep his job. The Ganalinis are selling their furniture. Cheap. Maybe you should take a look? I hear they're moving back to Italy."

Yacov shrugs. "What for? No one can afford to buy."

"Maybe there's something good you can get cheap. They're practically giving it away, I hear."

"All right. I'll stop in and take a look."

"You never know."

"I said I'll look."

"That's all I ask."

Since the big crash, more and more of their neighbours have been out of work. It's a struggle to wring even a few dimes out of people who owe them money. Yacov scratches the back of his neck. How much longer can the slump go on? Surely things have to get better soon.

Steam rushes out the top of the kettle. With a stained, quilted pot-holder Sophie removes it from the stove, and pours hot water into the silver samovar that was a wedding present from her parents. She has used the tea leaves three times already. It will be a little on the weak side, but she's trying to stretch out what little tea they have. It hasn't been a good week for business. Yacov barely brought home two dollars this week, and the boys are still in school for a couple more weeks. Their summer jobs won't start until the end of the month. Sophie goes to the cupboard for tea glasses.

Yacov nods his head repeatedly, up and down, up and down, and purses his lips tightly together. Here it comes, Sophie thinks. She knows the look on his face. The corner of his mouth upturned. Jaw clenched. Forehead set. He breathes in deeply and blows the air out. Bows his head. Scratches the back of his neck. She waits for the inevitable.

"I could have been a rich man," he says quietly.

"Of course you could," Sophie answers as if she hasn't already heard the story four hundred times before. "Mr. Rockefeller could stand aside."

"A multi-millionaire. Four times over." Yacov looks up at his wife.

"I know, Yacov."

He tells the story he has told her at least three times a week for fourteen years. She listens as if she doesn't know the ending. He speaks slowly, carefully, staring at the table. "My brother-in-law gave me a necklace. A beautiful ruby necklace. If I hadn't lost the jewel in the river I'd have come to this country a rich man."

"I know, Yacov." Sophie places the tea glasses on the table.

"Sure. In those days, a necklace like that was worth a million dollars."

"Only a million?"

"Instead I came here penniless."

"It's okay, Yacov. Have some tea." She pours the steaming tea into his glass, passes him a dish with sugar cubes. There are only a few lumps left. She'll take her tea without.

"How much you think a necklace like that was worth?" He grips a sugar cube between his teeth and sips on his tea.

"How should I know? What do I know from fancy necklaces?"

"A million dollars at least." Yacov nods to himself, drinks his tea. "Maybe two million. Who knows?"

Sophie sets a mixing bowl on the counter. Thank God, there's enough flour to make bread for the rest of the week. She tips over the flour jar and without measuring, dumps two cups of flour into the bowl. Fine white dust floats upward.

Sid marches noisily into the kitchen with Izzy on his shoulders.

"That necklace was priceless. A precious stone," Yacov recalls.

"Are you telling about the necklace again, Pa?" At the table Sid lowers Izzy onto a chair and sits beside him. "Tell the part about the border police shooting at you."

"Pow pow." Izzy shoots a finger gun in the air.

"Enough with the questions, Sid. You've heard the story before." Sophie breaks off a piece of bread for each of the boys.

"And how you had to jump outa the row boat and swim for your life ..." Sid stuffs the whole piece of bread into his mouth, eats quickly and waits for more. He is always hungry. His body grows a little every day. It worries Sophie. Four boys eat a lot of food. She can barely keep up. She notices Yacov is looking thin. She supposes she too has lost weight in the past year. They make sure the boys have enough to eat before eating themselves.

"You heard your mother," Yacov snaps at Sid.

"Sorry Pa." Sid lowers his eyes, picks at the crumbs on his plate.

"Me too, sorry Pa." Izzy chews slowly on his bread.

Sid looks expectantly at Sophie. Hungry. She plunks a piece of cheese and more bread in front of him, already worried about dinner. She has some potatoes and a couple of onions. She could stretch it into a soup. By tomorrow, she'll need something more. In late May, Sophie planted a small garden in the yard, but it will be a month yet before anything besides the radishes and early peas will be ready to harvest.

"Yacov, I need potatoes," she says to her husband tentatively. She knows how worried he is. "And maybe a few eggs." She cracks the last two eggs into the mixing bowl, holds the shells up, waiting for every last bit of egg to plop down.

"What? Already?"

Sophie frowns at her husband.

"All right. All right. A few eggs we can get, don't you worry." Yacov doesn't have a penny in his pocket, but he hides this from his wife. These days when he and Max go out collecting from their customers, they get more excuses than payments. "Can you manage until tomorrow?"

Sophie bites absently on her lower lip, thinking. Maybe she can borrow a few nickels from her mother.

Lenny strolls into the kitchen in woollen knickers, knee-length socks and a long-sleeved threadbare shirt.

"Oy, Lenny, you're making me hot just looking at you," Sophie says affectionately.

Lenny takes his seat at the table.

"Where's Sonny? One of you boys go and call him in. Enough with the exercise already."

Sid bolts up from the table, tramps down the hall to the bedroom, sticks his head out the window, looks down at the backyard. Squints to see Sonny on the grass, under the apple tree, bouncing up and down. Exercising. As if it's not hot enough as it is.

"Hey! Sonny. Ma says come in for breakfast," he yells.

Sonny continues his push-ups. "Forty-five, forty-six, forty-seven."

"Sonny!" Sid yells louder. "Come on, let's go!"

"Forty-nine, fifty! Hah!" Sonny lets his arms relax, and rolls onto his back, breathing heavily, sweat dripping down his face. "A record. Fifty push-ups," he brags.

"A record? Great. But if you don't get your *toches* inside for breakfast, I'm gonna eat your share!" Sid shouts.

Mrs. Pincinni raises her fist and curses the boys in Italian. She doesn't see why she has to live beside Jews. Look at them. Screaming out the window like animals.

Sid waves at her. "Morning, Mrs. Pincinni," he hollers. "Anti-Semite," he mutters to himself, drawing his head back inside.

Sonny trots to the front door and up the stairs. He dashes straight into the bathroom to towel off the sweat. He loves the feeling of a good workout. His muscles are pumped. He can see how much they've grown already.

"There he is." Yacov smiles at Sonny as he enters the kitchen. "Sit down,

Shmuel. Eat something." Sonny is named for Yacov's younger brother Shmuel, who died at the age of six, in Russia, in the pogrom of 1913, the year Yacov emigrated. Sonny only faintly resembles Shmuel — he looks more like his mother, with Sophie's liquid brown eyes and sculpted cheekbones, even her dimples when he smiles — yet every time Yacov looks at Sonny, he thinks of his sweet, serious brother, Shmuel, and he is overcome with love.

"Pa, can't you call me Sonny?"

"Sonny I should call you? I came to America so I could call my son by an English name?"

"Canada Pop," Sid corrects.

"Canada shmanada. What's the difference?"

"It's a different country," Sid continues, then stops short, wishing he'd kept his mouth shut. His father doesn't like to be corrected.

Yacov snorts disapprovingly and turns his attention back to Sonny. "You're named for my brother, may he rest in peace. My favourite brother. We were like this." Yacov twines his hands together.

"He was your *only* brother," Sophie points out. She doesn't approve of Yacov's favouring Sonny. It makes the other boys feel bad. Sophie leans over the table, places an extra bit of cheese on Lenny's plate. She knows how much he likes cheese. Sid eyes the cheese with envy.

"So you'll have a little respect for the dead." Yacov glares at his wife.

"Yes, Papa," Sonny says dutifully. Sid keeps his gaze on Lenny's plate. Lenny watches the scene with interest. No one speaks. They all know to remain silent when Yacov speaks of his brother Shmuel. He won't talk about what happened. Not the details. And the boys know not to ask.

"It makes your father too sad," Sophie has told them many times.

They know what happens when their father gets sad. Sid gets in trouble.

Sophie drops the last piece of bread onto Sonny's plate, pours tea and a little milk into glasses for the boys. She bites into a small hunk of bread, standing by the window. Sonny devours his breakfast, famished after his workout. Izzy sticks a finger inside his bread, pulls out the soft parts. Lenny sneaks Sid the extra cheese under the table.

FROM DOWNSTAIRS, a door bangs open, followed by Max's heavy foot
tread thundering up the steps two at a time.

"Morning everyone." Max passes through the kitchen on his way to
the bathroom. Max wears black, pleated trousers and a white sleeveless
undershirt. He carries a towel and a fresh cotton shirt over his arm.

"Morning, Uncle Max. Morning, Aunt Tessie."

Tessie leans against the top of the railing in her thin cotton housecoat,
baby Esty on her hip. Barefoot, four-year-old Lillian leans against her
mother's legs.

"You want a glass of tea?" Sophie asks.

"I got some downstairs already. You going to the market today?"

"With what?" Sophie tries to keep the anxiety out of her voice.

Tessie moves closer, whispers. "So, we'll go together. I can get credit at
Zimmerman's."

"Oy, Tessie." Sophie sighs, pats her on the arm, wishes they didn't have
to resort to that. Al Zimmerman has a crush on Tessie. He'd do anything
for her. Tessie is a naturally beautiful woman and even with no money
she always manages to look like a movie star. Even though they know
she's married, all the men flirt with her.

"Don't worry, Sophie. It's kind of fun."

"You won't take a glass of tea?"

Tessie shakes her head. "I have to feed Mr. Tepperman."

"You ready, Yacov?" Max strolls back into the kitchen, washed and
shaved, buttoning his shirt.

"All right. All right. I'm coming. I'm coming." Yacov stands, gulps the
rest of his tea.

"Here's your lunch." Sophie hands Yacov a paper bag. Inside is a hard
boiled egg and a hunk of bread. He pecks her cheek, reaches for his cap
from a hat stand near the stairwell, glances sternly at the boys. "Mind
your mother," he warns. "And go to school."

"Bye Pop," Sid says quietly, hiding the extra cheese in his hand under
the table.

"Bye Pop," says Sonny, bending his arm at the elbow to study his
growing biceps.

"Bye Pop," Izzy shouts, his mouth full of chewed-up bread.

Lenny merely smiles at his father, as he slices his bread into perfect quarters.

Max takes his wife by the waist and kisses her passionately, lingering on her lips like a man who doesn't want to leave.

"Max ... go already ..." Tessie pushes him gently away, playfully. He kisses her again on the cheek, plants a quick one on the heads of each of his daughters and bounds down the stairs after Yacov.

Smiling and singing a popular new swing tune, Tessie dances down the hall to the bathroom, with Lillian at her heels. "... and try a little tenderness ... la, la, la, la, la, la, la ..."

Nickels and Dimes
JUNE 8, 1933

AS THE NEIGHBOURHOOD is pulled into the undertow of the Depression, Max and Yacov struggle. People everywhere are out of work. Those who do have jobs, work longer hours for less pay then they did five years earlier. Max and Yacov work twelve hours a day, hauling their wares from door to door. Their usual clients can scarcely afford to pay a tenth of what they owe. When Max and Yacov knock on a door, more often than not, they hear the scurrying of feet on the other side and then silence, as the inhabitants peek out a side window. Upon identifying the cousins as bill collectors, they pretend no one is home. Other people try to get out of their debts.

This morning, Mrs. Goldstein pushes aside her living room furniture and rolls up the rug she bought two years earlier from Max for fifty cents down and twenty-five cents a week. At regular payments the rug should have been hers, bought and paid for, after fifty-one weeks, but she's missed so many installments already, and with interest, she's already bought the rug three times over. She still owes Max and Yacov several more payments. Max stands at the door while she rolls it up and drags it toward the hall, sweat from her underarms staining the sides of her flowered, cotton housedress.

"Mrs. Goldstein, *nu*? What are you doing? You'll hurt your back." Max takes a step farther inside.

"What can I do, Max? I can't make the payments," Mrs. Goldstein hollers without looking up. She is bent over, clutching the heavy rug in both arms, breathing hard. "Harry's been out of work for over a year already. A rug we can live without."

Max holds his hands up, as if to stop her. "Wait a minute. Wait a minute. Not so fast, Mrs. Goldstein. Maybe an arrangement we could make." Max doesn't want the rug back. He wants payments. Who's he going to sell it to next? No one else in the neighbourhood has a dime either. At this rate, he will starve. As he has done every day since October 29, 1929, he berates himself for throwing away all his money on the stock market and he curses his former friend Checkie Seigelman for leading him there. He has refused to speak to Seigelman since that day.

Mrs. Goldstein drops the corner of the rug. It lands with a loud thud by her feet in the narrow hallway of her duplex on Manning Avenue. "What kind of an arrangement?"

Max furrows his eyebrows. "How much can you pay me today?"

She shrugs. "Nothing. *Bubkes*. Today I haven't even got what to put on the table."

Max sighs, removes his hat, runs his fingers through his sweaty black hair.

"You see? That's what I mean." Mrs. Goldstein bends down and heaves the carpet up at one corner. "Take the rug, Max. Please. Do me a favour and just take it." She hauls it to where he stands and lets it fall. The edge lands on his shoes — an expensive pair, made in Italy. He bought them in 1928 at Eaton's when times were good and he was doing well for himself. The upper leather is beginning to pull away from the sole, but who can afford new shoes?

Sighing, he leans over and grabs the edge of the rug. Technically, he has every right to repossess it. That's their agreement. Max had all his customers sign their names in his account book, beside the amount owed to him when they first made their purchase. In the late 1920s when most of the merchandise he is now collecting on was sold, people saw no problem with the agreement. Folks had money in their pockets in those days, and the idea of a missed payment seemed almost humorous then. Now, his neighbours are practically starving. Max hauls the rug out to the porch. He will have to carry it to the car by himself and tie it to the roof. In the old days, Yacov and Max went out together. These days they can't afford to. Max takes one street and Yacov takes the other and one by one they make their house calls, hoping to scratch a few pennies out of their customers. As he heaves the rug onto the roof of the car, Max spies Mrs. Goldstein in the front window watching him. He curses himself for being soft at heart, then he climbs back up the stairs to her porch and knocks.

Tentatively she opens the front door and peers out at him suspiciously. "Now what?" her face says.

Max reaches into his pocket and pulls out twenty-five cents, which he hands to Mrs. Goldstein. He doubts he will sell the rug to anyone, but he says, "A little something, Mrs. Goldstein, for the resale back to me."

She smiles for the first time in weeks. "May God be with you, Max," she says, but he is already down the stairs and hopping into the front seat of the car. Max leans forward onto the steering wheel. His head aches with tension. He rubs the sides of his temples.

The rapping on the car windshield startles Max. He looks up, sees his cousin.

"Max. Why's that rug on the roof?" Yacov asks.

"Mrs. Goldstein."

"Mrs. Goldstein?"

"We repossessed it."

"She can't pay even a little something?"

"Not a penny. How's it going by you?"

Yacov reaches in his pocket, holds out some change. "A little here, a little there. If they say they ain't got a dime, I ask for a nickel."

Max frowns, nods. "Nickels and dimes."

"That's it." Yacov replaces the change in his pocket, scratches the back of his neck. "I'm walking up the other side. I'll go north."

"I'll find you."

Yacov nods, crosses the street to call on Mrs. Cohen. Her husband Hershel owns a fish shop in the market. She's usually good for two bits at least. And if she can't make the payment, she'll at least send Yacov to the shop for a piece of carp. Or maybe even pike.

Party Line
JUNE 9, 1933

YACOV SITS AT THE kitchen table with a glass of seltzer. He unrolls a copy of the evening *Star*. Sophie switches on the radio. Her favourite music program is playing. She hums along to "Brother Can You Spare a Dime," and steps back to the stove to check on her pot of cabbage borscht. She's added much more water than she wishes, to stretch it out, and a little extra salt to give it flavour. She can't remember the last time they've been able to afford meat. These days, watery soup and day-old bread is their staple diet. But at least they have a roof over their heads.

That afternoon Sophie had patted Mrs. Verducci sympathetically on the arm. Mrs. Verducci was standing outside her house, her furniture in the gutter, rain falling around her in large wet drops. Nine months earlier, her husband had been laid off from his job with the construction company he'd worked for since 1915 — eighteen years with the same company — and they were so far behind with the rent they were evicted. The landlord arrived first thing in the morning with a crew of unemployed men hired for the day. They systematically moved the Verduccis' belongings out beyond the edge of the front yard to the ditch. The family will move in with Mr. Verducci's brother's family, who live in a three-room flat farther south near Dundas Street. There will be no room for their furniture. Mrs. Verducci asked Sophie if Yacov would like to buy any of it.

"Going cheap," she added. Whatever they didn't sell that day, they would have to leave in the gutter. Sophie promised she'd send Yacov over later. She didn't have the heart to tell Mrs. Verducci that even if he wanted to, Yacov couldn't buy any of her furniture. The few nickels he and Max managed to squeeze out of their customers this week are going toward their own rent and groceries. More and more often, the cousins search the back alleys, gutters and abandoned lots for cast-off furniture and rags, which they repair or refinish and attempt to sell. Sophie couldn't bring herself to tell Mrs. Verducci that after her family left, Yacov might take whatever was left in the ditch and try to sell it.

It's a common sight: People standing on the sidewalk outside their homes, with all of their worldly possessions lying on the street beside them. Still, every time Sophie sees it, her heart crumples. This evening, in the kitchen, Izzy sits at the table beside his father reading quietly from an old picture book that had once been Sonny's. Izzy is a fast learner and has already learned how to read the simple text in the one book he owns. When he remembers, Lenny brings home picture books from the library for Izzy, who devours them; he's a good student already at five years old. Sid and Sonny are outside playing. Sophie opens the kitchen window to see what they're doing. Along with some of the other neighbourhood boys, Sonny and Sid are playing stickball in the middle of the street. Sophie wishes they would go to the park, but Sid has complained that some tough older boys called the Pit Gang bother them, call them names, sometimes even chase them out of the park. So they play on the road in front of their own house.

The milk wagon turns onto the street.

"Truck!" one of the boys screams and they all move to the side of the road. They wave to Mr. Robinson, the milkman, and pat his horse Glory as she walks by. She crunches lazily from the feed bag strapped below her mouth, leather blinders strapped to either side of her face to keep her from panicking at the sight of motorcars passing on her left.

Back in the street, Sonny steps up to bat, grinning. The pitcher throws the ball hard. Sonny effortlessly whacks it with the old broom handle they use for a bat. The ball arcs high in the sky and thuds against the brick of the Pincinnis' house, missing the window by inches. Sonny trots easily to first base.

"Watch the windows!" Sophie yells down. The boys look up, surprised to see her.

"Don't worry, Ma," Sid yells back.

"Don't worry Ma," she mutters to herself as she pulls her head back inside. "How can I not worry?" Four boys. Oy. A girl would have been nice. "Stormy weather ..." she sings along with the radio.

"Oy, a curse," complains Yacov, turning the page of his newspaper.

"La, la, la, la ... What is it?" Sophie pauses from her singing to taste the soup.

"It's that Hitler, the new chancellor of Germany. He's completely *mishugena*. The things he's getting away with ..."

"So? What has that got to do with us?" Sophie adds more salt.

Yacov shakes his head. He's not really sure how to answer her question. He only knows the news feels bad. Yacov can smell a pogrom from miles away. From across the Atlantic Ocean. From the Old World to the New. He is worried about his family in Russia. He wonders if there will be more pogroms.

He can still hear the pounding of horse hooves. Can smell the dust rising in the air. The shouts of Cossacks; smashed dishes; crash of tables being overturned. His sister Rachel's screams. He pictures himself at fifteen, running to the barn, leaving his little brother Shmuel hiding under a feather bed in the back of the house. Shmuel's young serious face so trusting. Big brown eyes looking up at him. That was the last time he saw his brother alive. Yacov shudders.

"Yacov?" Beside him, Sophie peers down to look in her husband's face. "What's it got to do with us?"

"I don't know, Sophie," he says. "All I'm saying is good luck to the Jews in Germany."

"As if the Depression isn't bad enough," Sophie says to the ceiling, addressing God more than Yacov. "Now, we need this too?"

Yacov turns the page and reads about people on relief. Opposite is a full-page ad for the new Eaton's College Street store. Gas ranges are selling for $37.95, four-piece bedroom sets cost $80.75 and a steel bed with a spring mattress is going for $12.95. Yacov would love a steel bed with a spring mattress. He and Sophie are still sleeping on a lumpy mattress he bought wholesale when they were first married. It rests on a wood frame he constructed himself out of scrap wood he found in an alley back in the twenties when abundance was everywhere and people threw out things like wood. These days, with the fuel shortages, a scrap of wood in an alley is unheard of. Last winter, people ripped down fences and broke apart kitchen chairs to burn in wood stoves, never mind throwing good wood into the streets. If things are as bad this winter, what will be left to burn?

Sophie hauls a basket of damp laundry to the boys' bedroom and opens the window. One by one she pins the clothing and bedsheets to the line that is strung from the house to a pole in the back lane. Lenny sits under the shade of the apple tree in the backyard, reading a book, *A Room of One's Own,* by Virginia Woolf. Just in case one of his brothers comes into the yard, he's hiding the book inside a copy of Hemingway's *A Farewell to Arms.* Sonny and Sid think it's bad enough that Lenny's all the time reading. If they see him reading a "girl's book," he'll have hell to pay, especially with Sonny, who takes great pleasure in teasing Lenny, even though he'll defend his brother to the death if any of the neighbourhood guys try to do the same.

Lenny looks up, sees his mother and smiles.

"What are you reading, Sweetheart?" she calls down.

He holds up the top book. "It's by Ernest Hemingway."

Sophie smiles at her scholarly son. She's never even heard of most of the books he reads, but she likes to ask. She relishes in his intellect. To think, she gave birth to such a literary genius. "It's almost suppertime," she tells him.

"Okay, Ma." He bends his head back into his book.

Sophie reaches into the basket for more clothespins. It's such a hot night, the clothes will be dry before it gets dark.

"OKAY, SUPPER'S READY," Sophie announces. "Do me a favour, Yacov, and call the boys in."

"Good. That, at least, I can do something about." Unlike the situation in Germany. Unlike the Depression or his family in Russia. Yacov folds his paper, places it on the table. A headline on page one reads "Shut German Schools to Weed Out Jews."

"Make sure they leave their shoes by the door. I don't want they should track dirt into the house. I just washed the floors yesterday."

The brash jarring ring of the telephone downstairs slices through the air.

Sophie listens. One long, two short rings. The call is for them. The phone they share with Max and Tessie is a party line. Tessie's sharp footsteps click on the floor below.

"Hello," she answers. "Oh hello, Mrs. Perodsky." Tessie's voice grows louder, more methodical. Channa Perodsky's hearing loss is particularly challenging over the phone. "It's Tessie … .No. Tessie," she says even louder. "That's right … I'm fine. How are you? … I said, How are you? … Uh huh. Uh huh. Sure. She's here … I said, she's here! Just a minute. Sophie!" she hollers up the stairs. "It's for you."

"I'm coming." Sophie sets her mixing spoon on the counter, runs past Yacov and flies down the stairs.

"It's your mother."

Sophie takes the black earpiece from Tessie's hand, puts it up to her ear. "Thank you," she mouths to Tessie and she leans forward to speak into the mouthpiece on the wall-mounted phone. "Hello. Mama?" She shouts. "Yes Mama! We're all fine. You just saw the boys yesterday. What could happen in one day?" Sophie glances at Tessie, who covers her mouth, trying to contain a laugh. "I said everyone's fine. Fine! What? A carp? You made it? Okay … no … no … I'll come by and pick it up … no, it's fine. After dinner. Lenny will come with me. Lenny. No Lenny. That's right. Okay … see you later. Bye Ma." Sophie hangs the earpiece on its hook.

"She made a carp?"

"Baked. We'll split it in half."

"Don't be silly. It's from your mother."

"So? I can't share with you?"

"Okay, but not half. Just a small piece. The girls don't eat much."

"All right. It's settled. I gotta go upstairs. I got a pot of soup on."

Sophie climbs back upstairs to put dinner on the table.

"I DON'T SEE WHY NOT," Sid answers back to his father after dinner, his thumbs hooked inside the elastic of his suspenders.

"You're only thirteen years old, Sid. You can't quit school."

"I'm a man. I already had my bar mitzvah."

"In the old country you'd be a man," Sophie declares from the sink, where she is washing the supper dishes. "Here, you're a boy."

"Come on, Pa, I could work with you and Uncle Max," Sid lobbies.

"You're staying in school. And that's that," Sophie says firmly. "You only got one chance to get an education."

"You heard your mother." Yacov reaches for his newspaper, the matter now closed.

"Pa, what's the point? I'm no good in school. Lenny's way past me already in reading and writing."

"Well ... Lenny's good at reading."

"Pa, even Sonny can read better than me. I'm not the schoolboy type. Can't I just work with you from now on? I'm good at selling. Remember when I went out with you when Uncle Max was sick with the flu last year."

Yacov nodded. It's true. Sid has the knack. He's like Max. Smooth. A real charmer. He's a better salesman than Yacov. Most of the ladies assume he's Max's son.

Sid can sense his father weakening. "Whadya say, Pop? I'm almost a grown-up now. Times are tough. That's what you and Ma always say. I could help out. It doesn't make sense for me to sit in school. It's a waste."

"A waste it's not, but ... on the other hand ..."

"I said no." Sophie moves closer to the table waving a wet spoon in the air. "He stays in school."

She turns back to her washing. Yacov pours himself more seltzer, takes a drink. The bubbles shoot up his nose, make him cough. "Okay Sid, tell you what. Every day after school lets out and on Sundays, you'll come work by me. And when school lets out in a couple of weeks, you'll work days during the week. Next year, we'll talk."

Sid smiles. It's more than he'd hoped for.

"What are you talking about, Yacov? He has to stay in school until he's sixteen. This is Canada. It's not Russia. They'll send the police over."

"Truant officer, Ma. Not the police."

"An officer is an officer."

Yacov slams a hand on the wooden table to show he's in charge, even though it's obvious to everyone that Sophie makes the household decisions. "I said we'll talk about it next year. *Farshtaist?*"

"Sure Pop." Sid stands.

"Three-thirty sharp I expect you to find me on my route." He points a threatening finger in the air.

"Swell, Pop. I'll find you on your route." Sid skips out of the room.

Sophie waves her dishrag at Yacov. "He can't quit school until he's sixteen. What are you telling him?"

"Acch." Yacov waves the back of his hand at Sophie, and opens his newspaper to the financial section. Ever since the stock-market crash Yacov has taken an interest in following the financial news, searching for signs of hope.

"Such *mishuges,*" Sophie mutters to herself as she scrubs the inside of a pot.

Sonny bounds into the room a moment later, sits beside his father and pulls up his socks, which are always slipping down and exposing the bare shins under his knickers. His feet don't reach the floor and he swings his legs nervously under the table.

"Pop. I want to get a job too."

Yacov sighs, looks over the top of his newspaper. "You're too young. Did you finish your homework, Shmuel?"

"Come on Pa, you were working when you were my age." The feet-swinging picks up in pace.

"What? How old are you?" Yacov knows full well how old Sonny is. It's a game he plays with the boys.

"Nine years old." Sonny puffs out his chest, full of self-importance. "Almost ten."

"Already?"

"Pop. Please. There's a job at the bowling alley. Davey Tittel works there. They need another boy. It pays real good." Sonny has it all worked out. He was planning to wait until the weekend to ask his father, but after Sid tore into the room with his news, Sonny figured it might be better to act now, while Yacov is in a good mood.

"I can make three dollars and fifty cents a week. Just after school and on Saturdays. Please, Pop."

"A bowling alley he's not working at," Sophie yells from the sink. "Gangsters and thugs it's filled with."

"Aw Ma, it's just a game. All kinds of people go to the bowling alley. Even women and kids."

Sophie sighs. He's right about that. Sort of. Her friend Ida Cooper had invited her several times to go bowling in the afternoon, a few years earlier, before times got so tough.

"Just after school and on Saturdays," Sonny pleads.

"No one around here is working on *Shabbes*," Yacov says firmly.

"You do," points out Sonny, absently kicking the table leg.

"That's different. Stop with the feet. You're upsetting the whole table," Yacov reaches forward, touching Sonny's knee to steady him. "I have to." Earlier that year, Yacov had given up his Saturdays in the synagogue to work and Max gave up his Sundays off. They really had no choice. They were barely making a living as it was. Yacov made his peace with God over the matter. He knew somewhere in the Talmud it said that if it was a matter of life and death, a man could work on the Sabbath. These days it takes working seven days a week to keep food on the table and a roof over their heads. On Sundays, they have to be careful of the police and the Gentiles, because of the Sunday Blue Laws — no work allowed on *the Lord's Day*. Yacov and Max make it a point to only call on Jewish customers on Sundays.

"Okay, just after school during the week," Sonny answers quickly, realizing his error in strategy. Absently, he begins swinging his legs again.

"No later than nine o'clock."

"Eight o'clock," Sophie corrects. "I want him home by eight o'clock."

"Okay." Sonny seizes his chance, jumps off the chair before his mother changes her mind. "Eight o'clock. Thanks, Pop."

Yacov winks at his son, proud of his initiative at such a young age. A fire burns in little Shmuel. Who knows how far he'll go?

Lenny already has a job as a paperboy. It's a good job for Lenny. He loves to read. Anything he can get his hands on. In books he can go to far-away lands and learn new things. He can't afford to buy books of his own, but Lenny visits the Shaw Street Public Library twice a week, where he can sign out books for free. Lenny reads two or three books a week. When he's older he'll buy his own books and line them up on shelves in his house. To Lenny that will be the greatest gift of all.

June 20, 1933

YACOV KISSES HIS WIFE on the cheek, and dashes out the door into the bright June morning, eating a cold piece of bread on his way out. Max sits in the car warming up the crotchety old motor, reading the morning edition of *Der Yiddisher Zhurnal*. It is five months since Adolf Hitler was elected chancellor and the Journal has published a lengthy editorial. Max usually only reads the financial section of the English papers, but since the new chancellor was elected he has been paying close attention to the situation in Germany.

Yacov slips into the passenger seat and pulls his cap lower on his forehead to shield his eyes from the sun.

"You see, Yacov," Max says without looking up. "This is exactly what I was talking about."

Yacov leans across the seat to read over Max's shoulder.

"Hah," Max slaps the middle of the paper. "That's what we should have done to the Cossacks in Russia."

"What? What does it say?"

With a flip of his hand, Max straightens the paper and scans the article. "It says the Jews in Germany should defend themselves with force. That's what I've been saying for years."

"I know, Max. I've been right here all along. But how can you fight against the government?"

"Armed resistance. This is 1933, after all. And in Germany people aren't as backward as we were in Russia. The Jews live in big cities. It won't be the same as it was for us." Max clenches his fist and punches the air as he speaks. He hopes the Jews in Germany will read the article and be encouraged to fight back. He doesn't consider that the Jews in Germany don't have access to *Der Yiddisher Zhurnal,* which is published in Toronto.

Every morning, the news grows worse. Max and Yacov sit and read the morning paper while the motor of their old car chugs. Sometimes they are numb with disbelief, other times eloquent with rage.

"You see, Yacov. It goes on and on. Thank God we're here. What a mess." Max shakes the newspaper as if it's to blame for the news.

"I don't know." Yacov sighs deeply.

"What?"

"Maybe I should apply to bring over my family ..."

"Yacov, what are you talking about? You bring them over, you have to sponsor them. Pardon me for bringing it up, but you can barely feed your own family these days. How do you think you could support a father, a brother and a sister?"

"Two sisters," Yacov snaps. "I told you. My brother died in the pogrom. I have two sisters."

"What about the butcher?"

"My sister's husband."

"You see? Also a sister's husband. They have children?"

"Two boys and a girl."

"There. That's ... seven people. Yacov, how do you think you could support seven more people?"

"We'd manage. At least they'd be safe."

"They're in Russia. All the trouble is in Germany. Don't worry so much, Yacov. Believe me, this will blow over. A madman. That's what he is. Give it a year or two, he will have to stop with the edicts, or he won't get re-elected. The Germans are a cultured people. Not barbarians like Russians. They won't stand for this much longer. You'll see."

"I haven't even heard a word from my family in two years."

"No news is good news."

"I should have brought them all over here years ago. When it was still possible," Yacov says. Now, even if he had the money, even if Pinchus, his stubborn brother-in-law, is willing to leave Russia and bring his sisters, father, niece and nephews to Canada, they cannot. When Mackenzie King was prime minister a few years ago, he was against all Jewish immigration. "None is too many," a senior official in King's government declared, when asked how many Jews would be allowed into Canada.

"Never mind. They won't come anyway. Your brother-in-law the butcher is a big shot in the village. He's respected. He has a good seat near the front in the synagogue. He even makes a nice living. Probably better than we do. Why leave that?"

"At least they could have sent Shoshana," Yacov sulks.

"Your sister is eighteen years old. She has her own mind to make up. Maybe she'll be getting married soon," Max counters.

"Oy," Yacov says, overwhelmed by it all. The last time Yacov saw Shoshana she was three years old. The day his brother Shmuel died. The day he hit a Russian soldier and was forced to leave his home. The day he left Tiraspol, Russia forever.

Dogs and Jews
JULY 1933

WHILE YACOV IS FRETTING over the fate of his family in Russia, another very different kind of immigrant community is concerned about its fate in the new world. Charles Geoffrey Bain Jr.'s grandfather immigrated to Toronto from Britain in 1870. He started off at the Great Western Railway company as a clerk in the accounting department, and quickly rose through the ranks to the position of chief accountant. He owned a home in the Annex, where he raised three girls and a boy. He wanted his son Gregory to go to university, but Greg married young and ended up following his father's footsteps, being hired on as a junior clerk in accounting in 1906 at the age of eighteen. When he married his childhood sweetheart, Elizabeth, they had just enough money for a downpayment on a small house in the east end of Toronto, on the shore of Lake Ontario, in a quaint neighbourhood known as Balmy Beach. What had been summer cottages for many years were being winterized and converted into homes. Now that the Queen streetcar ran all the way to Woodbine it was no problem for people to live in the Beaches and commute every day downtown.

Elizabeth and Gregory had originally intended to move farther uptown when they were more established, but they grew fond of living right on the lakefront. Balmy Beach was comprised of two streets north and south, and five streets east and west. A cozy neighbourhood. The folks who lived there were all good Protestants of British background. They all knew each other, and socialized together. Their children played together. They never locked their doors or their cars. Like their neighbours, the Bains had a boathouse for the two canoes they owned. In the summer after the kids were put to bed, the adults would gather on the small beach area, paddle out in their canoes, and later have big communal barbecues on the beach. Life was ideal for the Balmy Beach residents.

In 1932, Toronto mayor Sam McBride attempted to purchase the lakefront properties. When the residents refused to sell, the city expropriated the land and built a boardwalk and a park with newly planted young trees, opening the beach to the public. People from other areas of the city began to fill up the beach on weekends — mostly working-class immigrants from Italy and eastern Europe, who couldn't afford summer cottages or vacations out of the city.

The Bains were compensated handsomely by the City of Toronto for their small home and lakefront property, and they found a similar though larger house two blocks north. They were still *close to* the beach. But that wasn't the same thing as being *on* the beach. Not the same thing at all. Gregory Bain was bitterly resentful.

"Bloody foreigners," he cursed in his thick Scottish brogue that whole year and for years later, forgetting that his own father had come to Canada an immigrant. "Think they can take over the whole country. Come over here with their damn foreign ways and their damn foreign food, speaking some godforsaken bloody foreign language, can't understand a goddamned word they're saying. Have to move my family. Damn foreigners. Should just go on back where they came from."

Gregory Bain's fifteen-year-old son, Charles Jr., known as Charlie, is not immune to his father's xenophobia. In fact, he has learned his lessons quite well. In July of 1933, when his best friend George Patterson invites Charlie to a meeting of the Balmy Beach Swastika Club, Charlie says, "Sure. What's a swastika?"

"Come on, you'll see," says George, throwing a brotherly arm over Charlie's shoulder. Charlie and George have been friends since they were toddlers. In the fall they will begin the tenth grade.

The club meets in the back of a confectionery shop on Queen Street just a block up from the beach. It is a hot evening — the hottest night of the summer so far, although everyone knows it is going to get even hotter — and the air is thick and stale in the back of the narrow store. A faint sticky smell of sugar, licorice and chocolate hangs in the air. When Charlie and George arrive, there are twelve other boys from the neighbourhood and a couple of young men Charlie doesn't recognize. They say their hellos and take a couple of seats near the back, as the meeting is called to order by one of the older fellows. He is in his late twenties, says his name is Gordon Hill. He wears long pants tucked into high black boots — which Charlie finds odd footwear on such a hot summer night — with a long-sleeved brown shirt. He wears a black leather belt around his trousers and another leather strap slung across his chest diagonally. On his lapel is a chrome badge. Impressed on the badge is a red emblem, which looks vaguely familiar to Charlie but he can't quite place it. It resembles a tipped-over cross with extra "feet" on all four ends. When Charlie glances around, he notices several other boys in the room have the same badge pinned to their lapels. He tries to remember where he's seen the symbol before.

As the meeting begins Charlie learns that the badges are called "swastika badges," but he still doesn't know the origin of the symbol. The speaker talks a lot about the foreigners and the Jews who are, let's face it, "undesirable persons." He talks about how they're coming every Sunday to the Beach, and how they should just stay in their own neighbourhoods and leave the Beaches for the Beaches — meaning the residents of the area.

Charlie has to admit he agrees with the speaker. He remembers what it was like just the year before, when his family lived right on the beach and only local residents used Balmy Beach. There was lots of space to spread out. He knew just about everyone — friends of his parents, kids he went to school with, and people who lived right on his street. He could run down to the lake from his own back porch any time he wanted. He could look out his bedroom window and watch the lake. It just isn't the same now that the beach is a public park. It isn't the same living two blocks away. And the mess those people leave. It's disgusting: orange peels, old sandwiches, eggshells, fish bones, cigarette butts. Charlie has heard his father complain about the foreigners changing their clothes right out in public. His family would never do that. There are change rooms for that purpose, for heaven's sake.

At the end of the meeting when one of the boys walks around the room selling swastika badges for twenty-five cents, Charlie and George each buy one and proudly pin them to their shirts. They are members of the club.

July 16, 1933

THE SECOND WEEK of July in 1933 is scorching. Humidity hangs low in the air, sucking the life out of every man, woman and child. The only relief is by the lake, where sometimes there is a breeze. For years, people from the Lapinskys' neighbourhood have visited Sunnyside Beach in the west end. There is an amusement park, with a Ferris wheel, roller coaster, and games of skill. And there's a boardwalk and a long stretch of beach with fine brown and white sand. There are venders selling hot dogs, candy apples and popcorn. On weekdays the streetcars offer free fare to kids going to Sunnyside. In the summer, every inch of space on the beach is covered with people escaping the heat of the city. Some wear one-piece bathing costumes that cover the body from neck to knee. A few daring men bare their chests, although it is illegal. Others arrive fully dressed — the men in cotton suits and ties and the women in full skirts and blouses — then roll up their pant legs, tuck up their skirts above the ankle and sit under umbrellas, or in the shade of wide-brimmed straw hats. The year before, a new beach opened in the east end and this summer Balmy Beach is the talk of the town. New immigrants from the Ward and Kensington neighbourhoods begin visiting the east-end beaches for the first time. Some drive cars across the city on the newly built Danforth viaduct; others hop on the electric streetcar that quietly glides across Queen Street.

For the summer, Sid is working fulltime alongside his father and Uncle Max. Lenny is selling papers on Bay Street and Sonny's at the bowling alley. They hand over most of their earnings to Sophie each week. During the summer, she has enough money to serve her family decent meals for a change. Smoked fish, fresh vegetables, even meat or chicken on Friday nights. She secretly hides some of the money away, in a jar in the back of the kitchen cupboard, for the winter. For fuel and food. Just in case.

ON SUNDAY MAX, Yacov and Sid knock off work early. It's so hot they're wilting, dripping in sweat. Most of their customers have already fled to the lake. Max decides there's no point in working for the rest of the afternoon. Besides, his chapter of B'nai B'rith are having a picnic at Balmy Beach. He figures they should go.

"It's good for business," he tells Yacov on their walk home. "You never know who we could meet. This one talks to that one. That one talks to this one. And, boom." He claps his hands together loudly. "Next thing you know, we make a sale."

"I don't know about that, Max."

Sid agrees with Max, but says nothing out loud.

"It could happen." Max pulls open the front door. "Anybody home?" he calls.

"Where else would we be?" Tessie hollers back. "What are you doing home in the middle of the day? What's wrong? What happened?"

"Nothing happened. Calm yourself, woman."

Yacov climbs the stairs to his flat, with Sid on his heels. "Sophie," he calls, "I'm home."

"So early?" she hollers back. "What happened?"

The heat inside is practically unbearable. His family is scattered around the kitchen. Yacov wonders why they aren't outside, although really, the air is just as still outside as in. Sophie sits at the table with her sewing basket, darning socks and underwear. Lenny sits across from her, reading the front page of the *Star*. Izzy lies on the floor reading his picture book. Sonny rolls up little bits of paper from the sports page, chews on them until they are just the right texture and flings them across the room with a wooden ruler, aiming for the back of Lenny's head. So far, he's missed.

"Nothing happened," says Yacov, kissing his wife on the cheek. "Who wants to go to the beach today?"

"I do!" Sonny shouts, as he lets another spitball fly. It falls short, landing on the floor.

"What beach?" Sophie asks.

"Yeah, the beach!" Izzy shouts.

Lenny doesn't look up. He's deeply engrossed in an article written by the *Star's* reporter in Berlin. The headline reads, "Germany to Degrade Jews to Second Class Citizenry." It goes on to say that "All civil servants of Jewish descent will be retired except those in the service before August 1, 1914, and those who actually served in the trenches during the war."

"What about work?" Sophie is suspicious. Yacov has never come home in the middle of the day before.

"Never mind. What's a matter? A man can't decide to take an afternoon off?"

"You never take an afternoon off." She shoves her fist inside a black sock, holds it up to the sunlight streaming in through the window, looking for holes to darn.

"Now I do."

Sophie eyes her husband. He is acting strange. Maybe it's the heat.

"We're going to the new beach. Pack a picnic," he tells Sophie.

"Pack a picnic? Why all the way over there? What's wrong with Sunnyside?"

"A picnic. A picnic. Some food in a basket."

"You still haven't answered my question."

"Question? What question?"

"What's wrong?"

"Nothing's wrong. Max and I decided to come home and take our families to the beach. What's so terrible?"

"On a Sunday?"

"If not Sunday, then when? Pack a picnic already."

"A picnic he wants? Just like that?"

"Sure. We'll eat at the beach. Here, I picked up some herring." Yacov hands her a grease-stained brown paper package.

She drops the half-finished sock into her sewing basket, takes the package of herring to the counter to unwrap the paper. She will pack some bread and apples to go with it. "What's wrong with Sunnyside?" she asks again.

"What? Nothing's wrong."

"So? Why should we go all the way over there?"

Yacov hesitates. Sophie doesn't like Max's B'nai B'rith friends. She calls
them a bunch of greenhorns. Most are new immigrants from Russia and
Poland. Sophie feels like more of a Canadian because she came over from
Russia with her family when she was a child. She only has a slight accent,
unlike her husband, whose accent is thick.

"So *nu* Yacov? Are you going to answer my question?" Sophie lays out
a few apples and a paring knife.

Yacov wipes sweat from his forehead with his handkerchief.

"What's wrong with Sunnyside?" Sophie opens the pantry cupboard,
where she keeps the plums.

"Nothing's wrong. What's the matter we should try a new beach for a
change? Is that so terrible? Boys, come on. Get ready."

"Huh?" Sid asks.

"Your bathing trunks," Yacov answers impatiently.

Sophie searches for a piece of cloth large enough to wrap up a loaf of
bread.

"Oh yeah. Swell. Come on guys." Sid grabs Izzy's hand.

"Max and Tess are coming," Yacov informs his wife.

"So? Why shouldn't they?"

"Swell," says Sid.

"Can I bring my book?" Izzy asks.

"It'll get wet," Sid decides.

"Pow." Sonny aims and shoots. He watches the slimy wad of paper arc
through the air and hit Lenny right on the back of the neck.

"Hey!" Lenny looks up from his newspaper for the first time.

CHARLIE BAIN SPENDS the morning sitting on the back veranda of his
house, drinking lemonade and scanning the evening *Telegram*. He thinks
of trotting down to the beach for a quick dip to cool off, but it's a Sunday
and the damn foreigners will be there, messing up the sand as usual,
littering it with strange smoked fish and pickles. Speaking their foreign
languages. Polish, he thinks. Russian maybe. His father says the foreigners,
especially the Jews, are dirty. Charlie can't stand the thought of their filth

in his lake. He doesn't want to get into the water while they're using the lake for a bathtub. So he sits on his own porch, sweltering and fuming. On the front page of the newspaper is a photo of a group of Nazi storm troopers in Germany, marching down a street in Berlin. They have swastika armbands on their arms. It's the same symbol as the one on the badge he bought from the local Swastika Club. Holy cow. So that's why the emblem looked familiar. The article is about German Jewish intellectuals attempting to flee the country with their money and being caught by the Nazis and tortured, then murdered. Murdered? Charlie reads on. The article says they deserved to be punished. It's against the law for emigrants to take any money with them. Charlie has to agree; they broke the law. They must pay the penalty. But still, the punishment is a little stiff for the crime. Couldn't they just fine them? Or give them a short jail sentence, like his Uncle Buck got for "borrowing" petty cash from his company's register? Tortured and murdered just seems harsh. Still, he does admire how crisp and strong the Nazi soldiers look in their starched uniforms, proudly displaying their swastikas as a symbol of strength. They look like winners. Fierce and brave. Charlie fingers the metal swastika badge in his pocket. He feels proud to be part of something that is international in scope, something you can read about in the newspapers.

George calls on Charlie at 2:30 sharp, just like they'd agreed. George is wearing long pants and a white, short-sleeved shirt. Pinned to his collar is his swastika badge.

"Come on, Charlie. You ready?" George notices that Charlie is not wearing his badge.

"Just a second." Charlie leaves George on the front porch. "Mom?" he calls out. "Going to the beach with George."

"There's fresh towels in the linen closet," she yells back from upstairs, where she sits by an open window, with a cigarette, a romance novel and a gin and tonic.

"That's okay. We're not going swimming."

When they are a few steps from his house, Charlie fishes in his trouser pocket for his badge and pins it to his shirt.

"This is going to be great." George's enthusiasm is contagious.

Charlie feels excited and proud. He is doing his civic duty, helping rid his neighbourhood of the "undesirable visitors." His father would be proud, although some internal uneasiness warns him not to tell his parents. Not yet, anyway.

When they arrive at Balmy Beach, Charlie notices the usual crowds of Jews and other foreigners spread out on the picnic tables, swimming in the lake, and all over the beach. Huddled outside the Balmy Beach Canoe Club is a mass of young men and boys from several chapters of the Swastika Club, fully dressed in the ninety degree weather. Pinned to their shirts are Swastika badges. A couple of the boys wear white shirts with black Swastikas painted right over their chests. Tacked to the door of the clubhouse is a white sheet with a Swastika painted on it in black.

THE LAPINSKYS PILE into the Model T. It's extremely crowded, even with Sid and Sonny sitting in back, in the rumble seat. Max drives, while Tessie sits up front with little Lillian and baby Esty in her arms. Sophie squeezes into the back with Yacov and Lenny; Izzy is perched on her lap. Tessie has a basket of food by her side. Sophie has her own basket, which she crams by her feet.

On Queen Street East in the Beaches, there are rows of cars parked by the side of the road. Max circles around until he finds a spot and manoeuvres the car into it. They walk two blocks back to the beach.

"There they are." Max spots his friends from B'nai B'rith at a couple of picnic tables in the park area. Sophie glares at Yacov. So that's why here and not Sunnyside. Why didn't he tell her? Yacov smiles warily. They follow Max and join his table of friends. Tessie and Sophie change the smaller kids into bathing costumes out in the open by the picnic tables. The other boys are too big. Sophie sends them back to the car to change. Then the adults take turns changing in the car. It's tricky. They have to cover themselves with a blanket and change while sitting in the back seat, but they have nowhere else to dress. There is the Balmy Beach change room for members only, but membership is restricted to the Gentiles of the Beaches.

The older boys run down to the lake. Sophie orders them not to go in any farther than their chests — none of them know how to swim — but it's a great relief from the heat to splash around in the cool lake water. Yacov and Max join the boys, balancing them on their shoulders, splashing and playing. Tessie and Sophie take the little ones, Izzy, Lillian and Esty, into the shallow part where the water meets the beach. They sit in the sand while the kids play. Izzy, the oldest of the littler ones, organizes a game. They're building a castle out of sand. How he knows about castles is a mystery to Sophie. Maybe he saw one in a book.

After a while Max comes out of the water and joins the women. He wrangles some table space from his B'nai B'rith friends and Tessie and Sophie lay out the food they've brought. They call the boys and Yacov from the water to eat lunch. It's a beautiful afternoon. The sun shines high in the sky, hot, but there's a cool breeze blowing up from the lake. It is so pleasant, they almost forget there's a Depression on. Their picnic is not fancy — black bread with hard-boiled eggs, apples and a few pieces of herring — but just to have a day of rest by the water makes them all feel like millionaires. Like multi-millionaires.

"I came to this country in 1913," Yacov tells the boys. "It was a beautiful day. In May. I met your mother the day I got off the train in the city. The most beautiful woman I ever saw."

"Stop it, Yacov …" Sophie loves when he tells the story, but modesty compels her to protest.

"I fell in love right away. Only she was engaged to another man …"

"Saul Weinstock." Lenny provides the name.

"That's right. Weinstock."

"Tell about the river in Russia." Sid loves the shooting part best.

"No," Sonny jumps in. "Tell about the dry well. And how you had to stay in the bottom for seven days."

"Was it really seven days?" Max has always been skeptical. His own story is far less dramatic. He was also smuggled across the Dneister River into Romania. But his trip went smoothly. Their tiny boat evaded the border police. He made it across without incident. He walked, travelled by train, and hitched a ride in a farmer's wagon to make his way to Hamburg, where he boarded a boat that landed in Halifax five months before Yacov made a similar, though more hazardous, crossing.

"Seven days. Yeah," Yacov confirms. "The Russian police were looking for me. The Romanian police were looking for me. I was lucky. I found a farmer who saved my life. All day I had to sit inside the bottom of a dry well. And at night I climbed out and slept in the barn. Seven days. He gave me bread and water. And before I left a pair of old boots."

"Because you lost your boot in the river," Lenny says.

"And the ruby necklace," Izzy adds.

They can picture a black leather boot at the bottom of a muddy river. And inside the boot, gleaming and sparkling, sits the famous jewel.

"That's right. Then I walked and walked until I got to Germany."

"Tell about the spiders in the well. And the rats." Sonny is fascinated with the details.

"*Feh,*" Sophie says. "We're eating. Please, Yacov. Do you have to tell that story?"

"Okay. Okay." He turns to Sonny. "Your mother doesn't want to hear about bugs."

"Aw nuts."

"Eat your lunch, boys. Izzy, stop playing with your food."

CHARLIE LOOKS UP. Gordon, the man who led the meeting the other night, is making an announcement. Charlie and George move forward into the crowd. Charlie glances over one shoulder and sees a Jewish mother wiping sand out of a little boy's eyes. The boy is standing up on a picnic table, crying. Then the mother says something in Jewish, and the little boy giggles. Charlie involuntarily smiles at the sight, then forces his mouth into a deep frown. Disgusting, he thinks to himself. Standing on a table like that. *It's for eating, not standing,* a voice that sounds not unlike his mother's nags at him. He turns face-front to listen to his instructions. The leader informs the boys that they will have a peaceful demonstration. A couple of the fellows have written a song and handwritten song sheets are handed out. They will march along the boardwalk and back again. They don't want to cause any trouble, but if any trouble comes their way, well, "You fellows know what to do, don't you?"

Excitement crackles in the air. Charlie guesses there must be a hundred boys in the demonstration. Some of the Jews notice the gathering and stare. George and Charlie take their place in the parade and begin marching. Charlie follows along on his song sheet as they boys begin to sing to the tune of "Home on the Range."

"O give me a home, where the Gentiles may roam,
where the Jews are not rampant all day,
Where seldom is heard a loud Jewish word
And the Gentiles are free all the day."

SONNY HEARS IT FIRST. Boys singing. He stands and walks toward the voices. Stops a few yards away from his family. A parade of young boys and men. Sid joins Sonny. What kind of parade is this? The Swastika boys march closer. The Lapinskys stop talking and listen.

"O give me a home, where the Gentiles may roam,
where the Jews are not rampant all day."

"Hey," says Sonny. "What?" His fists involuntarily clench at his sides.
The parade marches in front of them. Sonny and Sid see boys dressed as imitation Nazis, with swastika armbands and badges. Boys at the front carry hand-painted signs:

Jews go home
No dogs or Jews allowed
Off our beaches

"Let's get them, Sid." Rage boils in Sonny.
"Shhh. Sonny, we're outnumbered. Besides, they're bigger."
Max and Yacov stand beside Sonny and Sid.
"Pop. Let's get them," Sonny urges.
"Don't make trouble," Yacov declares.
"What? They're the ones making trouble."

"We don't make trouble, Sonny."

"Uncle Max?"

"Let it go, boys. Better that way."

Rage burns in Sonny's belly. Frustration churns. How can they let those guys get away with this?

"Where seldom is heard a loud Jewish word
And the Gentiles are free all the day."

THE PARADE CONTINUES down the beach.

The tune is catchy and Charlie finds himself singing along in the second round, even though he normally feels shy about his singing voice. Then all hell breaks loose.

"Come on. Let's get them," the boys in front of him shout. Charlie can't see what's happening up ahead. He and George are right in the middle of the parade.

George and Charlie break free of the parade. The boys in front are chasing three Jewish youths toward the lake. Some pick up stones and hurl them at the running youths. The Jews stop suddenly and face their pursuers. The boys in front of Charlie charge on them, fists flying. Five against three. Charlie jumps in. He pulls a Jew off of John Gerrard, his next-door neighbour.

"Thanks Charlie," John says. John and Charlie pummel the Jewish boy.

Charlie spots the mounted police from the corner of one eye. He grabs John's shirt sleeve. "Police," he yells. Everyone stops.

"Damn." Charlie scrambles to his feet. His mother will kill him if she finds out he's been fighting. He runs away as fast as he can.

"Hey, Charlie. Wait up!" George calls. But Charlie keeps running.

SOPHIE AND TESSIE quickly pack up the rest of the food.

Sonny paces the beach. In the distance he can see a smaller group of boys chasing each other into the lake. The rest of the parade continues farther along the boardwalk.

"Come on Sonny," Sid urges. "We're going."

"Crap," Sonny kicks the dirt.

Lenny helps Sophie repack the dishes and the rest of their picnic. Izzy stands by Sonny and Sid.

"Why are they singing?" he asks his older brothers.

"They're Nazis," Sonny says with disgust.

"Do they hate us?"

"Yeah, but we're going to get them. Right Sid?" Sonny looks to his older brother hopefully.

"Another day." Sid's brown eyes blaze with supressed anger.

"They don't want us on the beach?" Izzy asks.

"It's not their beach." Sonny spits on the sand. "It's public. Right Sid?"

"Supposed to be." Sid's eyes are on the trailing parade in the distance.

"Boys!" Sophie shouts. "We're going home.

Sonny picks up a stone and hurls it as far as he can in the direction of the swastika boys.

Their ride across the city back to their own neighbourhood is a quiet one.

THE EVENING TELEGRAM's front-page headline screams, "Toronto Swastikas arouse Jews. Hundreds Don Swastikas in Drive to Rid Beaches of Undesirables." There are photos of club members wearing a white shirt stenciled with a black swastika. The caption explains that it's the emblem that Hitler carried to power in Germany. Another photo shows a sign bearing the swastika and the words "Hail Hitler." Yacov can't believe his eyes as he scans the paper that evening. The sign apparently was posted sometime after the parade, in front of Balmy Beach Clubhouse, just a few hundred feet from where they'd spent the afternoon. He reaches for his package of cigarettes, and lights one, glances over to see his wife unpacking the picnic basket. It's unbelievable that in Canada people are acting with such hate. If seemingly civilized people can behave like barbarians, what will the rest do?

Resistance

ON MONDAY, late in the afternoon, Yacov tells Sid to knock off early; it's so damn hot, he should go and get himself a soda with his friends.

Sid trots down Brunswick Avenue toward College Street. Sid and his buddies spend most of their free time at Manny's Deli. His friends all have summer jobs too, but it's four o'clock by the time he arrives, and some of the guys are already inside, sitting at their usual booth at the back. Manny Scheckstein is a swell guy. He lets the boys take over the back table, so long as they each order at least a soda or a cup of coffee.

"Why not?" figures Manny. "There's not exactly crowds lining up at the door to get in."

Sid pushes open the glass door of the deli. Manny stands behind the long counter at the front, pouring coffee and telling jokes to the customers. He waves at Sid on his way in. Manny likes Sid. A good kid. Helps out his father every day. Manny has seen Sid helping elderly women from the neighbourhood home with their groceries, even surly old Mrs. Pincinni. And Sid is always ready to help when the boys call on him. Every now and then there's a little trouble with one of the Gentiles. He's seen Sid on more than one occasion convince a Gentile boy to apologize for name-calling. Sid usually doesn't have to even strike the other kid. His bulky presence is enough.

SID'S BEST FRIEND Louie Horowitz leans back in their booth with Eddie Finkelstein. Louie has a summer job in his father's tailor shop, pressing pants, from six in the morning until three-thirty in the afternoon. It gets so hot in the backroom with the presser that Louie tells people he works in a sweatshop. It isn't nearly as bad as a real sweatshop. It's his father's shop and he only works nine and a half hours a day, instead of ten, with a half-hour for lunch and a break in the afternoon.

Still, Louie is right. It sure is hot back there. Sid went by to meet him one morning before he went to work with his father. It was only seven in the morning in the end of June, and it was already so hot that Louie was stripped right down to his undershirt.

Eddie is at the racetrack for the summer. He works for a bookie named Benny Hersh, out behind the official betting booths in an area known as "back of the tracks." Behind the tracks, there are guys selling hot dogs and soda pop, unofficially. You can buy a shot of rye or bourbon, cigars and cigarettes. Working girls ply their trade up against the side of stables. And there are poker games, crown and anchor, even craps. Bookies turf out permanent spots in the back of the tracks. A gambler willing to bet more than the maximum front-of-the-tracks two dollar bet has his pick of bookies with which to place a more a sizeable bet. Eddie is what's known as "a table." It's a hard job physically, and there are dangers involved, but Eddie is perfect for the job. At thirteen, he's only four foot ten, but he's stocky. His voice hasn't cracked yet, so he can impersonate a much younger boy. His job is to create an outdoor table out of a newspaper. He stretches a paper out with both arms, holding it perfectly straight and still. Customers place their bets on his "table." Al, one of Benny's yes-men, stands beside Eddie to collect bets and pay out winners. If someone spots a cop approaching, they scream "Cop!" and all the action back of the tracks magically disappears. Eddie expertly folds up his "table," money and all, tucks it under one arm, grabs a pile of newspapers waiting by his feet and acts the part of an innocent newsboy.

"Afternoon *Star*. Get your *Star* right here," he yells. Sometimes he even sells a paper to the cop. The girls pull down their skirts. Bookies fold up shop, the hot-dog man folds his wares into a specially designed portable suitcase. And everybody's simply getting some air, or engaged in a stimulating outdoor conversation. Of course, the cops are on the fix, paid to turn a blind eye to the crowds of people who all get the urge for some fresh air simultaneously.

After the cop turns the corner, Eddie scoots back to his place against the brick wall, near the public bathrooms, reopens the folded-up paper with the bets inside, and the betting continues. Eddie is paid a cut of the profits each day. He makes better money than any of the other guys.

Ralph Shapiro helps out in his family's poultry shop in Kensington Market, and Meyer and Jerry Glass act as lookouts for their father's small bootlegging operation, which he runs out of the family kitchen. Guido is a stock boy at his Uncle Vinnie's grocery store.

"Hey, Sid," Eddie calls out. "Come, sit down. It's a good thing you came by so early."

Sid plops down beside Louie in the booth. "Why? What's up?"

"We gotta go down to the Beaches tonight," says Louie. "Everyone. We gotta find all the guys we can. Ralph's brother's gonna be bringing the chicken truck. We can all pile in."

Ralph's family owns an old rickety truck with wooden sides for hauling live chickens to the store.

"Why?"

"There was a rumble down there yesterday."

"A rumble?"

"'Those Nazis in the Beaches," explains Louie.

"The Swastika Club," adds Eddie.

"I know ..." says Sid. "I was there."

"Hey Sid!" Ralph shouts as he emerges from the washroom in the back of the deli. He has a swollen lip. "Good thing you're here. You guys tell Sid?'

"Sure we did."

"What happened to your lip?' Sid asks Ralph.

"Those Swazis attacked a bunch of guys. I was with my brother Eli. We were driving back from a farm with a truck full a live chickens. It was so damn hot Eli says let's stop at the beach for a quick dip in the lake. We peel off our shirts and walk down the sand, minding our own business. Next thing we see this parade-like, full of Swazis, and they're singing ..."

"I saw them," Sid says.

"You were there?"

"Yeah ... but with my folks ... you know ... we just watched ..."

"Yeah, well they attacked some guys from the neighbourhood. Jacky Cohen and his brother. What's his name?"

"Dave."

"Right, Dave. Me and Eli rush over to break it up-like, then the cops show up and everyone scatters. First sight of the cops and they run."

"We heard the Swazis are going back tonight. Right, Ralph? So we're going too. Saul Berger's organizing. He put out the word. We're meeting at Woodbine and Queen," says Louie.

"What for?" Sid asks bluntly.

"What for?" Louie can't believe his friend sometimes. "To show them we're not gonna take it, that's what for. They say 'no Jews on the beach'. So we're going. To show them."

"Saul says all we're gonna do is walk on the boardwalk, show them our muscle," adds Eddie. "We ain't gonna do anything. But if they try and attack us, well … you know…"

Sid sighs. Why can't people just get along? He's heard stories from his father about the pogroms in Russia. He feels lucky to have been born in Canada. But look what they still have to put up with. Sid is sick about the reports his father reads out loud to the family in the newspaper about the Nazis in Germany. What if a Nazi party starts up in Canada?

"Okay, Sid?" Louie asks. "I'll pick you up tonight at your place. After supper. Eight o'clock. All right?"

"Yeah, sure." Sid stands. "I'm gonna order a soda pop. Anyone want anything?" He walks over to the counter and gestures for Manny.

"I WANNA COME," Sonny begs after dinner.

"Well, you can't."

The boys are in their bedroom. Sid is changing into long pants from his shorts. It's still hot as hell, but he doesn't feel as tough in short pants.

"Why not?"

Sid shakes his head at Sonny, who comes up to his chest. "Too little."

He stands in front of the cracked mirror hanging from a lone nail on the wall and combs back his thick wavy hair.

"Am not."

"You are too." Sid spills out a few drops of olive oil into one hand, rubs his palms together and smoothes the liquid through his hair, patting it down on both sides.

"Come on, Sid. Lemme come. I wanna take a crack at the Swazis."

Sid looks at Sonny. Itching to fight. He knows the feeling. Damn Nazis murdering helpless women and children in Germany, just because they're Jewish. It makes Sid feel so angry he wants to cry. A huge lump of grief churns in his chest, makes his rib cage feel too tight for his own body. Makes him want to scream. He understands his brother's anger, but Sonny is too young. He's only nine. His mother will kill Sid if he brings his little brother along to a rumble. "You can't come, Sonny. That's all there is to it," Sid says.

Sonny grabs his rubber ball and stomps out of the room. He thumps down the stairs and out the door. From the bedroom window, Sid watches Sonny run into the yard and hop the fence into the alley. He knows Sonny will probably find a stickball game somewhere in the neighbourhood and hit home runs all evening.

Sid tells his parents he's going to the pictures with Louie — a new show starring Jimmy Cagney. Sophie asks him to invite Lenny along. Luckily Lenny doesn't want to go. Instead he picks up a stack of books, says he's going to the library. Funny kid, his brother Lenny, thinks Sid. He'd rather sit in a stuffy library reading old books than catch the latest Cagney picture. Sometimes Sid feels sore at Lenny for being such a mama's boy. The other guys tease Lenny all the time, call him *faygele,* and sometimes they make kissing sounds with their lips when he walks by and call him "baby doll." Sid's had to teach a lesson to more than one character. He wishes Lenny wouldn't act that way. He *does* walk like a girl, kind of jiggly with his hips. He throws a baseball like a girl, underhanded. Instead of leaping up and trying to catch a ball coming right at him, Lenny ducks, or lets the ball hit him. Sid thinks his father should force Lenny to play sports more. Then he'd get used to it. Instead, Lenny's allowed to stay indoors with their mother, with his nose in a book. It isn't normal. No wonder the guys make fun of his brother. No way he wants to bring him to a rumble.

"Sid," Sophie calls from the kitchen. "Louie's here."

"Bye Ma." Sid kisses Sophie on the cheek as he races past her. "Bye Pop," he yells to Yacov, who sits in his undershirt by the front window drinking a cold glass of seltzer, reading the paper. Sid takes the stairs three at a time all the way down, pushing off with either hand on the wall.

"Ralph's brother's picking us up in front of the deli," Louie says when they're a block away from Sid's house and out of earshot. Even so, Sid glances back nervously. He swears his mother can hear from this far away. She knows things he thought were well hidden from her. He hopes she hasn't heard Louie. His mother is angry about the Swastika Club too, but she disapproves of fighting. Sid wants to make his parents proud. His worst fear is that he'll do something to bring shame on his family.

LENNY STROLLS DOWN Shaw Street toward the library, books tucked under his arm. He likes the quiet of the main reading room and the gentle tenor voice of Mr. Cornwall, the evening-shift librarian. He's daydreaming as he walks, remembering his favourite scene from the Fred Astaire picture he recently saw, "Flying Down to Rio," when he walks right into Jacob Moskowitz, the toughest kid in Lenny's grade.

"Well, if ain't the fairy," Jacob taunts. "Where ya going, Lenny? Ballet class?"

"No," Lenny says, trying to keep his voice even. Don't show your fear, Sid has told him, more than once. Don't let them see it. "I'm going to the library."

"Oohh," Jacob exaggerates. "The library. Ain't that sweet?" He puffs out his chest, blocking Lenny's way.

"Leave me alone." Lenny moves off the sidewalk to the road to walk around Jacob, who blocks his way.

"Come on, Jacob."

"Make me."

Lenny sighs. "Please …"

Jacob pushes against Lenny's chest.

"I don't want to fight …"

"Yeah? Well, maybe I do. Come on, Fairy. Put up yer dukes." Jacob assumes a fighter's stance, fists in front of his chin.

Lenny holds his hands out in front, palms out. Jacob jabs at Lenny's hands. It hurts. Lenny swings wildly with a loose punch. Jacob retaliates with a smooth hard right against his chin that knocks Lenny to the sidewalk. Jacob straddles Lenny's chest and slaps at his face and body. Lenny wraps his arms over his face to shield the blows.

SONNY TURNS ONTO Shaw Street, looking for some of the guys, tossing his rubber ball straight up in the air, catching it, throwing it. Instinctively he turns his attention ahead, where there is a fight in progress. He stuffs his ball in his pocket and hurries forward. Crap. It's Lenny. Sonny races down the block, shouting.

"Get offa him," he orders Jacob. "Get offa my brother."

"Make me, squirt," Jacob sneers. He's two years older than Sonny and a head taller.

Sonny puts up his dukes. "Come on, Jacob. *I'll* fight ya," Sonny challenges.

Jacob laughs at Lenny's younger brother. He could flatten the squirt without even trying. "Okay." He gets off of Lenny, assumes a defensive position, his fists covering his chin. Lenny scurries to his feet. Rubs his aching chest. Hopes Sonny knows what he's doing.

Sonny looks into his opponent's eyes. He and Jacob circle slowly around each other. Jacob lets fly a left jab. Sonny rolls under it easily. He sees it coming from a mile away. He grins, proud of himself. This is easy. Jacob fakes a left to Sonny's body. Sonny lowers his elbow. Jacob plows him hard against the chin with his right, knocking Sonny to the sidewalk. The impact vibrates up his spine, right to the top of his head. Sonny's belly hardens in anger. He sees red. He hates Jacob Moskowitz. Wants to kill him. Pulverize him. Make him hurt.

"Had enough?" Jacob sneers.

Sonny growls under his breath. He leaps to his feet and puts his fists up in front of his face.

"Oh?" says Jacob. "You want more, huh? Okay, shrimp." Jacob tries the same move again. He fakes a left to Sonny's body. This time, Sonny clenches his stomach muscles, absorbs the jab, sees his opening and throws a solid right, hard against Jacob's mouth, splitting his lip. Blood spurts down his chin and into his mouth. Jacob touches his lip, looks at the blood on his fingers. His wide eyes give away his surprise. Sonny feels a rush of adrenalin race through his body. He charges forward and unleashes a series of rapid-fire jabs and punches to Jacob Moskowitz's bloody face. With his left, his right and his left again, Sonny strikes out, as Jacob, stunned, stands with his arms at his sides. Two other boys run down the street to watch.

"Fight!" they scream. As if drawn by magnet, a small group of boys crowds around.

Jacob regains his composure, lifts his fists in defence. Sonny won't stop. He tries out Jacob's trick — he's a quick learner. He fakes a jab to the belly. Jacob falls for it. Already hurting, he drops his guard and Sonny goes in for the kill. It's hard for the other boys to follow his fists, he strikes out so quickly, catching Jacob on the chin, the eye, the ear, and a final right uppercut to the bruised chin that sends him backward onto his back.

"Come on. Get up," Sonny shouts. "Get up, ya sissy."

But Jacob doesn't get up. He lies on his back watching a series of silver stars shoot in front of his vision. His face is a bloody mess.

"A knockout," one of the guys yells. He grabs Sonny's arm and holds it high above his head. "The winner by knockout." He mimics a radio announcer. "Sonny Lapinsky of Clinton Street."

"You oughta try boxing, Lapinksy," says another boy.

Sonny stands among the boys, breathing hard, his heart racing in his chest, the red still circling in his brain. Why's Moskowitz just lying there? Why doesn't he get up? He wants to hit him again. It felt so good. Sonny punches his right fist into his left palm. He could take on the whole crowd of guys.

Lenny moves in beside him. "Thanks. That was amazing, Sonny."

Sonny glares at his brother. *Don't go and embarrass me in front of the guys,* he thinks. "Shut up, Lenny," he says, rubbing his chin, which is tingling from the one blow he took.

"Hey Sonny." Ziggy Levine pounds Sonny affectionately on the back. "Come on. We're getting a stickball game together. You in?"

"Yeah, sure." Sonny lets Ziggy lead him down the street, leaving Jacob Moskowitz to his stars and his brother Lenny to his books.

AT THE CORNER of College and Spadina, Sid and Louie jump into the back of the waiting truck. There are twelve other guys sitting on makeshift benches of flimsy wooden chicken crates. Most of the fellows are unarmed, but Eddie Finkelstein flashes Sid a piece of broken-off lead pipe he has stashed inside his shirtsleeve.

"Just in case," boasts Eddie.

Louie wishes he'd brought a weapon too, a baseball bat or something. Sid doesn't need one. His big body is weapon enough. The truck ambles eastward, jostling the boys against each other.

At the corner of Woodbine in the east end, just up the hill from Balmy Beach, the boys pile out of the truck. Fifty or sixty other Jewish boys from their neighbourhood are waiting. In lines of three across, they march toward the lake. The beach is quiet when they arrive. From the Balmy Beach Ballroom they hear live band music playing. There is a dance in progress for local youths. As arranged earlier, Saul Berger leads the way, with his snarling German shepherd straining against its leash. It is a peaceful protest. The boys march down Kew Beach Avenue, along the boardwalk and up to the Balmy Beach Clubhouse. The swastika flags have been removed. There is no sign of any of the boys from the Swastika Club. Sid and the Jewish boys follow Saul as they walk right past the refreshment counter. Residents of the Beaches stand about, but none are wearing swastikas. No one knows what to do next. They had expected to meet the Swastikas head-on.

"Now what?" Louie asks.

Sid shrugs, glances in the direction of Saul Berger. Maybe he has a plan. Saul's dog growls and everyone turns to see what's going on. Three mounted police head their way. Saul puts both hands out behind him, signalling his "troops" to stay calm. Sid and Louie move closer to the front.

"All right, boys," a police officer barks, a hard "b" on the word "boys." "Time to move along now. Go on home. There's nothing going on here tonight. We don't want any trouble outa you punks."

"Excuse me officer, Sir." Saul politely addresses the officer. Behind his back, Sid can see Saul's fist clenched in anger. "We don't want any trouble either, Sir. This is a peaceful protest. We have as much right to be on the beach as the Swastika Club, ain't that right officer?" Saul punches out the word "officer" like a curse.

The police officer smiles tightly. "Not on my beach, punk." He spits on the ground by Saul's feet.

"Excuse me Sir?"

"I said, go home. Now. All of you. Or else I'll run you all in," the officer orders.

"Beg your pardon officer Sir, but on what charge?" Saul pushes.

"Unlawful assembly, loitering, conspiracy to commit robbery, trespassing. Take your pick," the officer shoots back. The nerve of the Hebrew bastard, he thinks. "Now get lost. All of you."

A man in his mid-twenties standing beside Saul says, "Come on. Let's go. We've made our point. No sense getting arrested."

Saul considers for a moment, then turns his back on the officer. "All right guys. Job well done. We sure showed them Swastikas. They probably heard we was coming and they're too yellow to face us man to man. Let's go home." He holds one victory arm above his head and marches back toward the road. The others follow.

The officer stays put until the last of the Hebrew bastards have cleared their keisters off his beach.

TWO BLOCKS AWAY on Woodbine, Charlie Bain, George Patterson and two hundred other Swastika Club members are convening, armed with baseball bats, sticks, chains, and broom handles. There are some members of the neighbourhood lacrosse team, their lacrosse sticks clutched by their sides. They know the west-end Jews have come down to the beach — a younger boy ran over earlier with the news — and are preparing to head them off. Charlie stands with his friend George, gripping the broom handle he swiped from his mother's kitchen closet. He isn't planning on actually using it. If it breaks, he'll have his mother to deal with. He's carrying it to look tough.

At ten o'clock they start out, heading south to the beach. Excitement floods Charlie's chest. He loves the feeling in his belly, the adrenalin, the camaraderie he feels with the other guys, as they march down the street. As they march, some of the guys in front start yelling "Heil Hitler!" and just "Heil." From behind he can hear some guys singing "God Save the King." George shouts, "Heil Hitler!" with one fist thrust high in the air. Charlie turns his head and smiles at his friend. George looks scared and happy at the same time, a tight grin plastered on his face. He grips a baseball bat in his fist. Charlie hopes George isn't planning on actually using the bat. If he swings the heavy weapon at a guy's head, he could kill him. Charlie doesn't want to see his best friend go to jail. They're supposed to scare the Jews back to their own neighbourhood, not actually hurt anybody. He's just about to say something to George, but the guys in front of them stop short. It takes a few minutes for the news to reach the back of the line where Charlie and George stand. The Jews are gone. They were on the beach earlier, but the cops sent them away. The club members branch out into a semicircle. A guy Charlie doesn't recognize, but who says his name is Harold, stands up on a rock to address the crowd.

"Friends, comrades and members of the Swastika Club. We hear the Jews were here tonight, but they must have heard we were coming and they hightailed it outa here."

"Cowards!" someone shouts from the crowd.

"Sheenies!" someone else adds.

"Kikes!"

"We should mark this as a victory!" Harold shouts dramatically. "Let our slogan remain, the Beaches for the Beaches!"

The crowd begins chanting the slogan, "The Beaches for the Beaches."

Harold holds out his hands to quiet the crowd. "And don't forget to stop by the Balmy Beach Clubhouse and buy a Swastika emblem if you don't already have one. Makes a nice gift too." Laughter. "Even your girl might like one. Or your mother," Harold adds. Then he leads the group in a rousing chorus of "God Save the King."

From behind him three police officers appear. The singing peters out as one officer moves closer, towering over Harold on his horse. The crowd quiets.

"All right, boys." The officer smiles, indulgently. "Time to go on home." Harold makes a move to protest. The officer cuts him off with a fatherly motion of his hand. "You've done a great job tonight, boys. I'm sure your fathers are all proud of you, but it's late. Time to get off the beach. Go on up the street and have yourselves a soda. Come on now, boys, in an orderly fashion."

The Swastika Club breaks up and its members head toward Queen Street.

LENNY HAS BEEN following the skirmishes on the beach, as related to him and Sonny by Sid. They talk quietly in the privacy of their bedroom. The sense of injustice offends Lenny. Like his brothers, he feels they have just as much right to be on the beaches as anyone else. But the method of Sid and his friends are barbaric and primitive in Lenny's opinion. If he were older, he'd write about the situation. The pen is mightier than the sword, he believes. Besides, his altercation earlier with Jacob Moskowitz has left him frightened of physical violence and quite clear on his inability to defend himself. Not that being bullied is anything new to Lenny. Older, bigger, tougher kids have been teasing him and pushing him around since time began. Usually, though, they leave him alone after a bit of verbal teasing, maybe some shoving. Usually he is able to talk his way out of it. Usually they don't resort to hitting him, there being no sport in it.

Although in theory Lenny agrees with Sid's position on the Swastika matter, there is no way in hell he's going to get involved in the fighting. Besides, the new young librarian at the nearby Shaw Street Public Library, Mr. Cornwall, has taken an interest in young Lenny. Mr. Cornwall noticed Lenny right away. The boy appeared at the library like clockwork, every Monday and Thursday after dinner, to return an armload of books and sign out an armload more. Mr. Cornwall has never seen an eleven-year-old boy so interested in reading. A literary man himself, he appoints himself an unofficial mentor to the boy, recommending books, answering questions.

"You haven't read Charles Dickens?" Mr. Cornwall is astounded. Dickens, of course, is standard fare to anyone interested in literature.

Lenny shakes his head, slightly embarrassed, and at the same time, flattered with the attention from the neat and trim Mr. Cornwall, in his freshly pressed gabardine suit and tie.

"Well, then," Mr. Cornwall winks at Lenny, "let's start you with, let's see, yes, *Great Expectations.* I think you'll enjoy this." He hands a well-worn copy over the counter to Lenny.

"Thank you, sir." Lenny accepts the heavy, hard-covered book.

"We'll discuss it, after you've finished, shall we?"

"That would be fine, sir." No one, not even his teachers, who are all impressed with Lenny's good school habits, has ever made such a generous offer. Lenny beams with pleasure.

"Mr. Cornwall," says the librarian, offering a hand for Lenny to shake.

"Mr. Cornwall, sir." Lenny repeats.

"And your name?"

"Lenny, sir. Lenny Lapinsky."

Mr. Cornwall peers over his round glasses at Lenny's face. "You're Jewish, then?"

A sinking feeling spreads quickly through Lenny's stomach. Should he lie? Will Mr. Cornwall rescind the offer if he knows the truth? Lenny nods almost imperceptibly.

Mr. Cornwall smiles. "Course you are. I should have realized sooner. Makes perfect sense. Your people are great lovers of the printed word, is it not so, Lenny Lapinsky?"

Relief replaces the dread in Lenny's belly. "Yes, sir."

"Fine. That's fine. Well, then, perhaps you'd better get started," Mr. Cornwall suggests, gesturing toward the book.

"Oh, right," Lenny agrees.

"You may read here, if you like." Mr. Cornwall points to the two tables and chairs in the middle of the room.

"Thank you, sir." Lenny takes a seat, cracks open the book to page one, and begins to read:

My father's family name being Pirrip, and my Christian name
Philip, my infant tongue could make of both names nothing
longer or more explicit than Pip. So, I called myself Pip, and
came to be called Pip.

Lenny sneaks a peek at Mr. Cornwall, who is efficiently reshelving a cart-
load of books. Lenny is in deep admiration of Mr. Cornwall's suit and his
elegant manner. The librarian is more refined than anyone Lenny knows.

THE NEXT SUNDAY after work, Sid stops in at Manny's, with Sonny tag-
ging along. Sonny's chin is bruised from his fight with Jacob Moskowitz,
but it's nothing compared to Jacob's injuries. Louie, Ralph, Eddie, and
Meyer and Jerry Glass are crowded around the booth at the back.
Agitated. Eddie has a torn shirtsleeve and a fat lip. Ralph has a shiner on
his left eye.

"Hey Sid. Get over here," Louie calls across the deli.

Sid smiles at Manny behind the counter as he passes. Manny waves his
hand in a quick downward motion. "Acchh." Manny doesn't approve of
what the boys are doing. It's one thing to defend yourself when trouble
comes your way. It's another thing entirely to look for trouble. "Oughta
stay right around here, in your own neighbourhood," he told Ralph and
Eddie when they ran in all bloodied up. He dragged them into the men's
room in the back, pulled out the first-aid kit and fixed up their wounds.
Someone had to. He knew they weren't going to go home until they'd sat
around his place bragging and boasting for the rest of the evening.

Sid and Sonny hover at the end of the table. There's no room on
the seats.

"You should've been there, Sid." Eddie brags, with his dukes up.

"What happened?"

"Me and Ralph went down to the Beaches. My Pop said there was
gonna be trouble again. Half the Jews in the city were there today…"

"There was more of us than them," Ralph bursts in.

"The Swazis were all parading around the beach like they owned it or
something," Eddie continues.

"They don't," Sonny interjects. "Public property. Right Sid?"

"Shah," says Sid.

"And this time, they're all wearing those rotten swastikas. Red ones on badges on their chests. Some of the guys have them pinned on their swimming trunks. Even girls have them on their bathing suits," Ralph says, rapidly, as if he's seeing it all over again.

"So we go around ripping off their badges. And some guys are wearing white t-shirts with big black swastikas drawn on. We ripped their shirts right off."

"And they planted a big sign on the beach. Holy cow."

"What'd it say?"

Ralph juts his jaw out. "Said 'No Jews, Niggers or Dogs.'"

"Holy cripes."

"Wish I'da been there," Sonny pipes up. "I'd a shown 'em." Sonny put his dukes up and punches at the air in rapid-fire succession. All the guys watch him. For a little guy he sure is fast. They can barely follow his fists. After Sonny beat up Jacob Moskowitz, word spread throughout the neighbourhood. The guys have been slapping Sonny on the back and calling him "Champ" ever since.

"Sure you would've," says Louie.

"So what happened to your eye?" Sid grabs Eddie by the chin, tilts his head to get a good look at the shiner.

"Aw, caught a stray hand is all. It's nothing."

"Eddie ripped the sign out of the sand and we busted it up."

"Yeah, then they really got mad."

"Chased us into the lake."

"Every man for himself."

"Some bum threw a lucky punch is all."

"That sign's fish food now."

"I hope the fighting's on next Sunday too. I'm going next Sunday. I'd like to punch one of those Nazis right in the kisser." Sonny demonstrates again how he'd punch the guy. And everyone watches; they all know Sonny's going to be a prizefighter some day. The guys are as proud as if he were their own brother. He's one of them. They will be able to say, "I knew him when."

Die With Boots On
AUGUST 16, 1933

"WE HAVE TO PAY a shiva visit tonight. After supper," Sophie announces, as the family eats breakfast.

"Who died?" Yacov asks, surprised. The boys look up from their plates.

"I told you already yesterday. Always your head is in business, Yacov."

"Well if my head wasn't in business, we'd starve. These days, who can think of anything else? Sonny, stop kicking the table."

Sonny steadies his swinging leg.

"Morris Silverblatt."

"What?"

"He died. Remember? I told you yesterday. A heart attack, the doctor said. So, we gotta pay a visit tonight to poor Esther. A young man he was."

"He was older than you," Sid points out.

"Never mind. He wasn't so old. So I want you boys to stay in after supper."

"Aw Ma," Sid complains. "There's a ball game tonight at Christie Pits. I promised the guys I'd be there."

"And why, Shimon, should you be there? Baseball you don't play."

"Pop, can't you call me Sid?"

"Sid I should call him?"

"Pop," Sid pushes, "I have to go to the game. I promised. There could be trouble."

"What kind of trouble?" Sophie sits down across from her eldest son.

"Remember? I told you about the Swastika Club. Ralph says they're coming to Christie Pits tonight to make trouble. They say 'no Jews in the park.' They push around the guys, and wear swastika badges on their shirts. And two nights ago, they painted 'Hail Hitler' on the clubhouse roof."

"In Christie Pits?" Sophie hadn't heard this neighbourhod news and is shocked.

"We gotta protect ourselves. We got a right. It's our park too. You pay taxes, don't you Pop?"

Yacov sighs deeply. No matter where in the world you go, the trouble is always the same. "Look, Shimon …" He stops himself. "*Sid* … you can't fight with people like that."

"Pop, we have to fight back. First it'll be the park, then the street, then they'll kick us out of the country."

"They will?" Izzy wonders if they'll have to sleep in the bottom of a dry well on their way out of the country.

Yacov laughs, more out of nerves than because he finds anything funny. "We just got here. Already you think they'll kick us out? It's not right to make trouble with the *goyim.*"

"What should I do? Bow my head and take it, like you do?" Sid dares to say.

Yacov pulls back in his chair, stricken. Silence.

Sid groans low, under his breath. *Crap. Why'd I say that?*

Sonny involuntarily balls up his fists. Lenny's delicate stomach churns. Izzy looks down at his plate. Sophie watches her husband.

Yacov stares at Sid, eyes hard. "Talking back to me, Shimon? You want the strap?"

"No, Pa."

"Is that what you want?" Yacov stands, unbuckles his belt. "Cause you're not too old."

"No, Pa."

Yacov slips his belt from its loops, folds it in half, holds it up menacingly. "Is that what you want?"

"No, Pa."

"Sid …" Sophie says quickly. "Apologize to your father. "

Sid keeps his eye on his father, one hand gripping the edge of the table. "Sorry, Pop."

"You're sorry?" Yacov keeps the belt high.

Sid tries again. "I'm sorry I said that, Pa. I didn't mean no disrespect."

Yacov slams one hand down on the edge of the table. Lenny jumps slightly in his seat. Izzy is on the verge of tears. Sonny is eyeing his father, wondering how much bigger he will have to grow before he can stand up to him. To convince him to stop strapping Sid. Why's it always Sid who has to take the brunt? Just on account of being the oldest. It doesn't seem fair to Sonny. Sometimes Sid gets the strap for something Sonny's done wrong. Or Lenny. When Sonny grows up and has kids, he's never going to strap them.

Sophie lets out a breath; the worst is over. Yacov lowers the strap. "There are reasons, Shimon, for everything. A hothead is not always such a good thing to be. People can get hurt."

"Sorry, Pop." Sid breathes a sigh of relief.

"Sit down, Yacov," Sophie says.

Yacov places his belt on the corner of the table and sits.

"Sid's right." Sonny speaks up. "They want to run us out of the park. There's a game tonight. The Harbord Playground team — they're all Jewish. Meyer Glass is on the team."

"I didn't know an athlete he was," Sophie says.

"We're just gonna be there, see that nothing bad happens," Sid finishes.

Yacov sighs. Eats the last of his bread. Rubs his hands together, dropping crumbs onto his plate. "You two can go to the game," he says to Sid and Lenny, "but I don't want you boys getting into any fights. Sonny, you'll stay here after supper with Izzy. You can go out in the yard if it's hot, but that's it. Otherwise play on the porch or up here. *Farshtaist?*"

"I'm not going to the park," Lenny says quietly. "Ma, I'm going to the library."

"Aw Pop. I want to go with Sid. Please Pop. You gotta let me go," Sonny begs, kicking the table leg absently.

"You'll stay here with Izzy," Sophie orders.

"Ma, you can't make me stay. They need me. Tell them, Sid. Ain't that right?"

Sid shrugs, eyes down. "Listen to Ma, Sonny."

"Pop. Please." Sonny's big eyes plead.

"You heard your mother. And stop with the kicking."

Sonny steadies his leg. He hates being little. The guys need him. He can punch faster than anyone. He wants to pulverize some Swazis. He doesn't want to stay at home and babysit his little brother. It's not fair.

"You kids don't know what trouble is," Yacov says. "In order to leave Russia I had to cross the Dneister River under dangerous conditions."

The boys have heard their father's story before, many times over. Lenny, Sid and Izzy listen intently, in case their father adds something new. Sonny sulks, leaning back in his chair, arms folded across his chest, feet swinging back and forth.

"My brother-in-law Pinchus hired the smugglers to get me across the Dneister River. It separates Russia from Romania. The first thing you gotta do is get across that river. Let me tell you, such an easy thing it's not. On both sides you got the police. The Russian police are shooting at anyone trying to leave the country. The Romanians are shooting at anyone trying to get in. My brother-in-law Pinchus gave me ..."

" ... a ruby necklace," Lenny jumps in, excited. He loves this part.

"That's right." Yacov smiles at his second son. "A beautiful ruby necklace. It was a precious stone. It was my brother-in-law's grandmother's necklace. And he gave it to me ... because of what happened ..." Yacov stops. Takes a deep breath. "So that I would have money to start with when I got to America. If I hadn't lost that necklace in the river, I would have come here a rich man."

"A multi-millionaire," Lenny says.

"That's right. A multi-millionaire. Sophie, how much you think a necklace like that was worth?"

"Again with the necklace?"

"A lot of money," Yacov tells the boys. "A million dollars at least it was worth."

"Tell about the border police shooting at you," Sid says. He likes to think of his father doing something dangerous and exciting. So different from his life now, as a meek, mild-mannered peddler.

"I was inside the boat. It was a ... what do call it ... ? A rowboat. I was sitting in the bow seat. With the two smugglers who were paid to get me across the river. I had the necklace wound around my ankle, so nobody would find it and steal it. Inside my sock. I could feel it against my skin. It was sharp and heavy. We were almost across. I could make out the trees on the Romanian side. Suddenly, birds flew out from the leaves, flapping their wings. Then a shot. A loud bang from a rifle."

"... and you jumped into the water," Lenny helps.

"That's right. I went over right away, headfirst into the water. It was so cold. I remember to this day how cold that water was. It's a wonder I didn't freeze to death. I could hear the shooting all around, so I swam down far to the bottom, until I felt the mud and weeds. Then I had to breathe, so I pushed back up with my feet."

"And your foot got stuck in the weeds." Lenny sits up on his knees, leaning toward his father.

Sophie gets up and starts clearing the dishes.

Sonny's jaw remains thrust out. He's pretending not to listen.

"I pulled and pulled at my leg, because my lungs hurt so much I thought I was gonna burst. And finally I gave one good pull and my foot came right outa my boot."

"And that's when you lost the necklace," Lenny declares.

"That's right. I came up and took a breath of air. I can't tell you how good that air felt. But the police were still shooting, and I had to get as far away as I could, so I went back under and swam far far away."

"... and when you got out of the water the necklace was gone."

"That's it. It was gone. I couldn't go back. They were shooting. If I had gone back, they would have shot me."

"Killed you?" Sonny asks in spite of himself.

"Course, dummy." Sid answers.

"I'm not dumb," Sonny shouts back.

"Sonny's not dumb," Izzy affirms.

Sonny pats Izzy's head.

"No fighting, boys, "Sophie orders from the sink.

"What about the smugglers?" Lenny asks.

"The smugglers?"

"Yeah. What happened to them?"

"Well ..." Yacov glances at Sophie. He wonders if the boys are old enough for the truth. "I never found out," he says. "I couldn't go back."

"Were they shot?"

Yacov nods his head from side to side. "Could be."

"You mean they got shot right in the river?"

"Things were different then. The police could do whatever they wanted in those days."

"Did ya see them get shot, Pop?"

"I didn't see nothing. I was trying to save my life."

"But you lost the necklace way down deep in the river."

"That's right."

"And you couldn't go back to get it."

"I could have been shot."

"And you could have been a millionaire," Sid says.

"A multi-millionaire," Lenny corrects.

"Multi multi," Izzy says knowingly, adding up the zeroes as he speaks.

"All right. Enough with the stories. Finish your tea," Sophie says.

AFTER BREAKFAST, Sid leaves with his father. They meet up with Max a few blocks over.

"Okay Sid," Max says to the boy. "Take this." He tosses him a ten-pound sack of potatoes. Sid holds it against his abdomen. "Start on Brunswick and then head west. Three small ones for a penny. Or two big ones. No credit. Cash only. You got that?"

"Yeah, sure, Uncle Max. I got it." Sid admires his uncle, but he notices that he makes all the decisions in the business and his father always defers to him. Sid doesn't like that. He thinks Yacov should stick up for himself more. Not just take orders from Uncle Max. Aren't they partners? One of these days, Sid is going to do something about it. He's just not sure what.

"Okay, good boy. If you sell the whole bag, come find me. I'll give you something else to sell."

"Okay, Uncle Max."

"And keep your cap on. The sun's gonna kill us today." Max loosens his tie and opens his top button. Sweat stains are already forming under his arms. The air is hot and humid, no breeze at all.

Sid flings the sack over his shoulder, adjusts his cap and trudges down the street. On a day like this he's happy to be sent off on his own. He has a lot on his mind. He's worried about the ball game that night. Everyone knows the Swazis are planning to be at the game at the Pits later. It's bad enough they're trying to keep the Jews off the beaches of the east end, but now they're coming to the Jewish district to muscle us out of our own park, he thinks. What'll be next? Is Toronto going to become like Germany, Sid wonders. Will he and his brothers be kicked out of school? Will they be kicked out of their apartment? He's read about Jews being beaten in the streets in Germany. Isn't this the same thing?

Sid grits his teeth in anger and walks on, head bowed, the sack of potatoes riding on his strong back. He doesn't like fighting. It makes him feel awful when his fist connects with another guy's face. Almost like he's the one getting hit. He feels a twinge in his belly. A bad feeling. Like stepping on a big spider and hearing its body crunch. He worries that God is watching and He doesn't approve. Still, Sid will go to the park that evening. He's given his word. The fellows will be depending on him, but Sid hopes with all his heart that the game will be peaceful. Anyway, it's too damn hot to fight. Too damn hot to do anything.

At the corner he stops in at Cohen's Fish Market to ask Mr. Cohen for a glass of water. His throat is already parched, his chest and back are covered in sweat, and it's only eight-thirty in the morning.

AFTER HELPING SOPHIE clean up the breakfast dishes, Lenny walks over to Bathurst Street to catch the streetcar south to the *Mail and Empire* office and pick up his morning papers. Later he'll go to the *Toronto Daily Star* to pick up their afternoon edition. He used to sell the evening *Telegram* too, but Yacov asked him to stop. The *Telegram* was growing worse in its conservative dogma. It was almost as if the writers admired Hitler and his madness. The paper quoted the chancellor extensively and references to the Jews in Germany were tainted with disdain. When Yacov read a scathing editorial aimed at Communists he put his foot down.

"Pop, we need the money," Lenny begged.

"It's a matter of principle," Yacov said, the matter now closed in his mind.

Now Lenny just sells the *Star*—the most progressive of Toronto's newspapers and the most sympathetic to Jews and other immigrants — and the morning *Mail and Empire,* which isn't as conservative as the *Telly,* and covers mostly local news aimed at the working class.

Inside *the Mail and Empire* office, Lenny pays for thirty copies and kneels on the sidewalk outside, where he folds each paper and adds it to the neat stack in the canvas shoulder bag his mother sewed for him. When he's ready he walks toward the financial district. He sells most of his papers to the businessmen who rush by on their lunch hour. The richer ones toss him a nickel for the three-cent paper and tell him to keep the change. He can make a lot more money on Bay Street than just about anywhere else in the city. And he loves to watch the businessmen in their tailored suits, ties and hats. Lenny doesn't have a proper suit, just a tie for shiva visits and synagogue, but one day he's going to buy a fancy suit of his own. His will be navy blue with a thin white pinstripe. The trousers will be pressed just so, with a crisp seam in the front, and cuffs on the bottom. He'll have two-toned shoes, shined every day. His black felt fedora will be perched at a jaunty angle on his head. He will have tasteful silk ties, a different one for each day of the week. A sterling-silver wristwatch, a genuine pearl tie pin and a gold pinkie ring. When he grows up Lenny plans to be elegant. No one will know he grew up the son of a street peddler, sharing a bedroom with three brothers, in a run-down duplex on Clinton Street.

When Lenny arrives at the corner of Bay and Bloor he stops, pulls out one copy of his paper, and holds it out so the front page is visible.

"Morning *Mail and Empire,*" he shouts. "Morning paper. 'Hitler bans Jews from walking on City Sidewalks.'" Lenny screams out the headline. *Holy cripes. Banned from the sidewalks?* He peers down at his feet standing on a sidewalk and imagines himself in Germany. What would happen to him if he didn't move?

"Gimme a paper, kid," a man says abruptly.

Automatically, Lenny hands over the paper in his hand. The man is tall and thin. He has blond hair and steel-grey eyes. He flips Lenny a nickel, while looking hard into Lenny's eyes. Lenny meets his gaze. The corners of the man's mouth move into a small smile. Lenny has a strange feeling in his body. A churning, swirling, light-as-feathers, blizzard in his belly. Embarrassed and confused, he looks down at his feet. The man walks on. Lenny lifts his head and watches him go.

SONNY'S SHIFT AT THE College Lanes is from eleven in the morning until seven at night. At half-past ten, Sophie and Izzy walk with Sonny to the bowling alley. Sophie bends over to kiss her son on the cheek. Embarrassed in case any of the guys see, Sonny squirms and rushes to the door.

"See you later, Ma." He lowers the brim of his cap over his eyes.

"Be careful, Sonny," Izzy warns. He's only been inside the bowling alley once, soon after Sonny got the job as Monkey Boy. Just as Sonny and Izzy entered, Davey Tittel fell from his swing above the pins and broke his nose on the hardwood floor of the bowling alley. Blood poured down his chin as the boss, Sal, walked him to the men's room. Izzy was horrified and ever since has worried that something would happen to Sonny.

"Don't worry. I'm always careful," Sonny tells his little brother.

"Don't hurt your nose," Izzy warns, thinking of Davey Tittel.

Sophie watches as Sonny pulls open the heavy glass door and enters. She sighs. He looks so little against the spacious entranceway. She wishes the boys didn't have to start working so young. They should be spending the summer playing ball with their friends in the park, or going to the beach. But times are tough and the money the boys bring into the house during July and August is a godsend. She takes Izzy by the hand—at least he's still young enough to appreciate her affection—and they head for the market. Sophie wants to pick up some fresh summer vegetables for a cold salad to go with the nice pumpernickel bread she baked yesterday, and some cheese. It's too hot to light the stove in heat like this.

"Come on," she leads Izzy in the direction of the market.

"When I grow up, I'm not working at the bowling alley," he tells his mother.

"No?"

"I'm going to college, right Ma?"

"God willing." She squeezes his hand hopefully. By the time Izzy's old enough for college, the Depression will be over. Maybe Max and Yacov will be running the store they're always talking about. As they walk down College Street, Sophie allows herself to feel just a little bit of hope.

SONNY CAN THINK OF nothing but the rumble in the park later that evening. He squats on his twelve-inch-by-three-foot wooden perch that swings above the bowling pins, imaging a full-out fight in Christie Pits. In his fantasy, he's the hero. One of the guys is in a terrible jam, being beaten by a Swazi when Sonny comes barrelling down the hill and like the champion heavyweight boxer Max Baer, Sonny jabs the bastard with a hard right uppercut, followed by a series of well-placed punches to the stomach. The guy keels over. Six other guys leap at Sonny, who flails around, taking out some with a high kick; others he knocks out with one deadly punch. It will be all over in seconds and he will be a hero. All the Swazis will be passed out on the ground in a heap. The guys will lift Sonny up onto their shoulders and parade up and down Bloor Street, calling him the Champ. Maybe a fight promoter will be there and see the whole thing and he'll sign Sonny up for pro fights, even though he's just a kid. His picture will get in the paper. And even though his mother hates fighting, she'll be proud of him. Cause he knows how much she hates the Nazi bastards. He's heard his parents talking about the Nazis in Germany late at night. They're scared. He can tell by the way they whisper. Brittle with tension. Uncertain. But he will make the world safe for his parents and for all of his people.

"Hey Lapinsky!"

"Huh?"

Sal Carmello, Sonny's boss, struts down the lane gutter toward him. "What's a matter wit you? Look alive. We ain't paying you to have a pleasant swing up there. Come on, Sonny. Do your job will ya?"

"Sorry, sir." Sonny lowers his swing quickly and rights the knocked-over pins. He glances down the alley behind Sal and sees the bowlers glaring at him, hands on their hips. How long had he been daydreaming?

THE SUN BEATS DOWN relentlessly in a cloudless sky, and the humidity continues to rise throughout the day, so that by evening the air in the city is stifling, with no relief in sight. After dinner Charlie Bain grabs his cap and rushes out the door.

"Going to a baseball game, Mom," he yells on his way out.

In the kitchen his mother is washing up. His father sits on the back veranda drinking Irish whiskey on the rocks and reading his favourite newspaper, the *Telegram*. He's reading about the Kitchener, Ontario chapter of the newly formed Swastika Club. He's not sure what he thinks about the club, although he agrees something has to be done about the foreigners taking over their beaches. But he's a civilized man. There are courtrooms and police officers to keep the peace. No good will come from angry young men taking to the streets. That's just not the British way. "Don't be late, son," he calls out.

Charlie dashes up the street to wait for the Queen streetcar. He's heading all the way across town to Christie Pits on his own. The rest of the members of his chapter of the Swastika Club left together an hour earlier. But his father works later than most of his friends' fathers. His friends were all on the streetcar while his family was still eating dinner.

Standing in the aisle of the Queen streetcar, gripping a leather strap that hangs from the ceiling, Charlie hopes it won't be too hard to find George and the others. He rarely travels to the west end of town and has only been to Christie Pits once. He remembers it as a large hole in the ground. No wonder it's called a pit. He feels in his trouser pocket for his swastika badge. He is nervous to wear it when he's by himself. He'll pin it onto his shirt when he finds his gang.

ALL OVER THE NEIGHBOURHOOD of Ward 5, people sit on porches, hoping for even a slight breeze to pass by. Babies cry from the heat. Old people melt in their wooden chairs. Tempers soar. At Christie Pits, people are already gathering to watch the game. It's the quarter-final game of the Junior Softball League, so a large crowd is not unexpected. But Sid can sense it's more than that. There's a brittle tension twisting and winding all over the park, like a poisonous snake. The game has just begun. The predominantly Jewish Harbord Playground Team has scored two runs already against the St. Peter's Church Team. People are sitting in the stands and on the grass on the hills that overlook the park on four sides. Some have bottles of Coca-Cola and hot dogs. Others sneak shots of rye from hip flasks. There are some families with small children, some older people, some girls. But mostly there are young men and adolescent boys, numbering in the thousands.

"There they are," Eddie Finkelstein tells Sid.

"Where?" All Sid can see is a blurry jumble of brown and green.

"Right there." Eddie peers at Sid, like he's stupid or something. Pushing on Sid's back he steers his friend in the right direction.

"Oh yeah." Sid pretends he can see, allows Eddie to push him forward. When they are a few feet from the gang, he recognizes his friends. He grabs Eddie by the shirt aggressively. "Come on."

At the south end, near the top of the hill facing north, with their backs to their own neighbourhood, sit Ralph Shapiro, Jerry Glass, Fats Tenenbaum, Guido "the Arm" Toscano and Yossie Singer. Sid's gang. Meyer Glass is down on the field in his ball uniform as a member of the Harbord Playground Team. Sid and Eddie join their friends.

"Hey Sid. Hi Eddie. About time you guys showed up." Yossie smacks Sid on the back.

"Where's Louie?" Sid looks around.

"He's late. I don't know. We thought he was with you," Ralph says.

"No." Sid looks around the field as best he can. "So, what's going on?"

Ralph nods with his head to the north end of the park. "Over there. See those guys?"

Sid squints, trying to see all the way across the large park. He can't make out much detail. But he lies. "Yeah?"

"They're from the Beaches," Ralph says. "Those are them. The Swastikas."

"How do you know?"

"We went over there before," says Jerry. "They're wearing those Swastika badges. Even the girls."

"They're wearing them here?" Sid can't believe it.

"Something's going to happen," predicts Jerry.

CHARLIE BAIN JUMPS OFF the Bathurst streetcar at Bloor and hikes west to Christie Pits. Ahead of him he spots a group of boys carrying sticks and pipes. At the southeast corner of the park, Charlie stands, scanning the sea of faces for his gang. He enters the park and wanders through the crowd, searching. At the far northwest end he spots George with some of the other guys from the Beaches. They're all wearing Swastika badges and shirts. He scoops his badge from his pocket and pins it on.

"Hey Charlie!" George shouts. "Over here." He waves a baseball bat in the air.

Charlie smiles and waves. The game is in progress. Top of the second inning. Charlie sits on the grass with his friends and they watch the game. There is a jovial mood about the park, but underneath is a rippling tension. Brittle like broken glass. Charlie can feel it. The St. Peter's Team scores a point.

"Hail Hitler!" Shouts George, thrusting up his hand in the Nazi salute, imitating the real Nazis from the pictures he's seen in the *Telegram.*

"Hail Hitler!" roar a couple other guys.

Louie Horowitz enters the park at the north end. He had planned to meet up with Sid and the other guys earlier at the south end — closest to their neighbourhood — but just after closing the shop, his father asked him to deliver a suit to one of his Gentile customers who lives up the hill, north of Bloor on Crawford. Usually Horowitz's Tailoring doesn't deliver. Most of their customers live in the College-Spadina neighbourhood and wouldn't even think to ask. But Sam Horowitz has the occasional Gentile customer. He charges more for their tailor-made suits, and to them, he delivers. Just as Louie passes by Charlie Bain and the other Swastika boys, he hears them shouting,

"Hail Hitler! Hail Hitler!" The Swastika boys mispronounce the German word *heil,* their arms outstretched in the Nazi salute.

The blood in Louie's veins runs cold. Just the day before his father was reading the evening paper, clucking his tongue with his teeth, shaking his head, looking more worried than Louie had ever seen him.

"What's a matter, Pop?"

His father folded the paper and placed it neatly in his lap. "Sit down, Louie," he said, his German accent thick.

Louie sat.

"I never talked to you much about my family. It's a long story. When I left Germany they ah … let's just say they didn't agree with my decision to emigrate. You know, in all this time, not a card or a letter did I get from them, even though I wrote to them when I first got here. Now…" He sighed deeply.

"What is it, Pop?"

"Yesterday I got a letter from my sister-in-law in Berlin." He hesitated, pulled a handkerchief from his trouser pocket and blew his nose. "My brother and father were arrested. All the Jewish schoolteachers were arrested together. They sent them to a labour camp in the east. But, before they were sent, they were beaten. Very badly. My sister-in-law hasn't heard from them in weeks. No one knows where they are, or if they're even still …" He broke off, pulled out his hanky and blew his nose again. "No one knows what's going to happen to them. It's very bad in Germany. Very bad, Louie." His father's eyes filled with tears that ran down his cheeks.

Louie had never seen his father cry. He felt helpless.

"Hail Hitler!" the kids yell again. And though Louie is alone and these guys are older and bigger, he runs over and jumps on the loudest guy, knocking George Patterson flat on his back. Louie flails his fists, hitting George anywhere he can. On the face, the chest, the nose.

"Shuttup. Shuttup. Shuttup!" Louie screams over and over.

Charlie is on his feet in a flash. He throws his arm around Louie, gets him in a headlock, pulls him off George and punches Louie hard in the mouth, splitting his lip. Some of the other guys jump in.

"Hey, Stop that!" someone shouts. Louie hauls free and darts. Charlie and George chase him up the west-side hill onto Crawford and down toward Bloor Street.

"Get him. Lousy Kike! Damn. I think he broke my nose," George howls, gripping his baseball bat.

AT THE TOP OF THE second inning, there is commotion at the north end of the park. Eddie leaps to his feet, senses tuned, his anger quickly kindled.

"What is it?" Sid asks.

"Hold on ..." Eddie rises up onto tiptoes, cranes his neck. It's hard to see all the way across to the other side. "Looks like a fight, I think." There's movement, then a small clump of guys running, heading toward them. Closer. He can make out shapes. Two boys chasing one slightly smaller boy. One of the pursuers wields a bat that he waves over his head. "Holy cow."

"What is it?" Sid is frustrated. It's all a blur to him.

"What a couple of cowards!" yells Ralph. "Two big guys on one smaller guy. Come on, let's go!"

"Forget about it," says Sid. "We should stay here. In case something happens."

"Yeah," agrees Jerry, "We gotta watch out for Meyer."

"Yeah, guess you're right," Ralph says reluctantly. He watches the small dot of a boy run out of the park, trailed by the larger boys.

LOUIE'S HEART THUDS in his chest. The two guys chasing him are about two years older and at least three inches taller than he is. And the loud one is swinging a baseball bat over his head. What was he thinking, to jump them alone like that? *They're gonna kill me now.* He glances over his shoulder. Crap. They're gaining on him. Luckily they're in his neighbourhood and Louie knows the alleys and fences like he knows his own apartment. Half a block down Montrose he leaps over the Steins' fence, dashes through the backyard, past the whole Stein family who are eating dinner in the yard to keep cool. The Steins, used to the neighbourhood boys playing hide and seek in everyone's yard, barely notice Louie as he runs by. Twelve-year- old Beatrice Stein, who has a crush on Louie, waves and smiles at him.

"Oh my God," she says, noticing the blood running from his lip and down his chin. "Louie?"

He hops over the back fence and into the Zampinis' yard, just as George and Charlie follow him into the Steins' backyard.

"Hey!" Mr. Stein jumps up from his chair. "Get outa here." He yells at the strange young men who stop in their tracks in the middle of his yard. "Go on. Beat it," he says angrily when he notices the Swastika badges pinned to their shirts. Mr. Stein doesn't like the way the boy with the bloody nose is clutching that baseball bat by his side. "Scram, you lousy punks. I'll call the cops," he threatens through gritted teeth. George and Charlie peer over his shoulder for a glimpse of Louie, who is by now three backyards and a laneway over. Louie keeps running for several more blocks. When he glances over his shoulder and sees that he is alone, he stops and leans against the back wall of Cohen's Fish Market, breathing heavily, sweat dripping from his head and mixing with blood from his split lip. He is not far from Sid's place. *Gotta go get Sid*, he decides. He's too scared to walk back to the park on his own. *Maybe Sid's still at home*, Louie thinks. Taking the back way, he speeds toward the Lapinsky residence.

"Damn, where'd he go?" George's nose drips blood. He searches in his pocket for his handkerchief, holds it over his nose, pinches hard to stop the bleeding.

"Right through our fingers." Charlie bends forward, leaning his hands on his knees to catch his breath.

"Damn Sheenie," adds George, although truthfully, he doesn't even know what Sheenie means. He's heard his father calling a Jewish neighbour the word.

"Damn Sheenies," his father says. "Why don't they stay in Poland where they came from?"

The neighbours he refers to are actually from England, by way of Italy several centuries ago. They speak the King's English better than Mr. Patterson does. George thinks maybe Sheenie pertains to English Jews. He's not really sure, but it sounds good and feels powerful as he spits it out between clenched teeth, so he repeats it all the way back up Shaw Street to the park.

"Sheenie, sheenie, sheenie," he chants. His nose throbs now that the adrenalin isn't coursing through him. He keeps the handkerchief pressed against his face as he walks. "Come on, Charlie, hurry up."

Charlie, a few steps behind, is lost in thought. When he was pounding the little Jewish guy — who was about the same age as his younger brother Richard — in the face, it didn't feel good at all. It made him feel low, like a skunk. A one-on-one fight between equally matched fighters is one thing. But four guys pounding on one scrawny little kid ... Charlie shivers.

"We gotta get back to the park." George is agitated. "Remember the flag? I hope we didn't miss everything already. Why did we chase that little kike anyway?"

INSIDE THE LIBRARY the air is stuffy, even though Mr. Cornwall has opened all the side windows and switched on the big floor fan. Lenny, though, does not get hot easily and is not bothered with the heat or the humidity. Dressed in short pants and a short-sleeve cotton shirt, he is actually quite comfortable. There is practically no one else in the library. Mr. Cornwall is seated across from Lenny.

"And why," he asks, "do you think Miss Havisham never left her house again?"

Lenny ponders the question. "Shame," he decides.

Mr. Cornwall smiles at his charge. "Good, go on."

"She just couldn't face anyone, I figure, after her fiancé ran off. And she tipped over the edge."

Mr. Cornwall smiles at Lenny's colourful way of describing things. "The edge?"

"She went nuts, I mean, sir."

"That's right." Mr. Cornwall remains silent for a moment, apparently in deep thought. Ever polite, Lenny waits patiently. Usually when Mr. Cornwall thinks hard, what comes out of his mouth delights Lenny. "Lenny, have you ever attended a poetry reading?"

"Gosh no, sir," Lenny admits, "but I'd like to."

"Fine. That's fine."

The door opens and an elderly woman, Mrs. Brownsmith, enters, leaning heavily on her wooden cane. Mr. Cornwall raises his eyebrows in a secret signal that Lenny knows means "Here comes that annoying Mrs.

Brownsmith." Mr. Cornwall leaves Lenny to read alone while tending on the older woman.

Lenny discreetly watches Mr. Cornwall. He's the only adult Lenny knows who works with his mind, not his body, and who graduated from community college, with a certificate in English literature. Lenny imagines what Mr. Cornwall's bachelor apartment must be like. He would surely have a large bookcase filled with literature on every topic imaginable. He would have a radio, and framed original paintings by French artists. He'd have a wet bar in the corner of his living room, with a bottle of champagne chilling on ice, and a carafe of fine French brandy. Lenny hopes that one day Mr. Cornwall will invite him over to a cocktail party filled with sophisticated gentleman and ladies.

When he realizes that Mrs. Brownsmith is going to capture Mr. Cornwall's attention for quite some time, Lenny picks up his books, waves goodbye and heads for home.

SONNY IS PLAYING OUTSIDE in the backyard with Izzy. He's managed to forget about the baseball game and focus on his little brother. He's teaching Izzy how to catch a ball when Louie Horowitz climbs over the back fence.

"Hey, squirt, where's Sid?" In truth, Louie is not that much taller than Sonny, and Sonny's muscles are more developed. But Louie is four years older and that makes all the difference in the world. Sonny hates being called "squirt"; he's sensitive about being short. He puffs out his chest, shrugs and throws the ball to Izzy, who stands completely erect with both hands out stiffly in front of him. Izzy misses and the ball bounces off his chest and rolls toward Sonny, who bends down and skillfully scoops it up. He tosses it from one hand to the other. Izzy watches the ball, just like Sonny told him to.

"What happened to you? Holy cripes, Louie." There's a stream of blood running from Louie's split lip, down his chin.

"Where's Sid? There's a big fight at the Pits. We need Sid," Louie repeats, as he catches his breath.

Sonny's eyes light up. "There's a fight?"

"I just said so, didn't I? You don't know where Sid is?" Louie wipes at his chin with the back of his hand. He winces at the sight of his own blood and smears it onto the back of his trousers.

"He's there. He's at the park already. He went early."

"He's already there?" Louie licks at the cut in his lip, tastes the salt.

"Yeah."

"Then what am I doing here?"

"I don't know."

Louie grabs the ball from Sonny's hands and tosses it to Izzy, a little on the hard side. It bounces off Izzy's head. Izzy stands stock still, trying not to cry. Louie leaps back over the fence. "Bye, short stuff."

Sonny stands still for a moment. There's a fight. At the Pits. And he's stuck here, with his baby brother. He hates being little. He wishes he could have gone with Sid. Lenny should be babysitting, not him. Too bad Uncle Max and Aunt Tessie went out with their little girls, or he could leave Izzy with them. He looks next door. Mrs. Pincinni is in her chair as usual. Not doing anything. Just sitting and staring into space. Sonny can hear the rest of the Pincinni family behind her in the kitchen, talking loudly in Italian, and laughing. Sonny looks at Izzy, and then he decides. He has to go to the park. Just for a few minutes. If there's a fight, he has to get into it. Excitement vibrates through his body. His breathing speeds up. He literally sees red at the thought of the damn Swazis taking over Christie Pits. He balls his hands into fists. He needs to punch one of those damn Nazis; he's going to go crazy if he doesn't. He takes Izzy by the hand, leads him to the back porch and sits him down with his ball.

"Listen, Iz. I gotta go. Just for a couple a minutes. I think Sid needs my help. I'll be right back. Okay? You stay right here on the porch. Don't go off the porch. You got that?"

Izzy stares at Sonny with wide eyes. In a small voice he says, "You can't leave me alone. Pa said."

"Come on, Iz, if you need anything, go and see Mrs. Pincinni. See? She's sitting there like always. Okay?"

Izzy is frightened of Mrs. Pincinni. His lower lip trembles. "She hates us."
"Aw nuts." Sonny puts his hands on Izzy's shoulders. "All right. You'll
just have to come with me then."
Izzy's face lights up. "To the park?"
Sonny takes his hand. "Come on." He leads his little brother to the
back fence and clasps his hands together. "Hop up." Sonny pushes his
brother's bottom as Izzy climbs to the top of the wooden fence. Sonny
hops up and over, holds out his arms. "Come on, jump down." Izzy falls
into Sonny's arms. "Let's go." Sonny grabs Izzy's hand as they run through
several backyards onto Euclid Avenue, and race toward the park. They
can hear people yelling before they even reach Harbord Street.

Hell Breaks Loose
MINUTES LATER

THERE IS A HEAVY UNDERTONE in the air as the game progresses. It's
oppressive and thick as the humidity. Like wading through the lake, it
surrounds the body with pressure from all sides. Tension rises like mer-
cury in a thermometer — a thin red line climbing, climbing, pushing,
straining against a narrow glass bulb. Threatening to burst. Small slivers
of razor-sharp glass exploding, shooting pinpricks under the skin. The
evening air does not bring any relief from the scorching humidity of the
day. Men strip down to cotton undershirts and roll up their pants. Their
shirts lie beside them on the grass, limp piles of sweaty cotton. Women
hike their skirts up above their knees; perspiration gathers under their
breasts, between their thighs, and drips down the back of their necks.
Shoes are tossed off. The stink of unwashed sweat permeates the park,
hanging heavy like clothes left on the line in the rain.
Secretly, Sid hopes it will all end soon. He can see that the other guys
are crawling out of their skins to get in on some action.

"I'm telling you," Eddie keeps saying. "We're gonna show those Swazis." He's been carrying around a sawed-off lead pipe since the Swastika Club began kicking Jews off the east-side beaches. The pipe is shoved up his pant leg and stuffed into his sock. Every so often, he takes it out and slaps the end of it into his palm.

Jerry Glass keeps his eye on the game. His brother Meyer is second baseman and Jerry is worried that if a fight breaks out, the players will be first to get creamed. Also, he wants the Harbord Playground team to win. He is proud of his big brother, even if his rotten drunkard of a father isn't. His father should be here, but Jerry knows where the old man probably is. His favourite watering hole is on Queen Street East in the Ward, an old broken-down pool hall, where a man can drink cheap homemade whiskey, play poker in the back and make a bet on the horse races all in one joint. The place is owned by the famous neighbourhood gangster, Checkie Seigelman. Jerry cheers so loudly every time the Harbord team scores a run, he is starting to lose his voice.

Ralph Shapiro is engrossed in the game, but for different reasons. In April, he tried out for the team but didn't make it. He can hit pretty good, but he can't run. With his bum leg, the little one with its heavy steel brace, he takes two steps off home plate and he falls on his face. He can't make it around the bases before getting tagged. He plays in a recreational league, but the Harbord team only recruits the best, and he just isn't good enough. Ralph isn't bitter. His mother has told him all his life how lucky he is to be alive. He doesn't moan and whine about his rotten luck. Instead, he watches every play, studies the players, convinced that next year he will make the team. Unlike his friends, who don't usually attend the games and are only here because of the trouble, Ralph is an avid fan. He's seen every game the Harbords have played, followed every play, can recite every player's batting average, and theorize on how they could have won lost games.

Eddie doesn't care much for playing sports. He'd rather bet on the outcome than be one of the schmucks running around in short pants, chasing a ball, making a fool out of himself. Eddie would love to wrap his lead pipe around the head of a Swazi. His old man came to this country in 1910. Fought in the Great War in a Scottish Canadian regiment. He was gassed in the trenches. Took a load of shrapnel in the arm. He used to work in the needle trade, as a cutter. After the war he couldn't hold a pair of scissors. And now he can't breathe right half the time, on account of what the gas did to his lungs. Lucky he became acquainted with Benny Hersh or he'd have starved. Eddie's father is smart with numbers. He figures out the books for Hersh's numbers operation. Brings in more money than anyone else Eddie knows. It isn't exactly *according to hoyle,* but Eddie's old man isn't hurting anyone. He's making a pile of dough for lots of working stiffs and out-of-work guys. He was a hero in the Great War. Saved a man from sure death. With a shoulder full of shrapnel he carried his Sergeant, who'd been hit in the chest, all the way to the medics. He passed out from the pain only after he'd delivered the Sarge to safety. Never even got a medal for his bravery. At night, Eddie hears his Pa coughing, spitting up blood. His old man fought for this country. Eddie's got a right to use the parks same as anybody else. His nerves twitch with anticipation.

Meyer Glass hits a home run. His brother Jerry jumps to his feet in front of Eddie, screaming and whistling through his teeth.

"How about that? You see what Meyer did? You guys see that?"

"Yeah, yeah. Great. That was stupendous, Jerry."

"Sent it to the moon, he did. Huh, Eddie?"

"Yeah, Meyer's great." Eddie's keyed up. He gets to his feet, paces behind his gang.

"Hey, down in front!" comes a voice from behind.

Eddie spins around, hikes up his pant leg, whips the lead pipe from his sock, waves it around in the air menacingly. "Shut up! It's a free country," he shouts.

Sid is on his feet, towering over Eddie. "Hey, come on now, Eddie. Let it go." Sid peers at the guy at the back, who holds his hands out in front of him. "It's okay, Eddie." Sid places a hand on his friend's back. "Come on. Watch the game." He swivels Eddie around.

"I got a right to stand up," he tells Sid.

"Sure you do, Eddie. Sure you do."

"My father fought in the Great War."

"I know he did, Eddie. Your Pop's a brave man."

"Damn right."

Sid gently taps the lead pipe. "Come on, Eddie. Put it away."

Eddie kicks the ground, then shoves the pipe back into his sock, covers it with his trousers. He's angry. Sometimes Sid acts just like a grown-up.

Where the hell is Louie, Sid wonders. He should be here by now. It's usually Sid, with the help of Louie, who keeps the other guys in line. Bunch of hotheads. They'd all be in reform school if it wasn't for Sid keeping them out of jams. He cranes his neck around, searching for Louie in the crowded field. A St. Peter's player scores. Around Sid and his gang, Gentile boys roar to their feet, patting each other on the back. Goddamn it, thinks Sid. We're surrounded by Gentiles. Not a good position if anything happens. The first drop of dread lands in the centre of Sid's belly, and ripples through his body like a stone tossed into a creek.

Eddie wanders over, crouches on his haunches by Sid. Pulls a slightly bent cigarette out of his shirt pocket, lights it up, takes a deep draw, passes it to Sid. Eddie always has cigarettes. He gets them from his boss, or steals them from his Pa. Sid puffs on the cigarette, then passes it to Ralph. Sweat is pouring down the sides of Sid's face. He removes his cloth cap and wipes his cheeks with the back of his wrist. His hair is drenched. His shirt lies on the grass by his feet. His suspenders are damp against his cotton undershirt.

At the top of the ninth inning a player from the Harbord team scores a run, tying up the score. The crowd goes wild with excitement, shouting their team's name, jumping up and down, throwing fists full of popcorn out into the park.

"DID YOU SEE THAT?" George Patterson is up on his feet. "Lousy kikes tied it up."

Charlie Bain winces. He just can't get the image out of his head of smashing that little guy in the face. Split his lip wide open. Blood dripping down his chin. He's kind of glad the little fellow got away. The sound of hate on his friend George's lips is beginning to curdle in Charlie's stomach.

"Come on, Harold," George is more agitated than Charlie has ever seen him. Maybe he's just sore because his nose is probably broken. It must hurt. Charlie can see the beginnings of purple black bruising on either side of his friend's nose. "It's time for the flag. What do you think, Harold? The guys on the field'll see it. It'll give 'em faith. That way they'll know we're here behind 'em one hundred percent. Whatda ya say, fellas?"

"Yeah," says Harold rising up on his knees. "You're right Georgie boy, time to show our stuff."

Charlie and his friends are sitting on an elevated piece of ground at the northwest end of the park, known as the Camel's Hump. The hump can be seen from all areas of the park. Harold and George each walk to one end of a rolled-up piece of white cloth, about ten feet long and seven feet wide. They nod to one another and then ceremoniously unfurl the flag. Everything shifts into slow motion. Charlie notices some of the ball players looking up. Some take off their caps and scratch their heads. Others shout. All over the park, heads turn.

FROM THE SOUTH SIDE, Eddie spots it first. It is quiet and almost strangely beautiful for a moment. A small group of boys on the Camel's Hump slowly, carefully unroll a large white sheet. It spreads out like a grand statement on the brown grass, the white of the sheet reflecting bright in the light of a fading orange and pink sunset. It takes a moment for folks to recognize the huge black swastika hand-painted onto the middle of the sheet. Heads turn. Bodies stiffen. People begin to shout.

"Hey!"

"Oh my god!"

"Hail Hitler!"

"What the hell?"

"Hail Hitler!"

"Bastard Swazis."

"Stinkin' Jews."

It is hard to say where the fighting begins. Perhaps it starts all over the park simultaneously, in small pockets. It happens at the south end within seconds of the flag's appearance. Sid and his friends turn to the left.

Beside them is a small group of Gentile boys who seem as startled by the flag as they are.

"Let's get 'em!" shouts Eddie, whipping out his lead pipe.

Sid and his friends seize upon the Gentile boys. Sid throws himself fists first against the largest boy, knocking him to the ground, then sits on the boy's chest and holds him down. Ralph grabs another guy by the scruff of his shirt and socks him across the jaw. The first boy grabs a large rock from the ground and smashes it over Ralph's head. Ralph goes down, silver and white stars swirling across his vision. Eddie charges the boy, brandishing his lead pipe. He swings it like a baseball bat, catches the boy across the ribs.

Another boy grabs Sid by the shirt and hauls him up. Then the two boys start punching Sid in the face, the chest. His body absorbs the blows.

LENNY WALKS ALONG Bloor Street with a new stack of library books. He's taken the long way home so he can stare at the evening-wear display in the window of Smith and Sons Tailor Shop and imagine wearing the black tuxedo, tails and top hats. Lost in his own daydreams, he doesn't notice the commotion in the park until he is passing right by the south end of Christie Pits. He stops to look down the hill. Holy cripes. It's a madhouse. All over the park, guys are beating on each other. He sees Ralph lying on his back, then he spots Sid being held down by three guys who are pummelling him with kicks and punches. *I have to do something,* Lenny thinks. He moves forward a few steps down the hill. What will he do? Lenny tentatively reaches out to push one of the boys off Sid, when someone attacks him from behind. He can feel heavy hands against his shoulders.

"Hey!" Lenny spins around.

"What's a matter, Jew Boy?"

There are three of them. Lenny backs away, clutches his books against his chest. "Look, I don't want to fight."

The boys laugh cruelly. Lenny steals a glance out the corner of his eye at Sid, who is being kicked in the legs.

"Aw, what's a matter Jew Boy? Scared?"

"No," Lenny says defiantly. "I'm not scared of you. I just don't like to fight."

"Ohhhh," One of the boys says in an exaggerated tone and then curtsies. "You're not a fairy boy, are you? Look at that. A Jew and a fairy all in one. Maybe we should kiss him instead of hitting him."

"What, and get Jew germs?"

The boys laugh uproariously. Lenny shakes his head and turns away, determined to help Sid. One of the boys kicks Lenny hard in the back, sending him lurching forward. His books fly out of his grasp onto the grass. The others surround him. Their fury toward him is huge. Their hatred of him for being a Jew and a sissy-boy rises to the surface. Lenny hears a dull thud as one boy punches him across the jaw. He flies backward, lands on his butt, the hard ground sending shock waves up his spine. He feels dizzy. Shields his face with his hands. Someone kicks his arm. He feels a sharp pain in his wrist. He hunkers down against the dirt, hands covering his head. Prepares for more blows. Nothing happens. He peeks from behind his hands. Sid has broken free of his attackers, and has two of Lenny's adversaries under his arms in a headlock. Eddie moves in, grabs the other one by the shoulders, throws him to the ground like a sack of potatoes, strikes at the boy in the legs and chest with his lead pipe. Sid knees one of his captives in the groin. The boy crumples to the ground and curls into the fetal position, cupping his crotch and moaning. Sid holds the other in the headlock, draws back his right arm and smashes the guy hard across the nose. He slips from Sid's grasp, blood pouring down his face. Sid and Eddie fly flailing into a sea of arms and legs.

Lenny lays on the ground staring up at the clouds as blood trickles from his split lip. He holds his left wrist with his other hand. Sharp pain sears through it. Maybe it's broken. He doesn't move while the fighting continues around him.

SONNY RUNS HARD, dragging Izzy by the hand all the way up Euclid to Bloor, afraid to miss the action. By the time they get to the entrance of the park, the riot is in full swing. Sonny stops at the top of the hill for a moment to survey the situation. It's a mess. Down inside the Pits there are guys all over fighting. Some are using baseball bats and lead pipes. Some are using rocks, bricks, sticks and stones. Many are swinging with bare fists. A couple of girls run past him out of the park screaming. Sonny sees Louie Horowitz flat on his back. A bigger guy stands on top of him about to smash his face with a stick of wood.

Sonny turns to Izzy. "You stay put. Right here. Don't move. I'll be right back. You got that?"

Izzy nods. "Don't get hurt, Sonny."

"Ahhh," Sonny screams as he careens down the hill, his dukes up. He leaps up and socks the guy on top of Louie with a hard left to his stomach, followed by a clean, quick right uppercut to the jaw. The guy flips backward. Sonny hears a discernible crack. The stick flies out of the guy's hand, through the air and into the general chaos. Sonny holds out a hand for Louie.

"Come on." Sonny grabs Louie by the arm and drags him into the nearest skirmish. Izzy watches from the top of the hill, eyes wide. His thumb finds its way into his mouth.

CHARLIE LIES UNDER a large boy who has pinned him to the ground. *But I didn't do anything,* he thinks. It wouldn't make any difference to say the words. It is a free-for-all at this point. He strains against the weight and bucks the boy off, scurries to his feet. George rushes to his side with his baseball bat. He raises it high above his head and smashes the guy on the head. The boy goes down with a thud. George hoists the bat back up to pound the guy again.

"George, no!" Charlie instinctively yells.

George glances briefly at Charlie, a demented expression on his face. "Shuttup, Charlie." George brings the bat down on the boy. The wood blasts against the boy's jaw, breaking bones. George whacks the boy against the skull, then in the chest. The boy's face is a bloody mess. His nose is bent to the side. Charlie feels nauseous.

"Stop it, George. Stop it! You're gonna kill the guy," he shouts, tears of shame beating against the back of his eyes.

George ignores Charlie, bats the boy once more in the shin. "Sheenie lover," he mutters to Charlie under his breath. Then George charges down the hill waving his bat above his head, like a soldier in battle. Charlie stands frozen, watching his best friend unleash a furious, white-hot hatred. Charlie's never seen this side of George. He glances around. All over the park, guys are fighting. Fists, brass knuckles, baseball bats, lead pipes, rocks, sticks, stones, boots. Any available weapon is put into action.

Charlie feels a sickness in his belly that he can't place. He's not afraid. That's not it. He can fight like the best of them. It's something else. Something bigger. A sense of doom. This wasn't supposed to happen. They were going to show the flag and that was it. A peaceful protest. That's what Harold said. Charlie sees Harold to his left. He's pinned down a small Jewish boy. He's got him tight around the throat. He's choking the kid, who is red in the face and slobbering. Eyes bugging out. Damn it Harold. Charlie charges at Harold to stop him before he kills the kid. Charlie grabs Harold by the shoulders, hauls him off. Harold swings a heavy fist and slams Charlie on the jaw.

"What the hell?"

"Jesus." Charlie rubs his jaw, feels around inside his mouth with his tongue, checking for broken teeth.

Harold shakes his head, jumps back on the smaller boy.

Disgusted with his friends, Charlie stands and advances into the park. He walks through the fighting untouched. To his left and to his right boys are hitting, pounding, choking each other. Some guys are bleeding. Others are yelling. He proceeds clear through to the south end near Bloor Street, and up the incline. He spots a small boy, couldn't be more than five years old, standing alone at the top of the hill, sucking his thumb. Someone should send the kid home. He could get hurt. Charlie approaches the boy. When he's close, he smiles; he doesn't want to frighten the kid. From behind, someone whacks the back of Charlie's head with something hard. He swings around. Sees a lead pipe raised to smash him. Charlie deflects the arm with his hand. The pipe flies through the air. Charlie watches in horror as it falls back to earth, slamming onto the little boy's head. The boy drops to the ground, blood already pouring from his wound. Charlie runs toward the boy. Hands grab him, spin him around and a fist against his jaw knocks him backward. Charlie sees black dots swim in the air just before he sinks into blackness.

SONNY KICKS THE GUY wearing a swastika sweatshirt after he's knocked him to the ground. He kicks him over and over in the chest and belly with his boots, satisfied with the dull thud he hears each time he connects with the boy's crummy Nazi body. That'll teach you, Sonny thinks. He glances up the hill for Izzy. Crap. Where is he? He's not there. Where'd he go? Sonny charges toward the hill and walks into a baseball bat aimed at his chest. "Oof." Sonny goes down, as the boy with the baseball bat jumps on top of him.

Ralph Shapiro limps up the hill. His head is throbbing from the blow he took to the skull. Damn Swazis. Someone caught him across his good leg with a broken bottle. He doesn't think it's busted, but it's bleeding to beat the band. He figures he better at least wash off the blood before it gets infected. When he struggles to the top of the hill he sees Sid's little brother Izzy lying on the ground.

Ralph forgets about his leg and rushes over to where Izzy lies. "Oh my God." He picks up Izzy in his arms, limps to Bloor Street. Sirens. He looks up. Police cars head toward the park. Ralph stands in the middle of the road, flags down the first car he sees.

With all his strength, Sonny pushes at the boy who has him pinned down. He leaps up, dodges hands and feet, and roars to the top of the hill. Where the hell is Izzy? Sonny spins around in all directions. Damn it. Damn it. Damn it. Where'd he go? Sonny's heart pounds in fear. Sweat pours down the sides of his face. He stands on tiptoes, straining to see something, anything, amid the fighting. He spots his brother Sid, pushing off a guy with his right arm, while holding another guy by the scruff with his left hand. "Sid!" Sonny shouts as he runs down the hill. Sid releases both boys from his grasp, turns toward Sonny. The first scream of police sirens echoes through the park.

"Izzy!" Sonny yells, as Lenny crawls along the ground on hands and knees, searching. Lenny figures he'll see Izzy more easily this way. His ripped library books are tucked into the back of his trousers. Mr. Cornwall is going to be disappointed in him. He's hoping to tape them back together, later at home. His hurt arm aches. Sid looks above heads, while Louie, Jerry, Eddie, Meyer, Fats and Guido scour the park. They're all looking for Izzy.

CONSTABLE JOHN MILLER sits in the back seat with the little Jew boy, while his partner, Constable Bill Brooks, drives. The kid's out cold. A blow to the head. Blood's pouring from the wound. Kid's probably going to die. What the hell's such a little kid doing in a rumble? "Can't you hurry up, Bill. Kid's bleeding all over the seat."

Constable Brooks turns on the siren and speeds toward Toronto Western Hospital.

"WHAT'S WITH THE TRAFFIC?" Sophie asks Yacov. They've been waiting in bumper-to-bumper traffic to move along Bloor Street for the past twenty minutes. Between the lines of cars, streetcars are ground to a halt.

"How do I know? Maybe a bank robbery," Yacov answers.

"Again?"

"Who knows?"

They hear a siren and stare out the car window as a police car passes them, heading in the opposite direction.

"Maybe they already caught the criminals," Sophie muses.

"Good, then maybe the traffic will clear up."

"THAT'S IT. MOVE ALONG. Break it up." In the park, the police disperse the crowd, arresting anyone with a weapon.

"Why'ja leave him alone!" Sid screams at Sonny for the twentieth time.

"It was just for a second."

"You shoulda stayed home, Sonny."

Lenny glances at the cars moving slowly across Bloor Street. "Uh-oh."

"What?"

"It's Ma. And Pop."

Sonny and Sid turn and look in horror. Just across the street, their parents sit in traffic in the Model T Ford. The boys turn quickly away. "Crap."

SOPHIE AND YACOV stare out the window. There is a great commotion
in the park. It's hard to tell what's going on from across the street. They
see police officers dragging dirty bruised boys into a police car. A group
of boys from the neighbourhood run in front of Yacov's car. Sophie recognizes Sonny's friend Davey Tittel. He has been beaten. His face is
bleeding. His shirt is torn. The other boys look worse. Sophie looks
toward the park. "Oh my God."

"What?" Yacov looks at his wife. Her eyes are wide.

She opens the car door and gets out.

"Sophie. What are you doing?"

She crosses in front of the car, trots toward the park.

"Sophie?" Yacov puts the car in first gear, pulls on the handbrake, shuts
off the motor.

Sophie crosses the street and marches straight toward her sons.

Lenny peeks over his shoulder, sees her coming. "Uh-oh."

"Sid! Lenny?" Sophie calls.

"Hi Ma," Sid offers a weak smile to his mother.

"CALM DOWN," an officer says, reaching in his pocket for his notebook.
"Lets just start with the facts."

"Someone stole Izzy," Sonny shouts up at the cop.

The officer peers down at the scruffy Jew boy, flips open his book to a
blank page. "Stole him?"

"I left him right here." Sonny stomps on the spot with his foot.

"Uh-huh."

"Really, officer," Sid offers. "He was standing here, for a just a moment."

"And then he was gone," Sonny adds breathlessly.

Sophie glares at Sonny. "And you were supposed to be home, young man."

Sonny looks down at his feet.

"Look. I don't think anyone stole your son, lady. Maybe he went home.
Did you check?"

"No."

"Well …"

"I told him to wait right here," Sonny says.

"Look, all I can do is take a report." The officer waves his arms at the crowds in the park. "We got a big mess to clear up here. Maybe he's in there somewhere. You can call the station in a while and see if anyone turned up anything. And you should call the hospitals. Just in case. " He flips his notebook shut, tips his hat and walks farther into the park.

"Hospitals?" The first wave of terror spreads through Sophie's body.

"Sid!" Ralph Shapiro limps over, a pack of ice tied around his knee with a rag. "Your brother." Ralph is out of breath from running. "Izzy."

"Where is he?" Sid shouts.

"The cops took him to the hospital."

"Oh, thank God." Sophie clutches Yacov's hand.

"Which hospital?" Yacov asks.

"Beats me." Ralph didn't think to ask.

Canada Shmanada
THREE HOURS LATER

IN THE HOSPITAL waiting room, Yacov smokes one cigarette after the other and paces back and forth. The walls are a sickly beige, the floor a polished yellow linoleum. The chairs are wooden, hard and uncomfortable. There are several chrome floor ashtrays in the room, all overflowing with cigarette butts. On one wall there is an impressionistic painting of Lake Ontario and the beach. The strong scent of antiseptic covers other more primal smells.

"Sit down," Sophie says to her husband. "You're making me nervous."

He obeys, sinking into the chair beside her. His right knee twitches up and down. His chest is a stretched rubber band. He feels as though he is going to break in two. He puts one hand over his heart to steady himself.

After an hour the doctor, wearing a white lab coat over a shirt and tie, steps into the waiting room with a sombre expression on his face. Yacov stubs out his cigarette in the ashtray and stands.

The doctor looks down at his clipboard. His stethoscope clinks against the board. "Mr. Lap-in-sky ..." he says, "your son has a concussion. Possibly even a contusion ..."

"Concussion." Yacov repeats the unfamiliar word.

"I'd like to keep him overnight for observation. He took quite a blow to the frontal lobe."

"I thought he got hit on the head."

The doctor glances at Yacov over his bifocals. "Yes, Mr. Lapinsky. A cerebral contusion is a diffuse disturbance of the brain, characterized by oedema and capillary haemorrhages."

Yacov looks his wife in the eye. What the hell is he talking about?

The doctor continues. "Your son has been rendered unconscious. This much we know. He may recover completely or ... in the case of cerebral irritation, persistent and disabling symptoms are extremely common. Symptoms may include headache, giddiness, and mental disturbances. In extreme cases, violent conduct which may necessitate treatment at a mental hospital ..."

"Oh my God," Sophie's hands fly to her mouth.

"Normally we have no way of knowing how much damage the brain sustained. There are tests, of course. Radiography, lumbar puncture, but ... well ..."

"What ... ?"

"Well, Mr. Lapinsky, let's just say, these diagnostics are ... costly? And I assume beyond your means."

Yacov would like to hit the doctor. He folds his arms across his chest.

"We know so little about the human brain. Scientists are discovering more every day ..."

"Doctor Milne ... please ... I don't understand ..." Sophie would like to tear the doctor apart limb by limb, but she contains her rage inside a locked box.

The doctor sighs. "There could be permanent damage."

"Damage?"

"To the brain."

"Oh my God." Sophie clutches Yacov's arm.

Yacov's chest tightens. Sweat drips down his back and under his arms. "Doctor. What can we do?"

The doctor shakes his head and sighs meaningfully. "There's nothing much we can do right now. Just wait and see. We'll know more when the boy wakes."

Tears well up in Sophie's eyes. *My baby. My baby boy.*

"He needs to be kept well hydrated, especially in this heat. I've ordered a saline purge. The nurses will take care of that. And if he wakes they will administer a sedative and analgesic for the pain. I'll look in on the boy in the morning. Oh and … ." he glances at his clipboard. "Mr. Lapinsky, on your way out, please consult with the desk nurse. She will prepare your bill."

Damn doctors, thinks Yacov. *The bill. That's all they care about?*

"Can we see him?" Sophie grabs the doctor's sleeve. He gently but firmly releases her hold.

"Yes. He's in room 3B, down this hall. Good day." The doctor strides off in the other direction, his shoes clipping against the polished tile floor.

IZZY IS SENT HOME the next afternoon. The doctor concludes he has suffered severe cerebral contusion. There is no sign of infection or fever. This is good news. Even Izzy's appetite has returned. But the boy has lost the power of speech. His eyes are dull, his lips silent.

"Though a patient may recover rapidly and completely from the effects of a cerebral contusion," Dr. Milne reports to Yacov and Sophie, "these acute symptoms may or may not persist. There also may be a latent interval lasting days or even weeks."

"I'm sorry, doctor." Sophie has locked an iron clamp on her seething emotions. "What does that mean?"

The doctor shrugs. "He may recover. He may not."

Sophie's hand flies to her lips. The clamp blows apart. Her eyes fill with tears. "Oh my God."

"We'll just have to wait and see," Dr. Milne says cheerfully, attempting to pass a shred of hope to the distraught parents, but truthfully, he doesn't expect much for this boy. Probably end up in an institution.

"Wait and see." Yacov repeats the words, but they don't mean anything. The thumping of his heart drowns out all comprehension. "See what?" he manages.

"You might notice inability to concentrate, irritability, nervousness, anxiety, headache, dizziness. He may speak again. He may not. Modern science has come a long way, Mr. Lapinsky, but there is so much about the human brain that remains a mystery. I'm sorry I can't tell you more. We'll just have to wait and see."

Yacov stifles the impulse to mimic the doctor's *wait and see*. He is sick of hearing it.

"Mr. Lapinsky, on your way out …" the doctor begins.

Yacov holds up one hand. "I know, doctor. I'll check with the receptionist to go over my bill."

The doctor chuckles softly. Then he pats Sophie on the arm, gives Yacov a bracing squeeze on the shoulder, nods and heads off down the hall.

Sophie hits Yacov on the arm, as if it is all somehow his fault. Then she throws herself into his arms, where she lets her tears flow freely. When she is cried out, Sophie composes herself, and they walk down the long hall to collect their son.

YACOV DRIVES THROUGH a heavy rain, windshield wipers flapping rhythmically back and forth as rain pelts the glass. The rain is a welcome relief, cooling down a baking city, freshening stifling air. To Yacov it only adds to the surreal feeling of the past few days. Beside him, Sophie sits with Izzy in her lap. He is awake, but he hasn't said a word. Sophie tries to draw him out, asking him simple questions. "Are you hungry? Thirsty?" To which she receives no reply. Izzy just stares at Sophie's mouth as if he is trying to decipher her words. She points things out to see if he will react.

"See the rain? Oh, look at it splash the window." Izzy remains silent. He doesn't look out at the rain or at the window. Sophie's eyes fill with tears. She hugs him tightly.

The hospital bill feels like lead in Yacov's shirt pocket. He now owes $189. A fortune. You can buy a good used car for that price. The hospital has agreed to accept weekly payments, with interest of course, of $3 a week. Now Yacov is on the other side of the credit business. Max is not going to be happy. With this debt hanging over his head, there will be no way he can contribute a dime to their store fund.

Still, Max can't complain. He's the one who lost all their money in the crash of '29. A silent ache begins deep in Yacov's belly. It spreads throughout his body the closer they get to home.

SOPHIE LEADS IZZY into the bedroom to put him to bed. The other boys linger in the kitchen, chins to the floor. They are trying to understand the news. Izzy's brain was hurt. He will never be the same again. How could that be? What will he be like? What will happen to him? He can't speak and maybe never will again. It is unnaturally quiet in the kitchen. Yacov sits stony-faced at the table, with a glass of schnapps in front of him. He rarely drinks, but today he needs a glass of the warm liquid to cool the burning in his belly.

"I'm running downstairs for a minute," Sophie says quietly, as she passes by. "I can't read this thermometer. I'll see if Tessie can figure it out …" Holding the handrail, she walks slowly down the stairs.

Yacov downs his schnapps, looks up at Sid, who is sitting in the corner by the stove, head lowered. Yacov flashes on an image of himself as a boy. The pogrom of 1913. Back of the house. He never should have left his little brother Shmuel alone. He remembers the thunder of the horses, the sound of his mother's scream, the blank look in her eye. Shmuel's broken body sprawled on the dusty ground. The image won't fade, even after all this time. It is a jagged edge inside him that never leaves. It is a rough lump of coal, waiting to poke at him from the inside any time it wants to. It is poking him right now. Yacov downs his schnapps. Stares at his eldest son. Something in him snaps, the elastic band inside his gut, which stretches from the base of his throat to the centre of his belly. Someone has been twisting and turning it tighter and tighter these past few days until now it snaps, the two ends springing apart and ricocheting inside him, ripping out a small piece of his heart. There's only one way to get the piece back.

"It's your responsibility, Shimon," Yacov says quietly to Sid.

"Huh?"

"To watch out for your brothers."

"But Pop ... I wasn't anywhere near ... I mean ... I didn't even know Izzy was there ... I mean ... I know, Pa."

"You're the oldest."

"I know, Pa. I'm sorry."

"You're sorry?"

"I'm sorry, Pa." Sid's belly churns. He rubs it with one hand.

Yacov bangs an open hand on the table. "Tell that to your brother Izzy!" he shouts. "You wanna be sorry. I'll show you sorry." Yacov stands, unhooks his belt, rips it violently from his belt loops, folds it in half. Sid grimaces. Yacov raises one arm and whips Sid across his lower back with the leather belt, catching him across the kidneys.

"Ummph." Sid absorbs the punishment.

"I'll show you sorry."

Whack. Whack. Whack. The sound of leather on Sid's skin is sickening. A sweat breaks out on Sid's forehead. He huddles his body in tight, as he takes the beating. The other boys watch and cringe. Yacov strikes his eldest son again and again. Sonny hugs his body with his arms, feels every blow as if it's him. It should be him. Not Sid. It's all his fault.

Tears stream down Lenny's face. He can't stand it. "Pop. Stop it. It's enough. You're hurting him."

Yacov stops, turns in the direction of Lenny. Sneers at his son. "What'sa matter, crybaby? Huh? Now you're gonna cry, like a little girl. Huh? Like a *faygele. Feh.*" Yacov waves a hand down in disgust. "Maybe you need a lesson too, huh? Crybaby? Teach you how to be a man."

"No, Pa ..."

Yacov raises his arm and with the back of his hand, belts Lenny across the face, knocking him backward against the wall.

"How do you like that? Huh?" Yacov whips Lenny with the belt, first on one side, then the other. "Teach you a lesson. Little *faygele.* Stop crying, damn it. Act like a man. It's sickening," Yacov mutters, as he strikes Lenny once more.

Sonny grits his teeth. Sees red. It should be him. Not Sid. Not Lenny. Agitated, he steps forward and grabs at his father's sleeve. "Quit it, Pa. Stop it."

Enraged, Yacov jerks his arm free, and strikes Sonny with a closed fist, catching him on the jaw, knocking him back against a kitchen chair that topples over and crashes to the floor, just as Sophie rushes up the stairs with Max and Tessie behind her.

"Yacov!" she shouts. "What are you doing?"

Sonny sits on the floor against the chair, eyes wide. His father has never hit him before. He can't believe what's happening. Everyone is used to Sid being strapped. Even Lenny once in a while. But never Sonny. Never before. He can't believe it. The whole world's gone crazy.

Sophie scans the room, tries to make sense of the scene.

Yacov stares at the floor, breathing hard. Spent.

"Yacov. What happened here!?"

Yacov wheels around to face his wife, one hand raised. "Don't you start with me too."

"Yacov! What's the matter with you? Why are you hitting?"

"We need some discipline around here."

Sophie glares at him, her eyes hard.

"All right. All right. It's finished." Yacov unfolds his belt, slips it slowly into the loops around his trousers.

Sonny stares straight ahead. Tears flood his eyes. He has to get out of here. Has to leave. He wants to hit someone. If he doesn't get out of here, he will hit his father. He jumps to his feet and pushes past his mother, stepping on one of Max's feet as he runs by and thumps down the stairs.

"Sonny?" Sophie calls.

The door slams.

Sophie removes Yacov's hat from a hook on the hat stand, hands it to him.

"Get out of my house," she says calmly.

"Sophie, please."

"Get away from my children."

Yacov looks in her eyes. He has never seen her more serious. The chair Sonny had been leaning against lies on its side on the floor, accusing him. Ashamed and dejected, he walks to the door. Izzy has woken up. He staggers into the room from the bedroom, sees Yacov leaving. He tries to speak, but he just looks confused.

Sophie picks him up.

"Izzelah, what are you doing out of bed? Come on." She carries him out of the room.

OUT ON THE STREET Sonny runs as fast as he can. Tears run freely down his red cheeks. He runs smack into Louie Horowitz. His head thumps against Louie's chest, knocking a carton of eggs out of Louie's hand. The eggs fly up, then spatter on the sidewalk.

"Hey, Squirt. Watch where you're going," Louie shouts, staring in disbelief at the ruined eggs. "Goddamnit. Look at that."

"Shut up," Sonny barks back at the older boy. He hates Louie. It's all his fault. If he hadn't climbed over the fence looking for Sid, Sonny never would've gone to the park and none of this would have happened. "I hate you," Sonny yells, then charges at Louie, fists flying.

"Hey. Sonny!" Louie's outstretched hand catches Sonny's head, holding the smaller boy at arm's length, while Sonny lashes out in wide useless arcs. He can only reach Louie's arm, which he pounds with all his fury. "Quit it, Sonny." Louie leans his head back, trying to stay out of Sonny's range. But Sonny can't hear him. He strikes Louie on the arm and shoulder, from one side, then the other. With all his strength. With all his grief, as tears stream down his face.

"Hate you. Hate you."

Louie keeps his grip on Sonny's head, and with his free hand sneaks in one clean punch that connects with Sonny's jaw, knocking him backward onto the sidewalk. "Quit it, Squirt." Louie yells. "Or I'll really hurt you." He hovers over Sonny, his dukes up.

Sonny leaps to his feet, still crying, and runs away down the street. Louie watches, rubbing his arm, as Sonny disappears around a corner.

YACOV SPENDS THREE DAYS downstairs on the floor in Max and Tessie's flat. Mr. Tepperman sleeps on the sofa, so the only place left for Yacov is on a pile of blankets on the floor of the hall. On the fourth day Yacov goes home. Sophie watches as he walks tentatively through the door, hat in his hand. They stare at one another for a long moment.

"Well ..." she says, "aren't you coming in? This is your home."

Yacov hangs his hat on its hook.

"I'll make some tea," Sophie says, turning her back to him. Sophie has no idea how to fix her broken family. She is sick with worry. Everyone has been walking on pins and needles since the night of the fighting. She has been trying to make sense of it. She knows her husband has pressures. The Depression is bad enough. Now this. Izzy will never be the same. The hospital bill will never be paid. But all the boys are suffering. Sophie tries her best to comfort them.

"It was an accident," she says over and over.

But Sonny knows it wasn't an accident. "If only we hadn't gone," Sonny repeats over and over until he makes himself sick to his stomach. *If only we had stayed home. It's all my fault. Izzy will never be the same again.* Sonny can't sleep any more. He lies awake night after night worrying. He knows his father hates him. Everyone hates him for what he did to Izzy. Maybe he should be sent away.

Sophie has no intention of sending Sonny anywhere. She blames herself. Sonny is only nine years old — too young to be looking after his little brother. She should have taken them both with her, to the shiva visit. It's all her fault. She's the mother. She barely slept herself while Yacov was gone. Her family is breaking apart. It is hatred that caused it all: the riot in the park, the Swastika Club, Nazis and Jewish boys acting like thugs. Her own sons slugging it out. Her husband turning to violence. It is hatred that is tearing her family apart. The only thing that will bring it back together, Sophie knows, is love.

Yacov sits beside her at the table, his eyes searching hers for a sign.

She reaches over, takes his hand. He bows his head, raises her hand to his lips. "I'm sorry," he whispers.

"All right," she says, pulling her hand back. "But Yacov …"

The serious tone in her voice frightens him.

"Don't you ever lay a hand on my children again," Sophie says. "Ever."

A Rich Man in America

AUGUST 20, 1933

THAT NIGHT, Yacov stays up late, alone in the dark, at the kitchen table. It is still hot as hell. He sits in his boxer shorts and undershirt by the small window, smoking, remembering. The smell of Russia, the wind, the river, wheat fields, tall stalks fluttering in the breeze, and the mud. Never will he forget the muddy streets of Tiraspol. Especially after the spring thaw. Mud on his boots, his pants, everywhere. Mud in his eyes, his mouth, the taste of it. Mud clinging to every surface. And then the dust of summer, floating through the air: grit on his skin, over his teeth, in his hair, on his clothes. His last day in Tiraspol never leaves him. Over and over, it turns in his mind. If only. If only. If only he had hidden Shmuel better. If only he'd remained behind the house with the kids. He could have protected them. Saved his little brother. If only. But what of Rachel? If he hadn't left his little brother behind the house and run to the barn, what would have happened to her? He knows what would have happened. There would have been no one to stop it. To stop the sweating bear of a man, the soldier, as he lunged at her. Would he have killed her? Or just … the other. His beautiful sister Rachel. He saved her, at least.

Over and over he replays the scene. Every day for twenty years. It's the sound that sticks with him. The horrifying clang of metal on the man's skull. It sickens Yacov. The blood on the ground by his head. Sticky. With a wet iron scent. He'd never noticed before that blood had a smell. Metal on skull. On skin. On flesh and bones. The skull cracked, like stone crushing wood. It made Yacov gag. He remembers the heavy nauseous pressure in the back of his throat. Because of this man, Yacov had to leave Russia, leave his family. He was only fifteen.

He found out later that the soldier lived, but hadn't stopped searching for Yacov, who by then was in Hamburg, waiting to get on a steerage ship and sail across the ocean to America. If he'd stayed in Tiraspol, Yacov would have ended up in jail. Or Siberia.

April 3, 1913
TIRASPOL, RUSSIA

YACOV'S BROTHER-IN-LAW, Pinchus, led him deeper into the forest. Before they had left the house, Rachel had hastily put together a half loaf of hard pumpernickel bread, some salted herring, an apple and a pear, and wrapped it in a piece of cloth that Yacov slung over one shoulder. She had filled a tin can with water that he carried. He tried to say goodbye to his mother, but she looked right through him, as if he wasn't there. She was lost somewhere, deep in her own mind. It pained Yacov; for he felt responsible for his mother's grief. It was all his fault. Everything was his fault. At the edge of their yard, his father had embraced him.

"Only God knows when we shall see each other again," his father, Avram, said sadly.

"I will become rich in America, Papa, and I will send for you. For everyone."

"Yes, my son. You shall be an important man."

"A rich man, Papa. You know what we hear about the streets of America."

"*The Goldene Medina.*" The Golden Land. Paved with gold. You only had to get there to mine the streets of their treasure.

Yacov was keeping up a brave face for his father's sake. He had no desire to go to America. He loved his family. He hated the pogroms, the pale of settlement, the Czar's edicts and the poverty his people lived in, but he was convinced that things were going to change for the better. Already a member of the *Bund*, the Jewish Worker's organization, he had planned to be part of the change. And now he was being sent away. He would not even have a chance to say goodbye to Avichail, the girl he loved. He vowed to himself that he would send for her. And soon.

Rachel could not contain her tears as she clung to her brother.

"That should be enough food for the next few days, until you get to Hamburg. Maybe I should get you another piece of bread?" Rachel did not want to see her brother go. It was her fault he was leaving. He had clubbed the soldier to save her. A mountain of guilt had begun to fester deep inside her belly.

"Hey, come on, Rachel. Don't cry. Didn't you hear what I said? I will send for all of you soon. In America I will have enough money to bring our entire *shtetel* over if I want."

Which only made Rachel cry more.

Yacov bent down and kissed the top of his baby sister Shoshana's head. She stood beside Rachel, barefoot in a light dress. It was a warm evening.

"Look." Shoshana held up a stick to show Yacov.

"Yes," he said, choking back his tears. "What a nice stick."

"A horse," Shoshana corrected.

"Oh. It's a horse?"

"Yes." Shoshana nodded emphatically.

"What a beautiful horse," Yacov agreed.

Shoshana grinned proudly.

Pinchus gently took Yacov's arm. "We should go."

Yacov bit his lip.

"May God be with you, son," Avram said, clutching his son's hand for the last time. Avram knew in his heart they would never meet again. *Please God*, Avram beseeched silently, *keep my boy safe. See him to America. And maybe in the next life, we shall meet again.*

Yacov squeezed his father's hand, looked deep into his eyes. Rachel flung herself once more into Yacov's arms, held on tightly.

"*A be gezunt,*" she whispered in his ear. *Be safe.* Then she released him, wiping her tears with a handkerchief. Yacov looked in the direction of their house one last time, wishing his mother would come out and say goodbye. Then he turned and followed Pinchus toward the forest. Avram took Rachel's hand. Rachel put Shoshana on her hip and slowly they walked back to the house. Avram silently cursed the Russian Czar, his edicts and his pogroms, that had in a single afternoon ripped apart his family. His youngest son was dead, his oldest son gone. He would never know what kind of man Yacov was going to become.

PINCHUS LEIBOWITZ KNEW his way around the forest because he had been a member of *Hashomer Hatzair*, a Zionist youth group, as a boy. Many times they had taken trips into the forest to learn how to sleep on the ground, how to light a campfire, and how to find one's way out using only a compass. He knew exactly where he was going. Pinchus had convinced Avram that Yacov must leave at once. It was too risky for him to stay. If the soldier survived he would want revenge. If he died, well, Yacov would be charged with murder. Either way, things did not look good. Yacov would end up in prison in Siberia. Or conscripted into the army for a twenty-five year term, and there he would be treated badly, sent off on the worst dangers, and be maimed or killed. Self defence would be worth little in a Russian court. The victim was a Russian soldier, Yacov was a poor Jew. His motive would be of no relevance in a Russian court. Pinchus had assured Avram that he would lead Yacov to a hiding place in the woods. Yacov would wait there in safety. In the meantime, Pinchus would hire smugglers who, for fifty-five rubles, would get Yacov out of the country, across the Dneister river into Romania. From there he would travel west and north, all the way up to the port of Hamburg, where he would buy a ticket on a steam ship and travel across the Atlantic to America. Pinchus had promised Avram to provide Yacov with the necessary funds for his journey.

Dry branches crackled under Yacov's feet as Pinchus led him away from his home. So many emotions swirled inside him, he felt twisted and pulled by the force. He was frightened and excited, pained and filled with guilt. His senses were heightened. It was dark. There was only a quarter moon waning in the sky, but Yacov could see every tree and every leaf. His hearing was acute. He heard small wildlife in the trees, squirrels, chipmunks, birds, mice. He heard his own heart pounding inside his chest.

A branch snapped a few feet away. Pinchus grabbed Yacov's wrist and wordlessly advised him to be still. Perhaps they were being followed. They stood silent, barely breathing. Then they heard the scampering of a small animal. They breathed and walked on. After two hours they stopped.

"This is the place," Pinchus announced. Yacov heard faint sounds of rushing water in the distance. "The river's another half mile that way. We will stay here for the night."

"You will stay with me?" Yacov's eyes were wide with fear and relief. Pinchus smiled, patted the younger boy reassuringly on the back.

"Yes. Tonight I will stay. But tomorrow you will stay here by yourself. I will send the smugglers here to you. But you must hide when you hear them approaching, in case it is not them. I will give one of them my hat to wear. This hat." He touches the brim of his black wool workman's cap. "That's how you will know it is them. If anyone else approaches, you must hide until they leave. It could be a trick. Don't reveal yourself unless you see my hat. This hat exactly. *Farshtaist?*"

Yacov nodded.

"Now," said Pinchus, "we will build a fire, so we don't freeze to death tonight."

The fire was a small one, just large enough to warm Yacov and Pinchus, but not so big as to create a lot of smoke. They were deep in the forest; it was unlikely anyone would see them, but they couldn't be too careful. Pinchus unrolled the blanket he'd strapped to his back, and they huddled together against a tree, under the blanket. Yacov stirred, thinking he would unpack his small store of food. Pinchus covered Yacov's hand.

"No. We will eat what I have brought. You must save your food for your journey."

Pinchus had a small loaf of black bread with some fresh chopped liver in his pack. Yacov, suddenly starving, ate quickly. Pinchus produced a bottle of red wine and they passed the bottle back and forth. Pinchus had grabbed the wine before they had set out. He figured it wouldn't hurt to settle the younger boy's nerves and even encourage him to talk a little.

They drank in silence for a while. Yacov was deep in thought. Pinchus waited. Finally, Yacov sighed deeply.

"It's my fault, isn't it? I never should have left the children alone."

"Yacov," Pinchus began gently. "No one is to blame. Except for the murderers. This was your first pogrom, no? You were too young to remember much about the 1906 riots. I remember a little. Same as today. There is not much we could have done. How were you to know what savages those men would be?"

"But the other thing. That's my fault."

"Yes, my friend, and for protecting my Rachel I shall forever be indebted to you. It would have torn me apart if anything had happened to her."

"I didn't think about it. I just did it. I couldn't stand to hear her cries."

"Yes. And you are a hero. Do you know that?"

"A hero? But Papa is ashamed of me ..."

"No. He is ashamed of his blind faith in God."

"What?"

"Your father believes in God with all his heart, no?"

"Yes."

"And this is not the first time that God has taken away one of your father's children."

"Yes."

"Think of what your father must be asking God at this moment."

"Oh ..."

"You see. He is not ashamed of you. He is proud of you, Yacov. That was a brave thing you did."

"But it's wrong to kill ..."

"The man is not dead."

"But he might die."

"You had no choice. He might have killed Rachel. And your mother."

The thought of his mother made Yacov unbearably sad. His eyes filled with tears. "I'm scared. To go so far away. I've never even left Tiraspol before."

"You are a man now. I'm sorry it had to be this way. But I have faith in you."

"I will never see any of you again. Will I?"

Pinchus passed the bottle back to Yacov. "Who knows what the future will bring?"

"Pinchus. There is something you have to do for me."

Pinchus pushed Yacov's cap down over his eyes, playfully. "I know. You want me to take a message to Avichail Glickstein."

"How did you know?" Yacov had told no one about his feelings for Avichail.

"I have seen it in your face many times, my friend."

"You have."

"I have seen the way you look at her."

"Oh."

"She is a beautiful girl."

Yacov sat up, grabbed Pinchus by the arm. "I will send for her. Once I am settled in America. I will send the money for her ticket. Do you think her father will approve?"

"Of course, Yacov," Pinchus answered, although he doubted it would ever happen. America was a long way away. Yacov was just a boy. Pinchus knew that Yacov had never so much as even spoken with Avichail. He had a long dangerous journey ahead. Who knew what the future would hold for any of them?

"We should sleep now," Pinchus told Yacov. "You will need your strength for your journey. But first there is one more thing." Pinchus put one hand inside his shirt and pulled over his head a woman's necklace, with a large red stone, a precious ruby, set in silver. He handed the necklace to Yacov. The younger man held the heavy stone in the palm of his hand and studied it. He had never seen jewelry of this quality up close before. "This belonged to my grandmother, Ziporah Leibovitz, may she rest in peace. It was given to me when she died. That stone is a ruby, a precious one. It's worth a lot of money. It was to be a wedding present to Rachel, but now, you must take it."

Yacov pushed the necklace back to Pinchus. "No. I can't take it. It's for Rachel."

Pinchus closed his hand around Yacov's. "You will need money in America. The streets may be paved with gold, but somehow I have a feeling the golden streets are restricted."

"No." Yacov tried again to give back the necklace.

Pinchus smiled. "Don't you understand, Yacov? What you did — you saved Rachel from the worst fate for a woman. You gave her the most precious gift and for that you must leave your home, a fugitive. You are a young man. You should not have to leave your family like this. Rachel knows. She wanted me to give the necklace to you. Please. Take it." Pinchus gave Yacov's hand a final shove.

Slowly Yacov opened his fist. He took the necklace and slipped it around his neck. It felt strange, the heavy stone bumping up against his chest. And he worried that it could be seen there. So, he took it back off, lowered the sock on one foot and twisted the necklace around his ankle. It went around three times. Then he knotted it securely, and pulled his sock back up to cover it. That felt safer. If he came upon thieves, his sock would be the last place they would search for valuables. Yacov slid down to a lying position and fell asleep after a few minutes.

He woke with the morning light. Pinchus was already up. Stiff and sore from sleeping on the ground, Yacov struggled to his feet.

"I will leave you now," Pinchus said sadly. "Here." He handed Yacov his small tin of water and the rest of the bread and chopped liver. "I will try and send the smugglers today." Pinchus grabbed Yacov in a bear hug and held on for a moment, then he released him and turned to leave. "May God be with you, little brother. You are brave. That alone will carry you far."

Yacov watched Pinchus walk through the trees and when he could no longer see him, he listened for the footsteps and the crack of branches as Pinchus walked further into the distance. And then it was silent. The only sounds Yacov heard were the distant rush of the river, the fluttering of birds and the wind in the trees. He sat down with his back against a tree to wait.

AT THE TABLE in his second-storey flat on Clinton Street, Yacov drinks the rest of the schnapps in his glass. When he arrived in Toronto in 1913, the first thing he discovered was that the streets were made of cobble-stones and of mud, not gold. And if there were no pogroms here, there wasn't exactly a warm welcome for a fifteen-year-old Russian Jew. Thank God his cousin Max was already here, had arrived several months before. He'd come to avoid being conscripted into the Russian army where he'd have spent a twenty-five-year term, if he lived that long. Yacov never became the shoemaker he was destined to be. He had no money for tools or to rent a shop. Max was already in the peddling business. He joined his cousin. It was supposed to have been just for a few years, until he got on his feet. Then he would set up a shoemaking shop like his father. But a few years gave way to a few more and then the Great Depression took away any chance of fulfilling his destiny. Yacov hoped his father would have understood.

There had been a few letters from Rachel after he first arrived in Canada, spaced by many months. It was hard for her to write. The paper and postage were expensive, getting a letter into town to be posted was difficult. She was vague in her letters. *Everyone is fine. Thanks for the American dollars.* Rachel said little more. She'd written only one long letter — in 1921, the year his mother died. Yacov had wept in Sophie's arms when he read the letter. The mother he had never properly said goodbye to, was dead. He'd never have the chance again to look at her face, tell her he loved her, be held in her soft embrace. He and Sophie had been married a couple of years by that time. Sid was a tiny infant. Sophie had been so good to Yacov. She never made him feel weak for crying. She held him in her arms, stroked his head, rocked him to her like a baby. In 1931, Rachel's letters had stopped. Not a word since then. Yacov thinks about his family in Russia often. Deep underneath, out of reach of his conscious mind, he knows he'll never see any of them again.

EPILOGUE

Notes on *The Biography of Sonny Lapinsky*
by Moses Nino Lapinsky, Ph.D.
CANADA DAY, JULY 1, 2003, VANCOUVER, B.C.

IN APRIL OF 1954 a cooling-fluid explosion at Ontario Hydro caused one million dollars' worth of damage. In Jerusalem, tension was mounting between Arabs and Israelis. You could buy a baby stroller with shopping bag for $8.88, while an RCA Victor 21-inch console black-and-white television in a walnut cabinet was going for $349, and electric Frigidaire refrigerators could be had for $235. Kotex was ninety-eight cents for a package of thirty, white bread was fifteen cents per loaf, one dollar could start you dancing at the Robert Morgan dance studios on Dundas Street, "Guys and Dolls" was playing at the Royal Alexandra and you could purchase a pre-fab home for $4677.

In September, at the Canadian National Exhibition, you could see the fabulous Bendix Duomatic, the only washer in the world that turned into a dryer before your very eyes. Audrey Hepburn, Humphrey Bogart and William Holden were starring in "Sabrina," James Stewart was the star of Alfred Hitchcock's "Rear Window," Marlon Brando's "On the Waterfront" was playing at the Imperial, the fabulous though closeted Rock Hudson starred with Jane Wyman in "Magnificent Obsession." "Seven Brides for Seven Brothers," the Jane Powell, Howard Keel picture, was released in blushing colour. It was a wonderful year for film. On New York's Lower East Side, Marilyn Monroe had an audience of one thousand as she rehearsed a scene from the "Seven Year Itch." The scene called for her to stand over a subway grating under which dozens of electric fans were placed to blow her skirt up. Fifteen times.

I am ending my notes in the year 1954 because I realize now that it was the second turning point in my father's life, after 1933 of course. It was the year of his reconciliation with Yacov — which had begun slowly seven years earlier, when my grandfather first started seeing me and my siblings. And now that I've sketched out my notes this far, I think I see how the pieces might fit together.

In 1954 my father was still technically the middleweight boxing champion of the world, just as his health was rapidly deteriorating. Although his body — the one thing he'd counted on his whole life — was beginning to break down, his salvation was closer at hand than ever before, just somewhere over the rainbow, if only he could find his way home. The thing that had pained him for most of his adult life was the fact that he was shunned by his own father, simply because he had married my mother. The injustice burned in my father's heart until he thought he'd explode. On good days, he silently thanked his father for his stubborn Old World attitude. In some ways, the rage had won my father many fights. He had only to think of how angry he was, how wronged he felt by his family, to find the heart to fight like a demon. That's not to say the combination of his skill, experience and conditioning wasn't responsible for his success. But a fighter has to have the heart for fighting. And my father certainly had that.

How it must have pained him to be unwelcome in his parents' home for the greater part of his adult years, while he was making something of himself. He had three children and a beautiful wife — okay, she wasn't Jewish, but it could have been worse. He could have been a thief, a bookie, a gambler, a pimp or in jail, like many of his contemporaries. He was a world champion fighter. Famous, world-renowned, professionally respected and rich. And yet he couldn't go home. He couldn't visit his own mother and father. The one thing Sonny Lapinsky wanted most in life was to make his father proud. And it didn't seem as if that was going to happen.

In many ways I regret waiting this long to write this book. If I'd thought of it sooner, I could have interviewed my grandparents, Sophie and Yacov. It would have given the book so much depth to hear their point of view. But they've both been gone for many years. I've also wanted to interview my mother for months, to get her take on my father. She's been putting it off, making excuses. Finally last week, I pinned her down. I took her out for dinner, and we spoke for hours. I taped our discussion, thank God, because there were so many fascinating details. Even at seventy-eight, her mind is sharp, her memory intact. I think I am a changed man since our talk. There were so many things about our family I did not know, had not understood before. After talking to her, probing, asking hard questions, I feel as though a veil has been lifted, and I finally understand my family, especially my father.

How I wish he had lived longer, so I might have known him as an adult and given back some of what he gave to me. What did he give me? Pride. A love of history. Love, in his own way. Honour. Dignity. Even now, as I approach old age, I have only to speak my father's name, and my listener grows excited to know that I, meek and mild history professor at a university on the West Coast, am the son of one of Canada's greatest prizefighters ever. A national treasure. A Canadian hero.

What else did he give me? A sense of family. Since my father was shunned by his own father, his love of his own family was huge. Even after the divorce, even though he stayed away those first few years, I came to know he'd do anything for me, for my sister and brother, even my mother, the woman who had sent him away. And although he had affairs off and on for the rest of his life, he remained devoted in every way to my mother and to his kids.

My father's hard experience of being disowned taught me to be true to myself. And later, to my family. I knew when I came out to them as a gay man in 1969, I risked being banished, as Sonny had been by my grandfather. Perhaps that's the main reason I wasn't cut off. I'm not saying my father enjoyed the idea that his firstborn son was, in his words, "a fruit." He was, if anything, ashamed and disappointed. But he was clear on one thing. No matter what choices his children made for their own lives, the one thing he would never do was disown them.

My father, the 1948 Middleweight World Titleholder, was a stand-up guy. To be sure, he was dysfunctional emotionally, as were most men of his generation, but what he lacked in finesse, Sonny possessed in heart.

He had more heart than most men could dream of. He had more passion in his little finger than most people have in their entire bodies. And I miss him. I miss him so much.

Some days, the pain that is being dredged up as I write this book is too much for me to bear and I think about stopping. But I can't. I am conditioning myself emotionally the way my father conditioned himself physically to withstand the punishment of the boxing ring. If he could go fifteen rounds in a ring, take fifteen rounds of physical punishment, absorb hundreds of pounds of pain into his body, I can take the same punishment into my heart. It is with pride, and grief and a son's love for his father, that I proceed with this biography. I hope it will add to Canadian literature a small chapter, a piece of our national history, one man's story: world-champion fighter and son of a Russian Jewish immigrant peddler, Sonny Shmuel Lapinsky, Middleweight Champ of the World from 1948 to 1954.

NO PLACE LIKE HOME

Attack of the Heart
MARCH 26, 1954, TORONTO

A BLOCK AWAY from Lenny's House of Bargains, Yacov can already see the line of people waiting for the store to open for the day. It's nine o'clock, a full hour before opening. Wacky Wednesdays are always like this. Crowded, with people lined up for blocks, hours before opening. It was another of Sid's brilliant ideas. Sid has a knack for giving the customers exactly what they want. The partners are making money, hand over fist. Sid figures if they give the customers the "deal of a century," they'll buy anything. Whether they need it or not. Once you get them in the store and keep them happy, they'll buy more. They'll spend every cent they saved on the sale item and still go home thrilled with their purchases. Sid insisted on installing a phonographic sound system in the store, with loudspeakers mounted high on the walls. They play hit tunes, but only happy songs. People buy more when they're happy, Sid figures. He personally shops for the records. Yacov and Max didn't see the point in wasting money on music. What's that got to do with selling? But Sid argued until they finally gave in. Later, they had to admit he was right.

On Wacky Wednesdays from ten until noon, when certain items are marked at half price, people line up at seven in the morning, just to be first inside.

Yacov walks past the queue of people and enters through the back. He removes his hat and smoothes back what's left of his hair, which has thinned out considerably over the years. The lights are on. Sid must be in the back. Yacov loves walking down the aisles when they're empty of customers first thing in the morning, just to look out over their accomplishment. He never did become a shoemaker, but Yacov is pretty sure his father would have been proud of him just the same. When they started the store in 1946, it was one storefront, but they did so well that every time a store beside them went under, they rented that space, knocked down the walls and expanded. Now, Lenny's House of Bargains stretches an entire city block and encompasses two and a half floors. In the back is a large warehouse with three loading docks, where they stack the merchandise as it comes in, and prepare it for display.

Sid is at the loading-dock desk, poring over the daily delivery schedule. Sid's hair hasn't receded much, but his temples are now flecked with grey, giving him a distinguished, mature look. He glances up, sees his father.

"We filled out the application," Sid tells Yacov, solemnly.

"Good. So, how long will it take?" He looks over Sid's shoulder at the schedule.

"Who knows? They're sending a social worker to check up on us."

"What for?"

"I guess they want to see if we have a nice home before they'll let us adopt a baby."

"Course you have a nice home."

"I guess they have to check. It doesn't matter. But Ruthie is nervous."

"It's gonna be fine. Maybe you want your mother and I should be there for the visit?"

"I don't think so. But thanks, Pa." Sid and Ruthie are nervous enough about saying the right thing in front of the government social worker. The last thing they need is for Yacov to be there and blurt out something about Sonny or Izzy. Sid doesn't think the social worker would like to know that their father doesn't speak to one of his sons, or that Sid's youngest brother was brain-damaged years ago, because he took part in the Christie Pits riot. Sid just hopes it's not already on his record, maybe from Izzy's medical records. If this doesn't work out, Sid is worried Ruthie's going to have a nervous breakdown. She keeps it all inside.

Puts up a brave front. Helps Loretta with her children. But Sid knows his Ruthie is slowly dying inside.

A truck rumbles as it backs into loading bay one. Sid opens the heavy garage door and they wait for the driver to hop up onto the dock with the paperwork. It's a shipment of cookbooks. This was Sid's idea. Cookbooks are all the rage. There's a huge market in household items. Since the end of the war, most women have given up their jobs, gone back inside their homes and are taking care of husbands and children. So many women just want to be good housewives these days. Having the best recipe on the block is a symbol of status. He figures the cookbooks will go like hotcakes.

Nick, one of the stockroom boys, rushes over to unload the heavy cartons of books onto a wooden skid. The foreman, Pauly, an older man who has worked at the store since 1947, hustles Sid to the other end of the warehouse. There's been a mix-up. A row of boxes marked "ladies' slips" actually contains boxer shorts. They have double the amount of boxers and no slips. He's not sure if they should send the shorts back or mark them down and sell them off quickly. Sid wants to see the purchase order. Yacov hears their footsteps recede in the distance as they head for the opposite end of the warehouse. When he's sure they're at the far end, he steals a cigarette from Sid's pack, tossed haphazardly on the order desk. He lights it, inhales deeply with great satisfaction, then wanders over to help Nick unload the truck.

Nick stops, looks at Yacov warily. "Uh … Mr. Lapinsky, Sid says I'm not supposed to let you do that."

Yacov smiles, amused. Ever since Dr. Grossman diagnosed Yacov with high blood pressure the whole family's gone crazy. Sophie won't let him eat cheese or fried food, he's not supposed to smoke — he has to sneak cigarettes when no one's looking — Max looks at him with pity, and Sid won't let him help in the warehouse. Yacov has always been physically fit. He enjoys helping the stock boys unload the trucks once in a while, to keep in shape. And he's not about to stop now.

"Sid shmid. Move over. We have to get these onto the floor before we open."

"Pauly can help me." Nick's been given express orders from Sid.

Under no circumstances is he to accept help from Yacov.

"Move." Yacov grabs a carton, sets it on the skid, the cigarette dangling from his lips.

Nick doesn't like the looks of this, but what's he going to do? Yacov is his boss also.

Yacov grabs another box of books. No problem. It's the third box that gets him. It happens suddenly: a sharp pain in his chest. The left side. His arm goes numb. The box slides, thudding against the wooden skid. Nick rushes over in time to catch Yacov before he hits the concrete floor.

"Sid!" Nick's cry echoes across the cavernous room.

THE ADMITTING DOCTOR says it was a mild heart attack. By the time Yacov's ambulance reached the hospital he was in stable condition. They're keeping him for a few days, under observation. He's resting comfortably, an IV in his arm to keep him hydrated. Every hour the nurse takes his temperature, listens to his heart with a stethoscope, checks his blood pressure, peers into his eyes. It's annoying. Yacov just wants to go home. Sophie sits on the chair by his bedside. Still beautiful, her face has taken on a softer look as she's aged. Her hair was streaked with grey, but Tessie finally talked her into having it touched up at the salon, so now it's back to her natural deep brown. Izzy, a grown man of twenty-six now, though still with the mental capacity of a five-year-old, has already made friends with the head nurse, who allows him to listen to his father's heart through her stethoscope. Sid paces the small floor of the room.

"It's my fault. I should have unloaded the truck," he tells Sophie.

"What are you talking? You have stock boys. Let them do it." Sophie won't let Sid shoulder this one.

"I should have been back there supervising."

"I'm not an invalid," Yacov reminds them.

"You're not supposed to lift." Sophie is angry. What if he'd died?

"Stop pestering me." Yacov sulks.

"You shouldn't be smoking. Dr. Grossman said," Sophie continues.

"Who said I was smoking?" Yacov glares at Sid, who bobs his head to one side and instinctively glances toward the door when he recognizes the crisp click of Ruthie's heels marching down the hospital corridor. She sweeps into the room, efficient in her skirt and blazer, her work clothes.

"Oh my God," she says at the sight of her father-in-law, lying in bed, pale and thin with tubes in his arm. Yacov has never been sick a day in his life, that she can remember.

"I'm not dead yet," Yacov reports.

"I came as soon as I could get away. You know how crazy Wacky Wednesdays can be."

"I'm fine. I'm going home soon."

"What are you talking?" Sophie reproaches. "You're staying put. Doctor's orders."

"Acch." Yacov waves his hand at his wife. He just wants to get out of bed and back to work. Yacov has never had a sick day in his life. The admitting doctor was amazed when he asked Yacov when he'd last been in hospital. Yacov had to think about it.

"Nineteen twenty-eight," he said. "I dropped a metal ashtray on my toe. It was broken. They put a bandage on it and I went back to work."

Ruthie stands by Sid and takes his arm, to make him stop pacing. They exchange meaningful looks.

"I dropped it off," Sid tells his wife. "Did they phone yet?"

"No. Maybe we should paint, fix the place up a little before they come," Ruthie suggests.

"It's fine. I think they're more worried about us than the paint."

"Who?" Sophie buts in.

"The adoption agency."

"So you're going ahead?"

Sid nods. How can he be so happy and sad at the same time?

It was Ruthie's idea to adopt. Her empty arms ache for a baby. She is already thirty-five. Soon she'll be too old for children. Like Sid, her hair is now speckled with grey. She refuses to let the hairdresser touch it up, even though Tessie keeps at her to give it a try. Ruthie flat-out refuses. "What am I? A movie star? Who needs it?"

"Did you tell them the other?" Ruthie asks Sid.

He shrugs.

"Tell us what?" Sophie asks.

Sid looks uncomfortable.

Yacov eyes his son.

"Loretta's gonna file for divorce. She's hired a lawyer. The papers are drawn up. I told her to wait until after Sonny's title bout next week. So it wouldn't make him lose."

Yacov looks away.

"Oh God," says Sophie. "I thought it might come to this. How's your brother? He doesn't know yet?"

"Nurse!" Yacov yells.

"What are you doing?" Sophie asks.

"I'm asking the nurse to get rid of my visitors. They're not good for my weak heart."

"Sonny's not doing so good," Sid continues, despite his father.

"Do I have to listen to this?" Yacov turns to the window. A new pain bubbles up in his heart. Not the physical kind. The other kind. The old wound that's been his constant companion, that has never properly healed. That can split wide open at the mere mention of Sonny's name. It gnaws at him tenaciously.

"Sonny's sick." Sid doesn't want to upset his parents, but he figures they need to know. Might as well get it all out into the open now.

"What?" Sophie's hand instinctively reaches for her heart.

"Loretta says he has dizzy spells. He fainted even, one day," Sid continues. "All the years of getting punched in the head, I guess."

Even Yacov stops to listen now. How could Sonny be sick? He's always been young, strong and virile. He's knocked out some of the toughest, strongest men in the world. It's unthinkable to picture him frail or weak. Yacov turns to the wall as the old pain intensifies. It's the guilt he's harboured since he was a boy, the guilt that has nothing to do with Sonny. Nothing and everything. He thinks of his brother, Shmuel. Yacov can almost smell the dusty dirt roads of the town where he was born. Sid's voice melts into the background.

April 1, 1913
TIRASPOL, RUSSIA

IT WAS THE MORNING of Rachel's wedding. The whole family was up with the sun, preparing the house and yard for the evening celebration. It was an arranged marriage, but with God's blessing and no small miracle, the young man and the young woman were deeply in love. The agreement was informal in a way, because the bridegroom's father, Mendel Leibowitz, who was the village butcher, happened to have been friends since boyhood with the bride's father, Avram Lapinsky. And so it gave no small pleasure to both the father of the bride and of the groom that after the nuptials they would, technically, be relatives. Of course, the father of the bride was only slightly ecstatic that his daughter had the good sense to fall in love with Pinchus, who at the age of eighteen already worked in his father's butcher shop and would eventually take over the business. With times being as hard as they were, at least Avram was sure his daughter would never starve.

Fifteen-year-old Yacov Lapinsky lowered a wooden bucket into the river. His mother and his sister Rachel were scrubbing every surface of their thatched-roof one-room, dirt-floor house, and he had been sent to fetch more water. Yacov hauled his full bucket out of the river, plunked it on the bank and sat by the edge for a moment to think. He removed his cap and wiped sweat from his forehead with the back of his sleeve. He stroked his face, sure that a few more hairs had grown on his chin during the night. He was happy for his sister Rachel and excited about the celebration they would have later that day, but he also had other things on his mind. Almost sixteen, he was no longer a boy. He was an apprentice in his father's shoe-making shop. As the oldest son, one day Yacov would take his father's place as the village shoemaker, but he would not follow his father's footsteps in every way. He'd already decided to trim his beard in the modern Russian style — that is, when he had a beard — rather than let it grow, as was the Jewish custom. He'd been raised in traditional Orthodox ways, but Yacov was the newest member of a local chapter of the Bund. Only two weeks ago, his best friend, Dovid, had taken him to his first meeting. Yacov was swept away with enthusiasm. The older men in the group were talking in ways Yacov had never heard anyone speak before. Yacov's father was a religious, observant man.

"If it is God's will, then so be it," was Avram's answer for everything. "We must follow our traditions and get along the best we can," he would reason.

The men in the Bund had a very different approach, which was music to Yacov's ears.

"The Jewish working man must fight back," his new comrades informed Yacov, over endless glasses of strong, hot tea they'd drink over sugar cubes gripped between their teeth. "Religion is counter-revolutionary."

"If we wait for God to make things better, we'll be waiting a long time." They'd pound their fists on the dusty worktable in the back of Gershon Walensky's bookbinding shop.

The Bund was going to change things for the Jews in Russia. No longer would people stand by in poverty and fear. The Bund would work together and change would come. Yacov was delirious at the prospect. He was willing to do anything for the Bund. He went to meetings twice a week. He helped distribute the Bund's newsletter, he listened intently as the other boys and men argued politics, and he soaked up everything. All day long, as he glued soles onto boots and repaired holes in leather, Yacov thought about the Bund's ideals. He never said a word to his father about his new passion. He knew Avram would not approve. Avram was from the old school of Jews who had lived under the restrictive thumb of Czarist Russia for so long, they saw no alternative. Their faith in God was their solace. They lived for the Sabbath, the one day of the week when they would dress in good clothes and eat a special meal with their families. They lived for Saturday mornings, when they would gather in the synagogue to pray.

Yacov was a respectful son. Though he no longer believed that man should trust in God's will alone, he continued to accompany his father to the synagogue every Saturday. He played the part of the dutiful son, but his heart was not in it. As he sat beside his father in the small, shabby, one room synagogue, his mind raced with the new ideas he was learning. This was the beginning of the twentieth century. Great change was on the horizon. And Yacov knew he would be part of it all.

He knew exactly how his life would unfold. He would work alongside his father and eventually take over the shop. He would work with the Bund to improve the lot of his people, and he would marry Avichail Glickstein, the most beautiful girl in the village. Her father, Yitzchak, was a watchmaker, and a good one. The only trouble was, times being as hard as they were, for most of the villagers, if a watch was broken it stayed that way. Food on the table was hard enough come by. You could always look at the sun to figure out the time. Being the son of the only shoemaker in town, Yacov could have had almost any girl in the village — he didn't have to even look at a girl from a poor family — but Yacov was smitten with Avichail. She did not know about Yacov's feelings. He had never even spoken to her. Not yet. But in two years, when his apprenticeship was over, and he was a shoemaker proper, Yacov would ask Yitzchak Glickstein for his daughter's hand in marriage.

"Yacov, where's the water already? We've been waiting." Rachel lifted the edge of her skirt and bent down by the side of the river to peer into her brother's handsome face.

"What did you say? Water you want? I'll give you water." Yacov dipped his hand into the river and splashed his sister.

"Hey!"

Yacov sprang to his feet, threw his cap back on his head and raced toward the house with the bucket of water. Rachel chased him for a few feet, then she remembered it was her wedding day and she could no longer act like a girl. She was a woman now. She slowed her pace and walked in a dignified manner toward the house.

Her mother, Bayla, poked her head out the door. She looked tired already, and the day was going to be long. Bayla was only thirty-two, but she was the mother of four children, and hard times and hard work had aged her. Although she was still a beautiful woman, the lines on her forehead were deep. Her curly brown hair was streaked with grey. And the dark shadows under her eyes grew more pronounced with each passing day.

"So *nu*? Rachel, should I clean all by myself? Or maybe the bride can give her old mother a hand for a couple of minutes?"

"Yes, Mama. Here I am."

Inside the house, three-year-old Shoshana was sitting on the floor playing with a small piece of wood, which to her was a horse and rider. She could see the soldier sitting on top of the massive animal, as together they galloped from one end of the forest to the other. Shoshana made galloping sounds with her tongue, then giggled because it was a spectacular sight.

"Shoshana, you can't play here. We have to sweep the floor. Shmuel!" hollered Bayla. "Where is that boy?"

"Shmuel!" Rachel yelled, as she poked her head out the front door, looking for her little brother. "Yacov, go and find him. Mama asked him to watch Shoshana. Then come back and move the table and chairs outside. We have so much to do, and it's almost lunchtime already. Hurry."

"I'm going. Don't worry so much. You'll get lines on your forehead and who'll marry you then?"

"Mama!" Rachel yelled.

"Yacov, please. It's your sister's wedding day. It's not a day for teasing." Bayla pushed back the faded curtain that separated the family's sleeping area from their cooking and eating area.

Yacov shrugged, then went back outside in search of Shmuel. He knew exactly where to look. Shmuel was only five years old, but he was strong and agile. There was an ancient apple tree behind the house. Shmuel loved to climb the tree and sit perched in the highest branch, looking down at the world from this height. Yacov walked directly to the tree and looked up. Just behind a thick bunch of leaves, he could see his brother's thin legs swinging back and forth, the laces on his boots slapping against the leaves. Shmuel was small for his age, but his eyes were sad and wise, like those of someone much older. He was a serious child, prone to bouts of sadness, as if he alone were responsible for the world. Yacov smiled, then reached up for a thick branch and pulled himself up to it, so he was sitting in the tree, beneath his brother.

"Mama's looking for you."

Shmuel sighed. "I know."

"You're supposed to watch Shoshana while we get the house ready."

"I know."

"So, what are you doing up here then?"

Shmuel shrugged. Yacov studied his face. Shmuel was frowning.

"Are you sad?" Yacov tried.

Shmuel shrugged again. Narrowed his eyes. He hated that his brother could always tell what he was feeling.

"Is it because of Rachel?"

Shmuel's lower lip began to tremble. His eyes filled with tears. Yacov waited.

"We're never going to see her again!" Shmuel wailed.

"What? Who told you that?"

"Rachel."

"She did? What did she say?"

"She's going to live with Pinchus now. She's not going to live with us any more."

"So?"

"So we're never going to see her again."

Yacov suppressed a laugh. "Shmu … Pinchus's family live right here in Tiraspol. Remember? We see Pinchus all the time. At *shul*. At market. Just passing by. Right?"

Shmuel frowned.

"So, we'll see Rachel too. You'll see. They'll come for *Shabbes* dinner. And we can go and visit her in her new house."

"We can?"

"Sure."

Shmuel thought about it.

"So, come on. Let's get down. Mama needs your help." Yacov reached for his brother. Shmuel took his hand, turned backward and lowered himself down to Yacov's branch. Yacov leaped to the ground, held out his

arms, and giggling, Shmuel jumped into them. Yacov put him down and
took his brother's small hand in his. Together they ran back to the house.

AT HIS SHOP IN TOWN, Avram Lapinksy sat hunched over his sewing
table, daydreaming. He held two edges of a pair of boots between his
thumb and forefinger, waiting for the glue to bond. Avram's fingers were
stained with remnants of black polish and glue, years of working with
leather etched into the creases of his hands. It was his eldest daughter's
wedding day, and there was much to do at home, but Avram could not
afford to take a whole day off. He would leave a little early to go home and
help. Perhaps an hour before the wedding. In the meantime, there were
shoes to repair. Bayla had asked him to leave Yacov at home today to help
her and although Avram didn't exactly agree with her request, he obliged.
There were tables and chairs to be moved, buckets of water to fetch. He
supposed it wouldn't do for Rachel to be schlepping furniture on her own
wedding day. She was a woman now, about to become a wife. Avram
couldn't believe his first child was already getting married. It seemed like
only yesterday she was a tiny baby in Bayla's arms. Then, one after the other,
the younger children had arrived. Yacov. Eliezer, may he rest in peace, who
died at one year from consumption. Miriam, may she rest in peace, who
was murdered by the miserable Cossacks in the pogrom of 1906. Shmuel
and little Shoshana.

   Whenever Avram thought of baby Miriam, who had been torn from
Bayla's arms by a man on horseback, he felt a rage that threatened to blow
him apart from the inside out. His hands would tremble, and he would
have to stop his work and recite a prayer to God, for only He knew what
was best. It was a tragedy, but Avram knew it was God's will, and it was
not man's place to question God's will. Avram would sway back and
forth, stroke his long, scraggly beard, and recite his silent prayers until his
stomach settled and his hands stopped quivering. Then he would pick
up his needle and get back to work. He had, after all, four living children
and a wife to feed. A man could not quit working because two children
had died. Everyone in their village had lost someone at some time to the

hoodlums and thieves in the pogroms of late. They would do as they always had done. Somehow, with the help of God, they would survive.

As the first rumble of horse hooves sounded in the village centre, Avram was so immersed in his daydream that he mistook the sound for the beginnings of a thunderstorm.

Oh no, he thought to himself. Rain for Rachel's wedding. Not good. Not enough room for all the guests inside our tiny house. Bayla was planning to hold the celebration in the yard. He pictured his wife, her forehead tight with worry at the prospect of rain. It took a few more minutes for Avram to notice that the rumbling was coming from beneath his feet, not above his head. What was this?

By the time he realized it was horses, they were already clamouring down the centre of town, rushing past his window. He flung himself down on the shop floor, just as the window was smashed with a heavy wood plank by a man on horseback. Tiny shards of glass rained down on Avram as he lay on the wooden floor, hands shielding his head.

The rumbling faded. He could hear shouts, glass being shattered, laughter, screams. He should try and leave. Sneak out the back, make his way home. He raised his head and slowly crawled to the broken window to peer out. The men were riding on, smashing shop windows with sticks and rocks. There was only one door in the front of Avram's narrow shop. In the back, just a small window. Perhaps he could climb out the back way. His horse and wagon were in front, though. How could he get around to them without being seen? He could run home, but that would take a long time, and he would be more vulnerable on foot. He decided to risk it. Anything would be better than cowering here on the floor.

Quickly, he raised the back window and stuck his head out to check. Too late. The men were returning, speeding down the back alley. He pulled his head inside and ducked under his worktable, just as a flaming torch flew in through the open window. It landed on a pile of kindling by the wood stove, which immediately began to burn. He could smell kerosene on the torch, fuelling the fire. Avram had no water to douse the flames. He crept over, careful to stay low, then pulled off his jacket and beat at the fire. It grew stronger, smoke wafting into his face, burning his eyes, his throat. Avram stood to his full height and pounded his coat at the fire as if it were his enemy, a stand-in for the thieves outside. Over and over he whipped at the flames, until he was dripping in sweat and his arms ached. Only then did he stop, breathing heavily, leaning his hands on his knees, panting for breath. The fire was mostly out, smouldering. He wanted to laugh with relief. But he dared not.

Avram stood still for a moment, listening. It was quiet. He crept over to the back window and looked out. His neighbour, Simcha the baker, was on all fours outside his bakery, vomiting. There was no sign of the Cossacks. Avram ran to the front of the shop and peered out a crack in the door. All was quiet. Avram's horse Anya stood hitched to her wagon, unhurt. Silently, he thanked God for sparing his precious horse. She glanced over, saw him and tipped back her head. She whinnied loudly.

"Shhh," Avram whispered. Anya, who sometimes seemed more human than animal, quieted down. "Shhh, it's okay, girl." He opened the door and cautiously stepped outside. At the far end of town, he could see dust from the horses as the men rode away. He rushed around the back of the shop to Simcha and bent down beside him, placed a gentle hand on Simcha's back. Simcha lurched and whipped his head around in terror.

"Simcha. It's okay. It's just me. Come, can you stand?" Avram slung one of Simcha's arms over his shoulder and helped his friend to his feet. There was blood trickling from the corner of Simcha's mouth. He groaned and clutched his belly, as Avram lifted him.

"Come." Avram supported Simcha's weight and helped him onto the bench outside his shop. Glancing in the bakery window, Avram noticed that the place was a wreck. The wooden shelves had been smashed to the floor. Bread and baked goods were strewn all over the shop. Storage bins had been tipped over. Piles of flour were on every surface and white dust swirled in the air. All the bakery windows had been shattered. Avram could see little bits of glass mixed in with the flour.

Simcha was crying. Tears streamed down his face, mixing with the blood on his chin. "Beasts. Criminals."

"It's okay, Simcha, save your breath. We all know what kind of men they are. Are you hurt badly? Maybe you want I should help you over to see Shayna the midwife. Maybe she'll patch you up with herbs and poultice?" Simcha waved his arm down. "Never mind. I'll just rest here. Do you think they'll be back?" He reached inside his pocket for a handkerchief and wiped at his face.

For the first time Avram considered the direction in which the raiders had gone. They were on their way to the village. Where Avram's family was at home preparing for Rachel's wedding. "Oh my God!" He leaped up from the bench. "Simcha. They're headed for the village. Our families. Come. I have my wagon. By some miracle, they spared my horse. Come, I'll help you." Avram placed a protective arm around Simcha and they hobbled to the wagon.

INSIDE THE HOUSE, Bayla began dragging the heavy wooden table toward the door by herself. Dust rose from the floor. Where was Yacov already with Shmuel? Her youngest son was always running off somewhere on his own. But today of all days? When there was so much to do?

"Mama! What are you doing?" Rachel asked from the doorway. "Leave it. Yacov will move it."

"*Nu*? If your brother was here already, I wouldn't have to move it myself." Bayla sat on one of the kitchen chairs and mopped her brow with the dust rag in her hand.

Rachel flopped down onto the chair beside her mother, grinning ridiculously. She was deliriously happy. This was the most exciting day of her life. She was becoming a woman. She was marrying Pinchus, the boy she had loved since childhood. And yet, she was intensely nervous about the wedding night. As was the Orthodox tradition, she and Pinchus had not even touched hands, let alone kissed. Her mother hadn't told her much about what would go on between a man and a woman.

"When the time comes, you'll know what to do," was all Bayla would say. Maybe she should have better prepared her daughter, but the whole thing embarrassed Bayla. She didn't know how to talk about it. Her mother hadn't told her a thing either. It was up to the man anyway, to take the lead. Bayla liked Pinchus, had known the boy his whole life. She was sure he would be gentle with her daughter. Who knew what young people these days knew anyway? Probably a lot more than she had on her wedding day. Hers was a traditional, arranged marriage. She and Avram were married when she was twelve and he was fourteen. She moved in with Avram's parents, but they did not consummate their marriage until two more years had passed. Rachel was born nine months later, when Bayla was only fifteen herself. She remembered the wonder she had felt holding her tiny baby in her arms that first year. How could it be that Rachel was already grown up and getting married? Where had the time gone?

Shmuel and Yacov were giggling about something as they entered the house.

Bayla sprang to her feet. "There you are. Shmuel, take Shoshana outside and watch her. Hurry up. No wandering off now. We have so much to do. Yacov, you'll help me with the furniture."

Shmuel dutifully took Shoshana's hand and led her outside. Yacov grasped the sides of the table and lifted it.

"Go. Take it out, and the chairs too. We have to sweep the dirt off this floor."

Yacov was halfway through the doorway when the ground began to shake. He almost lost his grip on the table as he struggled forward. He placed the table down in the yard and looked up. About a mile down the dirt road, he could see a cloud of dust rising to the sky. He listened. Horses.

Terror shot through Yacov, freezing him to his spot. Horses stampeding so furiously could only mean one thing. Pogrom.

"Mama!" he yelled.

Bayla and Rachel were beside him instantly. Bayla's eyes were huge.

"Quickly, get the children," she said to Yacov.

He scanned the yard. Where had those kids gone? Yacov began to search, furiously.

"We should hide in the barn," Bayla said. Behind their house was a small rickety shed they called the barn. Avram kept Anya there and bales of hay.

"My wedding," Rachel whimpered.

"Come," Bayla grabbed her daughter's wrist. "Yacov, find the children and meet us in the barn." Bayla dragged Rachel across the yard.

Yacov ran toward the forest. Had the kids gone there? The thundering grew louder. He checked in the direction of the sound. A huge cloud of dust hung over the horizon. There were many men on the way. A knot of fear twisted in Yacov's belly. There had been no pogroms for several years. He didn't remember much about the last one, but he remembered the fear. And he'd heard the stories. He had heard about his infant sister Miriam, who had been snatched from his mother's terrified arms. Two men on horseback rode off with her, laughing. His father had tried to chase them, but it was no use. Her body was found by the river two days later. God only knows what they had done to her.

Where were the kids? Then he remembered: Shmuel's tree. Yacov ran frantically in that direction. The thunder of hooves reverberated from the ground into the soles of his feet, and up through his body. Adrenalin coursed through Yacov. As he approached Shmuel's tree, the first soldiers came around the bend. On the ground sat little Shoshana, still engrossed in her piece of wood. Up on a high branch perched Shmuel.

"Hey, Shmu," Yacov called up. "Come down right now."

"It's okay, Yacov. I'm not sad any more. We're just playing."

Yacov began to climb toward his brother. "Look, you have to come down right now." He didn't want to alarm Shmuel. "Mama wants you. Come on." He reached out one hand. Shmuel could sense the seriousness in his brother's voice. Reluctantly, he began to climb down. Once Shmuel was in reach, Yacov took him around the waist and pulled him. On the ground, Yacov scooped up Shoshana and began to run with the kids toward the barn. He could see soldiers approaching.

Running as fast as he could, Yacov swung around to the back of the house. There wasn't time to run across the small yard to the barn with the kids. They'd be seen. He'd have to hide them behind the house. With any luck the soldiers wouldn't come around to the back. What was there? Nothing but a broken chair and dust. He figured they'd search in the house for valuables, or food even. He had heard about other pogroms where thievery wasn't even on the invaders' minds. They would wreck prayer books, dishes, candlesticks, anything they got their murderous hands on.

He could hear a few horses in the front yard, and voices. Frantic to shelter the kids, Yacov stuffed Shoshana into an empty milk barrel.

"Shoshana. We're playing a special game," he whispered.

The little girl smiled and looked up at her big brother. So much trust.

"You hide in here until I tell you to come out. Okay?"

Shoshana nodded.

"Good. And be very quiet. Okay? It's a game. No matter what, you have to be as quiet as a mouse. And don't come out until I say. Got it?"

Shoshana's big eyes were huge with excitement.

Yacov put the lid in place, and even though he was no longer a believer, he said a small prayer to God to protect his little sister. He could hear the clip clip of hooves on the hard-packed earth and men's voices coming from the front of the house. He searched for somewhere to hide Shmuel.

"Crouch down here," he said, pointing to the side of the house behind the broken chair. Shmuel hesitated. Opened his mouth to speak. "Shhh," Yacov said, "Come on." He gently pushed Shmuel down to a kneeling position and covered him up with the feather bed his mother had been airing out. It wasn't the greatest hiding place, but he was desperate. "Did you hear what I told Shoshana?" he whispered.

"Yes." A tiny voice.

"Good. Stay there, until I tell you to come out. Okay?"

"Yes."

"And don't move."

There was a loud sound from the front yard. Wood breaking. Probably the table being bashed. Yacov's heart lurched. He hated leaving the kids alone, but he had to make sure his mother and Rachel were safe. If the kids stayed perfectly quiet, they'd be okay, he reasoned. It sounded like only a few men had stopped in their yard. Yacov paused at the corner of the house, near Shmuel's hiding place, flattened his body against the wall. He carefully peered out. He could see a long line of men on horses continuing to the next house, deeper into the village. This was his chance to check on Mama and Rachel. Another crash, from inside this time, and laughter. Rage coursed through Yacov's body. He took a deep breath and made a break for it. Ran full speed to the barn. As he approached, he heard screams. Rachel.

FROM UNDER THE feather bed Shmuel could hear a big racket. Dishes being smashed. Furniture being overturned. Then he heard loud voices. Men speaking in Russian. He understood only part of what they were saying. He heard them laughing. Shouting.

"Dirty Zhids. Where are they?" the men said.

Who were these men? Were they friends of Yacov's? Was this really just a game? Maybe it was Pinchus and Yacov playing a trick on him. He heard footsteps on the ground, getting closer. And a horse. The voices were right beside him. Should he leap out and surprise them? If it was Pinchus and Yacov, it would make them laugh. But it didn't sound like his brother. It didn't sound like anyone he knew. Shmuel decided to wait quietly until he knew for sure that Yacov was back. The men speaking in Russian were really loud now. Shmuel was getting scared. His family didn't know any Russian men. Who could they be? It was getting hot under the blanket. With his face on the ground, he could smell the mustiness of the earth. The air in his hiding place was already stale. It was hard to breathe. His knees were getting sore from kneeling on the ground. Shmuel shifted his legs slightly.

"Hey! What's that?" he heard one of the men say. "Look! It's moving."

Another man laughed. "Hah! Must be a stinking Zhid."

Suddenly fresh air enveloped Shmuel. Someone had pulled the feather bed off of him. He sat crouched in the dirt, exposed. Big men stared at him. One was standing. The other was on horseback. The man cleared his throat and spat on the ground.

"Look at that. A boy. Damn Zhids. What'd they do? Leave the child all by himself? Cowards."

Shmuel stared at his hands and pushed up against the house as tight as he could. Maybe if he didn't look up, they wouldn't see him. He was trembling. The men sounded so angry. He wished Yacov would come back.

From inside the barrel, Shoshana waited. She was a patient, observant child. Yacov had told her to stay put and be very quiet. And so she would do just that. There was a small hole in the barrel that was right at her eye level, and with her face pressed up against it, she could see out.

A big man she did not know had pulled the feather bed off Shmuel. He was kneeling on the ground like a little dog. He looked kind of funny. Shoshana wanted to giggle, but then she remembered what Yacov had said, and so she covered her mouth with her hand and laughed silently. Sometimes Papa brought home men from the village to eat *Shabbes* dinner with them. Shoshana knew it was a big day for Rachel. She didn't understand what the day was. But everyone said that a lot of people were coming over later. This must be them. Shoshana hoped Yacov would come back soon and let her out. She wanted to show her big brother her horse-and-rider stick. Through the hole in her barrel, Shoshana saw the man pick up Shmuel and hold him high in the air. The man laughed at him. Loudly. Shmuel began to cry. Shoshana didn't like this game any more. But she was too scared to do anything except wait. The man tossed Shmuel up to the other man on the horse, who caught him, laughed and threw him back. They pitched the boy back and forth many times. Hard. Over and over, as if he were a sack of grain. The first few times, he whimpered. Then he became eerily silent, tears streaming down his face. The rider kicked the sides of his horse and began circling the yard. He had Shmuel under one arm, dangling him over the side of the horse. The rider picked up speed, rode by and tossed Shmuel to the other man, who thrust out his arms to catch him, but misjudged by a few inches. Shmuel plunged to the ground headfirst. Shoshana watched her brother fall. She heard a horrible cracking sound. Then silence. Shmuel wasn't crying any more. He wasn't doing anything. Just lying on his back, like a sad, broken doll. His eyes were open, so Shoshana decided Shmuel was playing a funny trick. The men stared at him for a moment. The one on the horse climbed down and stood beside his friend, who kicked Shmuel in the stomach. Shmuel didn't move.

"You killed him, stupid."

"Nah, he passed out."

"No." The big man bent down and put his hand on Shmuel's throat. "I'm telling you. You killed the kid. Broke his damn neck."

"So? They shouldn't have left a little boy all by himself. No telling what can happen to children left alone. Come on. Let's look for their hidden gold."

"What gold? You think they'd leave it here if they had any? Let's go on. Find some women. Know what I mean?"

"Yeah. Okay." They laughed loudly.

Through all this talk that Shoshana couldn't understand, she kept her eyes on her brother. Boy, was he ever smart. Pretending to be asleep so the men would stop hurting him. Why didn't he close his eyes, though? He was so quiet. So still. Shoshana had never seen a person be so motionless before. It frightened her to her core. Terror sped through her little body. Shoshana squeezed her eyes shut to make it all go away. She wrapped her arms around herself, and rocked slowly and quietly back and forth inside the barrel, breathing hard and fast, in and out, through her nose.

AT THE BARN, Yacov crept inside and crouched behind a bale of hay as his eyes adjusted to the dark. He could see his mother lying on her back, on the ground, moaning softly. A small trickle of blood was running from her nose, which was bent to one side, broken. Yacov's heart pounded with fury. There was one man inside the barn. He was struggling with Rachel. He pushed her down on the ground and was mauling her body, trying to rip off her clothes. Rachel bit his arm. The man struck her across the face.

"Dirty Zhid! Think you're too good for me, huh?" He tore her skirt off. She struggled underneath him. He brought her hands together over her head, held them down with one hand as he fumbled with the buttons of his trousers.

"No, please …" Rachel begged.

"What's the matter? You're not a virgin, are you?" The man laughed in delight. Then leaned forward and placed his lips on Rachel's.

Rachel writhed and twisted, trying to pull free. She turned her face to one side to get away from his lips, then she spat in his face.

"Hey. What'd you do that for." He struck her again across the face. Hard. Ripped the front of her blouse. Grabbed at her breasts, roughly.

Holding her wrists together tightly, he slid his trousers to his knees and climbed on top of her, grunting.

"No," she pleaded.

Yacov wanted to tear the man apart. Sweat rolled down his back. He clenched his fists at his sides. The man wasn't looking in his direction, but he was ten years older, five inches taller and at least thirty pounds heavier than Yacov. What could Yacov do? He had to do something. Rachel's cries echoed through his heart. He scanned the dark barn. Nothing but hay. Then he saw it. The rusty metal spade. Leaning up against the wall in the far corner. He had to get to it. He raised himself up and peered over the top of the hay he was hiding behind. If the man opened his eyes he would see Yacov. But he was busy slobbering on Rachel and ripping at her undergarments.

"Please…" she begged again.

Vibrating with fear, Yacov crept to the other side of the barn, snatched the spade and silently slithered back over to Rachel and the man. Yacov raised his weapon high above his head. The man turned suddenly, his eyes on Yacov.

"Hey!" He moved to stand. Yacov brought the spade down hard, with all of his strength, on the man's head. The sound of metal on the man's skull was sickening. He slumped down on top of Rachel, out cold. Yacov grabbed him under the arms and hauled him off his sister. Rachel stood, backed away, staggered and bumped into a bale of hay. She wiped her mouth with the back of her hand and wrapped the remains of her skirt around her waist. Tears flooded her cheeks. Yacov kicked the soldier. He did not move. There was blood seeping from his scalp where Yacov had struck him.

Bayla stirred and moaned.

Rachel rushed over, and bent beside her mother.

"Mama?"

Bayla looked up into her daughter's face. "I'm fine." She touched her nose, brought her hand down, saw the blood. "Oh," she said. She eyed her daughter, noticed the torn skirt, her tears. "Are you all right?"

Rachel nodded bravely. "Yacov hit him."

Bayla sat up, saw the man lying on the ground by Yacov's feet. She said nothing, just pursed her lips, shook her head, looked at her son.

"He was hurting Rachel," Yacov explained.

Bayla nodded and glanced around the barn. Panic coursed through her body. "Where are the children?"

"They're fine, Mama. They're hiding." Yacov's heart was racing. He couldn't keep his eyes off the unconscious soldier.

Bayla was not convinced. "Please Yacov. Can you see anything?"

"Mama. Sit. Your nose is broken."

Bayla touched her nose, which was throbbing now. "It's okay. I'll live. Please, Yacov. The children…"

Yacov glanced down again at the man heaped on the floor. Slowly, the horrible truth washed over him. He was sure the man must be dead. He had killed him. Yacov felt sick inside. He'd done what he had to do to protect Rachel, but to take another man's life? This was not good. Not good at all. A dark cloud of dread hung over Yacov's head. Papa would be angry. How could Yacov explain? Thou shalt not kill, his father would say. He was a murderer. His father would be ashamed. His family would be disgraced. He was no better than the Cossacks. And what about them? The soldier had arrived with two other men. They might still be here. If they saw the body, Yacov would be arrested. He would be hanged for murder. They would make an example of him. There would be no mercy. He was a Jew.

Yacov tore his gaze from the dead man and stared at his mother. He felt ripped apart, as if someone had split open his skin and his insides were exposed to the air. He put a hand on his rib cage to steady himself.

"The children…" his mother urged gently.

Yacov nodded. With great trepidation, he crept to the barn door. It was quiet. He could see the dust from the other two soldiers as they rode away. They were leaving. His mind raced. There was much he would have to do later. He turned back to his mother and sister. "You wait here. I'll go and see."

Just in case there was one more solider hiding somewhere, Yacov ran through the open space between the barn and the house as fast as he

could, then threw his body against the side of the house. He looked
around. The milk barrel with Shoshana inside appeared undisturbed. He
took a breath and let it out, relieved. Then he looked beyond the barrel
and he saw Shmuel sprawled on the ground, his head bent at an unnatural angle. Terror raced through Yacov.

He rushed over to Shmuel. Put a hand on his arm. The boy did not move.
Yacov shook him gently. "Shmuel?" Nothing. Yacov's heart began to pound
furiously. He put his cheek up to his brother's nose. Nothing. He pushed his
ear against the boy's chest, listening for his heart. All Yacov could hear was
his own, thumping loudly. He put his arms around his brother's limp body
and lifted him. *This can't be happening. It can't be true. Not Shmuel. Make it
not be true*, he beseeched the God he did not believe in. *Take me instead.*

"No!" His scream pierced the silence of the yard. Yacov sucked air into
his lungs hungrily as his heart exploded. With his brother in his arms,
Yacov dropped to his knees and wept.

Shoshana watched the whole thing quietly from her hiding spot.
Slowly she pushed on the lid, tipped it off and poked her little head out.
She did not know why her big brother was crying, but it scared her so
much, she began to cry as well.

Yacov's anguish flew across the yard and inside the barn, stabbing
Bayla in the heart. Not again. Little Shoshana! My baby girl. With no
thought of her own safety, Bayla walked out of the barn, blood still dripping from her nose.

"Mama?" Terrified at what they might find, Rachel followed her
mother into the sunshine.

Heart already breaking, Bayla trotted toward the house. She saw Yacov
on his knees holding a child. Bayla ran full tilt, grasping a corner of her
skirt in one hand, her kerchief flying off her head as she ran. Rachel was
right behind her. Then they stopped in their tracks. Yacov met his
mother's eyes. Bayla moved slowly forward and gently took her youngest
son's body from Yacov's arms.

So heavy. Bayla hadn't thought her son was so heavy. When did he
grow so much? The child's eyes were still open. Even in death, he looked

wise beyond his years. Bayla's knees buckled and she sank to the ground, clutching her baby boy tight in her arms. The wail that came from the depths of Bayla's heart could be heard for miles in every direction. It mingled with the sorrow rising from the hearts of her neighbours, whose lives were also being torn apart.

"HELP!"

"Yacov, wake up." Sophie nudges him gently.

"Help!" Yacov shouts again, then opens his eyes. He stares at his wife. For a moment, he's not sure where he is. He looks around, sees the bland beige hospital walls, wood-framed window with its institutional venetian blinds, radiator, his plaid slippers on the floor, the IV tube in his arm. He remembers that Sid and Ruthie and Izzy had been in the room earlier, but now only Sophie remains. He must have fallen asleep.

"You were dreaming," Sophie tells him.

Yacov breathes, leans back against the pillows.

"Tell me your dream."

He sighs.

"It'll help to tell me."

He takes another breath. "Lenny was there."

Now it's Sophie's turn to breathe hard. All these years since Lenny's death and it still pains her. Just the mention of his name.

"And ..." Yacov hesitates. "Sonny."

Sophie raises her eyebrows.

"They were little boys. They were running toward me, but I couldn't pick them up. I tried, but they kept slipping through my hands. Then they were falling and there was no ground. They were just falling. And screaming, and crying for me. I couldn't help them. I tried, but I couldn't help them. Then I woke up."

Sophie pats his arm.

"I tried."

"I know you did. It's okay."

"I tried."

"It's okay."

And for the first time in many years, it is.

Technically Knocked Out

APRIL 4, 1954

SONNY AND RUDY ride the train together, back to Toronto, the Middleweight Title safely back in Sonny's corner. They had been in New York for only two weeks, but to Sonny it feels as if he has been away for years. Sitting next to Rudy, in the back of a Yellow cab, Sonny watches the city go by. He feels as if he hasn't seen clearly in a very long time. Like he's been in a fifteen-year fog. His surroundings have been a blur. And now everything is crystal clear for the first time. He notices the deep-red brick of houses, the grey steel streetcar tracks along Queen Street, a sign for the newly opened subway station. On College Street, he cranes his neck as they pass his father's store, Lenny's House of Bargains, plastered as it's always been with tacky signs: "We're not famous, but our bargains are;" "We're cheap and so are our prices;" "Wacky Wednesdays;" "Maniac Mondays;" and the worst sign, "Lenny Loves Low Prices." Sonny wonders what Lenny would have thought of that. Probably die of embarrassment, if he wasn't already dead. Once, a couple of years after the store opened, Sonny's curiosity got the better of him, and he put on dark glasses and went inside, his heart beating a million miles an hour, scared his father would see him and kick him out. He didn't stay long, just long enough to take a look around. He saw Lenny's picture in a place of honour, Lenny's Victoria Cross medal in a special glass case. It made him mad, because his picture should have been on display too. He was the famous boxer in the family. Sure, Lenny was a hero, but what was he? Chopped liver? He fled the store when he saw Ruthie emerge from an employee's door, quickly heading his way down an aisle with shoes piled haphazardly on a display table.

Now the store takes up an entire city block. He shifts his weight, faces forward as they pass the familiar landscape of his youth, the stores along College and Spadina. Manny's Deli, the Eppes Essen Restaurant, the Bagel, the confectionery and candy store where he'd taken Loretta for a soda on their first date. His body aches something terrible. He'd won the middleweight title back from Foster, but took one of the worst beatings of his career to do so. Three days since the fight and his eyes are still swollen and puffy, ringed in black. His nose is taped together, broken for the millionth time. He lost count years ago. He aches all over, and the dizzy spells have grown worse.

"All I'm saying, Sonny, is you should think about it," Rudy repeats.

"What else am I going to do? I've been fighting all my life." Sonny knows Rudy is right: Better to quit while you're ahead. He's just not ready to admit it. He'll have to fight a half-dozen more matches. Non-title bouts. To make it look good. Make it clear he won his title back fair and square, not on a fluke. And he'd better win them. Then he'll announce his retirement. It's the smart thing to do, at this point. But when Sonny thinks about hanging up his gloves, a terrible doom comes over him. All he sees is a big black emptiness. Sonny doesn't like to sit still for too long. As long as he keeps fighting, he doesn't have to think.

"I got a stash. Been putting it away for years," Rudy reveals.

"You do?"

"Yeah, don't you?" He eyes Sonny. Surely to God he's got some of his winnings saved. Over the past nine years of professional boxing, Sonny's made over two million in prize money.

"Sure I do, Rudy."

Thank God. He was worried for a second there. "Been thinking maybe I'll open a little place on Yonge Street," he tells Sonny.

"What kinda place?"

"A nightclub. Real jazzy. And classy. With live entertainment seven nights a week. What do ya think?"

"Swell."

"Why don't you come in with me?"

Sonny laughs. "What do I know about running a nightclub?"

"How hard could it be?"

Sonny takes it in. Not such a bad idea. What else is he going to do? "What'll we call it?"

Rudy hadn't taken the thought that far, but he's thrilled to see Sonny might be interested. He stares at his friend. "How about, 'The Boxing Glove?'"

Sonny bobs his head back and forth. "Sounds like a gym."

"Yeah, you're right. How about 'Sonny's Club?'"

"Sonny and Rudy's." Sonny corrects.

"Thanks, kid, but you're the one with the name. Not me. How about, 'The Athletic Club?'"

"Also sounds like a gym."

"Yeah, you're right."

The cab stops outside Sonny's apartment on Palmerston Boulevard. Out of habit, he glances up at the third-storey window, half hoping to see Loretta waving down at him. Rudy watches him carefully.

"You going to be okay?" he asks.

Sonny opens the car door. "Sure I am, Rudy."

"Take a few days off, kid. Lie around. Eat whatever you want. Buy a good bottle of Scotch. You earned it."

"Sure." There's a hole in Sonny's gut as he steps out of the cab and removes his duffle bag from the trunk.

He looks sadder than Rudy's ever seen him. "You want to go for dinner later? Get a couple of steaks?"

"Maybe tomorrow, Rudy. I'll be seeing you."

"I'll call you tomorrow, kid."

"So long, Rudy."

Sonny walks slowly away from the cab.

A MINUTE LATER, Sonny tosses his keys on the front table and closes the apartment door behind him.

"Loretta?" He knows she is not here, but calls for her anyway. His voice sounds hollow in the deserted apartment. On the floor is a single piece of mail, addressed to him, from the law firm of Rosen, Gelfarb & Klein.

Inside he finds divorce papers. A fury swirls in his belly and rises to his head, where it explodes red-hot anger. He rips the letter into pieces, throws the bits into the air, but that's not enough to tame his rage. He punches the wall. That's more like it. He hits it again. And again. He pounds the wall, with a series of low jabs, followed by a combination, then a dazzling right uppercut that knocks a hole in the plaster the size of a pumpkin and pops two of his knuckles out of place. That's better. The pain in his body overrides the pain in his heart. This kind of punishment, Sonny is conditioned for: the searing pain as he pops the knuckles back in their sockets, the dull ache in his wrists, still throbbing from the fight, the tender bruised fingers. This he can take. It's the emotional pain that knocks him out.

"Go to hell," he yells to the empty apartment. "Go ahead."

The spell comes over him so quickly, he almost falls over. He sees black spots in front of his eyes. Feels nausea and a dull throb in the centre of his head. His eyes roll back and he almost faints. He breathes and hangs on to the front hall table for dear life, until the dizziness passes. Leaning against the wall, he breathes deeply. The nausea is passing. That was a close one. He's going to have to tell his doctor soon. Was hoping it would just go away. The first time it happened, he was in the ring, a couple of months ago. It happened in the tenth round and it almost knocked him over. He would have lost on a technical knockout, but he was saved, literally, by the bell. He knew he'd have to get the fight over fast, so he charged out like a bull and knocked out his opponent in the first ten seconds of the next round.

Still in his dark trenchcoat, Sonny walks inside the apartment, heads straight for the bedroom. Loretta's scent still lingers in the closet, but all her things are gone. Her clothes, shoes, perfume bottles that used to line her dresser top, her jewellery. All gone. Only the white lacy doily on top of her dresser remains. In the bathroom, it's the same. The only things left are his shaving brush, one lone toothbrush, a tube of Brylcreem, a bottle of aftershave, a sliver of white Ivory soap in the dish. There's nothing left in Mary's room, except her furniture, white with pink trim. She picked it out herself. In Moses and Frankie's room with the matching twin beds and the blue and brown cowboys-and-Indians bedspreads, he spots a stray sweat sock under the bed, a discarded Lego piece, but the drawers and closets are empty. He sits heavily on Moses' bed, his trenchcoat still on, unbuttoned. He leans over his knees, head down. And he cries like a baby. For the first time in years, Sonny Lapinsky cries. But there are no witnesses to his grief. And so it doesn't cleanse his spirit or heal his soul. It merely hangs there in the air, like a bad smell. It is like the cry of an orphaned animal — the saddest, loneliest sound on earth.

SID AND RUTHIE'S apartment on Manning Avenue is just four blocks from Sonny's. The cool September air feels good on his face as he walks down Harbord Street, past the United Dairy Bakery, Cohen's Fish Market — now run by the Cohens' eldest son, Julius — past Zimmerman's Fruit and Vegetables and the Harbord Street Smoke Shop. It's a good thing Sonny beat up his wall earlier. Otherwise he'd want to kill Sid right now. He could knock out Sid in a heartbeat.

Honour Thy Father
ONE HOUR LATER

SONNY OPENS HIS EYES, looks up to find Sid hovering over him. Where the hell is he? He looks around. Christ. He's lying flat on his back, on the sofa at Sid's place. Must have passed out. Goddamnit.

"Sonny, you okay?" Sid offers Sonny a glass of water.

Sonny sits up, pushes the water away. "Got any more of that rye?"

"Sure, Sonny."

With the bottle and a couple of glasses, Sid joins Sonny on the sofa.

"You seen a doctor about that?" Sid sips on his rye.

"Shaddup, Sid." Sonny belts back his drink, pours another.

The brothers sit in silence for a moment. Sonny puts his feet up on Sid's coffee table.

"Pop's gone to your fights before, Sonny."

"What?"

"I know I shoulda told you before, but I couldn't."

"Aw, for Chrissake."

"This is the first time we travelled all the way to New York, but for the local ones, he's been more than once."

"You're full of it."

"It's true."

"He hasn't even spoken to me in what? Fourteen years." Sonny grabs a cigarette from a bowl on the coffee table, lights it with the large silver table-top lighter.

"He loves you," Sid says, reaching for a cigarette.

This enrages Sonny, who takes a deep drag, blows the smoke out through clenched teeth. "Up yours, Sid. He hates me."

"He loves you." Sid is calm. He's been wanting to settle this feud for a long time, never knew how before. But now it's clear. Tell Sonny the truth. It's as simple as that. Sid can't believe he's never thought of the answer before. "Every once in a while before he goes to bed, when he thinks Ma's not looking, he takes her scrapbook down from the top shelf of Izzy's closet."

"Scrapbook?"

"And he pores over the pages."

"What are you talking about?"

"You remember the scrapbook Ma starting keeping when you were a kid and fighting in the Smokers. Remember? She'd cut out every article, every single mention of your fights, and paste them in her book."

"Yeah?"

"She must have about ten of them by now. Maybe twelve. Got everything you ever done in it. Newspaper clippings. Fight reports. Ticket stubs. Photographs. Everything."

"She's still doing it?" He can't believe it.

"Religiously."

"Pop reads them?"

"When he thinks no one's looking. He brags about you."

"Stop it." Sid's got to be lying about this.

"At Manny's. He sits at the counter with a hot tea and holds court."

"Pop does?"

"Yeah, 'Sonny sure showed that Wop,'" he says.

Sonny grimaces. His kids are, after all, half-Italian. "He says Wop?"

"Yeah, but you know Pop. He don't know any better."

"Aw Sid, you're crazy."

"It's true."

The fury returns to Sonny's belly. "He don't even talk to me. He hasn't even met my kids."

"Sonny, if you ever went home once in a while … if you ever paid attention to your own family …" Sid shakes his head in disgust.

"What?"

"Sonny, Loretta's been bringing the kids to Ma and Pop's for years."

"Yeah, but only when Pop's out," Sonny says with certainty.

"Not always."

Sonny wants to deck Sid. Why is he saying this? Instinctively, he balls up one fist.

"The first time, I think it was an accident that Pop was home. After that, he'd show up on purpose."

"You're lying, Sid. I'm warning you." Sonny holds up his fist.

"What are you going do, Sonny? Knock my lights out? Go ahead. It won't change the truth."

Sonny jumps up from the sofa and paces the living room. "Why would he do that?" he asks slowly.

Sid shrugs. "Wanted to be a grandfather, I guess. Especially since me and Ruthie …" He trails off.

"Goddamn it." Sonny grabs the whiskey bottle, fills his glass. "God damn it to hell."

Back From the Dead
APRIL 11, 1954

SONNY STANDS OUTSIDE Manny's Delicatessen for a moment. He hasn't been inside for years. Yacov sits at the counter, with a glass of tea in front of him. Good old dependable Sid sits by his side. Yacov has the daily *Star* spread out in front of him, opened to the sports page. Sonny's been home almost a week, and still the sports pages are covering his title bout against Tommy Foster at Madison Square Garden. Accounts of the fight, editorials by the columnists, speculations on who the up-and-coming contenders might be, how much longer they figure Sonny can hang onto his title.

Sonny takes a deep breath and pulls open the door.

"Sure, Manny," Yacov says, "next time Sonny's home I'll bring him in."

"Hey Sonny! There he is now!" Manny shouts as Sonny enters the steamy restaurant. "Come on in, Champ. Sit down. We haven't seen you in the neighbourhood for a long time, Sonny. I'll make you a sandwich. On the house. What a fight that musta been. Wish I coulda been there." He stares at the bruising on Sonny's face. The swelling has gone down, but his face is still red from burst blood vessels and his eyes are now ringed in a dark purple with yellow edges. He still sports a piece of white tape to keep his broken nose cartilage in place while it sets. "Boy, Sonny. You sure got busted up."

Sonny shrugs. "Couple a lucky hits he took. No big deal. Next time Manny," Sonny says, "I'll get you a couple of tickets. Ringside." If there is a next time.

"You mean it, Sonny?"

"Sure, Manny."

"That's terrific, Sonny." Manny has never even been to New York City, let alone the famous Madison Square Garden.

Yacov sits perfectly still, his back to Sonny, shoulders tensed. He doesn't so much as glance in his son's direction. Is it really Sonny? Inside Manny's? Right behind him? Yacov doesn't know what to do. His heart flips over inside his chest.

Sonny steps forward and sits on the stool beside his father, reaches past him, extends his hand to Sid.

"Hiya, Sid."

Sid accepts his brother's hand. Grins at his father. Now, ain't this something? Sonny sure has balls. Just walks in here. Sits next to Pop. After all this time, acting like nothing is unusual at all. "Hiya, Sonny. What brings you to Manny's?"

"Missed Manny's smoked meat, Sid. Hi, Pop."

In front of his cronies, to whom he's been lying for years, Yacov remains outwardly calm, acting as though nothing unusual is happening. But he is trembling, his heart is crumbling, and there are tears forming in his eyes. He can't speak. He nods at the son he hasn't spoken to in fourteen years.

"Next time I fight at the Garden I'll leave tickets for you, Manny. You too, Pop. And Sid. Front and centre. I'll put you up in the hotel-like. Where I stay."

"Swell, Sonny. Right, Pop?" Sid prompts his stubborn father.

"Well ..." Yacov finds his voice, quickly wipes at the tears in his eyes. Hopes the others haven't seen. "I don't know if I can get away so quickly. The store ..."

"Pop, the store's fine. Uncle Max'll take care of things. We can go away for two days."

"What? And leave Max to run the store? Hah! We leave Max alone, he's liable to give the store away to those *goniff* friends of his."

"Pop, calm down. Your heart."

"What'sa matter with his heart?" Sonny is alarmed.

"Nothing," Yacov insists.

Sid sighs. "He had a mild heart attack. Last month."

"What?"

"It's nothing."

"He's not supposed to get excited."

"Aw jeez, Pop. I wish someone had told me. I woulda come and visited. Sent flowers at least."

"We knew you were busy, Sonny." Good old Sid covering for the awkward situation. They are, after all, in public.

"Still, I woulda come."

"I'm fine," Yacov grumbles. "It's nothing. Stop fussing. I'm not dead yet."

"All right, Pop. Calm down," Sid says.

"I'm calm. I'm calm. I'm so calm I'm falling asleep."

"Good."

"Hey, Sonny," Manny says. "Tell us about the fight." He plunks a huge smoked meat sandwich in front of Sonny.

Sid nods for Sonny to go on. Sonny is getting a little misty-eyed himself. It was so easy. Why hadn't he ever tried this before? All the wasted years. All the heartache. And here he is sitting next to his father like it's the most natural thing in the world. He takes a bite of the sandwich. God, he's missed Manny's smoked meat. They're all waiting for him. He sips on the seltzer Manny has placed in front of him.

"Well ..." Sonny says, "you know I coulda KO'ed him in the first round. I had him down for an eight count right off the bat. But I figured I'd hold off a little. Give the crowd a fight to remember, see?"

"Yeah?"

"So I let him get in a few shots for the next couple of rounds. But you know he's a heavy puncher."

"Yeah," agrees Manny. "That's what it said in the paper."

"He got me a couple of times with a hard right hook, see?"

"Yeah, go on Sonny."

"Like I was saying ..."

Acknowledgements

THE SEEDS OF THIS NOVEL began with my grandfather, Ben Tully, who was a storyteller at heart. As a child, I would sit beside my grandfather on the crinkly plastic of the living room sofa. As we sipped strong black tea, he would tell stories of his youth in Russia and his heroic escape across the Dniester River into Romania when he was a young man and his name was still Berel Tulchinsky. He would recount the same adventures over and over, but I never tired of the stories and they have stuck with me over the years.

In 1998, after my first novel, *Love Ruins Everything*, was published, I knew I had to go back and use *Zayde* Berel's stories as the beginnings of a novel. Yacov Lapinsky is loosely based on my grandfather, Berel Tulchinsky/Ben Tully. The family is fictional, yet the backdrop of their times — the riot in Christie Pits, the battle at Dieppe during the second world war, the existence of Jewish Boxers from Kensington Market, the Depression — are real.

I owe many thanks to the family members I interviewed for their stories and memories of the 1930s to 1960s, especially my parents, Jack and Marion; my aunt and uncle, Sybil and Shelly Jackson; my aunt and uncle, Judy and Norman Silver; my cousin, Professor Gerald Tulchinsky; and of course, my grandparents Ben and Mary Tully. I had the opportunity to speak with Mr. Harry Tepperman, who was a member of the Harbord Playground Baseball Team in the 1930s and who was on the field in Christie Pits on August 16, 1933, the day of the riot. I am grateful to Mr. Tepperman for speaking with me.

Many thanks to Ann Decter who read an early draft of this manuscript and provided me with editorial notes, as did Terrie Hamazaki and Marion Tully.

Dr. Joan Robillard guided me through a 1930s understanding of brain injury, and provided me with the medical terminology and prognosis for Izzy's brain damage. Roy Duquette spoke to me at length about the inner psychology necessary to be a professional boxer. In particular, he taught me about a boxer's "heart for fighting."

I owe thanks to the Isaac Waldman Public Library at the Jewish Community Centre of Greater Vancouver and librarian Karen Corrin;

Howard Marcus and The Ontario Jewish Archives; the Toronto Reference Library, where I spent many weeks poring over newspaper archives from the 1930s and 1940s; the Holocaust Centre at the Jewish Community Centre of Toronto; the Vancouver Holocaust Centre and the Vancouver Public Library.

My appreciation to cultural director Reisa Schneider, at the Jewish Community Centre of Greater Vancouver, who has supported this novel over the last several years by continuing to invite me to read excerpts from the book at the Cherie Smith Jewish Book Festival.

In researching the novel I read countless reference books about boxing, Canadian troops in the Second World War, the riot in Christie Pits, the Depression Era, the history of Toronto, the battle at Dieppe in 1942, the invasion of Normandy in 1944 and the liberation of the Netherlands by Canadian troops in 1945. I read biographies of boxers, Canadian soldiers' memoirs and fiction of the time period. During the process of writing, I was poring through so many reference materials, sometimes my office was stacked three-feet high in library books. Obviously I can't mention them all, but I would like to acknowledge several books which were of major importance to my research and helped me imagine my characters within these historical times. *The Riot at Christie Pits*, by Cyril H. Levitt and William Shaffir, was invaluable in teaching me about the riot, the circumstances that led up to the event and the prevailing mood in Toronto in 1933. *Call Me Sammy*, by Sammy Luftspring, gave me the inside story of a young Jewish boxer who grew up in Kensington Market in Toronto, and helped immeasurably with the forming of Sonny's character. I read so many books on the second world war I can't possibly mention them all, but these were extremely valuable: *Semper Paratus: The History of the Royal Hamilton Light Infantry* (RHLI Historical Association); *The Half-Million: The Canadians in Britain 1939–1945*, by C.P. Stacey & Barbara M. Wilson; *A Liberation Album: Canadians in the Netherlands*, by David Kaufmann and Michael Horn; and *Battle Royal, A History of the Royal Regiment of Canada*, by Major D.J. Goodspeed.

I must thank Lynn Henry, my editor, and Michelle Benjamin, publisher, at Raincoast Books for their enthusiasm for the novel and skillful guidance through the editorial process, as well as Allan MacDougall, CEO. Also, thanks to Tessa Vanderkop and Emiko Morita for their promotional efforts, as well as Ingrid Paulson for her design of the book, Teresa Bubela for the typesetting, and the dedicated production team.

Thanks to Brian Lam, Persimmon Blackbridge and Walter Quan for supporting my BC Arts Council Grant Application. And I'd like to express my appreciation to the small independent booksellers who have supported my work from the beginning, especially Little Sisters Book and Art Emporium, Women in Print, 32 Books, and People's Co-op Bookstore in Vancouver; and The Toronto Women's Bookstore, Glad Day Books, the University of Toronto Bookstore and This Ain't the Rosedale Library in Toronto.

Richard Banner has patiently helped me out of countless computer nightmares over the years. The fabulous author photo was taken by the talented photographer Daniel Collins.

This is a work of fiction and the imagination, and although I was careful to insert my fictional characters as closely as possible into the real events of the time, there are a few situations where, as a fiction writer, I had to stretch the facts slightly, mostly in regards to time frames, to fit the plot. I therefore ask any historians (professional and otherwise) to grant me a measure of creative license with the facts.

I am grateful to my partner, Terrie Hamazaki, who is thankfully also a writer and therefore someone who understands a writer's need to cancel her social life for the duration. Many a Saturday night at our house was spent watching fight movies from the 1930s or war movies from the 1940s. Many thanks to my friends and family, who were always there, even when they did not hear from me for long periods of time, and who provided me with support, conversation, inspiration, resources and shelter, especially James Johnstone, Dianne Whelan, Lois Fine, Rachel Epstein, Peter Demas, Claire Queree, Eunice Lee, Sara Graefe, Desiree Lim, Arlene Tully, Lynda Fisher, Jonathan Silver, Adam Silver and Adam Rose.

And finally, *toda raba* to *Zayde* Berel, for telling us his stories; to my parents, Jack and Marion, for immersing me in my culture when I was growing up; and to my extended family of uncles, aunts and cousins, whose voices are scattered throughout the *Five Books of Moses Lapinsky*.

Song Credits

"I'll Be Seeing You," words and music by Irving Kahal & Sammy Fain. Copyright 1938 by Williamson Music Company. Copyright renewed by Chappel & Co. Inc.

"When You're Smiling," words and music by Mark Fisher, Joe Goodwin and Larry Shay. Chicago: Harold Rossiter Music Co. Copyright 1928.

"It's Only a Paper Moon," words by Billy Rose and E.Y.Harburg, music by Harold Arlen. Harms, Inc. Copyright 1933.

"Over the Rainbow," (Wizard of Oz), words by E.Y. Harburg, music by Harold Arlen. Leo Feist Inc. Copyright 1939.

"There's No Business Like Show Business," words and music by Irving Berlin. Irving Berlin Music Co. Copyright 1946 by Irving Berlin.

"When I'm Not Near the Girl I Love," (Finian's Rainbow), words by E.Y. Harburg, music by Burton Lane. Crawford Music Corp. Copyright 1946 by the Players Music Group.

"Old Devil Moon," (Finian's Rainbow), words by E.Y. Harburg, music by Burton Lane. Crawford Music Corp. Copyright 1946 by the Players Music Group.

"Blue Moon," words by Lorenz Hart, music by Richard Rodgers. Robbins Music Corp. Copyright 1934 by Metro-Goldwyn-Mayer; assigned 1934 to Robbins Music Corp.

"Embraceable You," words by Ira Gershwin, music by George Gershwin. New World Music Corp. Copyright 1934.

"Tenderness," words and music by Harry Woods, Jimmy Campbell and Reg Connelly. Campbell-Connelly Co. Ltd. London, England/ Robbins Music Corp. Copyright 1932.

About the Author

KAREN X. TULCHINSKY is the author of *Love and Other Ruins*, a sequel to her bestselling novel *Love Ruins Everything*. She is the winner of the VanCity Book Prize for her collection of short fiction, *In Her Nature*. She was born in Toronto and now makes her home in Vancouver, British Columbia.